BLOODSTONE & DANDELIONS

THREADS OF AILIAR BOOK 1

Bloodstone and Dandelions
Copyright © 2024 by Elle Brockett

First Edition: November 2024

Second Edition: March 2026

Paperback ISBN: 9780645143669

Hardback ISBN: 9780645143676

Copyright by Elle Brockett

With special thanks to:

Editors: Kirsty Inic & C.H. Folan
Cartographer: Sirius Wesson

Want to stay in touch? Find me at:
Instagram: @biblioellegrpahy
TikTok: @biblioellegraphy

For Tristan, my husband and armourer.
You handed me the tools I needed, the time to learn how to use them, and the space I needed to thrive.
You are the reason Ailiar exists.

A Note from the Author

Please note that *Bloodstone and Dandelions* has on-page graphic depictions of violence and death, including the deaths of minors.

Bloodstone and Dandelions also has depictions or mentions of:

- past trauma

- gaslighting and coercive control

- sexual harassment

- inferences to racial prejudice

- parental neglect (of a young adult)

- displacement

- self-harm and self-mutilation

- enslavement and corporal punishment

- animal attacks

Please take care of yourself and your mental health.

The Division of Magic

SALDHRAOS

earth

primarily farmers

other careers include ceramics, construction, cannoneer, pharmacist

VISDHRAOS

water

primarily sailors

other careers include perfumer, pharmacist, farmers

AERDHRAOS

air

primarily archers

other careers include sailor, performer, healer

IGDHRAOS

fire

primarily blacksmiths

other careers include armed forces, cannoneers, glassworks

RUPABURG

Mountainous
Pass

Vaya

Peilach

Trostram
(Naval Base)

Ailiar

...ch

Dei'Nach

The Weeping
Wood

10MM : 500KM

PROLOGUE

SILKTIDE

IT WAS THE HEIGHT of summer.

The sun sat perched upon its throne at the highest point in the sky.

The day should have been bright.

The sun's rays should have been beating down upon the young woman below, colouring her pale skin pink and threatening to leave a burning sting. Instead, its light was smothered by thick plumes of dark smoke that stretched across the sky. It expanded its reach inch by inch, growing darker and thicker with each passing minute.

She had dismissed the smoke when she first left the home that she shared with her father earlier that morning. It was not uncommon, even in summer, for the air to have a hint of it. She had believed the heavy, cloying scent to be the result of a farmer burning dead animals, or crops that were unfit for consumption. Or perhaps it had been a bonfire hosted by other youths of the town, one to which she had either not been invited to, or had simply not deigned to attend.

After all, she was not one to attend gatherings often. When she was a child, her father had kept her close to the home. It helped that they lived far enough away from the village proper that the prospect of wasting so much time just to play with other children for a measly hour or two was not in the least bit tempting.

While her father had never given her a satisfactory answer as to why she was not allowed to wander and play like the other children were, she had chalked it up to their proximity to the Ailian border. If they had lived nestled within the confines of the seaside town of Silktide itself, she believed that her father would have been more lenient. If neighbours surrounded them, there would be less of a chance that she would be stolen away by the human-eating elves that lived on the other side of the border. As it was, their modest cottage was rather secluded, nestled in the outermost edges of the Edgeling Woods, surrounded by pine trees and wild mint.

Yet even as she grew older, her father had been reluctant to allow her to carry on the family business. He knew that it meant she would need to leave home regularly, and alone. However, he could not deny the talent she had as a seamstress, and so he had begrudgingly relented.

He allowed her to travel to the long, dirt road to the township of Silktide to discuss business with the townspeople on his behalf. Eventually, she took sole responsibility of delivering the gowns and trousers their customers had ordered. She spent market days selecting fabrics from the travelling merchants, and hours foraging in the Edgeling Woods for flowers and herbs to dye fibres.

Truthfully, he didn't have much of a choice in the matter.

No merchant in their right mind would waste their time going from door-to-door of the farms and cabins that stretched to the southeast of Silktide for an unlikely potential sale. And why would they, when they could park their carts in the town square and be surrounded by people already planning on parting with their coin?

He had fought his daughter on the foraging more times than he cared to count. But he was beginning to struggle with the walk, his old wounds came back to wreak havoc on his ageing bones. Though it hurt his pride to admit it, he was forced to stop every few feet to catch his breath.

But on this day, for once, the young woman was not racing towards the town with an armful of garments wrapped in slippery brown paper. She did not need to constantly readjust her grip on a new gown for the mayor's daughter, or make sure that the freshly re-dyed shirt for the tavern-keeper's teenage son did not end up in one of the many piles of horse dung along the way.

On this day, she had no responsibilities, save for three: get to town early, help the baker's family set up their tables for the mid-summer festival, and spend the afternoon with the baker's son.

If things went according to plan, that afternoon would stretch into the evening, and she could look forward to him asking her father for her hand. Her father, who had spent the night in the public house following a late consultation with a wealthy merchant, was sure to approve the match.

She could not imagine why he would not.

The baker's son was strong, kind, and handsome. He had his family trade, and bread was always needed, even in the harshest of times.

If only this smoke would clear, she thought.

If the air remained this thick, it was sure to cast a pall on the festivities. No one would want to spend hours milling about the markets and food stalls while smoke burned their throats and lungs, or stung their eyes.

As if to emphasise the thoughts in her mind, the young woman coughed.

It surprised her how hoarse the sound was. It was as though she had been coughing for hours, as though her throat was already ravaged and torn.

She slowed in her steps and looked once more at the sky.

There was too much smoke in the air for it to be from a bonfire, as she had previously suspected. The same was true for farmers burning off their produce. She frowned and set forth again.

There was a crest just ahead. There, she would be able to see over the land and determine where the fire was burning. Because she was sure that it was still burning. How else could the smell grow ever stronger with each step that she took? Why else would her head begin to feel light, and her vision twist and blur?

She pushed herself faster, determination cutting through the ache in her chest as her lungs laboured. She was certain that once she could locate the blaze, she would be able to convince herself that her symptoms were not so bad.

Perhaps she could even lean into them and be tended to ever so lovingly by the baker's son.

He could press a damp cloth to her face and mutter promises of protection that were as sweet as his glazed cakes.

That image fuelled her as she continued to climb.

At the top of the crest, she let out a short, relieved laugh. She had made it halfway to town, and now, she was going to be able to pinpoint the source of her agitation. The smile on her lips fell as she cast her eyes wide on the unburnt rolling hills of western Colosia. She spun towards the Edgeling Woods and saw no dark columns rising from within the thick trees.

It left only two other options.

Knowing that the smoke had only gotten worse the further away from her home that she had travelled, she was not going to insult her intelligence by looking backwards. With her heart pounding and her mind begging her not to, she looked towards the sea.

Towards Silktide.

Her scream would have echoed throughout the land if it had not been smothered by the oppressive blanket of smoke that rose out of what had been a bustling trade hub. Darkness reached out with claw-tipped fingers to the lands surrounding Silktide. The farmhouses that had been visible from the road were gone as well, leaving black smudges in the landscape.

Her memory did not serve her in the time that spanned between her decision to race towards Silktide and the moment she arrived. It returned only as she stood before the crumbled and smouldering remains of the wooden arch that had once welcomed visitors into Silktide.

The smell and smoke were unbearable now. Even as she held an embroidered handkerchief to her face, covering her mouth and nose, the blaze had erased every hint of the scent of salt and fish that was expected of a town built along the shore. It had utterly obliterated the warm, homely scent of fresh, daily baked bread that usually taunted and teased her, and wiped the memory of the perpetual lamb stew that was always bubbling over the fire in the tavern.

Even though, from what she could see, the fire had burned out, the tainted air continued to burn her nose and dry her throat. Her lips cracked in the vapourless air. Tears evaporated from her cheeks almost as soon as they were shed.

It felt like a dream.

No.

A dream implied that there was something good to come from this. A dream implied that the people she knew were about to rise from the ashes and greet her with open arms and wide smiles.

This was a nightmare.

This was where all her hopes and dreams came to die.

After another moment of hesitation, she stepped forward. She was keenly aware of the lack of arch above as she crossed the threshold into the township of Silktide. How she had never noticed how the feeling stepping beneath the beautiful carved wood before escaped her. She could not imagine having ever paid particular attention to it, but now that it was gone, she could see the carved fish weaving in and out of each other. She could see the white discolouration on the top, where the birds liked to perch and leave their mark.

And yet, she could not remember noticing any of it the last time she passed beneath it.

The first building to her left as she entered Silktide was a guardhouse. Or at least, it had been.

Like most of the structures in Silktide, had been made primarily with wicker and sticks, the walls filled in with mud and clay to keep the elements at bay. Now though, the only remnants of the guardhouse were eight stubs of what had once been the timber framework, burned down to various lengths. The walls were nothing more than rubble, reduced to small chunks of clay lost in the piles of smouldering ash.

Bile rose in her throat. She forced it back down and turned away to continue searching through the ruins for any sign of life. She had been here only two days before, and the streets had been buzzing with energy. Villagers had been milling about, carrying crates of decorations and baskets of food in preparation for the mid-summer festival. They had been hoisting lanterns – of which she could now see no evidence – and strings of flags and pennants in various shades of yellow, green and blue. The tavernkeeper and his preferred brewers had rolled barrels of alcohol through the streets to set up strategically placed temporary bars to alleviate pressure from the tavern itself once the festivities were in full swing.

She had needed to dodge and weave between people of all shapes and sizes on her way to deliver the gown she had made for the mayor's daughter. Now, she was stepping over debris and dodging smouldering piles of ash that glowed orange whenever a breeze stirred them.

The blaze may have abated, but it was still hungry. It threatened to devour even more than it already at the slightest provocation.

She gathered her patchwork skirt in her free hand to keep the hem away from the ravenous coals. It may have been a futile effort – there were already dark stains from the soot, and holes from embers carried on the wind – but she did so anyway.

She did not know when she decided what path to take.

Rubble crunched under her boots with each step, a stark contrast to the clean, sure *clonk, clonk, clonk* that she had grown to expect on the cobbled street. Her footing slipped more than once, but finally she came to a stop.

Like the guardhouse—like all the structures, buildings, and homes she had passed—the public house was no more. She could see smoking remnants of the foundations and framework. She could see the stone hearth in the centre that had provided warmth to the hundreds of people who had stepped inside.

A large iron caldron sat on its side; its lip crusted in the charred remains of the perpetual stew.

It's going to take hours to scrape that clean, she thought.

But it wouldn't, she realised.

Because there was no one left to wash it.

She didn't know how long she had been wandering the smouldering streets, but she knew she had not seen anyone. It was a blessing, she decided, to have not come across some poor soul begging for the pain to end.

She did not think that she could handle it.

But then, at least, she might have some answers.

Like where her father was. If he was still alive.

If there had been any survivors at all.

Her vision blurred again as tears once more rose to the surface. She could hold on to the hope that her father had made it out before the fire. She could imagine that the entire township had made it out. Perhaps they had evacuated on ships and would return once the smoke cleared.

Perhaps they were hiding in the Edgeling Woods, praying that whatever had started this was long gone.

Or perhaps they were all dead.

The voice inside her mind was cold and cruel.

She did not want to believe it.

What would she have left if she did? She knew which plants around her house were edible, but that was the extent of it. If the town was gone, if everyone that she knew was *gone*, how could she hope to survive?

Her breathing quickened, drawing more smoke into her lungs despite her handkerchief. Her heart pounded in her chest, threatening to break through the cage of her ribs.

Wood creaked.

Just as she turned around, a beam she had not noticed snapped and crashed into the ruins of the building below. The sound had been enough to startle her, but it was the eruption of embers that rained down in a biting shower that drew another scream from her lips.

In her attempt to avoid them, she took a quick step backwards. Her boot caught on something soft and pliable, and she fell, throwing her arms out behind her.

She landed within the white, ashy ruins of the public house. The many colours of her patchwork skirt were now muted, the patterns barely showing through the layers of grime and soot. There was still heat in the ground where she had fallen, but her mind was too preoccupied to consider the dangers of remaining where she was.

A pitiful, pained whine emanated from her.

She lifted her left arm gingerly. Pain coursed through the entire length of it, but the sharp ache came from her wrist. Bright red blood oozed from scrapes on her palm, mixing with the ash and soot to create some abhorrent sludge on her skin.

Gritting her teeth, she slowly flexed her fingers.

Though painful, she could still move them, which was a good sign.

With a whimper, she rotated her wrist.

Again, though painful, she was able to move it enough to rule out a break, even with her limited medical knowledge.

It was a small blessing, though one that she would gladly accept, all things considered.

She sniffed, and immediately regretted it as she felt the gritty snot run down the back of her throat. Curiosity was fuelled by a sudden wave of frustration; she pulled her feet away from the object that she'd tripped over.

Her eyes narrowed as she tried to make sense of the shape before her. But it was as though her mind refused to let her see it for what it was. Shiny, glistening red and thick, creamy, pale yellow swirled together. She had ripped off a chunk of whatever it was, revealing a bright white-

Her thoughts suddenly stopped.

This had never happened to her before, not without some external interruption to halt the flow of images and concepts in her mind.

Please stop, her mind seemed to be begging her. *Please stop looking. You do not need to see what this is.*

But she did.

She pushed through that mental block, unsure how it was even possible, and then she saw it.

Clear as the nose on her own face.

The red was blood and muscle, and yellow was puss and melted skin.

The white was bone.

She had tripped over a severed arm and, in doing so, had ripped up a chunk of flesh from the bone as easily as if it had been a stewed piece of meat.

She scrambled to her feet.

She rushed back out to the street, managing only three unsteady steps before she fell to her knees and vomited on the cobbled stones of Silktide.

Perhaps someone with more courage than she would have stayed longer and tried to investigate further. Perhaps someone with a stronger constitution than she would have attempted to find any potential survivor or determine the cause of this complete and utter destruction of such a beautiful, vibrant town.

But the tailor's daughter was not a courageous woman.

She had not so much as dreamed for a life of adventure, and she knew herself well enough to understand that she did not possess the correct frame of mind to help anyone even if she should find them.

And so, the young woman did the only thing that she could.

She lifted her skirts and ran back the way she had come.

She ran away from the blood and the smoke.

Away from the death and the carnage. Away from Silktide.

Away from the only home she had ever known.

ONE

AROS

THE EDGELING WOODS

FOR THE LAST EIGHT years, Aros C'Asad sat and watched as a curious wild bear wandered out of the Edgeling Woods to investigate the elven town of Luvrahn.

She was a large, brown beast with thick fur and an impressive set of claws that left grooves in the ground as she walked. Her curious nose had gotten into one too many baskets that unsuspecting villagers had left out. After a while, the elves of Luvrahn had stopped trying to scare her away, choosing instead to welcome her into the village as one of their own. Even the dogs had stopped barking upon her arrival.

Over time, Aros too had allowed himself to be lulled into a sense of security. With each visit the bear made to Luvrahn, Aros had found himself uttering fewer warnings to the children.

They had all paid for their hubris when the bear had killed one of those children in the town square.

Aros could not shake the overwhelming sense that he was the one to blame for the savage attack. After all, he had fostered Fisa's love for the creature from the beginning.

It had seemed poetic at the time.

The bear had first arrived in the village the day Fisa was born. It was as though the Ancient Ones had sent this creature to look after him from

11

the moment he drew his first breath. As the years passed, Aros had spent hours sitting with Fisa and watching the bear whenever she ventured near. In hushed tones, he would tell the sandy-haired child everything he knew about bears, no matter how small the morsel of information was.

If they were in a larger town, Aros would have found a bookstore and combed the shelves for a tome about the beast. Despite his years, his knowledge of bears was limited to only what a hunter would need to know for survival. There were scholars, he knew, that would have spent decades dedicated to watching the habits and movements of the creature before publishing their findings for all to read.

The thought of searching for a book had come when Fisa had first told Aros that he had "*already told him that*" when they were watching the bear figure out how to lift the lid of a barrel. The lid had been weighed down with rocks to prevent such a thief, but she had still managed to secure a prize of apples.

Aros had never forgotten how woefully inadequate he had felt in that moment.

It had not been a sensation that he was used to. In all his years, he had only ever experienced one other instance of such a feeling, and that had been half a century prior.

Elves were long-lived, but such emotions were not forgotten easily.

And it did not matter how Aros felt—they were not in a larger town. They were merely a settlement along the very edge of the queendom of Ailiar, so small that Aros was not sure if they even appeared on a map, days away from the nearest settlement.

For his part, Aros hoped they were not listed on any map.

Many people saw Luvrahn as a refuge, a place to which they could escape when their lives had all but forsaken them. The belief that they were so well hidden from the rest of the world kept some of them going.

He supposed that is what made Fisa's death so jarring.

This was a place where people were supposed to be safe, where they were supposed to be free of horror and torment.

Aros replayed the events over and over in his mind, trying in vain to figure out how no one had noticed Fisa inching closer towards the beast. He could not imagine that someone had seen him walk up to the bear and yet had not tried to stop him.

Aros could not even recall what he had been doing the moments before he had heard Fisa's voice ring out:

"Look, Ma! Look, Aros! Her fur is so soft and warm!"

Everything had moved both too quickly and too slowly after that.

Every soul that had been in the village square had turned around in what felt like same instant. Aros swore that he had seen the muscles in Fisa's mother's legs tense as she prepared to surge forward. He could remember how his own body had pressed down into the earth to propel him towards Fisa and the bear and stop the inevitable.

In the end, no one could have moved quickly enough.

The attack had been immediate.

Brutal.

It had taken three grown males to hold Fisa's mother back once they realised there was no saving him. Her wailing had bounced off the walls of the cottages, rung over the fields, and echoed into the ever-reaching sky above. It was filled with that singular note of pain and torment that was reserved only for mothers unfortunate enough to have their children ripped away from them before their time.

There were other screams, too.

Those were the screams of people who were witnessing a tragedy unlike anything else they had ever seen before. As horrific as they were, they paled in comparison to the soul-shattering cries of Fisa's mother.

Even Aros, who had a collection of horrific and gruesome memories that he had accumulated before he had settled in Luvrahn, knew that the image of Fisa's death would haunt him until his last breath. He would carry the memory of blood-soaked claws, the gurgled plea for help, and the mangled body until he could carry it no longer.

And if, gods forbid, he could carry his memories into the afterlife, into the gilded halls of Di'Tyan, Aros would replay the memory of Fisa's last desperate breaths for all eternity.

In the chaos and confusion, the bear had managed to escape to the Edgeling Woods.

The males holding back Fisa's mother eventually let her go, and she staggered towards her son's corpse. Fresh red blood seeped into her light-blue linen skirt. The stain grew and spread through the fabric as though tainting Fisa's mother with the horror of what had just happened.

She pulled the remains of her son into her arms. She rocked back and forth, much as she had done when he was younger, and wailed. The sound bore its way into the marrow of Aros' bones, weaving into the fabric of his being.

He tried to bear witness to her grief for as long as he could, but eventually, he found himself forced to turn away.

Movement from the corner of his eye caught his attention. Aros redirected his gaze to the three males that had held Fisa's mother back. They were huddled together now, engaged in deep discussion. Their hand movements were quick and violent, their faces turning red, and they were speaking in a very sure, confident manner. Over the wailing cries, Aros could not make out what they were saying despite the keenness of elven ears. So, he crossed the distance between them, and inserted himself amongst their ranks.

"What's going on?" he asked.

It was Dorsa who replied.

"We're going t' go aft'r th' beast," he said in that low, gruff voice of his. "And we're going t' do what's right. Life fer a life."

Aros' brow furrowed as the other two males nodded in agreement with the village's resident blacksmith.

"It was an accident," Aros tried to reason.

"Accident or no," piped up Rych. "That bear deserves what's coming to her. You don't just kill a kid and get to live your life free of the consequences."

Despite being half Aros' size, Rych held his chin high as he glared him down. Aros appreciated a male who held his own, regardless of who they were standing against.

He gave the youth a slight nod in acknowledgment of his bravery, and some of the tension disappeared from Rych's shoulders.

"You can't say that you don't want to go after the thing," said the third male.

Aros did not need to look at him to know that Holsten's grey eyes were casting accusations. He fought the urge to curl his nose into a sneer at the sheer implication that he would not want to avenge Fisa's death. But the bear was an animal, a creature unable to comprehend what she'd done beyond the simple fact that it had dispatched what she'd believed to be a threat to her survival.

She had no concept of revenge and would not understand why the villagers would be after her when they raised their weapons and magic.

"Or have you changed, C'Asad?" Holsten continued. "Have you lost your heightened sense of morality?"

A low growl rippled in Aros' throat. The wind, coaxed by the magic his unchecked emotions roused, whipped Holsten's mousey hair around his face. The beads in Aros' braids clinked together.

Holsten's face split into a wolfish grin.

He lifted his hands, but before he could direct the flames dancing on his fingertips towards Aros, they were both slapped up the back of their heads.

"Ow," Holsten complained.

"Who-" Aros did not need to finish his question.

Beside him, with her round face scrunched tightly in frustration, stood Aoife Reih. How she had managed to smack both males on the back of the head when the puffs of hair on the top of her own barely cleared their shoulders, he didn't know.

He wasn't sure he *wanted* to.

Aoife had ways of getting into places she shouldn't—it was what had made her so successful when she had worked for the Queen.

Aros sighed and lifted his hands, moving them as he spoke to the wife of his closest friend.

"What is it?" he asked.

When Aoife responded, it was with her hands only, but Aros felt the sting of her words as though she had shouted them.

"A mother is grieving the loss of her child, and you two louts are about to get into a fight?"

Dorsa snorted a laugh, and Aoife shot him a deadly look that made the tall, broad male look down at the ground in shame.

"The four of you need to take your business elsewhere if you are going to continue to cause a scene while Dania cradles her poor baby's body, or you will have me to answer to."

The four males muttered a chorus of *yes, ma'am*'s, earning a satisfied nod from the short, angry female. Aoife may be the homeliest of all the females in Luvrahn, but Aros would rather face a starved Kapriae than get on her bad side. She was the most respected member of their village and had a way of getting under your skin when she put her mind to it. Even the oldest and gruffest of elves dipped their heads in reverence to the mute storyteller of Luvrahn.

"Sorry," Aros muttered, signing the word for it as he spoke.

Aoife shook her head at him as though she was most disappointed in him of the four of them.

Heat rose to his cheeks and reached the pointed tips of his ears. He opened his mouth to apologise again, but he was cut off when Aoife gestured for him to follow her.

He obeyed. He did not entirely believe that it was a coincidence that Aoife had positioned them so he could see Dania, still rocking back and forth, wailing over her son's corpse.

"*You have to go with them,*" Aoife signed.

"You know I don't believe in killing animals for stuff like this," he said, voice low. He held his hands out to her, palms up. "You can't expect me to go with them, knowing that they will torture the bear for what she did."

"*That is exactly why you have to go,*" Aoife replied. "*You know the Woods better than anyone. You can find her before they do, and you can give her a good, clean death. You can make sure that they get their revenge without sacrificing the respect she is owed.*"

Aros clenched his jaw.

He hated that she was right. Hated that she was playing on his sense of honour to convince him to join the little hunt that Dorsa, Rych, and Holsten were planning.

He didn't mind the first two, but the idea of spending days out in the Woods with Holsten made his blood boil. His eyes slid over to the trio only to meet Holsten's gaze.

The other male smirked.

Aoife poked Aros in the gut, drawing his attention back to her. He glared at her and rubbed the aching spot.

"*You know I'm right,*" she signed. "*And you know that* he *will make her suffer as long as he can if there is no one there to stop him.*"

Aros took a deep breath before he eventually relented.

"It's what Fisa would have wanted," he said finally.

Aoife's smile was warm and kind.

"*It is.*"

Aros left with the hunting party later that afternoon, after Dania had been coaxed away from the sight of Fisa's death. The boy's remains had been laid in a grave in the meadow. The mound of dark earth had stood in high contrast beside the wildflowers, but it was where he belonged.

Dorsa pulled a cart behind him laden with enough food and provisions to last the four of them a few weeks. When Holsten asked why it was necessary when they were all strong and able enough to carry packs of their own, Dorsa had simply replied: "Do y' want t' carry a bear back on yer shoulders? Ye can if yer like, but I won't help y'."

Aros did not think it would take them weeks to find the bear, but he did not offer his opinion on the matter. As far as he was concerned, the less they knew about his hunches, the better. It would be easier to lead them astray when the time came if they believed he agreed with their plans.

They set up camp a few hours in. Holsten boasted about beasts he had killed in the past, animals that he had hunted for nothing more than sport. Dorsa bragged about obscenely large hammers that he had forged and wielded in the last war, and how easily they had caved in the skulls of full-grown Kapriaes.

Rych, to Aros' surprise, stayed quiet. He stared into the flames of the fire that Dorsa had lit with the magic his Affinity had gifted him, seemingly unaware of the conversations going on around him.

He only moved when Holsten nudged him with his elbow. Even then, it was to plaster on a fake smile.

Aros wondered what had happened to the male that had stood up to him earlier that day. Perhaps he had lost his nerve after the adrenaline had left his body.

It happened.

Aros had seen it many times. It was easy to rally people to a cause when they had just witnessed the cause of their anger. People were more likely to respond when surrounded by others who were just as enraged and hurt as they were. But take them away from the situation, give them time to think?

Many would question if they had what it took to live up to the heated words they had yelled mere hours before.

They did not see the bear the next day.

As the sun was setting on the third day, Aros had come across fresh tracks. His heart pounded in his chest.

He turned towards the hunting party.

"She went that way," he said, gesturing in the opposite direction.

There were tracks leading the way he pointed, and he hoped the other three either trusted him—or were dumb—enough to follow his direction blindly.

Although Holsten scoffed at him, he was relieved when the hunting party began walking the way he pointed. After an hour, they decided to set up camp for the night.

"We're going to get it tomorrow," Holsten said.

"We should ask Watren to tan its hide," Rych said. "And give it to Dania. Proof that we killed the beast that killed her boy."

"There he is," Holsten crowed. "And I thought you had gone all soft-hearted like pouty C'Asad."

"I am not pouty," Aros muttered.

Holsten chuckled.

"Sure you are," he said. "You're upset that we are going to kill one of the precious creatures of the forest. It doesn't matter to you that it deserves it."

Aros stared at the flames Dorsa had conjured. It would be so easy to call on the magic that ran through his veins and coax a rush of air to push the fire towards Holsten. He truly believed that Holsten would look better with one—or both—of his eyebrows missing.

But that would lead to trouble that he did not need. Not when they were so close, and they could end this gods-forsaken trip so soon.

"Leave 'im 'lone," Dorsa grumbled. "He came. He's 'elping, which is more th'n I c'n say fer y'."

Holsten made a sound that landed somewhere between a started stoat and an empty waterskin being thrown against a boulder. Aros bit the inside of his lip to keep himself from laughing.

Thankfully, the rest of the night passed without incident, and the others had drifted off to sleep with the aid of some ale Rych had brought along. Once he was sure they were well and truly passed out, Aros quietly picked up his bow and retraced their steps back through the Woods.

Ever since he had settled in Luvrahn, Aros had regularly disappeared for weeks at a time, camping, and hunting, generally keeping to himself. He felt more at home here than he did in the village. It was easier, surrounded by trees and gentle, bracing breezes, to forget the horrors he had seen over the decades. He did not see bloody bodies in his dreams when he slept under the canopy of trees.

Perhaps it was the open air that soothed the magic within him. His Affinity fell under the air element after all, making him a Aerdhraos. He supposed it made sense for him to feel more comfortable out in the open, much like a Visdhraos, whose Affinity fell under water, might feel more comfortable by the sea.

Sometimes, like now, when he was picking through the underbrush of the Edgeling Woods under cover of darkness, he wondered if he should just leave Luvrahn entirely.

He had played his part.

He had helped establish the settlement and had seen it grow into a self-sustained, thriving community.

He could leave right now if he wanted to.

Abandon the hunt and disappear.

But then he would be leaving the bear to the mercy of Holsten, and he would never leave a creature to that fate.

It was the one thing he held onto from his past. A voice, so melodic yet so commanding, reminding him that it was the responsibility of those with power to treat the creatures without it with respect and dignity. Otherwise, how were they any better? What was the point of having that power?

It was something Holsten could never understand. Aros had tried to explain it to him in a million ways, but each time had ended with them being pulled off each other, both covered in cuts, bruises, and burns.

Aros couldn't deny that seeing Holsten struggle for breath after Aros had finally relented and used his Affinity against him pleased him. He also would not lie and say that he did not like how his power changed the colours of the flames Holsten wielded. The only downside being that Aros was then unable to feign innocence.

His magic worked best when there weren't any visual cues to betray that he was using them.

Aros turned his face up towards the sky. Lifting two fingers, he motioned to the side. The wind obeyed his request and parted the topmost branches of the canopy to reveal the moon and stars. He had been following the tracks longer than he thought, his mind caught up in the possibility of running away from his responsibilities.

Again.

Aros cursed under his breath.

He needed to move quicker if he wanted to make sure that he didn't lose the bear. He needed to pay more attention if he didn't want the sun to rise before he found her and risk the others doing so.

He pushed on.

Doubt began to creep into his mind. Had he been mistaken? Had he read the tracks incorrectly?

He'd tracked and hunted many animals over the course of his lifetime, but he was not so naïve to think that the loss of Fisa hadn't affected him. Even though he was not allowing himself to grieve his loss until this hunt was over, his heart could not be expected to obey.

The anguish of losing someone so young and so dear and feeling wholly responsible takes its toll. Perhaps it had addled his brain so that he was seeing things that weren't there, or missing things that were.

Otherwise, how else had he not come across the bear already?

The tracks appeared fresh enough to suggest that she was nearby. He could have sworn that a pile of dung he had passed still emitted warmth.

Was it even bear dung?

The Edgeling Woods was riddled with different scents that he could have been mistaken. Despite his experience, the sickly-sweet scent of the night-blooms could have messed with his sense of smell.

Aros had been so caught up in the swirling, taunting thoughts that threatened his confidence in his abilities that he almost missed it. He stopped mid-step, rocked back on his heels, and dropped into a crouch.

Tracks.

New tracks, fresh ones. Made within the last few minutes.

Aros cushioned his steps with his Affinity to keep his approach silent as he followed them. It was not long before he heard the unmistakable snuffling of a bear rooting around for something to eat.

Aros hid himself behind the dying branches of a fallen tree. The bear was in a small clearing, bathed in the glow of the moon.

It looked ethereal and majestic.

Fisa would have loved to see her like this. He must remember to tell him when he—

Tears pricked in Aros' eyes. He would not be able to tell Fisa how beautiful the bear looked when the moon made the tips of her fur appear silver. He could not describe how nightblooms had edged the clearing like a fence of pale white.

Never again would he sit on an upturned crate with Fisa on his lap, watching the bear go about her business while the crafters of the village sang or while the scent of bread danced in the air.

With that pain crushing his heart in its iron fist, Aros understood the desire for vengeance. This creature had taken away such a bright and beautiful light from the people who loved Fisa the most. It would be so easy to give in to the desire to make her feel a fraction of what they did.

A fraction of what Fisa had felt.

But that was why Aros was here—to stop emotions from getting in the way and to give the bear a clean, quick, dignified death.

He took a steadying breath before returning his attention to the scene before him.

The moonlight had played its part in making the bear look magical. What Aros hadn't noticed the first time he looked was the body that lay in the clearing as well.

He could not tell if the body was dead, or if they were simply pretending to be. Either way, the bear was growing more insistent in its pawing at them. Soon, those claws would not just be trying to get the person to move, they would be cutting into the flesh as easily as they had cut into Fisa.

Aros loosed a breath.

The world fell away as Aros lifted his bow and knocked an arrow. The trees fell silent, the distant brook stopped bubbling.

Even his heart slowed its beat as Aros took aim.

When he was sure and ready, he shifted his foot to press down on a fallen stick. The *snap* rang out through the Woods, and just as he had planned, the bear swung her massive head towards him. There was something poetic about the fact that she was providing him with the perfect shot.

He loosed the arrow, and with the aid of his Affinity, it found its home deep in her eye. She was not even able to utter a roar of pain as that simple, single arrow ended her life. Her large body fell to the ground. Her paws twitched once, twice, and then she stilled forever.

Aros waited for the count of fifteen before he moved. He did not bother to mask his footsteps with magic as he approached the creature.

There was no reason to hide what he had done. He had killed, and it had not been for his own survival.

Aros crouched by the bear's head. Her eyes were still open, and the one that did not have an arrow through it stared blankly at him.

"I am sorry," Aros said quietly. "May Di'Tyan welcome you into his golden halls. May you feast on salmon and honey in the fields eternal."

It was still hotly debated amongst the faithful whether or not the god of Death—one of the oldest of the Ancient Ones—allowed creatures and beasts into the afterlife. Aros himself was uncertain of his own thoughts on the matter.

Just in case, he ensured that he always said a prayer over each animal he killed. He could not shake the sense of responsibility to at least open the pathway into an afterlife for the lives that he took.

A whimpering sound caught his attention, and he turned toward it. The stranger—not body, as he had originally thought—was lying on their side, curled tightly around a pack.

Aros offered one more silent apology and prayer to the bear before he moved over to them.

The moon allowed him to see three things immediately: she was a woman, she was severely injured, and most importantly – she was a human.

Aros swallowed hard.

He was sure that he hadn't crossed the border. The air in Colosia smelled different. He couldn't explain how, but he had been there before, and it had felt wrong. He had chalked it up to the hatred Colosian humans had for elves, to a general feeling of animosity that had tainted the air around them.

But the air was still sweet here, still cool and calm.

No. He was certain that he was still in Ailiar.

So why was she here? Where were her shoes? Why were her feet and legs shredded and torn as though she had been walking through the Woods for weeks without the appropriate footwear?

Why were their burns and tears in her skirts, and knots and debris in her hair?

What had driven her to Ailiar?

She whimpered again. Aros reached out to gently rest his hand on her shoulder.

"Are you alright?" he asked.

She didn't reply. She did not even flinch at his touch.

She simply remained curled around her pack, sobs racking her slight frame.

"It's going to be okay," Aros said softly. "The bear can't hurt you now, and neither will I. But you can't stay here. It's not safe out here."

He rubbed his face with his free hand as though the motion could solve the situation at hand. Rough stubble grazed his palm. Sweat and grime coated his fingers, and he wiped it off on his linen pants.

"Can I help you up?" he asked. "I have a camp nearby. Our village isn't far either, and we have a cart if it hurts to walk too much. We have a very good healer, and she'd be able to help you."

The human still did not respond.

Could she even understand him?

He had been sure that humans spoke in the Common tongue, but his experience had been limited. Perhaps knowledge of the Common tongue was reserved for the nobles, royals and merchants of Colosia. Perhaps the common folk of Colosia had their own language.

Aros should know if that was the case. Even if he had not stepped foot in Balliach in fifty years, he should still know—

The human nodded.

She unfurled her body and, with Aros' arm around her, tried to stand.

She cried out in pain, and her legs buckled from under her.

Aros caught her before she hit the ground, pulling her against his chest. Her sobs began anew.

Aros looked at her feet again and grimaced. There were more glistening patches of infection than patches of skin. Mud was caked over it all, stretching up her leg.

There was no way she would be able to walk without making matters worse.

He was going to need to carry her.

Aros looked at the bow in his hand and sighed.

He had not expected to find someone out here and had certainly not expected to have to carry them back to camp. Not wanting to risk damaging the bow, he held it out to the human.

"Carry this," he said. "And I will carry you."

Thankfully, she gripped the bow and held it as tightly as she did her pack.

Aros decided that once they were back in Luvrahn and her wounds had been seen to, he would ask her what was in it. In her position, he would have thrown the pack across the clearing in the hopes that the bear would go after it. If it had food inside, it made sense why the bear would be interested and further cemented the rationale behind using it to create an escape. If not, it must have something so sentimental that even after travelling for weeks, as he was sure she had, she still held onto it with such ferocity.

"Are you ready?"

The human nodded again. Perhaps, like Aoife, she was mute. That was fine if so. Almost the entire population of Luvrahn knew Common sign language to some degree of fluency. She would not be alone, and Aros could figure out what had happened to her.

Perhaps he could even fix it.

He knelt on one knee to better get a hold of her. The ground was damp with the dew that came with such early hours of the morning. It seeped into the fabric at his knees, and he found some relief in the knowledge that the wetness he felt as he lifted the human into his arms was not entirely from blood.

It was a small blessing, but it was not one that he was going to ignore.

He straightened and readjusted his hold on her as gently as he could. Aros could not completely prevent all movement, and the human's pained whimpers tugged at his heart.

"I know," he said as he turned around and carried her past the bear's corpse and out of the clearing.

"You should have thrown the pack," he told her as he walked.

The colours of the Woods shifted as the sky above lightened. The dark blues, greens and purples of the night were slowly giving way to the more vibrant, varied shades of green, red and brown. Morning would be here soon, and Aros would need to figure out how to explain to the other hunters why he was returning to camp with a human.

"If you had thrown it," he continued. "She would have been distracted enough to go after it, and you could have escaped."

The human shook her head.

"No," she rasped. "It was going to eat me. I know it."

That answered the question about her being mute.

"I am going to assume that you do not usually spend much time out in the wilderness," he said. "But animals, even ones as large as bears, prefer to steer clear of people. Unless they are desperate or feel threatened, they would prefer not to risk running into us."

The human sniffled again but did not answer one way or another. It didn't matter. Even though her clothes were hanging off her too-thin frame by threads and tatters, he could determine well enough that they were not designed to be worn on long journeys. The fabric seemed to be finer than the thick linen or wool from which his own clothes were made. And though the skirt was a patchwork of different colours and patterns, the blouse did not have any evidence of mending or reinforcement.

Either it had been new before she ended up in the Edgeling Woods, or she was accustomed to a quieter lifestyle.

Which meant she was running from something terrible.

He clenched his jaw as he began to prepare himself mentally for the unrelenting teasing that he was inevitably going to receive from Palis when they returned to Luvrahn. He could already hear his friend's voice in his head, as clear as if she were walking beside him.

"You just couldn't help yourself, could you? You just had to save a damsel in distress. Really Aros, this quiet village life doesn't suit you. You should go back to the capital. We both know Meitranis would take you back in a heartbeat."

"Who is Meitranis?"

Aros' steps faltered.

Had he really said all of that aloud?

Perhaps he did spend too much time out in the woods on his own if he voiced his thoughts so loudly.

In response to the human's question, he shook his head.

"She is an old friend of mine," he said dismissively. "It doesn't matter, I was just thinking out loud. You don't need to worry about that."

He looked down at her.

In the gradually brightening light, he could see that her hair was red. Once free of the mud, twigs and knots, it was probably quite beautiful, with tight curls that he could imagine bounced with every step she took.

An image of another woman he had known with similar hair came to mind—one that he quickly banished by forcing his attention elsewhere. It landed on the pendant that nestled against her throat. It was a deep red stone, carved to resemble a flower with many petals, nestled in a gold setting.

It was a beautiful piece of jewellery that would have cost a small fortune. Perhaps she had come from a wealthy family.

But that did not explain the patchwork skirt or the general plainness of her clothing.

Perhaps she had stolen it.

That must be why she was in the Woods. It made sense. If she had stolen from a wealthy family, she might be hiding from the rightful owners. Her pack could be filled with other gold and jewels.

If I were to have stolen precious jewels, Aros thought. *I would not be wearing them around my neck for anyone to see.*

Every answer that he considered only raised more questions. Frustrated, he decided to simply ask.

"Why are you out here anyway?"

The human did not answer. Instead, she curled up tightly once more and turned in his arms to bury her face against his chest.

The motion set his heart racing.

He continued walking, trying to ignore the sensation in his chest of having someone once more curl into him for comfort. He did not notice that the human was crying until a wet patch blossomed over his tunic. He pursed his lips.

With each step back towards the camp, Aros could feel the heavy weight of responsibility form and settle in his gut. He had just saved this girl's life, and now, he was honour bound to protect her. With his own life, if necessary.

You are not bound by those old oaths anymore, a voice from deep within his own mind said.

But what else was he supposed to do?

He could not just leave her there. Her legs and feet were covered in so many gaping, open wounds that it would take weeks for them to heal. He could not imagine how long it would take before she could walk without pain again. There would be other wounds too, ones that he had not yet seen that would certainly need tending to.

The bags under her eyes were so large and dark that Aros wondered when she had last been able to get restful sleep. She was so thin that her shoulders were poking painfully into his chest.

And even if she were not treading the path toward Di'Tyan's gates, bears were not the only creatures that roamed these woods.

And creatures, Aros knew, were not the only beasts.

Without his intervention, the human likely would not have survived another day.

So, Aros had done the only thing that could be done.

He had saved her. There was no undoing that now.

With that in mind, he pushed away the thought that he would soon grow to regret his decision.

Two

DI'ATH

ZADANAI

PRINCE DI'ATH ADARNA OF Zadanai sat hunched over a heavy wooden desk. The surface was covered in layers of parchment and paper. Piles of varying heights threatened to fall over the edge at any given moment—as though obstructing his view of the glistening sea through the large window wasn't enough.

He flexed his hand, trying to work out the cramp that had begun to form from the hours he had spent pouring over his outstanding accounts. There were, he had concluded long ago, far too many. Di'Ath vowed that once he was done here, he would never again make purchases with a line of credit.

Slap.

Slap.

Slap.

The muscle in Di'Ath's jaw twitched.

He focused on the ledger in hand. How had he spent 15 gold dragons at a tea shop? He didn't even particularly like tea. He much preferred the rich, warm taste of coffee. Di'Ath would have understood if he had amassed a debt of 15 gold dragons at Yu'San's coffee emporium, but *tea*?

He only drank tea with his family or when...

The long, pointed tips of Di'Ath's ears warmed and the corner of his mouth curled up in a lopsided grin.

He remembered how he had amassed such a debt.

Tea, he had discovered, was a wonderful way of wooing ladies. After some experimenting, Di'Ath had concluded that the more varieties of tea one presented to a woman they were interested in, the more likely she was to give her attention.

He had never worked out the reason why this happened. Tea was common enough. It was used daily, even by the poorest of Zadanai's citizens. Di'Ath could travel to any village in the country and have no problem finding a hot cup of tea.

It was used by everyone, for seemingly everything.

You just woke up and are greeting the day? Cup of tea.

Standing behind a market stall in the blazing heat? Cup of tea.

Meeting foreign dignitaries to discuss trade agreements? Cup of tea.

There were even vendors on the docks that sold nothing but tea.

Slap.

Slap.

Slap.

Di'Ath took a deep breath. In. Hold. Out.

He counted out fifteen gold dragons from the large leather pouch on the desk, and deposited them into a smaller, silk pouch. On a clean piece of parchment, he copied the itemised list of his purchases, the total amount owed, and the amount the tea shop would receive. He folded the copied page and added it to the silk pouch.

Pulling the golden drawstring closed, he added it to the pile of pouches in the basket beside his chair.

Another one down, he thought to himself. *And a thousand more to go.*

He couldn't imagine why anyone would choose to do this for a living. As a prince, Di'Ath was not accustomed to balancing his accounts. He simply purchased items, and the royal treasurer would take care of the rest.

If you had not reacted so childishly, they would have taken care of this, too, he reminded himself with a groan.

There was no going back and changing things now. The only thing to do was reach for the next ledger again and again until they were all completed, and then he could pay the merchants what he owed.

He reached forward, fingers outstretched to grasp the next ledger.

Slap.

Slap.

Slap.

Di'Ath twisted in his chair to glare at his sister, unable to take it anymore.

Princess Sy'da was lying comfortably on his bed, surrounded by plush cushions and colourful throw blankets. She threw a red ball into the air and caught it was a loud, obnoxious *slap.*

Di'Ath clenched his jaw so tightly he thought the pressure may soon break his teeth.

"Is that really necessary?" he ground out.

Sy'da turned her wide, dark eyes on him. She pouted, and Di'Ath wondered how often she had used that exact expression to get her way.

"Of course it is," she said. "I would simply *die* if I could not play with my ball."

She draped her arm dramatically over her forehead, the many bangles on her wrist jingling and clinking against each other as they slid down. The gold stood out stark against the deep olive tone of her skin and the long, black curtain of hair that pooled around her.

"As it is," Sy'da continued. "I can already feel my very life force draining from my body at this small interruption. I am already feeling so ill and weak. Dear brother, you do not wish me to *die,* do you?"

Di'Ath groaned. He pinched the bridge of his nose.

His sister was known for having a flair for the dramatic. It served her well when she performed on the silks, pretending to fall from the ceiling only to be caught by the large, colourful lengths of fabric right before she hit the ground.

He only wished that she wouldn't use it with him.

"I am very seriously considering its merits," he groaned. "It would make what I am doing so much quicker, and it would save me a lot of trouble in the future."

Sy'da poked out her tongue and sat up with an exaggerated grunt. The bangles clinked together again, and the bells that circled her ankle chimed in unison.

"You're no fun," Sy'da said. "Ever since you got engaged, you've been dreadfully boring and dull."

Di'Ath's expression darkened. He did not like to talk about his engagement. His pending nuptials to Princess Calliope of Ailiar were not on the list of things he looked forward to.

It was why he was balancing his accounts himself. *To teach you some responsibility*, his father had said.

Apparently, being upset that you were being sold off like cattle to marry some foreign princess in a country across the sea meant that you lacked responsibility. According to the King of Zadanai, if you showed your displeasure at not even being so much as consulted on the matter meant that Di'Ath lacked a sense of duty to his family.

Di'Ath was not proud of his actions following that 'conversation.'

Not only had he doubled his already outstanding debts in a foolhardy attempt to inconvenience his father *after* Di'Ath had already left, but he had allowed his emotions to get the better of him in a more destructive manner as well.

Like the other members of the royal family of Adarna, Di'Ath was a Visdhraos, with his Affinity falling under the water element. And, like the other members of his family, his magic was stronger than most. The Adarna's were renowned for having unique manifestations of their Affinity. His father, King Di'San, could summon tidal waves and conjure whirlpools in the shallowest of puddles. His eldest brother, Di'Wen, was able to conjure torrential rains even on cloudless days. His mother could see the future in the water, and Sy'da could freeze anything.

But Di'Ath...

Di'Ath just brought destruction.

"You heard father," he said, voice low. "I must be responsible now. I must represent the family to the highest standard."

Di'Ath was never supposed to be a representative of the family at all, save for a handful of royal functions throughout the year. He was the youngest son of the King and Queen and the second youngest of all their children. He had seven older brothers who had all been raised to bear the weight of responsibility and three older sisters who had the ferocity and tenacity to take their place should they fail.

Even Sy'da, the youngest of all Adarna children, would be better suited to taking on any role remotely akin to leadership than Di'Ath.

Di'Ath had grown up expecting to live a life of luxury, worrying only that his magic did not get the best of him. He was not prepared to marry the crown princess of another country. He was not prepared to one day become King himself. The idea of being responsible for the wealth, safety and happiness of an entire country had been so far out of reach, that to see it on the horizon now had Di'Ath feeling trapped.

It was as though he were back in the Salt Room, where the water was drawn out of the air and his magic was tamped down and starved until Di'Ath could regain control of it.

Sy'da slid off the bed and crossed the room. The bells on her ankle chimed with each step she took, a reminder of the greatest decision Di'Ath had ever made. He had bought the anklet for her to stop his sister from sneaking around the palace like a cat and jumping out at him from around corners at the most inopportune moments.

Sy'da reached over his shoulder and freed a small, framed portrait from the piles of paper and ledgers.

Di'Ath turned back around in his seat and buried his nose in the next set of numbers. He did not need to look at the portrait that now sat nestled in Sy'da's manicured hand. He did not want to think of the woman that was depicted, or their pending nuptials.

He supposed that she was handsome, to a degree. Her hair, a dull brown, had been curled and styled in such a manner that was probably considered the height of fashion in Ailiar, but if she were to step a foot in Zadanai? She would be ridiculed. The ribbons and pearls were used far too liberally, and the princess was almost lost in the pomp and frill.

Perhaps it was for the best, though, the horrific gown providing a distraction from the woman's countenance. Princess Calliope's mouth did not look as though it were capable of smiling, and her eyes were of such a muddied green Di'Ath could not imagine looking into them long enough to complete the wedding ceremony, never mind gaze into them lovingly.

But maybe Di'Ath was being too harsh. He had not received this portrait until after his father had announced their betrothal after all, and Di'Ath was not too proud to admit that his emotions could cloud his judgement.

It was not truly fair to judge her before he had even met her.

Just as it was unfair to compare her to the women of Zadanai, whose complexions were warm, their smiles wide, and who adorned themselves in rich colours and beautiful jewellery. Princess Calliope was so pale he had wondered if she had ever walked under the sun. He could not imagine any of Sy'da's gold bangles suiting the Ailian princess' complexion.

No. The women of Zadanai and the princess of Ailiar were as different as night and day. But just because Di'Ath had a fondness for night did not mean that he did not see value in the blue sky of day.

"What do you think she's like?" Sy'da asked.

Di'Ath sighed and slumped in his seat.

"Does it really matter what she's like?"

Sy'da shrugged. "It only matters if you are going to be spending the rest of your life with her."

She gasped, and Di'Ath's attention snapped towards her.

The feigned expression of shock and horror on his sister's face did not waver as she continued to speak.

"Oh!" she said. "That's right! You *are* going to be spending the rest of your life with her because you are going to *marry* her! You are going to have hundreds of pale little Ailian babies, and my big brother is going to be *King Di'Ath of Ailiar*."

Di'Ath groaned. The silk of his coat rustled as he slumped further down in his chair.

"Don't call me that," he whined. "Or I shall order you to go wander into the sea."

"Oh, how wonderful it would be," Sy'da continued. "To be the sister of the King."

Di'Ath raised a brow. "You are already a daughter of a king," he reminded her.

Sy'da waved a hand dismissively.

"Being the daughter of the king in the country you were born in is nothing," she said. "Not when you compare it to being the sister of the king in a land across the sea. My company will be sought after by everyone, from Queen Meitranis herself down to the common folk. Not only can nobles attempt to curry favour with you by creating friendships with me, but they will be so excited to learn about our home and customs that I will be able to talk about Zadanai to my heart's content."

Di'Ath's eyes fell on the portrait in her hand.

"That is only if I do not change my mind," he said. "I could tell father that I no longer wish you to join me on my journey. I am sure he would be thrilled to keep his youngest daughter at home."

Hoping his threat had distracted her enough, Di'Ath tried to snatch the portrait out of her grip. But Sy'da, in contrast to her magic, was too quick. She stepped back and held the framed picture high out of Di'Ath's seated reach.

"Uh-uh," she admonished with a wagging finger. "No snatching. Really, that kind of behaviour is unbefitting of a future king."

She giggled as Di'Ath's lip curled into a snarl.

"And besides," she continued. "You wouldn't dare tell father that you don't want me to go on the off chance that he would believe you. You seem to forget that I was there when you got down on your knees and begged him to let me join you."

It was not one of Di'Ath's finer moments. He had scuffed the toes of his favourite shoes and stained the knees of his favourite pair of white pants as he had begged his father to at least consider sending Sy'da to Ailiar with him.

Perhaps he would not have needed to beg if he had not responded to the news of his engagement by destroying the sitting room with his magic. If he had only accepted his fate with humility and grace, as his older siblings had done, he would have been able to request Sy'da's company without needing to make a complete and utter fool of himself.

Perhaps, a mocking voice in his mind said. *If you were a stronger man, you wouldn't need your younger sister to hold your hand.*

"I *suggested* that you accompany me," Di'Ath said through clenched teeth. "So that I would not be surrounded by Ailian idiots. If you recall, I was the one who suggested that it would be beneficial to search for a suitor for you in Ailiar seeing as the wells here are running dry, thanks to our multitude of married siblings. But as I said, I could always change my mind if you wish to stay behind."

The muscle in Sy'da's jaw twitched. Di'Ath felt a chill run down his spine, and his breath came out in a puff of white fog. He was pushing his luck, and he knew it. Sy'da had only come into her Affinity a few months ago, and although she had not needed to spend time in the Salt Room, it was still dangerous to push an elf who had not been given the time to master their magic.

"You will want to keep that in check if you want to go to Ailiar," he warned, voice low. "We do not know how casual they are with their magic. Someone could see you doing something like this as a threat. And even if they didn't, we don't want to start a war by freezing the wrong person."

"*We don't want to start a war by freezing the wrong person*," Sy'da mimicked.

She set the portrait back down on the desk. Warmth seeped back into Di'Ath's bones and tension left his shoulders as Sy'da released her magic. She leaned against the desk and crossed her arms over her chest as she watched him with those dark eyes of hers. Eyes that, like his, were set beneath thick, dark brows and seemed to drink in the sight of everything around them.

Di'Ath had always thought Sy'da looked just like their mother, until he stood beside her in a mirror, or passed a portrait. As the youngest pair of Adarna siblings, Di'Ath and Sy'da looked more like each other than they did either of their parents. They could have passed for twins, if Di'Ath were not nearly two full years older.

"Do not take this as me being anything other than completely ecstatic about the prospects of seeing the world," Sy'da said. "But... why are you marrying her?"

Di'Ath had asked himself the same question every day since he had learned of his betrothal. His gaze flicked back to the portrait of the Ailian princess. Her dull green eyes stared out at him, devoid of emotion.

He doubted that even the finest tea set from the finest store in the Zadanese capital would bring light to those eyes.

"Because it is my duty," Di'Ath recited his father's words as a reply.

"Your duty?" Sy'da scoffed. "Your duty is nothing more than drinking away our wealth and bedding too many women to keep track of the bastards you bear. How has this fallen to you?"

Di'Ath managed a weak smile. Had he not followed the same thoughts himself? Had he not tried to use it to devise an excuse to defy their father?

He would even go so far as to join the crew of a ship, providing a royal presence to increase morale and stoke the fires of patriotism. After all, what worked better to invoke feelings of loyalty to one's governing body than by fighting alongside someone who was a part of it?

But the Tide had other plans.

He would never forget the night he had been called into his father's study. His mother's eyes had shone with tears as his father sat straight and proud behind his desk. There had been no room for argument as the King of Zadanai told his youngest son that come autumn, he would be sailing across the Zadanese sea and marrying the crown princess of Ailiar.

He would never forget how sorrow morphed into horror on his mother's face when Di'Ath had lost control of both his emotions and his magic, or the way the blood had dripped down his father's face.

The memory had Di'Ath hanging his head in shame.

"I must marry her because Rupaburg is building an army," he said quietly.

Sy'da's breath caught.

"And their alliance with Ailiar means that whoever Rupaburg takes up arms against... will face Ailiar too," she whispered.

Neither Di'Ath nor Sy'da were ignorant of the stories of surrounding Queen Meitranis. Known as the Blood Queen, Meitranis of Ailiar was responsible for ending a centuries-long war with Rupaburg after killing no less than five Rupaburgan kings with her own hands.

"We are a strong nation," Di'Ath said gravely. "But we cannot withstand the might of both Ailiar and Rupaburg. We stand between them and the rest of this continent. If they wish to push East, we cannot risk the lives of our people. The best way to protect them is to broker an alliance, and marriage is the easiest way to do that."

Sy'da reached the conclusion much faster than Di'Ath had.

"And you," she said. "Are the only unmarried son."

THREE

AROS

LUVRAHN

THE HUMAN DID NOT speak a word on the two-day journey back to Lu-vrahn.

Aros supposed he did not blame her. He was not sure how he would feel about being dragged through the Woods on a cart that also carried the pelt, meat, and skull of a bear. No matter how many supplies had been packed between her and the beast's remains, Aros could not imagine it being comfortable by any stretch of the imagination.

She refused to answer any questions from the hunting party as they trudged home. She cowered amongst the packs and supplies whenever any one of them came near, except for Aros himself. That was not to say she did not appear completely terrified of him, but she accepted food and water when he handed it to her. He wondered, briefly, if her limited trust in him had something to do with the part he played in saving her, or if it lay somewhere in the fact that he did not try to get her to speak.

Holsten kept trying to ask her why she was out here all alone. Rych repeatedly asked her for her name, and Dorsa kept talking about his conquests in war in a misguided attempt to make her feel safe and protected. Aros did not bother to explain that an injured human in elven lands would not likely find comfort in learning of all the lives an elf had taken in combat.

Aros was relieved when they finally broke free of the tree line and could see the village nestled at the base of the small hill. Smoke rose from chimneys. The smell of baked bread filled the air and Aros could hear the thunderous bleat of Jon the kapriae in the paddock. The only thing missing was children running through the streets, laughing, and screaming as they played.

It was to be expected, given the village's recent loss.

And yet, despite that, Aros realised it was the first time he had ever felt truly relieved to have come home.

He turned to look over his shoulder to the human.

She did not appear as happy as he was to have arrived. She sank down further into the packs and blankets until only some matted red curls were visible. He sighed. He could not imagine the next few days were going to be easy, for either of them. He silently vowed to keep his people away from her until she seemed comfortable enough to face them.

Palis was certain to pose the most resistance to his goal.

"They're back!"

Aros looked towards the voice to find the small figure of a young boy standing in the middle of the main street of Luvrahn. The boy, a year older than Fisa had been, waved at the returning hunters enthusiastically.

"I'm surprised Nanos wasn't camped out waiting for us to return," Rych said with a laugh.

"After what happened to Fisa, I'm surprised Thalia let him out of her sight long enough to spot us," Holsten replied.

Dorsa snorted in agreement and continued to pull the cart towards the village. As the hunters neared, the people of Luvrahn pooled out of their homes and into the streets.

Aros could see Dania, Fisa's mother, standing between Aoife and Palis. The expression on her face was one that he had seen far too many times—the blend of pain, relief, and guilt that the survivors of any great catastrophe felt.

Pain that she had lost someone that she loved. Relief that the cause of that loss was gone too.

And guilt that she had felt relief at all.

"Dorsa!"

Beside him, Dorsa grunted and picked up his pace. He was eager to return to the arms of the female who had called his name.

"Let me take the cart," Aros said. "You go see Windra."

Dorsa gave him an appraising look before relenting and handing the cart's carved handles over to Aros. Aros watched with a smile on his face as Dorsa's hulking frame closed the distance between himself and the love of his life.

Windra all but disappeared from view as Dorsa picked her up and enveloped her with his body. From where he stood, Aros could only see the red leather of Windra's shoes as they poked out first from one side of Dorsa's legs to the other, like an elven pendulum swinging from side to side.

Aros shook his head and turned away from the blacksmith who appeared intent on making his lover seasick.

While Aris had been preoccupied with that scene, Rych had pulled away to run towards his parents. Their arms enveloped their son tightly, and Rych's mother was sobbing. Rych seemed both relieved and embarrassed with the greying female looked him over from top to tail.

For Aros, it was jarring to remember that Rych was young—so young that he had not experienced war and its effects like so many of the other adult elves in Luvrahn. And yet, Rych's mother was fussing over him as though he'd been away on a months-long campaign into the frigid north, holding the line at Rupaburg.

There was an odd sensation that came with the realisation. Hope for the future and pride for the part he had to play in achieving this peace were at the forefront, but resentment and jealousy reached out with clawing fingers, threatening to taint them both. It was unfair to feel any sort of displeasure at the sheer idea that this young male had narrowly escaped the devastation of war.

But Rych had been one of the first children born in Luvrahn, back when Aros, Palis and Aoife had first settled the area fifty years ago. He was the very image of the new generation, the sun rising on the dark night that had been centuries of war. It was the life that Aros had fought for new generations to have.

"You're brooding."

Aros jolted to a stop. He glared at the tall, golden-skinned female that stood before him. He glared at the smirk on her face, and the way her hands sat on her hips.

"You need to stop sneaking up on people, Palis," he grumbled.

Palis Reih—Aoife's wife and Aros' oldest friend—beamed in response.

"I wasn't sneaking," she said. "Holsten even tried to tell you he was going to see Dania, and you didn't respond. Far too preoccupied with *brooding*."

"Find a cliff, Palis," Aros replied.

He twisted to look over his shoulder. The human was still in the cart. Her hair was still poking out the top. As dirty and matted as it was, it looked like embers nestled among the hessian, wood and hide.

"You wouldn't survive two days on this earth without me in it," Palis said with a dismissive wave of her hand.

Sunlight glinted off the multitude of rings on her fingers, and Aros was unlucky enough to turn back at the most inopportune moment. He swore as the light was reflected into his eyes.

"Stop whining," Palis said. "I swear, you want people to remember that you were the Queen's most trusted and yo-"

Palis' words cut off. Her gaze fixed on a point behind Aros, and her expression shifted from glee to shock. Aros watched her warm, brown eyes as his friend took in the scene behind him. Palis' eyes were always the key to whatever it was she was feeling. No matter how schooled her expression, Aros could always find the truth plain as day if he just looked into her eyes.

That was how he knew the moment Palis realised what was in the cart. That was how he knew, without her so much as uttering a single word and without turning back to see for himself, that the human had lifted her head enough for Palis to see her rounded ears.

"Aros," Palis breathed.

"I know," he said. "Help me get her to my cottage, and then I'll need you to get Sordi. She's going to need medical attention, and I would like for her to get it without being overrun by the well-intentioned."

Palis nodded, and with her help, Aros pulled the cart through the crowd and towards his cottage. They weren't entirely successful in remaining undetected, and by the time Palis had opened the door for Aros to carry the human inside, the townsfolk of Luvrahn were buzzing with gossip.

Aros C'Asad had been pleasantly surprised when Palis had not pushed her way into the cottage with the village healer on that first day. Though he had been able to hear the residents of Luvrahn on the other side of his door murmuring amongst themselves as they tried to determine who or what Aros had taken into his home, no one had stepped through that door after him except for Sordi.

Aros had laid the human on the bed, explained that a healer was coming as he smoothed back her matted hair, and held her hand while Sordi attended to the wounds on the human's feet, legs, and arms.

Sordi's withered, wrinkled hands had cleaned blood and grime out of deep cuts. They had worked tirelessly to cut out as much of the yellow, seeping infection that had already set in as she could. She stitched shut as many of the wounds as she could and finished by wrapping the human's legs in bandages up to her knees.

The human, to her credit, did not cry out in pain. She whimpered, and sobbed, but for the most part, she quietly squeezed Aros' hand as though she could transfer the pain that she was feeling to him.

If he could take it from her, Aros would. It was his failing, his fatal flaw, always taking the pain and suffering of those around him whenever he was able.

Sordi had left them with a jar of salve and a tea that would ease the pain and help the human fall asleep. As the healer left, Aros spotted a basket of food and a bucket filled with water that had been left on the doorstep. Relief and gratitude had filled every last inch of Aros' tired body and soul. Sordi had brought some water with her, but it had been used to clean wounds and needed to be thrown out. He was not yet comfortable enough to leave the human alone to collect water from the well or find food.

He carried both water and basket in and set them on the wooden table he had made for himself all those years ago. It had been a project designed to keep his hands busy more than once with the intention of having a useful piece of furniture at the end of it. He did not entertain guests in this cottage he called home, and so the table had been constructed to seat two people.

He supposed it could sit four if he pulled it away from the wall where it sat nestled under a window. But he had only made one bench to go with it, and his home was so small anyone on the other side would need to sit on his bed if they did not wish to stand.

"I'll heat up some water," Aros said. "Then you can wash more, and I'll make the tea. We have fruit and bread here for you. I have some dried meat stored, and tomorrow I'll get some more food so we can have something more substantial."

He turned towards the bed, waiting for an answer.

It came with a small nod of the human's head.

She had been crying again, and she quickly wiped away the tears from her cheeks.

Aros did not know what to say next, so he simply narrated what he was going to do as he did it. He lit a fire in his small fireplace, and when it was good and hot, he filled a pot with water and hung it from a hook over the flames.

He had never been uncomfortable in silence before, but as the cracking of the fire became the only sound to fill the space around them, Aros felt increasingly unsettled. He opened his mouth a few times in an attempt to initiate some sort of conversation. No words came, and he decided that it was probably for the best.

The human had been through a lot, whatever it was that she had been through, and she did not need someone like him bumbling his way through small talk.

Eventually, the water boiled and he made the tea. After letting it steep for as long as Sordi had instructed, he gave the cup to the human, alongside a plate of summer berries and fruits, and a roll of bread.

She ate and sipped slowly, but it was not until she held the cup and plate back to him, indicating she had eaten her fill, that Aros dared take a bite of anything himself. As he ate, he watched the human try to defy the effects of the tea until her eyes eventually fell shut.

Aros did not sleep.

It had nothing to do with the fact that there was a human in his bed. He had slept in worse conditions before and could make the bench at his table work if need be, even if this meant his legs would be hanging off the edge. Worst case scenario, he would simply lie on the floor. Though hard and made of dirt, it would work. He could lay down blankets and furs and still be decently comfortable.

But he did not sleep.

Throughout the rest of the day and all through the night, Aros C'Asad watched the human sleep. She tossed and turned. She whimpered and curled tighter against herself.

He warred with himself, flitting between the impulse to pull her against his chest and give her warmth and comfort and the argument that it was entirely plausible that she would not want to be touched any more than she had been. That internal debate waged on inside him as the night drew on and well into the wee hours of the morning.

Aros watched the image of her slowly become clearer as the sun rose and he no longer had to rely on the light emitted from the fire to make out any details of her sleeping face. When he realised it was dawn, Aros also noted with surprise that she had slept through the night. He had not expected it. He did not know the last time she had slept, nor how long she had been in the Edgeling Woods alone.

Once the sun had risen enough for the time to be considered *morning* rather than *dawn*, there was a gentle knock on the door.

The human stirred, her brow furrowing in annoyance at being disturbed. Aros shared her sentiment.

As much as he wanted to ignore the visitor, it was possible that it was Sordi again, coming to check on the human's wounds and replace the bandages. So, he stood, his knees groaning in protest at the movement after spending so many hours seated on that bench. He crossed over to the door as quietly as he could and opened it a crack to see who was on the other side.

He glared at the knocker the moment he laid eyes on her.

"Your impatience is unprecedented and legendary," he grumbled, then stepped aside to open the door wide enough for Palis Reih to walk through.

"I myself am unprecedented and legendary," Palis said, beaming her signature sunshine smile.

She tossed her long braids over her shoulder before stepping over the threshold. She carried a basket of fruit and bread on the crook of one arm, and the smell of warm, fresh bread filled the tight space.

Aros' mouth watered instantly, and it was almost enough to have him forget that he was supposed to be angry at the intrusion.

"Aoife thought you two would appreciate something fresh," she said. "Seeing as our contribution yesterday afternoon was really only what we had left."

"Keep quiet," he said. "She's asleep."

Palis peeked around Aros' shoulder to the bed and shook her head, the beads in her braids clinking together.

"No, she's not."

Aros spun on his heels and found himself staring into the eyes of the human. She was still bundled in the blankets and furs that covered his bed, but the top half of her face was visible, and she was watching them intently.

"Good morning," Aros said. "I am sorry if we woke you."

The human did not respond. It seemed that whatever strained trust she had in him while Sordi had been to attending her wounds was gone. Aros was not prepared for how painful the idea of that was.

He was no one to her, a stranger, and yet he felt guilt coil around his heart and constrict as though *he* were the one who had put her in this position.

He could hear Palis behind him. She set down the new basket on the table before turning to stoke the dying fire. Aros wished she hadn't. It was already warm in the cottage, and if he had read the colour of the sunrise correctly, it was going to be a hot day.

But he kept his mouth shut and moved to sit at the table. He focused his attention on Palis. She was dressed in the same manner she usually was—loose linen pants that were brought in on the calf by long, colourful strips of thick cotton and a white, billowy shirt cinched in at the waist with a wide leather belt that covered most of her stomach. Pouches hung from the belt with varying degrees of fullness. Her long, pointed ears were adorned with countless golden rings, delicate chains, and precious gemstones.

Aros' own ears housed almost as many piercings as Palis'. They had sat together for most of them, gripping each other's hands as thin, hot needles were pushed into the delicate cartilage. Unlike Palis, though, Aros had chosen silver-toned jewellery. He found that it complimented his complexion more than gold ever could.

"Are you going to introduce me to your new friend, Aros?" Palis asked, snapping Aros out of his thoughts.

"I would," Aros said. "But I cannot introduce someone I do not know."

Palis turned to him. The frown was so motherly one would mistake her for having had children. Aros snorted a laugh.

"Are you telling me that you have been in such close quarters with someone you have never met before and you have not so much as asked her what her name is?"

Aros shrugged. "She needed medical attention, and then she needed rest."

He didn't like that they were talking about the human as though she weren't there. Especially when he could feel the heat of her gaze on him like a brand. He rolled his shoulders in a vain attempt to relieve some of the tension.

"Two hundred years," Palis said, shaking her head. "Two hundred years and you still do not have basic manners or common decency. Why I am still friends with you, I do not understand."

"You're friends with me," Aros reached for a bread roll as he spoke. "Because otherwise all your attention would be focused on Aoife, and she would put you to work."

"And I suppose you're only still friends with me because of the baked goods?" Palis asked.

Aros couldn't stop the second snort of laughter. "Aoife would still bake for me, even if you and I were no longer friends. Your wife loves me almost as much as she loves you."

"Ah!" Palis said, a twinkle in her eye. "But she gets *me* to deliver the goods. I could just as simply pass them along to someone else. Or, if I were feeling particularly petty, I could stand outside your window and have you watch me feed them to Jon."

Aros frowned. It would be a cold day in Di'Tyan's realms when he would let that beast get baked goods that Aoife had made for *him*. Especially when he knew both females well enough to know that the supply of baked goods was as much an apology for being unable to keep Palis away for longer than a single night as it had been a gift. While Aros had known Palis for far longer than he had known Aoife, the latter had immediately added Aros' care to her list of responsibilities. He would not hesitate to admit that Aoife's practice of reigning Palis in whenever she got too overbearing was one of his favourite things about the mute storyteller.

"You would have no one to bother if you let me starve to death," Aros reminded Palis. "Which would, in turn, lead you to die of boredom. Keeping me alive and feeding me your wife's delicious baked goods are in your best interest, and you know it."

"You say that, but I am seriously considering the merits of disinviting you from dinner," Palis hummed. She tossed the roll she had been holding at Aros' head.

Aros caught it before it landed.

"We both know Aoife wouldn't stand for that," he replied, then bit into the roll.

The crust was thick and crunchy.

He could hear Palis move. He heard the rustle of blankets and the shift in the mattress. He was certain that if he opened his eyes again, he would see Palis perched on the edge of the bed, smiling warmly at the pale human.

"Good morning," Palis said. "I am sorry to have woken you. That was not my intention. My name is Palis, and although you may not believe it, I am a friend of Aros."

The human did not reply.

"I hope he is being kind to you," Palis continued. "He usually is, even to those who aren't damsels in distress. Between you and me, Aros is a bit of a magnet for those in trouble."

"I seem to remember you having a problem with the phrase *damsel in distress*," Aros muttered.

"Because in most cases, it is demeaning and suggests that a female cannot protect herself. However, in your case, I know that you have learned time and again that females are just as strong as males—in some cases, more so."

Aros huffed. He knew exactly which specific female she was talking about—a female, daily, he fought to push from his mind. He tried to wave the memory of a tall, proud female away with little success.

"But in this instance, the poor thing needed help, and just like always, you were there to provide it. I doubt Holsten would have even noticed she was there if it had been him," Palis continued. "And I doubt Dorsa would have been able to stop himself in time before trampling her."

Aros brushed the crumbs off his lap.

"What about the other one?"

The human's voice was hoarse and quiet. Aros and Palis both whipped their attention towards her.

Aros' breath caught in his throat as the human slowly pushed herself up into a seated position, her face twisted in agony. Aros stood, and filled the pot with water again, placing it back in its spot above the fire. He berated himself for not realising that this was likely why Palis had brought it back to life sooner.

"There were three," the human continued. "What would the third one have done?"

Palis smiled kindly at the human, the skin creasing at the edge of her warm, brown eyes.

"Rych," she said. "Is still a child by our standards. He is old enough to have come into his Affinity, old enough to consider starting a family, but he till has many years to go before he can call himself wise. I love him, but I don't think Rych would have ever found himself close enough to take the bear down. As such, you would be safe."

"From him," Aros said. "Can't say you'd be safe from the bear."

The human appeared to ponder this for a while. Aros cocked his head to the side as he tried to decipher the expression on her face. She wasn't screaming, even though she must be in excruciating pain. She wasn't pulling away from Palis, but her mind was mulling something over.

But what was it?

"I didn't catch your name," Palis said.

Aros frowned. The human had never—

"I didn't give it," the human said.

Palis nodded as if in understanding. She pressed her hand to her breast. "I'm Palis," she said, introducing herself for a second time. "And this grumpy old thing is Aros."

Aros glared at the hand now outstretched towards him. He wasn't grumpy. And he didn't *brood* either, thank you very much.

To stop himself from slapping away her hand, Aros crossed his arms over his chest.

Silence fell between the three of them as the human refused to give her name freely in return. Palis, who could be as equally diplomatic as she was impatient, cut straight to the point.

"What is your name?" she asked the human.

"I don't have one."

The words had tumbled out of the human's mouth as if she had been keeping them balanced on the tip of her tongue behind closed lips. Her eyes widened ever-so-slightly, and her breath hitched.

"What do you mean?" Aros asked. He took a step forward, arms still crossed over his chest.

Water bubbled in the pot behind him.

"I mean," the human said. "That I do not have a name."

Aros frowned. He'd only experienced limited dealings with humans in his time at the capital, but each one he had met had possessed a name. Even the small handful of humans that had passed through Luvrahn over the past half-century had been named.

If they had gone back in time, when the bloodstone mines were still in operation and using human labour, perhaps coming across a nameless human would have been expected. But the mines hadn't used human labour in centuries and had soon closed after the establishment of the human territory now known as Colosia.

Palis' heartbreak was plain on her face.

"You do not have a name?" she asked.

The human shook her head. "No," she replied. "My mother died before she could give me one, and my father was too heartbroken by her death that I suppose he forgot."

The human looked down and picked at a loose thread of one of the blankets before continuing.

"By the time he realised he had not yet given me a name, I was half-grown, and there was no point."

Aros' eyes narrowed. Just as when she had said she didn't have a name, the human's breathing had hitched, and he could see more of the whites of her eyes. She was lying – he was sure of it – but he couldn't figure out why or what about. What could she possibly have to gain from lying about having a name?

"Where did you come from?" Palis asked, voice soft.

The human's eyes watered and she shook her head.

"It doesn't matter," she said. "It's gone. It's all gone. Everything is…"

Her words trailed off. Her lip trembled and her shoulders shook.

This was not a lie. Aros was certain of it. Something terrible had happened, and that was why she had braved crossing the border into Ailiar.

"Well," Palis said, clearly not wanting to push the matter further at the moment. "You're here now, and you're safe, and we will just have to find a name for you. We will take out time and find something that truly fits you—a name that is yours."

Aros turned and set about making tea for the human.

"And what do we call her until then, Palis?" he asked. "We can't just keep calling her *the human*."

Palis fell silent for a moment, thinking.

"I really don't like it," she said eventually. "But I think that it will help motivate us to find a name for you sooner rather than later, if we call you Dhuina for now."

Aros nearly poured the boiling water on himself as he laughed.

"Dhuina?" he asked. "You can't be serious."

The human looked at him quizzically.

"What's *Dhuina*?" she asked.

"Dhuina means *human*," he said. "In Elvish. Palis has just said *I don't want to call you* human, *so I'm going to call you* human *instead*."

"It is temporary!" Palis argued. "And it's better than straight up calling her *human* in common, or gods forbid *damsel*."

The human chewed her lip, deep in thought.

"I don't mind being called Dhuina," she said finally. "And it is only temporary."

Palis nodded.

"Good. Now then," she said. "I promised Aoife that I wasn't going to overwhelm you and I have other errands to run. I will leave you in Aros' brooding yet capable hands for now and will bring by some more food later. If you need anything, you can let me know, and I will do my best to make it happen. And if you would prefer to stay with my wife and myself, our door is open to you."

Palis smiled as she stood, the leather of her belts creaking with the motion.

"Aoife would be here too," she continued. "But she—"

"Has boundaries?" Aros cut in.

Palis shot him a deadly glare.

"She did not want to overwhelm our new friend," she said through a forced smile. "However, she did insist that no one recovering from such an ordeal as yours, my dear Dhuina, should be subject to a strict diet of dried meats and nuts."

"I eat my greens!" Aros protested.

"Vegetables in soups only count if you do not pick them out and leave them to the side," Palis chided. "And do not try to argue with me. Remember how long we have known each other, C'Asad. You are worse than a child when it comes to what you eat. You need more than meat and potatoes to be healthy, you know."

"I have survived worse than a limited diet," Aros muttered under his breath, pulling a mocking face as he did so.

"There's nothing wrong with meat and potatoes."

Aros and Palis both looked at the human in the same instant.

Aros' lips curled into a smile, thankful that the human's words had distracted Palis from whatever retort she was planning on slinging his way – and that he finally had someone on his side.

Palis, on the other hand, looked as though she had witnessed a horror beyond imagination.

"No," she said, lifting a warning finger towards the human. "No. You are not allowed to be on his side. You are on my side. You and I are going to be the best of friends, and by the time of the Wishing, you and I will be so close that Aros will regret that he ever introduced us. That plan does not work if you are on his side with these sorts of things."

Aros raised a brow.

"I didn't introduce you at all," he reminded her. "And I am already regretting the fact that the two of you have met."

Palis waved a dismissive hand. Her bright, sunshine smile still plastered on her face.

"I will see you two later," she said. "Don't let your brooding rub off on her."

And with that, Palis let herself out, leaving Aros alone with Dhuina once more.

Four

MAIDA

LUVRAHN

THE BEST KINDS OF lies are the ones that hold a kernel of truth.

Maida Tailor had been taught as much by an elderly woman named Oleanna Wyve. The grey and wizened weaver had given Maida countless pieces of advice throughout the years. It had never escaped Maida just how much of that information could be applied to the once-seemingly impossible event of meeting an elf.

Never stray past the river to the east of Silktide, for you will find yourself in the land of elves.

Always leave a small imperfection in your work, so you do not trap your soul within it.

Remember that you and you alone have the power to determine your destiny.

Never tell an elf your name, for they will use it to control you to do their bidding.

Maida had already failed in keeping to the east bank of the river. That was how she ended up here, battered and broken and at the mercy of two rather imposing elves. The decision to cross had not been easy. Two parts of her mind had warred with one another, each demanding she do the opposite of what the other was saying.

On one hand, she had the rules Oleanna Wyve had taught her. On the other, she had her father's instructions.

Should anything ever happen to me, he had said, while the rain beat down outside their warm, cozy cottage. *I need you to run west. There are settlements on the other side of the Woods with people that will help you.*

Maida had not understood then. In truth, she did not understand now. She could not imagine that her father meant that elves would be the people that she was supposed to run to. The fact that she had been saved and had her wounds tended by these ferocious, nightmare creatures was merely a coincidence.

She must have made a wrong turn as she ran. She had never before strayed far enough into the Edgeling Woods to lose sight of her home. She was not particularly adept at reading the sky for directions, nor could she remember which side moss preferred to grow on trees.

No. It was not the elves that her father had sent her to.

It was Maida's folly, her own inability to follow simple directions.

She wished she had listened to the old weaver. She wished that she had not run through the river, that her steps had not been slowed immediately as the fabric of her skirts greedily drank from the water and weighed her down. She would not soon forget how it was to feel like her skirts were trying to drag her down into the very riverbed. How the patchwork skirts she had made herself, so lovingly crafted from pieces left from the coats, pants and dresses she had made for the townsfolk of Silktide had worked against her in those first desperate, terrifying moments.

Perhaps, if she had not left a single imperfection, her soul would have been bound to the to the damned garment, and it would not have tried to be her undoing.

She had fallen twice, the second time nearly bringing her to the dark, unknown lands of the dead. Still, she had clawed her way to the muddy western bank. She had brought herself to stand, and she had run again.

Now she was here, in unbelievable pain, and watched by two fearsome creatures she had never hoped to lay eyes on.

Maida did not know which one to fear most—the tall, slender female who looked like the sun personified with long, brown braids, and adorned with beads and rings on what seemed to be every inch of her, or the male. From having been carried in his arms, Maida knew he was muscled. But he was not broad and had kept his distance as often as he could.

Perhaps it was an opinion tainted by the memory of him saving her from the bear. Still, given the option between the two elves before her, Maida would throw herself out of this bed to stand behind *him* before she trusted the female sitting within arms' reach.

The female tilted her head, braids falling over her shoulder and beads tinkling like wind chimes. Briefly, Maida wondered how long it took to braid hair that long. They were so delicate and thin; it must have taken hours.

But this was not the time to get distracted by the intricacies of hair.

The female elf had asked her a question – *the* question, to which the answer was the only thing Maida could never share if she wanted to have any hope of survival.

You alone have the power to determine your destiny.

"I don't have one."

The best lies hold a kernel of truth.

"My mother died before she could give me one, and my father was too heartbroken by her death that I suppose he forgot."

And there was the truth in her lie.

Maida's mother had died shortly after giving birth. It had happened so quickly that she was unable to speak a name over the baby she had just borne. But she had already ensured that Maida's father knew what name she intended for their daughter. Cillian Tailor, a man of his word, had bestowed the name upon the child.

As far as Maida knew, it was a name that had been passed down for generations within her mother's side of the family. Maida had lost count of how many times she had asked her father if it had been her mother's name. His answer was always a short and curt *no*.

He had promised that when she was older, when she was ready, he would reveal her mother's name.

Years passed, and not a syllable was uttered.

And not, he would never be able to.

Maida's breath caught in her throat as images of limbs and ash rose to the forefront of her mind. Of all the memories she could conjure, charred and peeling flesh was the clearest. Still, she could not help but note that the flesh had pulled off the bones as easily as a well-roasted leg of meat on a spit.

While Maida's mind raced, the elves had begun talking again. The female had asked her where she had come from.

It didn't matter where Maida had come from because she could never go back. Silktide had been all but struck from the map of the world, and Maida was on the wrong side of the Colosian border.

It did not matter that her father had told her where to run. Maida had made a mistake somewhere along the way, and every rock and fallen branch she had tripped or cut her feet on had been for naught. She was sure to die here, surrounded by these knife-eared creatures who lived to torture humans. Even if the two that were filling the cramped space had not made a move to hurt her yet, Maida was still untrusting.

The male chuckled. Maida whipped her head in his direction and a few of the matts in her hair swinging to hit her in the face.

"What's *Dhuina*?"

Human. It was human. Nothing more or less than what she was. And as the female elf made sure to remind her, it was only temporary.

Just like being here.

Maida did not know where she had found the courage to come to that decision, but the resolve was taking root deep within her.

Maida Tailor would allow the elves to heal her wounds. She would allow them to feed and clothe her. She would allow them to name her if it came to it, but she would take nothing more. Maida would accept only what was necessary for her survival. She would stay only until she recovered.

And then?

Then, she would return to Silktide. She would find whoever had stolen her life from her, and she would find a way to make them pay.

Until then, Maida could not allow herself to dwell her father's fate. There had been no way of knowing who she had seen on the streets. For all she knew, Cillian could be alive and well, searching for his daughter.

Until then, Maida could wait.

"There is nothing wrong with meat and potatoes," she said.

Even though Maida was sure she would trust the male more than she would the female, she found herself wishing that latter had not left them alone. She could feel the weight of the male's gaze on her every time he cast his eyes in her direction.

She could feel the shift in the air when he opened his mouth to speak, and though it was surely nothing more than her imagination, Maida could not shake the idea that it became cold whenever he closed it again.

Aros.

What a strange name. Perhaps, if she were not completely terrified and waiting for the moment that *Aros* decided that she was no longer a novelty worth entertaining, Maida may have indulged in the curiosity that was brewing beneath her skin. It may well have been a possibility if she were not plagued by the stories of her childhood, wherein elves tricked humans to do their bidding and where humans were imprisoned and enslaved, turned into nothing more than caged animals still living for the sole purpose of providing entertainment.

It was why she had lied about her name.

Oleanna had told her stories about how the first humans had been captured by the elves, long before Colosia had existed. The humans, trusting and welcoming of the creatures that looked like them save for pointed ears, had willingly given their names. The elves had used this knowledge and their magic to take control of the humans.

No matter the order, the human was unable to disobey.

If they had a human's name, an elf could instruct them to crush their own child's head with a rock until it was nothing more than a paste of brain, flesh, and bone. The human would be powerless to stop themselves. They would do as commanded, begging ceaselessly for it to stop.

Maida was powerless enough as it was. She could not risk giving up complete autonomy.

But what does Aros mean? Was it a name chosen by his parents in the hope that he would grow up brave and strong? Is it a common elven name, like Peter among humans? Are there stories about famous Aroses rescuing damsels in distress?

Despite herself, Maida could not stop her mind from wandering to the male elf. She could not stop her thoughts as they turned towards his parents, whether he got his wide, strong nose from his mother or his father, or if he could see his ancestors in his heavy brow. And what did his parents think of all those silver rings in his ears? Were they still alive? If so, did they live here with him? Would she meet them?

What would they think of their son embarking on a hunting trip only to return with a human?

How had those full lips looked when he was a child, grinning and laughing without the weight of years to taint the sound?

Aros lifted his gaze to meet Maida's. He arched a dark brow in query, though he did not give voice to any question. It was then that Maida realised that she had been staring at him. As her traitorous mind had wandered, her treasonous eyes had followed suit, and now human and elf were holding each other's gaze.

Maida's cheeks warmed, and she turned her attention away. She sent a silent thanks to whatever gods or deities ruled over this land that the bed she was nestled in had been tucked under a window. Otherwise, she would have been stuck staring at the wall or furs in her lap. The thin, plain curtains were drawn shut—to keep the curious children from looking in at her, she guessed—but there was enough of a gap that Maida could look outside.

Granted, the view was not forgiving. It did not allow her to glean much information that would allow her to determine where exactly she was, and much less in terms of how to leave this place far behind her.

Maida could see the corner of the neighbouring stone cottage. Grass grew tall along the home, swaying gently in the breeze. But that was all she could see in terms of the dwellings that made up this village unless she was prepared to open the curtain further.

And Maida was certainly *not* prepared to open the curtain further just yet.

So, instead, she focused on the rolling hills and fields that she could see without needing to risk revealing herself to whomsoever might be lurking on the other side of the window.

Fields, at least, looked the same no matter where in the world you were. They were easily recognisable for what they were, even if you could not recognise the crop itself. Maida's breath came easier seeing the familiar cultivated lines and the discarded plough off to the side.

It was strange, she thought, that she would feel comforted by the sight of something so simple, so universal.

Beside the field of crops was a paddock. The grass was low, suggesting a grazing animal resided within. Curious, Maida reached up, and gently pulled on the curtain, widening the gap ever so slightly. What animals did elves keep? Horses? It made sense with the plough.

Cows? Sheep?

If they had sheep, surely she would be under more woollen blankets than animal furs. If they had cows, perhaps it had been cheese that she had glimpsed in the basket, alongside the bread, fruit and berries.

Perhaps they had goats, though her own experience with the nuisance animals had her dismissing the thought immediately. Even if the horrific sound she had heard when they had first broken free of the tree line of the Edgeling Woods had sounded like a possessed bovid, she could chalk it up to the fear of being led to an entire village filled with human-eating creatures.

It must be cows or horses. Maida was certain that it was one of those two options.

And there!

The creature's back was to her, head down as it grazed. Its tail was short, flicking from side to side to ward off flies. It was unlike any horse or cow Maida had ever seen. It was certainly large enough, but even from this distance, the coat seemed too coarse. Perhaps it was a breed of horse that she had not seen before. Or it was a magic creature that did not exist anywhere else. It made sense for elves to have imbued creatures with magic, resulting in strange and unnatural beings.

Maida leaned forward, her brow furrowed. If only it would lift its head. If only it would reveal itself to her.

As if the creature were in tune with her thoughts, it lifted its head. Not only that, but it turned its face towards her. Maida's breath caught painfully in her throat.

She must be seeing things. She must have slept too long, and her mind must be struggling to keep up with what her eyes were seeing. She had just been thinking about goats, so that had to be the reason why she was seeing a giant one now. That had to be it.

Maida could not fathom any other explanation for the large, horned beast that seemed to be staring deep into her soul across the paddock.

"What is *that*?" she breathed.

The curtain was pulled from Maida's fingers and pushed open. Maida looked up to see Aros leaning over her to peer out the window. Her heart and mind seemed to race hand in hand with one another.

How had he crossed the cottage without her hearing his footsteps? How had she not heard the clinking of beads in his braids?

How had she not smelled the pine and earth scent of him, when it seemed to wash over her now?

"Do you mean the *kapriae*?" he asked.

Maida frowned. She watched the twitch in his shoulders and wondered if he was holding back a sigh of annoyance.

"The large goat thing?" Aros reiterated.

Maida nodded and turned her attention back to the creature outside.

"It is called a *kapriae*," Aros continued. "They come from up north, in a country called Rupaburg. We use them instead of horses on farms and for travelling. They produce milk as well, so not only do they work the fields, but we can use them to make cheese and soap. It limits the amount of space we need for livestock and reduces feed costs for the beasts."

He pulled away and let the curtain fall back to its original state. He continued to speak as he returned to the table.

"Generations ago, one of our Queens began to breed them for war. They are stronger and faster than horses. They can travel over more treacherous terrain, can carry more riders, and their diet is more diverse. That one out there, whose name is Jon by the way, has eaten more deer than I care to count."

"It eats meat?" Maida's voice was airy with wonder and fear.

"*Kapriae* eat anything and everything they can. They are very opportunistic."

Aros picked up another hunk of bread and tore off a corner with his teeth. When he was done chewing, he said:

"When you are up to it, I'll introduce you to Jon."

Maida could not imagine ever being up to meeting a giant war-goat with a taste for blood, but she did not voice such thoughts. Not that she would have had any opportunity to, as beast let out a monstrous, nightmarish bleat that had Maida pulling the furs over her head. But that was a problem she would have to face later. For now, she was alive, and she was safe enough to heal. Until she could leave, she would hold on to that.

Maida reached for the pendant on her throat, gripping it so tightly the petals from the metal flower bit into her fingers, and began to plan her escape.

FIVE

ANIAIJA

THE SEA BETWEEN SEAS

SAILING DIRECTLY INTO A storm has never been an act worthy of the title of 'good idea,' but neither was disobeying a direct order from the ship's captain. So, the crew of *The Mercy* set to work, securing the sails, working the ropes and cranks to manipulate the large sheets of canvas back against the masts. Once they were done, there was still much work left. There were other things to tie down, barrels and boxes and cannons, all to prevent them from being cast overboard by the raging sandstorm rapidly approaching.

Though it was certainly easier to salvage things that ended up in the sand-dunes of the Sea Between Seas, not a single member of *The Mercy*'s crew was eager to be sent off in what could still be a futile search.

At the ship's bow stood Aniaija Bahra, flanked on either side by fellow Saldhraos. Their task was easier on parchment than it was in practice—keep the ship safe from sand, rocks and other debris lifted by the storm while still parting the sand below to mimic the rolling of waves on a true sea.

To increase their chances of success and survival, Aniaija had split the Saldhraos into two groups. The first group would maintain their regular daily duties and focus their magic on shifting and guiding the sand to part and roll to allow *The Mercy* through. The second group—her group—would focus on protecting the ship.

The Mercy groaned in protest as it sailed through The Sea Between Seas.

If the storm had not posed such a risk to the sails, the Aerdhraos would have been able to fill them with air and push the ship faster. But the storm did pose such a risk, and if their sails tore too badly for mending, they could not simply make port and purchase more canvas. So, the Aerdhraos were forced to work in greater numbers to push the ship from behind. Unfortunately, it also meant that there were fewer Aerdhraos below deck, working on keeping a solid wall of air over the gaping hole in the hull to keep the sand out.

Aniaija could not allow herself to think about how much sand would be getting through that wall, and how much extra weight they were taking on. She could not dwell on the overwhelming possibility that they would not survive this.

Not when she knew that they would not survive the other option.

The wind whipped harsh grains of sand into her face. Ropes cracked and snapped like whips, reminding her to check the thick rope tied around her own waist. She hated being tethered to the ship—to anything, really—but after they had lost as many elven lives as they had in the first storm they had endured on the Between, it had become mandatory to tie oneself to *The Mercy* whenever a storm even appeared to be brewing.

Thunder rumbled, echoing throughout the ever-darkening sky. Lightning arched through the seemingly impenetrable wall of sand that they were heading towards. Not for the first time, Aniaija missed the storms of the true sea, where waves, seawyrms and pirates were their biggest threat.

Shouts were drowned out by the roaring of the wind. Aniaija hoped that Captain Geomar was regretting giving the order to sail right into the storm. She hoped that when it had revealed itself to be worse than anticipated, he had prayed to each one of his Ailian Old Ones, begging for the survival of his ship and crew.

Perhaps, she thought. *He is praying that they don't survive, to save him from the tidal wave of pain I am going to rain down on him.*

That is what she would be doing in his shoes—praying that her first mate was not plotting her demise should they survive this potentially suicidal endeavour. She would also be praying that every life they may lose would be worth surviving what was behind them, chasing them into the raging storm.

But this was not the time to dwell on the future or possible lack of it.

It almost did not matter that Dapsa had commandeered a small group of Aerdhraos to create a shield of air around the ship for sand continued to blast Aniaija and the crew in the face, slowly and methodically removing layers of skin from every exposed area of skin.

They were at the edge now, and any chance *The Mercy* might have had of turning away was gone.

"Brace yourself!" Aniaija yelled. She had no way of knowing if she was heard over the roar of the wind. She could only sink down onto her haunches and hope.

The sandstorm hit the barrier of air and the ship with such ferocity that the ship jolted violently. Each soul aboard *The Mercy* was knocked off their feet. Pained cries melted into the crack of thunder and groan of wood.

The rope around Aniaija's waist had kept her from being sent sprawling to the other side of the deck, but it bit into the soft space between her rib and hip and threw her roughly against the railing. Pain bloomed from her shoulder, a strange, electric sensation creeping down her arm as it reached for the tips of her fingers.

"Fuck," she groaned.

Squinting, she scanned the crew as she tried to regain her breath. She could not see anyone possessing any immediately urgent injuries. There were some scrapes and a few dashes of red blood flowing from cuts, but no visible broken bones.

No dead bodies.

The storm continued to whirl around them, hitting the sides of the ship and sending jolts through the creaking wood. They needed to do something else, something *more*. Simply diverting the sand was not working when the wind could whip it up again and send it back their way a moment later.

Her crewmates were too far away for her to tell them her plan over the noise. Aniaija tried to wave to get their attention, but the sand and dirt in the air made it too difficult. With another groan, Aniaija realised that she would have to trust that they would follow suit with her change of plan: to make the sand too heavy for the wind to lift.

Aniaija gripped the length of rope that tethered her to the railing with both hands. Despite the protest in her shoulder and swiftly forming bruise around her middle, she pulled herself back to her feet. If she saw another sunrise, she knew it would come with stiff joints and an ache that would reach her very soul. But for now, Aniaija focused on the feeling of her magic.

An elf's magic fell under four Affinities—Earth, Air, Water and Fire. It was not until they came of age that an elf would have any hint of where they would fall on the scale. Aside from royal bloodlines, it appeared that not even parentage had an influence on which Affinity an elf came into. Aniaija's mother's Affinity fell under Water, making her a Visdhraos, and her father's fell under Fire, meaning he was an Igdhraos. They had all been surprised when Aniaija had come of age and been able to turn dirt into rocks, shape clay with nothing more than a thought, and influence the growth of crops.

And according to Aniaija's parents, each Affinity *felt* different. To her mother, magic felt like it flowed in her veins. Her father claimed that his fire came from his heart, the flames flickering with every beat.

For Aniaija, magic felt like roots. She could feel it reaching out from her fingertips while manipulating dirt, stone, or grit. She could feel the ground beneath her curl around her feet, as if begging her to sink down into it.

With the storm whipping the sand around her, she felt like she was drowning in the most glorious way possible. It was like being wrapped in a hug so warm and comforting that she did not care that it was drawing the breath from her lungs.

Aniaija took as deep a breath as she could muster and planted her feet wide. She once again sank into her centre of gravity and hoped that by the time she ended up on her ass again, she would have bought herself enough time to make a difference.

Aniaija lifted her hands, facing their palms out towards the surrounding storm. She felt the tangled roots of her magic reach out to their element, bouncing from one grain of sand to the next. Her brow furrowed. Her magic was too erratic; it needed to concentrate.

She needed to concentrate.

She rolled her shoulders, ignoring the sharp surge of pain that shot from her injured one, and turned her palms towards one another.

Slowly, she curled her fingers and brought her hands closer together. Her magic reacted in kind, gathering grains of sand, and compressing them together. The roots of her magic zigged and zagged through the air, taking more and more from the storm. The boulder she was creating grew heavier. It began to sink towards the ground, and Aniaija let out a whoop of victory.

A little more.

It just needed a little more, and the boulder would be on the ground and too heavy for the wind to pick up.

Aniaija could feel other pockets in the storm where her crew must have caught on to what she was doing. More boulders were being formed and lowered to the ground.

"Just a little more," she rasped.

Just a little more, a voice seemed to echo in her head.

A voice she had never heard before, dark, low, and gravelly.

She opened her mouth to question the voice when her magic shifted. Instead of Aniaija feeding her magic and tending to it lovingly, it felt like the storm was *taking*. Like it was tearing saplings out of loamy soil, like taking a dull axe to the roots of ancient trees, or tearing the petals off a flower in some sick game.

This was not the first time she had experienced her magic taking control, but unlike before, it came unexpectedly. A new terror gripped her heart, sending frigid cold racing down her spine. Last time, she had been feeding magic into a golem until it had enough magic to sustain itself. What was stealing from her now? What could she possibly be creating?

There was too much power in the storm.

Too much.

That comforting blanket of power and magic threatened to reach down into Aniaija's very soul and drown her from the inside. If only she could take just a little of that rage and power for herself. If only the roots of her magic weren't tangling around themselves, and if only the storm were not tearing them from her fingertips.

Ifs are useless. They will not save you. Do not ask yourself if something else could have been done. Ask yourself what you can do to change your fate.

Aniaija's mind raced as she tried to come up with a possible solution. What could she do to turn the tide? The storm was overpowering her and the magic was going rogue. How could she possibly take control again?

She laughed maniacally when the answer came to her.

She could simply take the magic away.

Aniaija looked down at her hands. They were almost touching, making a sphere. Slowly, painfully, as though her hands had been bound in twine and she needed to break the bonds, Aniaija pulled her hands apart. The connection between her and her magic shuddered. Her breath became laboured, and the pain in her shoulder doubled.

"I will not let you take over," Aniaija growled.

With one final grunt of pain, she pulled her hands apart. The violent pull of the magic ceased, and she let out a nervous laugh and threw her hands high.

Her relief was short-lived. A dark shape was rapidly approaching her from the depth of the raging sand.

Aniaija barely dropped below the railing quickly enough before the boulder sailed through the air. She heard the explosion of wood, the raining of debris on the deck, and a terrified scream. She turned and felt the blood leave her face. The boulder had narrowly missed Nori. Wood chips and splinters still danced menacingly around the young elf, whipped into a frenzy from the wind.

Blood trickled down Nori's dirt-streaked face from cuts left by the exploding railing. And, judging from the gaping hole in the railing, Nori was lucky to have only received a few cuts. If the boulder had hit an inch to the right, it would have knocked out the space he had tied himself to, pulling him to the angry dunes below. Two inches, and it would have torn right through his middle.

And it would have all been Aniaija's fault.

She knew, without a shadow of a doubt, that the boulder that had nearly ended Nori had been the one she had created. She had nearly killed him.

It will not do to dwell on near misses.

They were still in the thick of the storm.

Aniaija cast her eyes over the deck of *The Mercy* as despair threatened to swallow her whole. Crew members were trying to hold on to their ropes for dear life while still manipulating their magic. Visdhraos were trying to weigh down the sand by wetting it.

Igdhraos looked helpless as they held on to one another to keep them on board.

This was it. It had to be it. She had never seen the crew of *The Mercy* look so terrified. Not even when the Queen's guard had shot cannons at them as they were leaving Balliach harbour, when a broken vow had almost seen the crew and their families at the bottom of the ocean.

Each face looked certain that they were sailing directly to their end.

But this was not the end.

No. Aniaija vowed that this would only be a new beginning.

It had been hours.

How many, Aniaija did not know. She was certain it had been more than two and probably less than five. But any guess more specific than that would be a stab in the dark.

When the wind had died and the top layers of her skin were no longer being blasted off with sand, Aniaija let go of the magic she had been using to direct the worst of it away from her and her crewmates.

Exhaustion flooded her body, weighing down each limb. Even the strands of her hair that had been pulled free from her tight braid felt too heavy where they rested on her face and shoulders. Now more than ever, she wanted to sink into the warm embrace of the ground below. She wanted to let it swallow her whole, wanted each grain of sand to fill her lungs and veins until she was one with earth.

But she could not do that. She had too much left to do in this life.

She really should preserve the rope around her waist. It was not as though it was easy to come by in their exile upon the Between, but she was too tired to care. Aniaija pulled the obsidian-hilted dagger from its sheath on her thigh and cut through the rope to free herself before storming across the deck with as much anger as her exhausted and spent body would allow.

She passed crewmates in various stages of recovery. Some were slumped against the mast, chests heaving. Others were helping their friends to their feet and checking each other for wounds.

Normally, Aniaija would stop and help. But her rage kept her pushing forward, searching for the source of the destruction she saw around her. She would catalogue it later, make lists of what they would need to search for the next time they came across a merchant ship.

A flash of bright blue caught Aniaija's attention, and she turned her eyes to a woman who climbing the rigging.

Dapsa.

The relief of knowing that Dapsa had survived eased some of Aniaija's pain. The two women locked eyes for a moment. They each nodded in acknowledgement of the other before Dapsa continued to climb, and Aniaija continued to search for Captain Geomar.

She ascended the stairs leading to the platform that housed the ship's wheel and found what she had been looking for.

Rols Geomar—captain of *The Mercy*—stood with his grey head bent over a map. Sand coated his red jacket, the grains glistening in the setting sun and dropping to the deck with each of the captain's movements. His hair was so thoroughly coated with the stuff that it sparkled like gemstones.

Aniaija had no presence of mind to question why the captain already had a map unrolled on top of a crate when the storm had only just dissipated.

She had no presence of mind to consider anything outside of the burning rage within her and the one question that demanded to be heard.

She rounded the crate and slammed her tan hands on the map as she forced herself into Geomar's field of vision, foregoing the expected salute to her superior.

"Have you lost your fucking mind?" Aniaija hissed. "You could have gotten us all *killed*."

Geomar continued to ponder the map, seemingly oblivious to the fuming woman before him. The long points of his ears, scarred and jagged, poked through the wiry hair on his head. After another moment of consideration, he placed a marker on the map and grunted with approval.

He straightened in a smoother motion than one might expect by such an ancient-looking man and brushed the front of his jacket with the back of his gnarled hands.

Sand fell onto the map. A shiver ran down Aniaija's spine.

"But I didn't," Geomar said calmly. "We are alive. And it worked."

Aniaija could feel how tight her brow furrowed, how wide her mouth had fallen open.

"It *worked*?" she asked. "What the fuck are you on about? If you're talking about damaging our ship when we have no way of getting supplies, then yeah, I guess it worked."

Geomar's pale blue eyes gleamed with mischief.

Aniaija always hated that look. It meant that whatever crazy ideas they had endured were only the beginning.

Geomar lifted his sabre and pointed it towards the horizon.

Aniaija's frown deepened impossibly further. She turned and followed Geomar's gaze. For longer than she cared to admit, she could not see what Geomar was talking about. Had the old coot finally lost his mind?

And then, as if the ripples of sand that concealed so much in this desert deemed her worthy, Aniaija could make out the form of another ship.

No, she thought. *Not just another ship. The Other ship.*

The one that had been on their tail for weeks now, finally sailing in the opposite direction.

"They gave up," she breathed.

"For now," Geomar said.

Aniaija turned back to him.

"What do we do now?" she asked.

Geomar shrugged. "We can go to the Oasis," he said. "But we have nothing for them. I can imagine that it might raise morale for the crew to see their family, but I don't know how well if it is empty-handed."

Aniaija chewed her lip.

The Oasis was a rocky outcrop in the middle of the Between. It was riddled with tunnels and caves, and when they realised that they would never be able to pull into a port and find safety in Ailiar again, the crew of *The Mercy* agreed that it would be safer for their families if they stayed in the Oasis.

They all would have stayed if the Oasis had been hospitable. But even with Water and Earth Affinities working together, they could not sustain crops. So, the families of the crew stayed in the tunnels and caves, staying as safe and hidden as possible, while the crew roamed the Between and raided passing ships for food and supplies.

She did not have any family of her own in the Oasis, but she could easily imagine how daunting it would be to wake up each morning, wondering if you would see your loved ones again and how terrifying it would be to go sleep wondering if they had survived.

"What were you marking?" she asked, unable to make a suggestion one way or the other.

"Where we are," Geomar said.

He gestured to the marker, and then pointed to a port. "It will take us a few days to get close enough that we can watch and set upon any ships leaving here. That is, after we've made the necessary repairs."

If they could make the necessary repairs.

With each storm, with each loss of a panel of wood or a nail, *The Mercy* was inching closer to never being able to move through the Between again.

And no one had been brave enough to have the conversation about what would happen when that day came.

"We don't know how long that could take," Aniaija said. "It would take hours alone to catalogue everything. Then we would have to set up teams, delegate, determine what is a higher priority..."

"I know," Geomar said. "You better get started then, right, Ani?"

Aniaija pulled a face. She opened her mouth to retort when she saw someone over Geomar's shoulder.

"Gillie?" she asked.

Gillie was a small, mousey boy who had recently joined *The Mercy* the last time they stopped at the Oasis. He had been only a toddler when *The Mercy* had first left Balliach. Aniaija had been hesitant to allow him to join the crew, even with his father's blessing.

"Aniaija, ma'am," he said.

His voice wavered, and he wrung his hands nervously.

Aniaija made a mental note to have a conversation with him about remembering to salute those above him in the chain of command – even if she had just refused to do so herself.

"Yes? What is it?"

"It's... it's Raisa," Gillie said. "She... she's not accounted for."

SIX

CALLIOPE

BALLIACH

CROWN PRINCESS CALLIOPE AILIAR had done her best to hold back the yawn that had been building for the better part of the last hour. It wouldn't be ladylike to demonstrate just how bored she was of the dreary, repetitive lessons that Councillor Doren Sancor delighted in torturing her with. But it wasn't just his lessons that were dry and dusty.

While the rest of the keep within Balliach Castle was so thoroughly polished that even the flagstone flooring glistened in the right light, Calliope often wondered if the cleaning staff even knew this room existed. She sat on the edge of the creaking wooden seat so as to not cover her entire gown with the thick layer of dust that surrounded the small space that she had claimed for herself. Her seat and desk were the only two things that were not smothered in dust and dirt. She kept her elbows pinned tight to her side to avoid brushing up against any of the cobwebs that draped themselves over the edge of every piece of ancient, rotting furniture like a tragic damsel. She kept her breathing shallow, lest the dust grew fingers and decided to reach up through her nose to scramble her brain.

Perhaps it already had.

Her brain did feel thoroughly scrambled. She was finding it more difficult than usual to listen to the raspy ramblings of the decrepit old man. Why did her father insist she take lessons from him? She should be taking lessons with the official royal tutors, like she had as a child, not having long-forgotten wars and battles shoved down her throat by someone who was supposed to be advising the King. Though, Calliope conceded, being the advisor to a king when a queen ruled the realm likely wasn't the glamourous position Sancor had dreamed of for himself. Playing tutor for the next Queen of Ailiar was certainly a step up.

But that didn't explain the dirty, draughty space that he insisted they take their lessons in. It didn't explain why he seemed so gleeful when she kicked a spider off her embroidered shoes, or why he seemed to take so much pleasure in her discomfort.

It certainly did not explain why her father didn't do anything about it whenever she complained. Calliope was not even sure that her mother, the Queen, would deign to intervene should Calliope manage to so much as get an audience with her. Was this what it was like for all daughters? To fight and claw for a scrap of attention from the only woman in the world who was supposed to lavish it upon them?

Or had she done something wrong?

Calliope certainly felt wrong.

The list of everything that Calliope failed to live up to her mother with was extensive, even at such a young age. It started with her hair—limp, straight, and as dull brown as the mice that scurry along the twisting hallways. It was the opposite of her mother's tight, red curls. Her rounded face and thin lips had been inherited from her father, and she had not received her mother's straight nose.

How was she, the First Daughter of the First Daughter, supposed to live up to her bloodline and her fate when she did not look anything like her mother, or any of the women that had come before her?

"I am so terribly sorry."

Councillor Sancor's high-pitched whine of a voice cut through Calliope's runaway thoughts, taking her with hands as gnarly and bony as the man's own and ripping her away. Only when her mind was completely back where it belonged did the princess realise that she had failed in her attempt to keep her yawn behind closed lips. Her fingers were splayed over her open mouth. Her nose was scrunched, and she could feel her lungs expand to their fullest.

Worst of all, Councillor Sancor was seated on the bench beside her, his hunched body twisted in her direction. Slowly, as though by moving too quickly, she would be opening herself to attack by the creature beside her, she closed her mouth and lowered her hand into her lap.

Perhaps she was being too harsh on the old man, for he *was* quite elderly, even by elven standards. When she was much younger and dim-witted, Calliope had even asked him if he had been born during the time of the Ancient Ones. It had earned her another two hours in this forgotten room and been the day she had realised her father would trust this man's decisions when it came to her discipline.

If only he would lay a hand on her. If he struck her, the Bloodmaids would dispose of him. She could imagine his too-airy voice begging for mercy as the red-clad warriors that tended to and protected the Queen and her heir advanced upon him.

But she was getting away from herself. Once again, her mind was taking strings of thought and running through the corridors of her innermost self, leaving knots and tripwires in its wake for her to get caught in later.

She lowered her gaze, hoping against all hope that so long as she looked remorseful for her distraction, he would not keep her cooped up here longer than he was supposed to.

"Is the culture of your intended not interesting? I would have thought that you would be clamouring for as much information about Zadanai as you could possibly retain in order to ensure a smooth transition into married life. Though I suppose I could be wrong, you never were one for knowledge, were you?"

Calliope's gut tightened. She could feel the soft linen of her chemise follow her body as the muscles pulled the softest part of her inward. She could feel each crease of the fabric move and shift beneath the heavier cotton outer dress. It was too much. Too much, too heavy, too cloying.

She closed thin fingers around the fabric at her lap, clenching until her knuckles turned white, and the cold, stale air of the room found the new opening around her ankles and climbed up her stockinged legs.

It was all almost enough to ignore how close Councillor Sancor was.

Almost.

Calliope was sure that no amount of discomfort that could compel her to ignore that his breath that smelled of urine, or the overarching scent of sweet rot that she guessed had something to do with the limp that always got worse after large feasts and celebrations.

It took everything that she was not to curl her nose in disgust.

"I am sorry," Calliope said. "I did not mean to imply that your teachings—and certainly not my betrothed's heritage—were tiresome."

She blinked rapidly, as she would if she were trying to keep tears at bay. At least Sancor's rancid breath was good for one thing—her eyes watered anyway, and a single tear broke free, racing down her cheek.

"I..." she continued, letting her voice waver. "I have not been sleeping well. Ever since my father announced that I was to marry, I have lain awake, staring into the darkness and wondering so many things. I want our union to be happy and fruitful, but more than anything, I want our union to be for the good of my country."

There was truth to her words. She had been restless, her sleep broken, but she was not worried about the male she was supposed to marry. She did not care if their union was a happy one, especially not if being unhappy meant that her country was safe.

Calliope took a shaky breath and blinked up towards the cobwebs hanging from the ceiling.

"I am so worried that I am not ready," she breathed. "I have not even seen a hint of what my Affinity will be once I come into it, and yet I am to be married within the year. How many women are married before they come of age? How many queens in our past have taken husbands before their power was assured?"

She should stop. She shouldn't be spilling so much truth to this horrid male, but her attempt at placating him seemed to have opened the floodgates. Truth spilled from her lips like wine from an overturned goblet, and she wished so desperately to scoop it all back to where it belonged.

Beside her, Councillor Sancor shifted in his seat. Calliope didn't move as he reached out and lay one of his knotted hands atop hers, even as bile rose in her throat.

"You are carrying a heavy burden," Councillor Sancor said.

Calliope was certain that the concern she heard in his voice was false.

"But you have nothing to worry about," he continued. "You are the daughter of the Blood Queen herself, and you also have your father's blood running through your veins. His Affinity is nothing to turn your nose up at, even if he is not Gods Blessed."

Calliope frowned. Certainly, she must be imagining the sneer she heard. Councillor Sancor could not possibly be mocking the generations of the Ailiar line, the Maiden's line, which had been chosen by the Ancient Ones to rule the land. She almost turned her head in his direction to see for herself.

Almost.

"And it is a little unorthodox for you to be married before coming into your Affinity, yes, but it is not unheard of. Queen Dierma was married before she came into her Affinity, as was her daughter. They both came into their Affinity as Saldhraos, just as the queens before and after them. They both controlled Bloodstone with ease, and both possessed the Maiden Sword. You have nothing to worry about, your Highness."

Councillor Sancor's words did nothing to soothe Calliope's fears. If anything, they served as fodder, feeding them and encouraging them to grow to titanic proportions. After generations of the Maiden's bloodline ruling Ailiar, the weight of her destiny lay heavy on Calliope's shoulders. The Queens he had given as examples were not comforting. Queen Dierma had gone mad and had been assassinated to put her daughter on the throne.

The attempted platitudes only served to stoke the flames of doubt, changing Calliope's question of *what if I don't come into an Affinity* to *what if I do, and I go mad?*

What if she were the one to break the long chain of Ailian history? What if the Ancient Ones found her lacking and the country—the world—was thrown into chaos all because *she* could not meet the expectations that thousands of years of tradition had thrust upon her?

Calliope gripped the skirts on her lap tighter. The stiff, metallic fibres of the brocade poked into the soft pads of her fingers. It was not as jarring as pricking oneself with a pin or needle, but the discomfort lay within a similar vein, and it was one that Calliope knew all too well.

She honed in on the feeling, directing all of her attention to it so that her lungs could continue to function as they were designed to, and her mind could be reined in. As she did, she turned her face towards Councillor Sancor and offered a polite, demure smile. If she could convince him that his words had allayed her fears, perhaps he would stand again, leaving the bubble of space around herself that she claimed as her own.

"I know that it is a heavy burden for one so young," Councillor Sancor continued. "I know that excitement and anxiety must be waging war within you, demanding top billing."

Calliope wanted to scream at him that there was no way that he could possibly know what she was feeling. He was not in line for the throne. He was not expected to marry for politics—though she would make sure to thank the Ancient Ones during the Wishing for this small blessing. She would do so, on behalf of every female who had been saved from the misfortune of being tied to him for the rest of her life.

Doren Sancor was not a young girl expected to give her hand to a stranger, to bind herself to someone she had never met for the rest of her long, elven life.

But she could not scream those words.

To do so would be so unladylike, so very beneath her station and a disappointment to the line of the Maiden. She would have failed to live up to her destiny before she was even crowned.

She would be no better than the Mad Queen.

So, instead of yelling or screaming, and instead of picking up the heavy tome Sancor had been reading from and bringing it down on his head over and over again, Calliope continued to smile at him.

"Thank you," she said. "It is so very overwhelming. I admit that I have been allowing it to get to me more than I ought to. I know that I should be taking this time to forget about all of that and take advantage of the remaining lessons that we have."

Calliope could not imagine that she would be expected to continue with her lessons with Sancor once she was wed. She even dared hope that their number would decrease once Prince Di'Ath of Zadanai landed on Ailian soil, though that may be asking for too much.

"For now," Calliope continued. "My mind feels far too muddled. I cannot keep a thought straight, no matter how hard I try."

Councillor Sancor nodded. He lifted his hand to brush a stray strand of Calliope's hair away from her face, disturbing dust with the long, billowy sleeves of his cloak. The particles danced in the air, threatening to work their way up Calliope's nose as they inched closer and closer.

It took everything she had to keep still and not jerk away. The conversation seemed to be going in Calliope's favour for once, and she was not about to let herself lose the hint of opportunity that seemed to be presenting itself.

"How about," Councillor Sancor began. "Just this once, we forget about the lessons for today. You can spend time with your ladies, rest, and clear your mind. I am sure that if you take some time to sort through your thoughts, you will find that they will not plague you so."

Calliope couldn't believe it. The corners of her mouth pulled upwards.

"Are you sure?" she asked.

"Yes," Councillor Sancor said, nodding his head. "Go—I suspect that there will not be many solitary afternoons once you are married. Go, enjoy yourself."

Not wanting to risk letting the man change his mind, Calliope stood and offered him a hasty, shallow curtsey before rushing out of the dusty room as quickly as possible.

The relief of clean air was instant.

Calliope closed her eyes and took a deep breath, filling her lungs. Not for the first time, Calliope marvelled at the difference a door could make. On one side, one could be suffocating, contemplating the merits of leaping off a parapet, and on the other, the very same person could be imagining the birds that they would see in the gardens should they desire to visit.

The tension that had gripped her shoulders so firmly was melting away like butter on baked potatoes. It would have continued to do so if there had not been a heavy clunk of armour behind her when she took a step away from the door.

Calliope's jaw clenched, and she straightened her back. Twenty years of it, and still she forgot that she would always be shadowed by a Bloodmaid. She couldn't decide which was more humiliating—the fact that she had forgotten that one of the red-clad warrior women had been waiting outside the door for her to finish her lessons or the knowledge that the only reason why she had heard the women at all was because she had *wanted* to be heard.

Calliope turned to face the Bloodmaid, lifting her chin.

The other woman would have made the princess feel small enough with her height, but with her blood-red dragon-scale tassets covering the red-embroidered skirts of the court-gown and the breast-plate bearing the likeness of the Maiden-Sword on her chest, she was downright imposing. But it was not the woman's stature or her armour that unsettled Calliope.

It was the mask.

All Bloodmaids wore a mask covering the top half of their face. Like their armour, it was made of Bloodstone, forged by the Queen herself for the elite group that had been selected for the sacred duty of protecting the Queen and her heir. The mask itself was a relatively plain affair, with no decoration save for the carving of tears running from the eyes, and a veil that was attached to the very top. The veil, made of a plain, opaque fabric that matched the same red as the Bloodmaid's gown, covered the woman's hair completely. Between the mask and the veil, it was impossible to tell who was standing right in front of her.

Calliope hated that.

She hated that she was supposed to trust that this woman would protect her against all harm when she did not even know her name. How could she not be certain that it was not someone that had snuck into the castle, stolen the warrior's garb and posed as her protector in order to be her ultimate demise?

What she hated most, however, was the masks that the Bloodmaids wore, covering the top half of their faces and leaving their mouths free. It didn't make sense, seeing as they were forbidden from speaking. Calliope couldn't make heads or tails of it, and yet, it was so.

You can spend time with your ladies, Councillor Sancor had said.

How was she supposed to *spend time* with someone she couldn't even identify out of the group? The only way that Calliope knew how to differentiate between any of the Bloodmaids was whether their veils were embroidered or not. This one, she could tell, was an apprentice. One step above recruit—a rank of which Calliope had never seen—and likely hoping against all hope that the Queen was planning on elevating her to one of the Twelve should a position open.

"Did you have something to say?" Calliope asked.

The apprentice Bloodmaid didn't respond.

"Oh, you're silent now?" Calliope continued. "Seemed like you wanted to make yourself known with that *clack-clack* of yours. Why didn't you dampen the sound? We both know you can. It's one of the first things you learn, right?"

The only reply Calliope received from the Bloodmaid apprentice was the clink of iron against iron as the other woman clasped her hands in front of her. Bangles of varying thickness covered her wrists. Matching iron rings donned her fingers.

Even though she was still an apprentice, this Bloodmaid had made her mark. The more iron worn by a Bloodmaid, the more accomplished they were.

At least I have not been assigned someone who doesn't know what they are doing, Calliope thought.

Frustrated with her unanswered questions, Calliope huffed and threw up her hands. She turned on her heels and stormed down the hallway.

Despite the lack of footsteps and the absence of all other sounds, Calliope knew that the Bloodmaid apprentice was following close behind, destroying any idea that Calliope may have entertained about enjoying a solitary afternoon.

SEVEN

ANIAIJA

THE SEA BETWEEN SEAS

IT WOULD NEVER MATTER how violent and terrifying a storm was while it raged over the Between. The stillness that followed was always worse.

On the true sea, when the waves took hold of any poor soul fallen overboard and dragged them down to the dark and unforgiving depths, there would be nothing left for the survivors to do but mourn. The true horror did not come from the storm itself. It came after, when Aniaija and a small team would be lowered onto the sand below, tasked with the most daunting responsibility of them all.

They were the unlucky ones, known as the Dead Crew, sent to the sand to search for those that they had lost.

As heartbreaking as it was to lose a friend, a fellow crewmate, or even a rival you had made while aboard the ship, it was easier when they fell to a watery grave. Survivors would send prayers to Di'Tyan—the God of the Dead—on behalf of those buried at sea to ensure that the fallen would be welcomed into the gilded halls of the afterlife. It was a truth known by all that those who spent their years on the water desired for their bodies to return to it after death. It was a fitting end to a life dedicated to the power and unpredictability of the waves.

But on the Between, there was no current that carried the dead to Di'Tyan's realm.

The *Mercy* had sailed by far too many rotting bodies of fallen crewmates over the first few months of sailing on the Between, and so they had come to the decision to refuse to leave them to the sands.

Instead, the Dead Crew had been formed. Since its conception, the Dead Crew had consisted primarily of Saldhraos, those able to feel the energy within the sand, rocks, and dirt that made up the Sea Between Seas and use their power to find the bodies of the fallen.

In the beginning, the Dead Crew had been a large group. Many had been eager to search for their lost loved ones and to bring their bodies back to the ship, where their remains would be burned during a ceremony honouring their lives. But as the years wore on and the crew and families aboard the *Mercy* dwindled, so did the willing participants of the Dead Crew.

Not even additional rum rations were enough to keep the ghosts of the dead at bay.

Aniaija couldn't blame them. As a founding member of the Dead Crew, she herself felt the toll of bringing up yet another dead body. The hollow, empty feeling that a corpse made when surrounded by the vibrant, vibrating energy of the earth around it seemed to creep along her skin in the dead of night. It threatened to consume her, to draw out her magic like salt draws out water, and with each death she brought to the surface, the hollowness grew hungrier.

As the Dead Crew assumed their positions on a small wooden lifeboat, waiting to be lowered to the sand below, Aniaija cursed both the Ancient Ones and the Tide for the cruel trick they appeared to be playing on her. Beside her, bouncing his knee with nervous energy and still-raw cuts and scrapes on his cheek, sat Nori.

Guilt bubbled within her. It rose in her throat like bile, threatening to spill over her lap. She could still see that boulder sailing through the air like a cannon ball. She could hear the splintering of wood as clearly as she had when it happened.

She had nearly killed him.

And he seemed none the wiser.

She turned to face him properly. The scrapes on his cheeks had stopped bleeding, but there was a deeper cut that ran beneath his eye. It seemed to follow the curve of the orbital bone beneath, and although it had clearly been tended to by healers, shiny, off-white pus oozed out from between the stitches.

Aniaija's mind was quick to fill in the image of what might have happened if the offending object had been any bigger and sharper. Bile rose in her throat as she imagined watching the top half of Nori's head separate from the lower.

She swallowed and redirected her focus to her hands. She toyed with the toggle on the back of her glove, securing and loosening the flap that covered her palm. She knew that she shouldn't, for the more often she undid the flap, the weaker the threads holding the toggle would get. Thread and fabric had become one of the more difficult resources to get their hands on.

At least it wouldn't matter if she lost the bone toggle itself. The *Mercy* had a surplus of bone needles, toggles, and buttons. Many crew members had created jewellery out of beads carved from the ribs and spines of the animals they slaughtered for food or found wandering the Between. But thread? The handful of thread that remained was off limits for anything other than medical use.

Like the stitches in Nori's face.

"No one would blame you if you stayed behind this time," Aniaija said to him. "Not after you nearly ended up in the sand yourself."

Nori snorted. "I'm fine," he said. "I'm not going to shirk my duty just because of some near miss."

Aniaija could not begrudge him the drive he had or the desire to do his part that he held onto so tightly. She could understand it. She felt it herself long before Geomar had appointed her his First Mate.

Before she had redirected that cannonball a decade ago.

Ropes creaked as Jora and Tinen lowered the lifeboat. The pulleys squeaked. The wood groaned.

Aniaija grunted as the lifeboat finally hit the sand with a jolt, jostling the Dead Crew. It was a sensation that she would never get used to. No matter how many times she went down to the sand, no matter how much she braced herself for impact, she could never get used to it.

But at least, she reminded herself. *It was easier than what was to come.*

Across from her, Fredericks and Eila stood and untied the ropes. Fredericks was a tall, broad blond man with notches in his pointed ears. Aniaija did not know whether they were intentional, in lieu of piercings, or evidence of a life lived violently. Eila was almost as broad. She had sailed with Geomar for decades, and had permanently sun-reddened skin and callouses to show for it.

Once the ropes were untied, Eila fixed her field green eyes on Aniaija.

"How many are we looking for?" she asked, her voice as sand-worn as her skin.

"Just one," Aniaija said. "Raisa."

As if losing 'just one' was an accomplishment, she thought.

While Geomar had been proud of their success in the storm, proud of how they had not only outpaced their pursuers but scared them into turning away, Aniaija had felt the guilt of suffering a casualty grip her with an iron hand. She knew, somewhere deep down, that it was stupid to take each loss personally. But she didn't understand how Geomar had not even reacted to the news that Raisa had not been accounted for, save to nod at Aniaija. It had been a silent order to gather the Dead Crew and search for her.

After having their own injuries tended to, the four of them had split up and interviewed the surviving crew to establish how long she had been missing for.

To Aniaija's horror, they had concluded that Raisa had gone overboard no more than fifteen minutes before the storm had died down.

Aniaija climbed out of the lifeboat and rolled her neck. The sand crunched beneath her boots and slid just enough to give her stable footing. She barely noticed when her magic did that now. It had been so confusing when she had first come into her Affinity when the uneven ground that she had been so used to navigating began to give way to her.

"Ready, boss," Fredricks called from behind her.

Aniaija looked over her shoulder as she undid the flaps of her gloves and buttoned them against the back of her hand. Fredericks, the strongest of the four, was responsible for dragging the lifeboat behind him as they searched for their dead. He had secured the ropes to a leather harness that he had created with Les, the ship's leatherworker. It had been designed so that he could pull the boat without restricting the use of his hands.

Aniaija nodded, and after receiving nods of affirmation from both Eila and Nori, turned her attention forward again. The *Mercy* had left a deep scar in the sand as it sailed through it, but it was quickly filling with sand picked up from the wind that still blew. They would need to rely on their navigation very shortly.

"Same procedure as always," Aniaija said. "Fan out, and call out if you find something."

If Aniaija Bahra had been a betting woman, she would have put money on the odds of it being her to find the body of Raisa Heartstrom. She would, as a result, become the richest person on board the *Mercy*. It just seemed inevitable. Out of each person who had ever been part of the Dead Crew, Aniaija had found the most bodies. She supposed one could attribute part of the reason to how long she had been at it, but to her it always felt like bad luck.

She just seemed to be the one who walked in the right direction, who looked in the right place.

Perhaps it was for the best.

It was always startling to come across the voice that signified a dead thing buried beneath the surface. As with all Saldhraos, each grain of sand, every piece of dirt, each rock and stone and mineral sang out to Aniaija. It was almost as though she could see the energy that emanated from the smallest speck of dust, and so, to feel the void of something that was not earth was like walking past an open window in a warm room. It was that shock of cold that seeped into your very bones and settled at your core.

It was a sensation that she wasn't sure she would ever truly forget. Even if the *Mercy* were one day able to dock, be repaired and leave the desert, Aniaija wasn't certain that she would ever be truly warm again. If she could protect others from feeling the same way, she supposed it was a small price to pay.

They had been searching for almost two hours when she found that cold hollow in the otherwise vibrant energies of the ground beneath her feet. There had been many times in her life when Aniaija had wished that she had come into a different Affinity. And this moment—the mirror of all the moments when she had found the bodies of lost crewmates—would always sit atop that list.

She let out a shaky breath and turned her face towards the sky. Only when she was sure that no tears would fall did she call out to the rest of the Dead Crew.

"She's here!" Aniaija called, voice cracking. Clearing her throat, she yelled it again.

It didn't take long for Fredericks to be by her side, boat in tow. Nori was next, his tanned face unusually pale beneath the red scrapes and cuts.

Eila arrived last, having been spread out the furthest away.

"Are you sure?" Fredericks asked.

Aniaija craned her neck to look up at him.

Fredericks had been pale upon first joining the crew of the *Mercy*. Now, his shoulders and cheeks were as brown as his hair. He had not lost the kindness in his face though, and his blue eyes had not lost the grip of the shine within them.

Aniaija wished she knew how he kept hold of it all these years.

She nodded.

"I'm sure. She's here. The dead spot in the ground is the right size. She's not that deep, but it would be quicker to pull her up than it would be to dig her out."

Fredericks nodded, and the four of them made a circle around the void of energy in the ground.

"Ready?" Aniaija asked.

Eila rolled her shoulders and nodded.

"Ready," Nori answered.

"This shit never gets easier," Fredericks muttered.

Aniaija offered him a sympathetic smile before reaching down into the sand with her magic once more, palms open and down towards the ground to guide it. The sand's energy reached back with glee, but she ignored it in much the same way a mother ignored a needy child while she was cooking dinner. She would have time for it later, but for now, she was busy.

She felt the magic of her companions brush up against hers. Nori's felt like moss-covered rocks. Fredericks' reminded her of craggy cliffs.

Eila's felt like caverns that stretched deep within the earth, housing bats and unknown, story-book creatures that thrived on darkness.

It had taken a few tries over the years for the Dead Crew to settle on the best method for bringing a corpse to the surface. For the ones closer to the surface, they would simply use their magic to scoop the sand away in a shovelling motion, as if they were digging them out. In order to reach those who were as deep as Raisa, they needed to be creative to make the process as quick and efficient as possible. Aniaija had learned from experience that having sand constantly fall into the hole you were digging to retrieve the body of a friend only served to make the process more traumatic.

So, it had been decided that the best practice was to separate the Dead Crew into two groups, each with a very specific goal. One group would focus on the sand directly beneath the corpse. They would use their magic to stiffen the grains and interlock them together like a board. This always left Aniaija feeling drained and lightheaded, and at times, she was unable to let go of the magic before the slab of sand became permanent. She much preferred being on the other team, pushing energy into the grains of sand to make them vibrate and dance. She had always thought it was like turning the sand into liquid.

Aniaija considered it a small blessing that she was in the latter group this time. Her magic branched out beneath the desert's surface like roots, eagerly reaching out to the sand like greeting old friends. Her heartbeat quickened as the sand began to dance. She could hear music that was not playing, could feel the press of bodies against her own that were not there.

It was intoxicating.

A mound formed in the sand as the body was brought closer to the surface. Steadily, the mound began to take the familiar shape of an elf's body as sand fell to either side.

Finally, it broke open to reveal the twisted remains of Raisa Heartstrom.

Bile once again rose in Aniaija's throat.

Raisa's eyes were still open. They stared into nothing, as if without the right prayers, they would never fall upon the wonders of the Gilded Halls of Di'Tyan.

But it was not those grey, sightless eyes that would haunt Aniaija. She had seen far too many dead eyes for another set to warrant a spot weighing on her conscience.

It was her mouth.

Raisa's mouth was still agape in a silent, soundless scream. Sand was packed firmly in her throat. It coated the inside of her cheeks and nestled in the cracks of her lips. It had worn away at the dead sailor's front teeth, leaving their surface oddly flat.

Raisa had not simply gone overboard and died. She had drowned in the sand, and she had been terrified throughout the whole process.

Death was an easier inevitability to know when they sailed on the true sea—when it was rare to see the horror of what it truly meant. On the true sea, you didn't find your companions frozen as they were in their last moments. They weren't left in place for death to set in and immortalize their fear of meeting their end.

Nori swore under his breath. Fredericks cleared his throat awkwardly.

Eila, mercifully, stayed silent.

"Let's take her home," Aniaija said.

With a nod of agreement, the Dead Crew lifted Raisa's body into the boat, and silently escorted their lost companion back to the waiting *Mercy*.

Raisa Heartstrom had been wrapped in the hammock she had slept in every night since she had joined the crew of the *Mercy*. It was always difficult to let go of something as precious as canvas, but it had been decided years ago that this would be how the crew honoured their dead—just as they had decided that they would not leave their crewmates to rot in the dunes.

Raisa's body had been dressed and prepared by her two closest friends, Arga and Tumo. They carried her through the belly of the *Mercy*, gaining an ever growing following of mourning crew with each room they passed. By the time they reached the gaping hole in the hull, all but one of the entire crew of four hundred and eleven souls were behind them.

Aniaija watched as Dapsa, who had been maintaining the wall of air over the hole, bowed at the waist. The tail of her headscarf slipped over her shoulder with the depth of her bow, the too-thin green fabric pulled by the brass weight at the end. She said something that Aniaija couldn't hear.

Arga and Tumo's response was just as inaudible, but it was enough to satisfy the unwritten ritual that had developed over the years. Dapsa straightened and turned towards the hole. The light that shined through lit up her face like candlelight through amber. Even as far as she was, several rows of people away, Aniaija's breath caught in her throat at the sight.

Dapsa raised her long, calloused hands, palm towards the shield of air protecting the *Mercy* from taking on too much sand. Then, as though she were grasping curtains, she tugged downward.

Immediately, sand rushed in, no longer restricted by the wall of air. It flooded the interior of the hull with a hiss. The first few rows of sailors each took a half-step back to avoid the encroaching wave. It was an odd habit, one that stemmed back to the days when they sailed upon the true sea. Aniaija grimaced as the people in front of her pressed back, sandwiching her against the people behind. Even though the crates and barrels had been moved towards the rear of the ship to protect them from any sand that might break through the barrier, the hull was not designed to have the ship's entire crew down here at once.

Someone's breath washed over her shoulder. It ran down her neck, and she closed her hand around the hilt of the dagger on her belt. True, these people were her friends. They were also the closest thing she had to family if she were being honest. But if she thought for one moment that they would trample her, Aniaija wouldn't hesitate to bring some of them down with her.

Thankfully, it wouldn't come to that.

Arga and Tumo climbed out of the *Mercy*, carrying Raisa with them. Slowly, the pressure around Aniaija lessened, and the crew moved forward. She followed the flow, walking out of the ship via the gaping hole.

The hole *she*'d had a hand in creating.

Moving like cattle, the crew of the *Mercy* followed Arga and Tumo until they were a safe enough distance away from the ship. They gathered in a circle around the pair and their fallen friend.

At least it was still summer. At least the sandwyrms would be buried deep underground and not waiting for this veritable feast that was all but gift wrapped to them. Aniaija cleared her throat and refocused her attention. It would be rude and disrespectful to let her mind wander right now.

Captain Geomar stepped forward from the crowd. He bowed his head to Arga and Tumo before turning towards the wrapped body of Raisa which had been set on a mound of sand. To her, Geomar bowed deep at the waist. He spoke to her, words unheard by any other—words designed to comfort

Raisa's soul.

When he stood, a broad, scar-riddled, flame-wielding Igdhraos by the name of Piet stepped forward. Piet followed Geomar's example, nodding to Raisa's two friends, and bowing to Raisa herself. Then, he raised his arms, pressing his hands to his chest.

This part had always intrigued Aniaija. While most Igdhraos needed a flame or a spark to access their magic, Piet was one of the few who could create it. Aniaija watched as Piet seemed to pull the flame out of his very body. Threads of fire followed Piet's fingers as he drew his hand away from his chest.

He draped them over Raisa's corpse like ribbons.

It wasn't until the shrouded body was covered in an intricate lacework of flame that the fire even began to burn the canvas. Piet had managed to contain the fire's hunger for destruction until he had laid down the last ribbon of heat.

The gathered crew watched as the flames burned hotter, burned brighter, coaxed by Piet and his magic.

Not a soul would move, not a soul would leave, until there was nothing left of Raisa on the sand.

EIGHT

DI'ATH

ZADANAI

THE POUCHES OF COIN tied to Di'Ath's belt had slowly dwindled throughout the day as he visited the last of his creditors. For three weeks, he had been working to pay off the debts that he had accrued over the last few years. Funny how easily one could amass a debt when they weren't anticipating being the one to pay it back.

At least, not personally.

While Di'Ath had known that his purchases had not come without a price tag, he had not expected to be the one spending hours counting out each individual amount after the days he had spent going through the mountains of paperwork to determine exactly how much he owed, and to whom.

Sy'da, of course, had not helped.

Even if she had been allowed to, Di'Ath was certain that she still would have sat there, watching as he wrote out the labels for each establishment and attached them with a length of cord. Each night, he had tossed and turned in smooth, silken sheets, debating whether it was best to get all the repayments delivered as quickly as possible or to select only a few to set out each day until the day he was due to set sail for Balliach.

In the end, he'd settled on the former. Even though he still had over a month before he was to leave his home, this would be the last day he would need to drag himself through the streets, depositing the pouches of coin.

It had been more embarrassing than he expected. Every acceptance of his outstanding balance at each vendor had crushed his ego. Di'Ath had never considered humility to have a physical substance before, and yet now here he was, weighed down with it so thoroughly his steps dragged, even as the weight around his waist lessened.

He didn't understand it.

His black leather boots felt as though they were made of stone. They seemed to pull him into the pavement beneath his feet, threatening—no, *promising*—to keep him here forever, only if he just let them. It felt the same as being in the water did. Like his Affinity was calling out to its element and begging to be allowed to become one with it.

He wondered if this was how those with an earth Affinity felt. Did the ground offer to hold them close and keep them safe? And what about fire? Did Igdhraos dream of walking into the flames?

At least those three elements could be avoided, to an extent. An elf with an air Affinity must feel constantly pressured by their power to give in and melt away on the wind.

Despite the urge to dive into the sea and let the Tide carry him away, Di'Ath conceded that it was a mercy that the place he was leaving his sea-bound home for was built along a shore. He would be able to visit the water whenever he pleased—or, at least, when duty permitted.

He was not to be landlocked.

As relieving as this revelation was, Di'Ath was certain that the streets would not have as many brightly coloured banners draping above the pathways as the Zadanese capital of Wylden. No other country could have such a love for colour and pattern, he was sure. Whenever he had read about the great cities of other countries, they always seemed so grey and bland.

But Wylden?

The people decorated their city as brightly as they decorated themselves. Windchimes and bells hung from doorways. Coloured glass caught the sunlight and reflected beautifully crafted images onto the pavement below. The salt-air was filled with the rich scent of spices, roasting meats and fragrant gravies. Each stone and plank of wood felt alive.

He could not imagine Balliach thrumming with as much energy. He could not picture the comforting scents of vanilla and cinnamon warming him from their very presence alone.

But then again, he supposed it could have been worse.

Di'Ath could have been promised to a Rupaburgan princess. He could have been bound for Huidon, high in the snow-capped mountains and weeks away from any shore.

His magic would not necessarily be hindered, but Di'Ath was certain that it would just as torturous as the time he spent in the salt rooms.

Perhaps he should find a Rupaburgan noble to introduce Sy'da to. Her control over ice would thrive in a place like Huidon. Perhaps she could follow the legends of the Ailian Queens and rebuild the city out of ice.

Perhaps she would become a legend, engrained in the country's very history if she were able to accomplish such a feat. Perhaps she would even be deified, all while Di'Ath was to stand by the side of his future Queen, keeping his own magic tamped down for the sake of peace.

After all, he couldn't have such destructive power loose in a foreign country. He doubted that a moment of lost control would be seen as anything over than treasonous.

As such, Di'Ath was resigned to be, at best, forgotten, lest he be remembered as a villain.

"What do you think the food is going to be like in Ailiar?" Sy'da asked.

Di'Ath turned his head to watch her lick the last remaining drops of sticky honey off her fingers. He regretted asking her to join him, especially when the sweets vendor had offered her layered pastry treat simply because she had commented on how wonderful the melted sugar smelled. Sy'da looked like a child with the way she licked her fingers clean, not like the 21-year-old royal that she was.

She had always been like this, caring more about a sweet treat in her hand or some fun that could be had, rather than how she was perceived. Di'Ath had no doubt that this had led to her popularity among their people.

Di'Ath had not cared about how he was perceived either, but the attention he received was far different than that of his sister. Di'Ath was popular with beautiful women and with the kind of men who wanted the chance of alleviating the prince of his burden of coin. He received bowed heads and respectful conversation. Sy'da received warm, welcoming smiles, and familial hugs from everyone she came across.

I think the food is going to be bland, Di'Ath thought, in response to her question.

He had read about the popular meals of Ailiar. Most of it was roasted meats and vegetables, with the same herbs and sauces just arranged in different ways. The only meal he was interested in trying was a pie.

It seemed the closest thing to Zadanese meals, with meat slow cooked and swimming in gravy, all contained neatly in a little bowl of pastry with its own lid.

Even if it was not something that would ever make its way onto his plate in the castle, Di'Ath swore that he would scour the city for a vendor or tavern that sold it.

He would try it, just once, even if it killed him.

"I do not think that they will have the same sweets," he answered. "Perhaps you should return to the confectioner and buy some more of those while you still can."

He gestured to her slick, glistening hands. Small flecks of pastry and nut clung to the mixture of honey and saliva on her palms.

How anyone recognised her as a member of the royal family was beyond him.

"I can ask the cooks to make them," Sy'da said brightly. "Or I could make them myself. So'Sha taught me how, you know. And I could make them when I find a suitor, too, and offer them as a gift. Or we could share them together in a garden, or a forest while we talk about our plans for our future together."

She sighed wistfully.

Di'Ath envied her positive outlook on marriage. Sy'da had always been promised that she would have the final say in who she was to marry. She also had always had her nose buried in great romantic sagas and had babbled many times about the perfect wedding and marriage she was looking forward to.

She had even tried to comfort him in regard to his own pending nuptials. She had reminded him that many of the greatest love stories came from those who were unwilling to be wed to one another. *It is the most sought-after plot*, she had told him. *You can ask the bookseller if you don't believe me.*

Di'Ath shook his head.

"As far as I know," he said. "There will be a lot of roasted meats. So, if you truly want to find yourself a suitor, you will need to practice *not* tearing the meat from the bone with your teeth like an animal."

"Aw," Sy'da pouted. "But that is the best way to eat it! You just hold onto the bone and *riiiip!*"

She mimicked the action, holding an imaginary cut of meat to her face and baring her teeth in a feral grin.

"You belong in the wilds," Di'Ath teased. "We really should have left you in them when we found you."

"Perhaps," Sy'da said. "But then you would be so lonely, and you would mope so much more than you do now."

"I don't mope!" Di'Ath protested.

Sy'da shrugged, and wiped the remainder of the grime on her hands onto her skirts before skipping ahead of him.

She bent to talk to a young child, and before long, she was surrounded by the people of Wylden. Proud and honoured parents smiled at the princess. Children reached out to play with her long dark hair and pointed to the bells on her ankle. After the least bit of coaxing that Di'Ath had ever seen, Sy'da shook her foot to make the bells chime.

While it was true that Sy'da had a wild, unladylike side to her, she did not belong out in the wilderness. She belonged here, among her people, bringing joy to the future of Zadanai. Guilt clawed at Di'Ath from within his chest.

Di'Ath knew that taking her with him was in Sy'da's best interest. Of this, he was certain. If she were to remain here, the only eligible matches available were far too old and far too slimy to grant her happiness. But when he watched her interact with the people who loved her so dearly, he could not shake the feeling that Sy'da would regret agreeing to join him.

He hoped that the people of Ailiar would be as open and welcoming to her as the people of Zadanai were. He was sure that Sy'da would wilt quickly if she could not spend time with the common people and make true friends among them.

Even if he achieved nothing else—if his marriage were loveless, or if he were to fade into obscurity and act as nothing more than a token of peace between two nations—Di'Ath would have succeeded in his life if he could ensure Sy'da's happiness.

Sy'da must have caught sight of the shift in his expression, because he heard her say:

"I must go. My brother and I have some errands to run, but it was lovely seeing you all!"

As though the gathered crowd were noticing him for the first time, children and parents alike turned their attention towards Di'Ath. The prince offered a wave and a smile, while Sy'da took advantage of their distraction to pry herself free from the little hands gripping her skirts and hair.

She returned to Di'Ath's side with the same skip in her step. She looped her arm through his and waved goodbye to the children as he led her down the path towards the last vendor on his list.

"What are you going to do once this last one is paid?" Sy'da asked.

Di'Ath frowned. "What do you mean?"

Sy'da tugged on his arm as if to say *isn't it obvious?*

"You have been so singularly focused on paying off your debts that you have not made room in your days for anything else. The moment you hand over your last purse, you will not know what to do with yourself. That is not something you know how to handle."

Di'Ath scrunched his nose at her words.

"I will be fine," he said.

But she was right. He didn't do well with boredom. That was why he sought out so many women and he spent so much money. It was why he entered into bets with nobles and common men alike, waging coin on who was the strongest, smartest or fastest in any given thing.

He was mourning the duty-free life of the youngest son and yet the life had never truly suited him.

"I am sure you will be," Sy'da sighed. She didn't believe him. That much was clear in her tone. But she didn't press the issue further. "So, did you bring anything else with you?"

Di'Ath was getting a headache with all the frowning he was doing. Though he should be accustomed to such pain whenever his sister was concerned.

"What do you mean?"

Sy'da's smile turned devious. Di'Ath immediately began thinking of ways to prevent the inevitable trouble she was brewing.

"Did you bring any coin to spend, or did you only bring what you had to pay back?"

Di'Ath glared at his sister.

"Why?" he asked, tone accusatory. "I am not buying you more sweets, if that is what you're hinting at. If you want them, you can spend your own money."

Sy'da laughed, throwing her head back with mirth.

"No," she said. "I was just thinking that if you *did* happen to bring something extra with you, we could spend the afternoon searching for a gift for your future bride."

"We are already taking gifts," Di'Ath said.

"No," Sy'da said. "Well... yes, technically. But *you* aren't taking her gifts. We have jewels from the family vault for Queen Meitranis and Princess Calliope, but *you* should find something to gift the princess. You should pick something that will remind you of our home, something that will show her that you are open to sharing both your culture and hers."

Sy'da rested her head against his shoulder as they walked. It couldn't have been comfortable, but Di'Ath didn't ask her to stop.

"It can be something you give to her in private," Sy'da continued. "Something to keep between just the two of you. You know how it feels to be pushed into a marriage without your consultation. Show her that you are willing to let what started out as mere diplomacy grow into something more meaningful."

Di'Ath wasn't certain that he was willing to commit to such a promise. But had he not already admitted that he did not want a loveless marriage? How could a union borne of politics grow into one filled with affection if he did not show a desire for it to be such?

And when did Sy'da become so wise in the affairs of the heart?

"I think you should become an advisor," Di'Ath said.

"I thought that I was to be appointed as *your* royal advisor the moment you were crowned King of Ailiar," Sy'da teased.

Di'Ath laughed.

"As much as I would be happy to have you be my advisor, do not keep yourself closed to other paths. The world has been waiting for someone like you, Sy'da Adarna."

NINE

MAIDA

LUVRAHN

MAIDA TAILOR HAD ONCE believed that she—like all Colosians—would rather die than accept help from an elf. It was common knowledge that to accept anything, including something as simple and mundane as an outstretched hand, meant that you were subjecting yourself to a life of constantly looking over your shoulder, wondering just when and how you would be required to return the favour.

In the three weeks since Aros had found Maida in the Edgeling Woods, Maida had accepted the help of elves no less than a handful of times each day. She did not want to consider how much debt she was putting herself into by letting Aros save her life. She didn't want to know what horrors she would have to endure for sitting silently while a too-youthful healer applied a salve to wounds on her legs.

Maida had decided that she would need to suffer a great deal to repay the relief she felt when that salve kissed her torn and broken skin. In the three weeks that she had been laying in this bed, watching the monstrous *kapriae* from the window and ducking beneath the sill whenever one of the elf children caught sight of her, each cut, each slice of flesh had almost completely healed over.

The pale skin was still marked with pink and white scars, but Maida was able to take several laps around Aros' tiny cottage without assistance before the aches and pains began to settle in. She had caught herself just staring at her feet more times than she cared to admit, marvelling at how they had gone from frayed ribbons of flesh and blood to once again looking normal in less than a month. She was not well versed in the world of medicine and healing, but she was certain that if she were back in Silktide, she would still be cleaning out open, angry, weeping sores.

Maida was not completely back to her old self yet. It would take weeks, perhaps months, for her to regain her strength and stamina. Only then, when she was certain that she could brave the Edgeling Woods again without falling and failing and needing to be saved, would she attempt escape. But even if Maida were able to prepare her body for the journey back to her homeland, it would be for nothing if she did not plan properly.

Which is where Palis' daily visits came in handy.

Despite her discomfort at being outnumbered by the immortal, pointy-eared beings, Maida looked forward to Palis' visits. Not only were the fresh-baked goods more delicious than anything she had ever tasted in her twenty years, but Palis spent as much time trying to convince Aros that Maida was ready to meet the rest of the village as she spent fussing over Maida.

Come on, Palis would say. *You know that it is the best thing for her. The threat of infection is gone if you don't consider your brooding as being contagious.*

Palis had pled her case so many times that Maida was able to mouth the words behind her back each time she revisited it. Aros had choked on a hunk of bread the first time he had caught her doing it, and when Palis had whipped her head back towards Maida to see what he had found so funny, Maida had schooled her expression into one of concern.

She had earned a withering glare from the female elf as payment for distracting Aros It had felt like spiders running down her spine, like ice forming around her fingers and toes, like that horrific, giant goat waiting just outside the window, preparing to eat her.

Aros was much better at hiding his reactions now, no matter how hard Maida tried to make him lose control. With nothing else to do other than walking exercises and staring out the window, toying with Aros had become Maida's favourite past-time.

This time, however, Maida had a different goal.

She had been standing in the kitchen that took up the corner of the cottage opposite the bed, stoking the fire to boil water. She didn't understand why the flames did not seem to want to respond to her the way they responded to Aros. Whenever he tended the fire, it was as though he were using bellows to bring the heat higher than Maida ever could.

Or perhaps he was using magic.

She had never seen him command any sort of magical power, but then again, she didn't know what it would look like. For all she knew, he could use his mind. Or he could be whispering words she couldn't hear, or gesturing with his hands while she wasn't paying attention.

The more she tried to figure out whether he was commanding magic or not, the more uncertain she became of its existence.

Palis knocked on the door once before letting herself in. The sleeves of her airy, linen shirt were folded up past her elbows, and the same woven basket she always brought hung from the crook of her arm. The smell of freshly baked bread filled the tiny space, and Maida's mouth watered. She would need to meet Palis' wife and thank her for all the food she sent Palis over with, she decided. Perhaps if today went well, she would be able to meet her sooner rather than later.

"Good morning, Dhuina," Palis said with a bright, glowing smile. "I see you have grown tired of letting Aros make you sub-par tea."

Aros, who had been sitting at the dining table and mending the fletching on his arrows, grumbled something under his breath that Maida did not catch. He did that a lot—grumbling and muttering loudly enough that she could hear that something had been said yet too quietly for her to determine what that something had been.

It was frustrating, even if she had eventually figured out that they were not aimed at her.

"I don't like being waited on," Maida said. She wiped her hands on her skirts and turned to return the smile to Palis.

It still felt odd to smile at an elf. Every fibre of her being was screaming at her to turn the other way and run, no matter how nice they were. Maida still did not understand their motives for saving her, for being kind to her, and for not asking for payment in return.

No one did anything nice for free.

"But the palatable tea is certainly a benefit."

Palis' laughter filled the cottage like sunlight. The space got warmer and brighter, and the few pieces of painted crockery that Aros possessed seemed to shine.

Maida did not trust it. Nor did she trust the way her body relaxed in response.

"Well, I am glad to see that you are up and about, Dhuina," Palis said. "And not just because I would also like a cup of tea."

Maida nodded in response to the not-so-subtle request and pulled down a third cup from the shelf. She had considered it lucky that Aros had more than one to begin with. But over time, she had learned that he likely only kept the other two for the occasions Palis and Aoife decided to visit.

Perhaps I should find a cup for myself, she thought. Then, angry at herself for even considering such a thing, she pushed the thought out of her mind.

"Anyway, I am glad to see you up and about because I have a proposition for you," Palis continued. "The two of you, really, seeing as I can't imagine Aros letting you out of his sight for more than a moment. But don't let any lack of enthusiasm on his part deter you from accepting. I know you must be going crazy staring at his ugly mug all day."

"I am not ugly," Aros grumbled with a frown.

His voice was almost drowned out by Maida's exclamation: "I do not stare at him!"

Palis' perfect brow arched. She flicked warm brown eyes from Aros to Maida and back again in an accusatory manner; however, if she had anything to say about Maida's particular outburst, she did not give voice to it.

Instead, she tapped a long finger to the table.

"No," she said. "Enough is enough. You two are developing some weird wavelength thing—do not even try to deny it, because I have seen it with my own eyes!"

Maida looked over her shoulder to see Aros with his mouth open, ready to protest. He snapped it shut and slumped down into his seat.

"I do not like it," Palis continued. "You two speak at the same time. You share looks. It's weird. It's odd. It's like something out of a novel and I will not stand for it. You, Miss Dhuina, need to step outside this cottage and make more friends before you end up like Mr Grumpy Britches."

Aros once again muttered something under his breath. Maida caught the way his nose scrunched, and his brow rose, and this time, she didn't need to hear what he said to know that he was mimicking Palis.

"Otherwise, I will just kidnap her and she can come live with myself and Aoife."

"She is not going to live with you and Aoife."

Silence fell over the cottage. Even the boiling water seemed to stop in its bubbling to ensure that Aros' hastily spoken words would hang in the air. Maida knew she was staring. She could feel Palis watching her stare, but she could not take her eyes off him.

Aros' green eyes flicked to Maida's for only a moment before they settled on Palis. When he spoke again, it was measured, and carefully thought out.

"Fine," he said. "We will... go outside. Now, what is it that you have planned?"

Palis clapped her hands in delight. With the now tension eased, Maida returned to making tea.

"Tonight," Palis said. "Is the absolute perfect time to introduce Dhuina to Luvrahn. Aoife will be hosting a storytelling night at the tavern, and everyone will be there. They will also be so focused on Aoife and too scared of upsetting her that they won't crowd Dhuina or bombard her with questions."

Maida poured the tea and set two of the cups down on the table. The third she kept for herself, and nursed in her hands as she perched on the edge of the bed.

"Are you sure it's a good time for Aoife to host a storytelling night?" Aros asked. "Fisa-"

"Fisa has been gone for almost a month," Palis said. "I know. The whole village is still reeling from it. But we can't let the children see us wallowing in our grief. And you know Fisa would not want us to. I'm sure his mother would take comfort in seeing you again too."

The muscles in Aro's jaw tightened beneath his dark skin. Maida fought the urge to go to him, to lay her hand on his shoulder and offer whatever comfort she could. She did not know much about Fisa other than him being the reason Aros had been in the Edgeling Woods the day he found her.

Maybe she would ask him one day. Maybe she would keep her mouth shut. As she should.

Palis sipped the tea and hummed with delight.

"This is much better than anything Aros can do," she said. "I don't know how you manage to make tea so incorrectly."

"I don't mind tea how I make it," Aros replied, his tone curt and short.

Ice inched up Maida's spine and she checked the distance to the door.

"You would also eat the same dried meat every day for the rest of eternity if you didn't have anyone looking out for you, so I don't think your opinion counts for much," Palis replied.

The two continued to go back and forth. Maida tuned them out, slowly sipping her tea. Finally, Palis finished her tea and stood.

"I will see the two of you later this evening. I am going to tell Aoife the good news. I know she is dying to meet you," she said.

She closed the distance between them and pressed a kiss to Maida's forehead. "You are going to love Luvrahn. And Luvrahn is going to love you. I promise."

She smiled and turned to wave to Aros before leaving.

The warmth and light seemed to dim when she left, and silence fell over Maida and Aros like a woollen blanket—comforting but heavy, and slightly itchy. Despite Palis' claims that the two of them had been on some strange wavelength with one another, Maida and Aros rarely spoke when they were alone. It wasn't uncompanionable, it just seemed that they didn't have much of anything to say.

Maida had considered trying to start conversations on occasion, especially when he was grumbling away. She always changed her mind at the last possible moment, just before sound left her lips, convincing herself that getting closer to him would be detrimental to her efforts of escaping and returning to normalcy.

"You don't have to go."

Maida looked up at him. Aros' attention was back on the arrows he had been fiddling with. He held one up to his eyes, and looked down the shaft, presumably checking how straight it was.

"Oh," Maida said, frowning a little. "No, I want to go."

Aros looked at her. A spark of surprise was in his eyes, and Maida's spine straightened in response to the attention.

"Palis is right," Maida explained. "I need to stretch my legs more, meet more people, and not be such a burden to the two of you."

Aros snorted. It was a sound usually reserved for Palis' visits and it surprised Maida so much that she had to fight to keep the smile off her face.

"I dare you to tell Palis that you feel like a burden," he said, waving the arrow in her direction. "Just please, make sure I'm watching. That will be some well-needed entertainment."

Maida's control over her smile faded, and the corners of her mouth tipped upwards. Her cheeks warmed.

For a long moment, her mouth opened and closed as she tried to come up with a retort worthy of the banter she had seen between the two old friends. She considered and reconsidered the words that danced on the tip of her tongue before finally speaking.

"Only," she said, allowing a teasing tone to her voice. 'If you tell her that we have decided to forego the whole naming thing and revert to calling me *Damsel* again."

Aros' mouth gaped. Then, he laughed. And it was the most beautiful sound Maida had ever heard.

TEN

CALLIOPE

BALLIACH

A BEAD OF BRIGHT red blood formed on the tip of Calliope's finger. She brought it to her lips with a frown, using her unpricked hand to secure the offending needle into the loosely woven fabric on her lap. The sweet, metallic taste spread over her tongue as she tried to stifle the flow of blood.

She stared at the likeness of the First Queen—standing in the Weeping Wood with the Maiden Sword drawn and gleaming red—that she had been attempting to create with the tiny, stitched crosses of coloured thread. She had been working diligently on this piece for the past three months, and each time she held the needle and thread in her hands, a horrid, vindictive voice in her head hissed at her to toss the wretched thing in the fireplace. She had come close a number of times, standing by the hearth with the hooped fabric illuminated by the flames.

It would have taken nothing to toss the whole thing, to stand there and watch it burn. She could toss everything—the cloth, the threads, the meticulously planned design that had taken the better part of a week to create. It could all be reduced to ash, and no one would know that she had ever made the attempt in the first place. No one would know the number of mistakes that she had made, or the number of times she had taken a thin blade to cut and undo hour's worth of work. Every instance of realising that she had used the wrong colour, or placed a stitch in the wrong place, would be erased.

No one would know the lengths Calliope had gone to ensure that the final piece was perfect.

Or that now, the princess' blood stained the once pristine, white gown of the Maiden.

Her eyes pricked with hot tears.

Hours of work, wasted by her incompetence. Hours more lay ahead, unpicking each and every stitch that she had made with that particular shade of white. She could not simply cover the stitches with new thread without making it look bulky and out of place. She could not simply remove the stained stitches either. Calliope had used the last of the white thread, and to buy more would mean to buy from a new dye lot. Doing so ran the risk of the colours being off. Even if the shade was off by a smidge, a discerning eye would be able to notice at a glance.

And then, it would not matter how perfect her stitches were. The work would be subpar. Unworthy.

Burn it.

Calliope shuddered. Even if there was no fire burning in the fireplace, the urge to set one alight and watch the fibres of her work turn to ash blazed within her.

Perhaps now was not the best time to listen to such thoughts. Her finger ached, throbbing at the point where the needle had pierced her tender skin. She still had not formed the callouses on her fingertips like she had seen on the royal embroiders and wondered how many more months she would need to work at her needlecraft before she did.

Perhaps she needed to stop using the rose-scented lotion that sat on her vanity. Perhaps, if she stopped wasting time on such things as lotion or perfume, or making sure her cheeks were the perfect shade of pink, she would not be so soft.

Perhaps then, her mother might look at her.

Burn.

Calliope pressed her lips into a thin line. Her thoughts were not working well with her this afternoon, it seemed. Deciding that it would be best to approach all of this with a clear head, Calliope tucked her needlework into the woven basket in which she kept all her threads and notions. With her foot, she tucked the basket back underneath the overstuffed chair.

She stood and rolled her neck in an attempt to work out the tension that had been building over the last few hours. Her chair had been comfortable enough when she had first set about her work, but she had lost track of time. She had been curled up for hours, barely noticing the arc of the sun outside her window or how the light swept across the rugs that covered her floor as morning gave way to noon.

She stepped towards that light now. Her footfalls were silent, padded by the thick woven rugs. But the silk of her gown rustled like a forest canopy in an autumn breeze. Lifting her hand to the light, Calliope inspected the finger she had pricked.

The bleeding had stopped, but the tip was still unusually pink.

Calliope pinched her finger between the thumb and forefinger of her other hand. She pinched hard, her nails biting into the delicate flesh.

No more blood came to the surface, the wound offering nothing to make the pain worthwhile.

She scrunched her nose in disappointment before turning her attention out the window. The sun's warmth penetrated the thick glass, bathing the princess in light and heat as she gazed down to the bailey below. It was a bustling courtyard with stalls and merchants eager to sell their wares to the upper echelons who had coin enough to spare. Once upon a time, the Queen would throw lavish parties and balls that spilled out onto the bailey, with performers of all sorts, and guests from around the world.

Parties were still thrown now, of course. But they were few and far between, and they only served to celebrate holidays and welcome guests. They were no longer spontaneous.

And they were no longer a place where one could find themselves dancing hand in hand with their Queen or drinking alongside her.

And Calliope had never been old enough for those parties at the time.

"Your Highness?"

Calliope jumped. She pressed her hand to her chest and turned to face the palace guard that stood in the doorway. She stared at the blond-haired youth for a heartbeat before her eyes flickered over to the masked Bloodmaid in the corner.

The woman hadn't so much as moved at the intrusion.

Calliope's lips pursed and returned her attention back to the palace guard.

Unlike the Bloodmaids, the palace guards wore silver-coloured steel armour. They wore a plate cuirass that bore a depiction of the Maiden Sword along the centre. This was the only touch of red that they wore, a stark contrast distinguishing them from the Bloodmaids.

Of course, it was not the only difference.

One of the most obvious differences being *that* Bloodmaids were only ever women. There had never been—and there never would be—a man bearing the famed and coveted title of *Bloodmaid*.

Another, being that they were hand-chosen by the Queen.

Calliope doubted that her mother had ever set eyes on this particularly sorry creature.

The guard looked positively uncomfortable where he stood. The plates of his armour *thunked* against each other as he nervously shifted his weight from foot to foot. His grey eyes darted between Calliope and the Bloodmaid, unsure where to look.

"H-his Majesty, King Oprianos has requested an audience with you, your H-highness."

The guard's voice cracked as he spoke. He swallowed hard; the movement visible from where Calliope stood.

She couldn't help the taste of satisfaction on her tongue that came with seeing such a thing. Even if the discomfort was not due to her presence, she took an unladylike amount of enjoyment from seeing men squirm.

"Why?" she asked, layering on a thick coating of boredom to her voice.

She swore she saw the guard's face grow paler still.

"I... I do not know, ma'am. I could go ask..."

The guard looked over his shoulder, out the door and towards the hallway. Calliope was certain that if she pressed the issue, the shaking whelp would indeed return to the King's chambers and request clarification.

Even if it risked making himself a target for the King's wrath. As the First-Born Daughter of the First-Born Daughter, Calliope's wishes trumped those of the King.

At least, it was supposed to.

"There is no need," Calliope said with a sigh. "I will go. Take me to him."

The guard's shoulders loosened and his chin stopped quivering as relief washed over him.

Calliope crossed the room towards him. The moment she stepped out of the sun's light, unseasonable, bone-biting cold took hold of her. She clenched her fists at her sides. Her buffed nails bit into her palms.

The guard did not move from his position in the doorway as Calliope approached. She raised a brow.

"Well?" she asked.

The guard's eyes tracked movement from the side of the room to just over

Calliope's shoulder. Whatever colour he may have regained was lost again, as the Bloodmaid took up position behind Calliope.

The princess wanted to scream. She wanted to yell, and curse, and push this *boy* out of her way. How dare he give more reverence to the Bloodmaid than she? *She*, who was to be his Queen, who was to carry on the Ailian legacy, the descendant of the Maiden. She wanted to shake him and demand to know if some warrior was of greater interest than the gods-blessed Blood Heir?

But she would not lower herself to such antics.

"Shall we?" she asked instead.

The guard blinked and shook his head before returning his full, undivided attention to where it belonged.

"Of course," he said. "If you would follow me, your Highness."

He bowed his head and turned, then walked out of the room, his armour telegraphing every step he took.

Calliope frowned. The guard should not be making so much noise. The other guards were far quieter, even when they wore a full suit as this one did. Once, while Councillor Sancor had been droning on about something she did not care about over dinner, Calliope had stared long enough at a palace guard to notice thin strips of leather carefully placed between the plates of armour. She had watched as the guard rolled his shoulders, and seen first-hand how the leather not only muffled the noise, but helped the steel move more smoothly over itself.

She had supposed that was why the Bloodmaids wore a bastardised court gown with their cuirass. Calliope was certain that there were more layers of steel and leather beneath the flowing red fabric, and the shimmering embroidery. She figured not knowing exactly how armoured they were fed into the fear that the Bloodmaids instilled in their opponents.

Calliope just wished they would do something to hide the ugly, iron bracelets they wore.

But the guard that had come to tell her that the King requested an audience? He wore no strips of leather between the plates of his armour. The closer Calliope looked, the more she was certain that he was too small for the suit he wore. Plate was supposed to be fitted to the wearer, and this boy—for Calliope had settled on the fact that he could not be any older than she was—was not wearing armour that was fitted to him.

She slowed her steps, falling behind just enough to put herself in line with the Bloodmaid.

"Have you seen him around the castle before?" she asked.

The Bloodmaid lifted a closed fist to chest height and rolled it forward twice in a knocking motion. The iron bracelets clanged against one another.

Calliope clenched her jaw.

"You know I don't understand you when you do that," she hissed. "If you're not going to give me a simple yes or no, at least nod or shake your head."

The Bloodmaid nodded.

"Okay," Calliope said. "He's been seen... Is he actually one of our palace guards?"

The Bloodmaid nodded again.

"Then why isn't his armour fitted properly?"

Clank. Clank. Clank.

Calliope pressed her nails into the palm of her hand. She wished she had come into her Affinity already, so she could bury this guard and his ill-fitting armour just to get some peace and quiet.

"Fine," she said, when she realised that she was going to need to word her question differently. "Is he so new that he has not had a chance to get his own armour?"

She could have sworn the Bloodmaid stifled a laugh beside her. But she accepted the nod that she received in answer, even if it drove a dagger right through her heart. Because why was someone so low and so new being chosen to fetch for the heir? Why had her father not sent someone more experienced? Why had he not sent one of his advisors?

Did he not care about her? Had her mother's all-but-complete withdrawal from court led the King to dismiss the traditions and hierarchy of their queendom?

That had to be the reason. Otherwise, she would not be following some inexperienced whelp who had not been in service to the crown long enough to get a proper suit of armour. Otherwise, she would not be the one being forced to weave through the corridors of the keep to her father. *He* should come to *her*.

Perhaps her secret fears were right all along. Perhaps she had already proven herself to be unworthy of the crown, unworthy of the Maiden's bloodline.

It made sense.

Her mother no longer spoke to her, and she no longer deigned to look in her direction. There were no smiles, no love, no stolen moments in her mother's suite, where Calliope played with her mother's makeup.

More than a year before she would come into her Affinity, Calliope had already proven herself a failure.

There was no other reason or explanation that she could fathom.

Even the betrothal made sense. If she were to produce an heir of her own, Calliope would never need to sit upon the throne. They could dispose of her. They could use her to bring a new, more viable queen into the world and dispose of her.

She tried to swallow, but her throat was too dry. She tightened her fists and was sure that her nails would break the skin. She tried to focus on her breathing, but her lungs were traitorous and refused to bring in enough air to be filled.

Just as she was sure this would be the end and that it would be her body that betrayed her, the guard came to a stop. Calliope looked at the large, heavy wooden doors that marked her father's study. On either side loomed tall, buff palace guards. Their armour was clearly made for them, and both looked highly trained and experienced.

But that was not Calliope's focus.

She was far more concerned with the doors.

Despite her fears, there would never be a time when the princess did not hold on to a secret hope that she would find her mother behind them. It was a childish hope—Calliope knew better than to wish for something that she knew would never happen. Even before Meitranis had locked herself away in her rooms, Calliope had never seen her in Oprianos' study.

But fact rarely altered hope.

"Are you ready, your Highness?"

Calliope looked at the guard. She steeled herself with a deep breath before nodding.

The young guard opened the door, and stepped to the side to allow Calliope to enter her father's study.

"Your Majesty," the guard said, addressing the man sitting behind the imposing desk hewn of black crystal. "Her Highness, Princess Calliope Ailiar."

Calliope did not curtsey or bow her head towards her father. The thought of doing so did so much as cross her mind. Her mind was far too preoccupied with the realisation that her father was not alone.

The Goddess of Fate seemed to be laughing at Calliope.

A young, blonde woman rose from the chair across from the desk. Her long, corn-silk blonde hair flowed around her as if in water as she turned to face Calliope.

The woman lowered her large, doe-like eyes and curtsied. The layers of butter-soft silk and tulle pooled around her like a pastel cloud. Her rosebud lips formed the most perfect, brilliant smile. It was as if the Gods had taken the very best of every woman that had ever existed and put them all into one person.

Whether it was a gift or a taunt to the mere mortals that walked the earth, Calliope could not decide.

"Ah," King Oprianos said, rising from his own seat. "There she is, my darling daughter. Calliope, my dear, come and meet our guest – Lady Jaena Cu'Sar."

Lady Jaena straightened from her curtsey. Her smile widened, and it looked far too comfortable and familiar for Calliope's liking. Why did it not betray a hint of fear and reverence for the youngest of the Maiden's line? Why did it not show a touch of distaste or suggest that a lie lay beneath it?

"Your Highness," Lady Jaena said.

Calliope wished she had not spoken at all. Lady Jaena's voice was sweeter than honey. It was as cheerful as the bells around the wrists of street performers. It was as warm and inviting as the sun on a clear, mid-spring day.

It made Calliope never want to open her own mouth again.

"It is an honour to meet you," Lady Jaena continued. "I have heard so much about you from my father."

"Jaena is your cousin," Oprianos explained. "From Rupaburg. I have been writing with her father—my brother—for quite some time now, and we were both in agreement that it would be best for both of you if Lady Jaena were to join your court as one of your ladies."

Calliope frowned.

How could one join something that did not exist? Calliope had expected the girls she had grown up with to be her lady's maids, but the older they all got, the less she wanted to spend any sort of time with them. The daughters of nobles had been her companions, once, but when they began to gossip about the Queen, Calliope had withdrawn.

Now, she sat alone when she worked on her needlepoint and her embroidery. Now, she read in solitude, finding company only in whichever Bloodmaid had been scheduled to watch over her at that time.

How pathetic, that horrid voice in her head whispered. *You don't even know the name of the company you keep.*

She pursed her lips and lifted her chin as she looked over the pastel cream-puff of a woman before her. Lady Jaena seemed out of place in this room, with the sharp edges of the furniture Oprianos preferred, and the black stain on the wood.

Perhaps she will not survive, she thought. *And beg to return home before too long.*

"Seeing as you are to be married," Oprianos continued, pulling Calliope's attention away from Lady Jaena. "And that there is still much to prepare, I thought you would benefit from having someone to share the burden with. I know I struggled with the preparations and anxieties that come with such a momentous occasion, and I know I would not have been able to make it through it all without the support of my companions."

Lady Jaena continued to smile sweetly. Lady Jaena, Calliope decided, must have inherited her looks from her mother. She was too soft in the face, her hair too pale, her blue eyes too bright.

The antithesis of Calliope's father, whose dark hair, and muddied green eyes had been mercilessly passed on to Calliope.

The princess swallowed hard as she realised that if Jaena's hair had been red, she would look more like the next Queen of Ailiar than Calliope could ever hope to be.

Perhaps this was it. Perhaps Jaena had been brought to Ailiar to take Calliope's place.

No.

It was impossible—only the First Daughter of the First Daughter could sit upon the Ailian throne. The only way to replace Calliope was to have her bear a daughter of her own.

Still, Calliope did not trust the radiant beauty standing before her. She could not shake the feeling that this *Lady Jaena* would cause her nothing less than heartbreak and pain.

King Oprianos did not appear to notice or care that his daughter was having an internal struggle over the very presence of this woman. He continued speaking.

"While she is here, assisting you," he continued. "Lady Jaena will be searching for a suitor of her own, right here in Balliach, though that is of a lower priority than her assisting you in preparing to become a bride."

He clasped his hands together and grinned with delight.

"I hope the two of you will become fast friends," he said.

"I am positive we will be," Lady Jaena replied.

I am certain we will not.

ELEVEN

MAIDA

LUVRAHN

NERVES HAD BEEN BUILDING within Maida since the moment Palis had left that morning.

She had expected that they would, but she had not expected just how severe they'd be. A hollow ache burned its way into her chest, replacing whatever courage she had once possessed. Her breath seemed to catch in her throat, refusing to follow its designated path down into her lungs. Her legs, which were blissfully pain-free with a new, thick layer of salve underneath long strips of cool, undyed linen, suddenly felt heavy and unwilling to carry her as far as the front door.

"Are you ready?" Aros asked.

Was she? Maida looked up at him, rooted to the spot where she stood. How could she be ready? She hadn't spoken to another living soul outside of Aros and Palis for almost two months, and now she was supposed to rejoin society as though she hadn't stood in the burning ruins of her hometown seven weeks prior?

And to top it all off, Maida was not only going to be surrounded by people, but by *elves*. She may have developed a temporary trust for Aros and Palis, but the others? She didn't know if they would extend the same kindness and understanding towards her. She didn't know if they would wait for a moment when Aros was distracted to strike and steal Maida away, to tie her a spit and roast her over an open fire.

She didn't know if there would be a town when she walked out that door, or if she would be walking into crumbling, smouldering ruins.

She didn't know anything.

Maida's eyes stung. Aros' dark brow knit together, and his beautiful, forest-green eyes held a tinge of an emotion she couldn't quite place. He had been so far away – as far away as he could have been, in this cottage of his – with his hand on the knob of the door. And yet suddenly, he was directly in front of Maida.

She could feel the heat radiating from his body. She could smell the earthy, pine scent of him, mixed with the sour lemon tang of the soap they shared.

All she could see was *him*.

Aros lifted his hand, and Maida wondered why she didn't brace herself for contact. Had she been so good at acting over these last three weeks that she was able to endure his touch without thought?

When had this happened?

Three weeks was not a long time. Had three weeks been enough to undo twenty years of warnings about the elves? And if she was no longer worried about Aros' touch, how long before she abandoned all hope of returning to Colosia and searching for her father?

Maida stared into Aros' eyes. Perhaps she should just tell him that she wanted to go home, that she wanted to find her father, that she had lied about not having a name.

She wondered what it sounded like on his lips.

"Dhuina?"

The word brought Maida out of her thoughts. She looked down, and noticed that while Aros had reached for her, that calloused hand had never come to rest upon her skin. It hovered between them, the unfinished motion glaring at both human and elf.

Aros had only ever touched Maida when it was completely necessary. Maida could still remember the sound of his heartbeat beneath the hard muscle of his chest when he had carried her through the woods. She could still conjure the perfect image of him bent over the bed, working to clean and redress her wounds. She could still feel his hands in her hair the day that she had finally allowed him to comb out the matted knots and give it a thorough washing.

She doubted she had the energy yet to do that by herself. Even tying her hair back into a thick, single braid had been exhausting.

But outside of those moments when Maida was helpless and in need? They had not so much as brushed fingers while passing a mug from one to the other.

"I…" she said, voice shaking. "I'm fine."

"We don't have to go," Aros reminded her.

It was a tempting idea. They could simply stay here, maintaining the quiet routine that they had established.

Maida offered a tired smile. "Palis would drag us out by the ears," she said. "And you know it. I'm sorry, but I am far more scared of her than I am of you."

Aros laughed. The sound washed over Maida, filling the hollow in her chest with warmth, coaxing the air into her lungs.

It drew her eyes to his lips.

She averted her eyes.

This wasn't her. She wasn't developing a fondness for the elf. It must be some magic that he was wielding, or some mythical pull that his kind had on humans to make it easier to lure their prey. That was why she wanted to ask him to hold her. It was why she wanted so desperately to hear him whisper her name against the shell of her ear, or to feel his heart beating in his chest again.

It had to be.

"We should go," she said.

Maida stepped around Aros and walked to the door. Her hand closed around the doorknob. She could have sworn that it was still warm.

Keep your head, she told herself, and opened the door.

She should have expected to find Palis waiting on the other side of it. Palis was dressed in her usual attire of a cream, puffy-sleeved tunic and brown pants. As she bounced up and down in delight like a child about to receive a sackful of sweets, the golden bracelets on her wrists and the beads in her hair made a joyous jingle.

"Oh, you look just *marvellous*," Palis exclaimed. "Absolutely darling! And that colour brings out the fire in your hair!"

Maida tugged on the hem of the deep green tunic Palis was talking about. It had been among the many bundles Palis had brought over.

Gifts, Palis had said. *To welcome you to Luvrahn, and to make you feel more at home.*

Maida had tried not to be too critical of the clothing that she'd received, but having grown up with the town's tailor, she had never once worn an item of clothing that hadn't been made to her exact measurements. Even though her clothes had been regularly made of scraps and offcuts from the clothes she and her father had made for the citizens of Silktide, they had all been made with her preferences in mind.

While the green tunic was beautiful both in colour and in the softness of the linen, Maida felt as though she were swimming in it. It wasn't quite as large as the tunic she had borrowed from Aros in the early days, but she felt as though she would become quite immodest if she were to bend over too far.

If only she had a needle and thread, she would be able to close the neckline enough to solve that problem. While she was at it, she could taper in the sleeves, so that the fabric didn't gape quite so much around her wrists.

Maida's mind was running away with itself again.

At least this time, it wasn't focusing on Aros, who had closed the door behind him as he followed her out onto the street.

The hair on the back of Maida's neck rose as she realised once again how close he was.

Palis reached forward and lifted Maida's braid. She inspected it closely and hummed in approval.

"I have so many plans for this hair of yours, you know," Palis said. "And so many plans for you, of course, but I must admit I cannot wait to get my hands on that hair of yours without any limitations."

Aros cleared his throat.

Maida jumped, her braid falling from Palis' hand.

"If Dhuina wishes to place a limitation on anything, especially her hair," Aros said, voice low with warning. "Then you will adhere to those limitations. She is not a doll, and you will not treat her like one simply because you convinced her to step outside for one night."

And yet, Maida thought, *here you are, talking about me as if I were a doll, and could not understand what you are saying.*

Palis waved a dismissive hand. More jingling accentuated the movement, commanding Maida's attention, despite the curiosity that was building within her.

"I know that Dhuina is not a doll," Palis said. "But I do not see you spending time attending to her hair."

"It is washed," Aros countered. "It is braided."

A rush of cool air alerted Maida to Aros' movement as he gestured towards her hair. It sent a shiver down her spine, chasing away the warmth that had lingered in the autumn evening once the sun had begun to descend over the horizon.

"It is washed, yes," Palis conceded. "And one braid does not constitute her hair being *braided*. Look at her hair and those curls. They need to be taken care of properly. I know you know this."

Aros muttered something under his breath.

Eager to diffuse the situation before it ended up in another hours-long conversation about who was right, Maida looped her arm through Aros'. Palis looked down at their entwined limbs, golden eyes wide.

Aros tensed.

Just as Maida decided she had made a terrible decision and she should let go, he used their connection to pull her tighter against him. His warmth bled into her, and she was all too aware of every inch that their bodies met.

She forced a smile as if that would be enough to change it.

"Are people not waiting for us?" she asked.

Palis clapped her hands together, sufficiently distracted.

"Yes," she exclaimed. "They are, and we should not keep them waiting!"

Palis motioned for them to follow her, and turned away, heading down the gradual hill towards the village centre. Maida let out a small laugh when she realised that Palis was not going to so much as check to see if they were following.

She couldn't decide if it was Palis' faith in them, or perhaps that Palis knew she was scary enough that they would eventually comply.

"Are you alright?"

Maida's face snapped up towards Aros. She had moved so quickly that a twinge of pain shot down the back of her neck. But his voice had captivated her again, and she wanted nothing more in that moment than to watch the way his lips moved as he spoke.

"She's gone," Aros said. "We can go back inside and lock the door; all it will take is one word."

Maida shook her head. "I want to meet her wife," she said. "I want to know what kind of stories she has to tell. And Palis is right. I need to get outside if I am going to get stronger. Autumn is already here, and by the time winter arrives, I will be stuck inside again."

A truth in a lie, just as Oleanna Wyve had taught her.

The first week of the first month of autumn had already passed. While the days retained the heat of summer, the nights were all too eager to give way to cooler air. This winter would be cold, and if Maida had any hope of reaching Silktide alive, she would need to leave soon.

Or wait until the coming Spring.

She took a step, tugging Aros along with her. For his size and strength, he moved easily according to her desires. As the dirt path crunched beneath their boots, Maida could almost imagine that she was walking side by side with Eoin, the baker's son.

The village of Luvrahn wasn't so different from Silktide. Sure, the air did not smell of fish and seawater, but cottages lined the path on either side. Many had low, wooden fences sectioning off patches of grass and garden to demark their private yard. All were bigger than Aros' humble home, and from the path Maida could determine that they were large enough to have the living spaces separated from the sleeping spaces. Like her home. Like the cottage she had shared with her father, buried in the Woods, two hours' walk away from the town proper. There had been two bedrooms in their home. They'd had a kitchen looking out onto the lush green woods, they'd had a large living space, and a dining table that was used more often for cutting fabric.

Maida had fallen asleep at that table more often than she cared to admit. She had fallen asleep at the table that last night...

Maida shook her head and leaned closer into Aros, trying to distract herself from the memories that were surfacing.

"It's okay," Aros said. "I've got you."

Tears pricked Maida's eyes.

"The tavern is not far," Aros said. "But if you need to rest, or if you wish to turn back, we will. Do not strain yourself for Palis' sake. She does not always take into consideration the boundaries that others may have set. It worked well when she was in the capital, but not so much here."

Maida frowned, and Aros must have been watching her face because he chuckled.

"You can ask her about that later. Just know that before she came here, it was her job to cross boundaries and learn people's secrets."

"Is the street always this empty?" Maida asked, diverting the conversation.

She wasn't upset that it was. She could hear conversation and laughter wafting up from the tavern in the town square, but not seeing another person on the path save for Palis – who was far too far ahead now to catch their conversation – meant that Maida was able to look at the homes of Luvrahn without worrying that *she* might also be looked at.

She wondered why some had chosen thatched roofing, while others had chosen wicker. Perhaps the wicker-roofed houses had been here first, and it had been all that they could use. But the placement didn't seem to make sense to her, nor the idea that the wicker wouldn't have been replaced with thatching over the years. And she was, for now, going to pretend that she didn't see the one particular home that had vibrant green vines instead. Maida did not yet want to know if it was magic or madness that had led to the creation of such a thing.

So instead, she redirected her attention to the flower boxes that hung outside the windows of some of the homes. They were empty now, the flowers that had bloomed over spring and summer dead and gone. A seed of pain took root in her chest as Maida realised that if she were successful in her attempts to escape, she would never see those boxes overflowing with bright, colourful flowers.

Maida realised then that she was in danger. Luvrahn felt too normal, too human. If she could imagine Eoin by her side right now, she could imagine she was back home. She could ignore the pointed ears and pretend she was surrounded by humans. She was already starting to forget how much of a danger Aros posed. Three weeks here, and she was already faltering.

She could not wait until next spring. She needed to get out now.

Tomorrow.

Tomorrow she would ask Aros to show her around, and she would get a feeling for the layout of the village. She would start squirrelling away food and other resources and prepare to leave before the weather turned too cold.

She took a deep breath, and tried to ignore the pine and lemon scent that filled her nose. She needed to refocus, especially now that her wounds had all but healed.

Finally, the road evened out beneath their feet. Much in the same manner as she had pulled him forward earlier, Aros tugged gently on her arm, and she followed him to the right. Homes gave way to public structures. Coals glowed in the blacksmith's forge, finally resting from a hard day of heating steel. A lantern hung by the well, illuminating the space around it with an unnaturally bright light and casting nightmarish shadows into the depths of the well.

To the left, in the centre-most part of the square, lay a pile of toys and flickering candles.

"What's that?" Maida asked.

Aros tensed beside her. She fought the urge to look up at him, to see what emotions were playing over his face. She couldn't risk seeing him in pain.

"That," Aros said, voice softer than usual. "Is a memorial. About a month ago, we lost one of our children. That is where he died."

There was more to it than that, Maida was sure. But she didn't have time to ask before Aros urged her on, past the memorial and towards the largest structure in Luvrahn.

Maida craned her head back to look at the building before her. It was two stories high, and even in the waning light she could see the beautiful, intricate carvings that made up the doorway and the windowsills. This building had not just been made for purpose, but with love.

"This," Aros said. "This is our tavern. It was the first building constructed here in Luvrahn, by those of us who founded it."

Warm light spilled out of the windows. The laughter and conversation within seemed to weave themselves into the tavern's very woodgrain. The air was thick with the smell of hops and stew.

Despite having eaten before they had left, Maida's stomach growled.

"Don't worry," Aros said. "Everyone reacts the same way when they smell Pso's stew."

Silence fell between them for a moment more. Maida was grateful that Aros was letting her choose when she was ready, and when she was, she pushed open the door and stepped in.

TWELVE

MAIDA

LUVRAHN

IF MAIDA HAD THOUGHT the smell of 'Pso's stew' had made her hungry when she was standing outside the tavern, then she had no choice but to admit that the smell of it once she had stepped inside made her ravenous. It was hearty, and fragrant. The very scent of it seemed to reach down into her belly and force the memory of the dinner she had shared with Aros away. Her stomach felt hollow and desperate, yearning to taste what her nose could smell.

At least Palis had been correc—the elves of Luvrahn were too preoccupied with each other to pay much attention to the arrival of a human. Maida suspected that this did not do much to soothe Aros' reservations. They were not completely free of stares either and Maida's cheeks burned as she watched knife-eared elves lean over to whisper to their companions.

She lifted her hand to close tightly around the pendant at her throat.

"There are seats at the back," Aros said.

Gently, he tugged her along.

Their clunking footsteps on the wooden floor was almost drowned out by the chatter around them. Elf children ran in and out of the rows of seats that had been set up facing a pile of pillows and blankets, shrieking in delight. A young girl with ribbons braided into her black hair, pushed past Maida without a care in the world. Her yellow ribbons trailed behind her, and a young boy pushed past Aros.

"'Scuse me!" he called out behind him, not so much as bothering to look over his shoulder.

"Are the children always like this?" Maida asked.

"Are human children not?"

Maida chewed her lip. She couldn't answer Aros' question honestly. She hadn't been raised alongside the children of Silktide. She could not even remember a time when she had played with other children. Her father had raised her on his own and kept her close whenever he needed to visit the town. By the time he allowed her to go on her own, she was well into her teenage years, and her peers were beginning to learn trades or searching for a suitable match.

"I... I actually couldn't tell you," Maida replied.

She followed the path of the girl with the ribbons. She climbed over anything and anyone in her path. Her laughter was bright and unburdened. Would Maida have run through a tavern with ribbons in her hair if her father had let her?

Would she have scrambled over the lap of the citizens of Silktide with no care for who it might be?

Maida felt the weight of a new layer of longing and loss settled over her shoulders. Not only did she miss her home and her father, but she missed the childhood that she didn't have. Even the small handful of times that her father had agreed to stay and listen to the tales of Oleanna did nothing to mend the now gaping wound in Maida's heart.

Aros did not seem to notice that Maida's mind was running away with her. That was a good thing, she decided. She was teetering on that ledge where she was okay just so long as no one asked her if she was okay. If all she had to do at this moment was focus on putting one foot in front of the other while

Aros guided her to the back of the tavern hall she could do that.

She tore her attention away from the little girl with the ribbons, intending to look forward. As she did, her gaze met with cold, grey eyes. Maida pressed against Aros as recognition set in.

She had seen those eyes before. They belonged to the grumbling elf male who seemed to find fault in every decision Aros made, especially in the decision to bring Maida to Luvrahn.

Holsten's jaw was clenched and his brow furrowed as he glared at her with what Maida could only interpret as hate.

She was relieved when they passed him and found seats at the very back of the tavern. It seemed that those who could not get seats closer to the mountain of pillows had preferred to take their seats upstairs, sitting with their legs dangling through the balustrade. As Aros guided her to sit, Maida craned her neck up to marvel at the dozens of shoe and boot soles that swung back and forth above her.

"Do you want some of the stew?" Aros asked.

Maida nodded. She barely registered that he left her side at first. She was too preoccupied with how beautiful the tavern was. The carving from the doorframe and windowsills had been mirrored inside. Above her, the ceiling created by the second floor had been painted lovingly by hand. Swirls of colour chased each other around, forming endless, looping patterns. The paint seemed to move and dance in the candlelight, and Maida wondered if elven magic was playing a part.

Elven magic.

Maida's throat tightened. She was surrounded by elves. Those feet swinging above, belonged to vicious, man-eating creatures. The backs of heads she could see in front of her were mounted atop the shoulders of nightmarish beings who had taunted humankind for centuries.

Maida had been stupid enough to let the one elf she trusted keep her safe.

She rose from her seat to peer over the waiting sea of pointed ears and hidden, unknown magic. She looked over the rows of braided hair and flowing conversation, searching for a sign of Aros.

Instead, she saw Palis standing at the front with a short, plump female. The shorter elf's hair was styled in two fluffy puffs on the top of her head. Even the very top of those puffs barely met Palis' shoulder. Her clothes were loose and flowing, with a skirt hiked up and tucked into a brown leather belt. Her complexion was a rich, warm brown, and Maida was certain that if she were any closer, she would be able to see dimples in her cheeks.

But it wasn't appearance that had caught Maida by surprise just enough to distract her from the panic that had risen within her. It was her hands.

They moved in front of the woman with such intensity and deliberateness, that it was clear this was not simply motioning to accentuate what she was saying. In fact, Maida could not see the woman's lips move at all, whereas Palis' was clearly speaking, even as her own hands danced before her.

Maida's brow furrowed.

"Pso told me to say hello," Aros said, reappearing by Maida's side with two steaming hot bowls of stew in his hand.

Wooden spoons rested atop the thick gravy beside hunks of bread, and the aroma urged Maida's stomach to growl again. Maida offered Aros a tight smile, accepting her bowl gratefully.

"What are they doing?" she asked, gesturing towards the front with her chin.

Aros lifted a spoonful of stew to his lips, blew on it, and then ate a mouthful. He chewed while he looked over to the front of the tavern, and then nodded and took his seat again.

"That's Aoife," Aros explained after he had swallowed his food. "Palis' wife. She is mute, and so she speaks with her hands."

Maida's frown deepened.

"She doesn't speak?" she asked.

Aros shook his head. He set the bowl on his knees and picked up the hunk of bread. He tore off a piece of it and scooped up some of the gravy. Before he plopped it in his mouth, he said:

"She was born mute. She has never spoken a day in her life, but she is one of the most outspoken, witty people I have ever met. Back in Balliach, there is a warrior class that communicates solely with sign—the hand language that you're seeing Aoife and Palis use now. They raised her, despite the rule of *no attachments*. It's the only time in history where any one of them had broken such a rule and not been expelled."

Maida didn't understand. Not only did the town's storyteller not speak, but there was an entire class of warriors that didn't speak either? Surely, of all the people in the world, warriors would need to be able to communicate verbally. How else would they give and receive orders?

"How..." Maida began, unsure how exactly to word her question politely. Her mouth opened and closed as she kept trying to find ways to ask the burning question on her tongue.

Instead, she settled on:

"But I don't know or understand Sign. How am I supposed to talk to her?"

Aros nodded, already chewing through another mouthful.

"Most of us here have learned sign," he said, gesturing to the crowd of elves. "For the children, it is much easier. They get taught sign alongside Common. The adults tend to take a little longer, but most of us are fluent enough that we can hold our own without needing to call in someone else for translation. There are maybe one or two elves that don't know any sign language at all, but they mainly keep to themselves on the outskirts and don't talk to anybody."

"So, they're like you?"

An elf in the row in front snorted a laugh, and Maida bit back the budding satisfaction.

"And *anyway*," Aros continued, pretending to ignore both Maida's comment and the laughter it had inspired. "Aoife can hear just fine. So, it was an easy decision for us to learn how to talk to *her*, rather than try and figure out a way for her to talk to *us*."

"That still doesn't answer my question," Maida pointed out. She picked up her spoon and chased a piece of carrot around in her stew. "How can I listen to her story if I don't understand sign?"

Aros smiled at her, setting off butterflies in her stomach.

"I'll translate for you."

As if on cue, the chatter and laughter in the tavern died down. Even the children settled, gathering together on the floor, watching as Aoife sat on the pile of pillows and blankets.

"It's starting," Aros said.

It was. Aoife lifted her hands, moving them in front of her in a manner that Maida could only describe as artful. After a moment, she could feel the heat of Aros' breath as he leaned close and whispered in her ear as he began to translate Aoife's story for her.

"*Tonight,*" Aoife began. "*I have decided that I am going to tell you one of my favourite stories. Tonight, I am going to tell you the story of the First Queen—the Maiden of Ailiar.*"

Excited whispered rose from amongst the children. The blond boy that had run past them earlier proclaimed in a loud whisper to a wild-looking boy with brown hair that this was his 'most favourite story ever.' Chuckles washed over the crowd, and even Maida found herself stifling a laugh.

"*Long, long ago,*" Aoife continued. "*In the time when the Ancient Ones still walked the Earth, a large, dark stone was discovered in the heart of the Weeping Wood. Of course, it is not uncommon to find rocks and boulders in woods. It is expected that you would be able to find one if you were only to look, but this stone was extraordinary. It was magical, for out of it grew a sword. Like the stone, the sword was also extraordinary. It had not been forged from steel. No blacksmith had laboured over it. Instead, it had grown from the stone, and was made of the very same. Many kings, lords and common men alike tried to draw the sword from the stone for centuries to no avail. No matter who tried, it would not budge. Not even magic could persuade the unexpected sheath to relinquish the blade it housed. So, for centuries, the sword remained unclaimed, growing a thicker cloak of moss with each passing year.*"

Maida tried to picture the sword in her mind, but all she could imagine was a long, thin rock. It was quite ridiculous. She couldn't imagine anything remotely resembling what her mind had conjured attracting so much attention for so long.

Though, she supposed, it might be an effective club to bring down over someone's head if she were out of other options.

But even though Maida had been trying to decide what a stone sword would look like, she had not missed the confirmation that elves had magic. Because surely, that was what Aoife had meant, right? If magic had been used to try and pull the sword from the stone, it meant that elves had magic.

Unless this was nothing more than myth, in which case, how much stock could she put in what she was learning? If this was nothing more than a cautionary tale, should she bother paying attention?

She could be tuning Aros out. She could be focusing on figuring out how she was going to escape this place without being caught by one of the elves in this very tavern.

"*Now, as you may know, before the Maiden ascended to the throne, Ailiar was known as Bermilan, and it was ruled by Kings. Like our neighbours to the North, the crown was once passed down from father to son, following a patriarchal line that stretched back generations. The last King of Bermilan was called Thar Moir. He was a cruel man, feared throughout the land. He himself had tried to draw the sword from the stone when he was young, but when he had failed, King Thar decreed that anyone who attempted to do so after would be charged with high treason. At first, people left the sword alone out of fear. As decades passed, they forgot its existence altogether, and soon, all the paths through the Weeping Wood towards the heart became overgrown and impossible to traverse.*

"*For all those decades, King Thar ruled without a Queen by his side, but eventually, his advisors convinced him of the need to marry and sire a legitimate heir. Elves may live long lives, but without a clear successor to the throne, the King was at risk of losing both his life and the power his family had held over Bermilan for centuries. So, he travelled across the land, visiting even the smallest of villages to search for a bride. He did not want to marry a noble lady, fearing the influence of her family. He wanted to marry a woman that would be loyal to him, and only him. He searched every corner of the kingdom before he came across a small village by the edge of a large, dark wood.*"

Any thoughts of tuning out had fled Maida's mind. She found herself leaning forward in her seat, focusing on the cherubic face of Aoife.

"*In this village, he came across the most beautiful woman that he had ever laid eyes on. The Maiden was beyond compare and beyond comprehension. Never had an artist been able to capture her likeness with enough accuracy to do her justice. And from the very moment the King laid his eyes on her, King Thar was determined to make her his bride.*"

A shiver ran down Maida's spine.

"But the Maiden knew of King Thar's cruelty. No crown, no throne, and no amount of riches or jewels could persuade such a horrible man. And so, the Maiden refused the King. Unfortunately, King Thar was not a man who would accept such a rejection—at least, not without retribution. He ordered his men to arrest the Maiden, determined to marry her whether she wanted to be his bride or not. He had expected her to fight, as many did before they finally fell to the whims of their king, but he did not expect her to run.

"The Maiden was as swift as she was beautiful, and despite the decades of training the King's men had endured, they were not fast enough to catch her. She knew all the back alleys. She knew all the little twists and turns of the village, and by the time the King had mounted his steed and given chase himself, the Maiden had already broken free of the village proper. She raced across the field between the village and the wood beyond."

Maida's heart was racing in her chest. Her breaths came quick and shallow, as though she were racing through a maze of streets herself. Had the King been mounted on a horse? That would be terrifying in and of itself, but her mind seemed determined to push the boundaries of how much horror she could handle.

She could imagine all too clearly what it would feel like to be chased down by a tyrant king riding astray one of the giant goats, like the one that lived in the paddock near Aros' cottage.

She could hear a bleating battle cry, gaining on her with each desperate step that she took.

She swallowed hard, and took hold of the pendant at her throat.

"Once in the field, the King urged his mount into a gallop. He nearly closed the distance between them, but the Maiden had managed to gain such a head start that the King's fingertips barely brushed the ends of her wild red hair as she leapt into the Wood."

Maida was picturing herself as the Maiden now, running from the evil king. She swore she could even feel a tug on the end of her curls, despite the braid that held them back.

"*Now,*" Aoife continued. "*I pray that none of you will ever have to see the Weeping Wood. It is a cursed place, forsaken even by the Ancient Ones, and even when the Maiden was fleeing King Thar, the paths were too overgrown for even the most skilled rider to traverse while mounted. So, the King was forced to dismount and follow the Maiden on foot. While most men of worth would have been honourable enough to accept the Maiden's decision and leave her be, the King saw her refusal as nothing more than an obstacle he must overcome.*"

Maida stole a glance at Aros. Even though he was an elf, she could not imagine that he would be the type of man to force a woman to marry him. Despite those pointed ears, he had a kind face, and he had been nothing but kind and generous to her.

She wondered—for the first time, and only briefly—why he lived alone. Surely, there were many elven women who found him handsome. Or men, if that was his preference. If women could marry women, it stood to reason that men could marry men.

But the story was continuing, and Maida did not want to miss a moment of it, so she returned to watching Aoife.

"*Perhaps if the King had realised which Wood the Maiden had run into, he may have abandoned his pursuit of her. It had only been two hundred years prior when he had declared the Weeping Wood off-limits. But blinded by his rage, he did not. Many scholars have argued about whether or not the Maiden had lured the King into the Wood with the intention of slaying the King. There are some who suggested that she had a vision, a gift from the Ancient Ones, showing her where to go to survive her pursuer. Then again, as with all great stories where the odds are stacked against the hero so tremendously, there are some to argue that the Maiden had nothing but unadulterated luck that had led her to the clearing."*

Maida could see it as clearly as if she were there herself. She stood in a green clearing, the canopy above forming a heart-shaped hole to direct sunlight down upon a grey, moss-covered stone. The sword jutting out of no longer seemed like a long, thin rock in her imagination. The hilt was defined and intricately carved.

In her mind, she turned to face the tall man who broke through the tree line. He was tall and wore blackened steel over fine black cloth. The crown upon his head was skewed, and his breathing was ragged and erratic. As though she were seeing through the eyes of the Maiden, Maida saw King Thar raise a hand and point it at her with a snarl on his face.

"No one knows what words—if any—passed between King Thar and the Maiden. What we do know is that the King had lunged for her. In desperation, she reached for the hilt of the sword, and drew it from its stone sheath in one fluid motion. It was with this sword that the Maiden slew the King, cleaving his head from his shoulders with a single swing.

"As the King's body slumped to the ground, the Maiden watched his blood seep into the earth beneath her feet. The earth was thirsty, and it drew every last drop from the King's corpse. It flowed like a river through the grass towards the stone, where it ran against the rules of nature up its surface. The Maiden watched in fascination as the very substance of the stone changed before her eyes. What once had been grey, cold, and unfeeling transformed into a beautiful, translucent red crystal. The sword had been changed as well. It was no longer grey rock, nor was it silver steel. It, too, was glistening red, from tip to pommel. Does anyone know what this crystal became known as?"

The blond boy, who loved this story, shot up his hand. Aoife nodded to him, and he clambered to his feet. Maida bit back the grin at the display of importance this child was putting on the name of a crystal.

"It's bloodstone!" he said. "And the King's blood went through all of Ailiar to become *more* bloodstone! And only the descendants of the Maiden can control it!"

Aoife smiled.

The boy turned to present a triumphant grin to the crowd before retaking his seat.

"*Very good,*" Aoife said. "*Yes, King Thar's blood had mixed with the land itself, and created bloodstone. Though she had seen this miracle first-hand, the Maiden was unable to marvel at the majesty of it. She had slain the King, and there was no hiding what she had done. She was not prepared to spend the rest of her life on the run, fearing discovery from any who may wish to avenge King Thar's death. The Maiden had no choice—she must return to the village and hope that the punishment would be swift.*

"*To ensure that there was no doubt of her victory, the Maiden picked up the King's head and carried both it and the sword on the long journey back. Soldiers and villagers alike had gathered along the Wood's edge, too scared to step foot inside. Whispers rose among them when the Maiden came into view. Gasps echoed through the trees when she tossed the King's head at the foot of his soldiers with all the ceremony of casting off a mud-covered cloak.*

"*The Maiden was exhausted. Her whole body ached, but she was as determined to find her death on her feet as she had been to avoid marrying the King. So, she raised the sword in challenge, and bared her teeth, ready for certain death.*"

Maida gripped her pendant tighter until the petals of the carved crystal flower dug into her palm. She didn't loosen her hold. She didn't particularly care if she was drawing blood. All Maida could focus on was how her heart seemed to sing as the story took root within her.

"*But,*" Aoife continued. "*No death came. Instead, the King's soldiers lay down their arms and they bent at the knee. The villagers quickly followed suit. The Maiden did not know what to make of this. She stood, the sword still raised with shaking arms, staring at all those who knelt before her. It was not until the captain of the guard lifted his head, and declared her Gods-Blessed that she finally lowered her weapon.*

"*You see, long, long before King Thar was born, there was a prophecy that claimed the true ruler of this land would be chosen by the Ancient Ones, and there was no doubt that they had played a part in ensuring the safety of the Maiden.*

"*And so, she became the first Queen. Upon her coronation, the realm took on her name—Ailiar—and the succession rules changed. The Maiden told her new queendom how the Ancient Ones had visited her the night before her coronation and told her that the realm would be safe so long as the first daughter of the first daughter sat upon the throne. Since then, the crown has only ever been passed down according to those rules. There have not even been any attempts to overthrow the Ailian line, for fear of the chaos that was sure to unfold.*

"*Along with the crown, the sword that the Maiden pulled from the stone is also inherited by the heir. Much like how only the Maiden could draw it in the first place, only the true heir to the Ailiar throne will possess the power to wield it.*"

The boy who had answered about the bloodstone spoke up again.

"So does that mean Queen Meitranis is a daughter of the Maiden?" he asked.

"*Queen Meitranis is a daughter of a daughter of a daughter, in a line that stretches back generations. And her daughter, Princess Calliope, will be Queen after her. Calliope will go on to bear a daughter herself, and the line of the*

Maiden will remain unbroken."

Aoife's smile was radiant as she looked over the children. It was clear that she cared for all of them very much. Maida couldn't imagine such an expression on Oleanna's face. Had anyone, other than her father, ever looked at her like that? Eoin had been interested in courting her, and his family had been welcoming enough, but Maida could not recall a moment of genuine warmth.

And yet you want to return to them, a voice taunted.

She pushed away the thought. She was tired, so her mind was pulling her towards ideas that should be left unacknowledged. In the end, it didn't matter how well she fit into the fabric of Silktide. Maida Tailor was human, and she belonged in Colosia.

Not here.

Not surrounded by elves, regardless of whether they were truly as dangerous and bloodthirsty as Maida had been raised to believe.

And certainly not by Aros C'Asad's side.

Thirteen

Di'Ath

Zadanai

Di'Ath Adarhna had expected his final day in Zadanai to begin the same way as the previous 8,595 days had begun, however no servants came to open the heavy curtains to let in the warm, golden rays of the morning sun.

There were no trays of cold fruits and warm pastries being carried in and set on the table by the window. His tutor—a surprisingly strong man for someone so thin and tall—did not barge in mid-citrus to tell him he needed to pick up the pace and get ready for a day of studying, training, and sitting in on council meetings.

Instead, the young prince of Zadanai woke to his mattress shifting under the weight of another elf, and the feeling of a gentle hand on his brow.

Di'Ath opened his eyes to find his mother smiling down at him.

"Good morning, my little whirlpool," the Queen of Zadanai said, and immediately, Di'Ath's eyes watered.

His mother had not called him her *little whirlpool* since he was a young child. Though by elven standards he was barely an adult, he could not remember a time past fifteen when she had used the name at all. He felt that young now—felt completely and utterly foolish for letting something so small get to him.

He would, if pressed, blame being so emotional on still being half-sleep.

He quickly lifted the edge of his blanket to wipe the tears away, but it was futile. His mother would never miss such a thing on one of her children, no matter where they fell on the list.

"Oh, my darling," she cooed. "There is nothing wrong with being a little emotional today. You are about to face a great many changes, and you will not be able to accept them if you do not let yourself feel everything you need to feel."

More tears fell, and once again Di'Ath was adamant that it was just too early.

He shifted to sit up, and frowned when a bright shard of light assaulted him. Di'Ath glared towards the blue, gold-trimmed curtains accusatorily. They had allowed for the room to remain blissfully dark, but perhaps it was not as early as he originally thought. Especially if, as he could so clearly see, his mother had taken the time to get dressed in all her finery.

"Morning is not the right time for philosophy," he grumbled.

The bangles and jewels around his mother's wrist jingled and chimed as she reached up to brush his hair back. He watched as the fabric of her embroidered shawl shifted with the movement, and felt those traitorous tears heat once more.

"Morning philosophy," she said. "Along with everything that is to come, is nothing that you cannot handle. I have seen you stomach more than a few pretty words in hours much smaller than these."

His mother was right. She had been the one to pull Di'Ath out of difficult situations in the past. Despite the truth to her words, Di'Ath felt the impulse to say that in order to get out of those situations, one did not require a functioning cognition higher than a fluke. It was an unfair statement, and he knew it. He did not want to mar the last few hours he had with his mother, so he kept his mouth shut on that matter.

"Did you come to make sure that I did not bribe one of my attendants to let me slip away?" he asked her.

The thought had crossed his mind, but he could not name a single person who worked in the castle that would go against his father. King Di'San was a fair king, but his punishments were nothing to turn your nose up at.

Not to mention that he would not get very far if he did manage to slip away.

Still, his mother laughed. It was an airy, carefree sound that seemed to take Di'Ath's heart in its hands and lift it out of the pit of burdens.

The Queen shook her head and leaned back on her hands. When she did, Di'Ath could see so much of Sy'da in her. Sy'da was, arguably, the only one of the Queen's children to take after her at all, and if Di'Ath had not yet realised how grateful he would be to have his sister by his side before, he realised it in that moment. To face what was in store for him alone would surely be his end.

"No," his mother said. "I wanted to come and wake you, because it is my last chance to do so. And as your mother, I decided that I have a right to that one last chance. I dare you to try and hold that against me."

"Does that mean that I should let you go, so you can wake Sy'da too?" Di'Ath asked.

The Queen laughed again.

"My darling, your sister is already awake and dressed. I am not certain that she slept, if I am to be honest. I poked my head into her room before coming here and I could not recognise it. I do not think that she is leaving me anything to remember her by, wretched thing."

Di'Ath smiled.

"She is very excited to see more of this world," he said.

"I wish you were as excited as well," his mother replied. "You are going to bring so much pride to your country, and to our family. But I want you to know that I am already so filled with pride for you."

His family and his country—two things that he would never see again.

And aside from Sy'da and the small retinue of advisors, Di'Ath would have no more ties or contact with his home until his wedding. And then, after he was tied forever to a girl he did not know for a country he would gladly never step foot in, he would never see them again.

But the more he thought about it, the more Di'Ath realised that it was not where he was going that was worrying him the most.

He looked down at his blanket and picked at a loose thread.

"What if," he asked haltingly. "What if I cannot love her, mother?"

He had never voiced this fear before. Not even to Sy'da.

He had not expected to utter the words while still upon Zadanese soil if he were to ever utter them at all. And he certainly had not expected his mother to smile.

Perhaps he could have imagined a worn-out, tired speech about how she had not loved his father when they were first wed. He could have foreseen a recitation of *duty has to come first, but love is sure to follow*. But the curve of his mother's lips was not designed to reassure him or allay any of his fears.

Instead, there was a playfulness behind it—a telling sort of look, as though she knew something that he did not.

"What is it?" he asked, brow furrowing.

"You," his mother said, leaning to one side so she could lift a hand to point at him. "Will love her."

Before he could speak, she held up her hand to stop him.

"The Tide has shown me," she continued. "You will have an instant connection with the woman you will marry. From the moment you see her, you will be drawn in. You will know that she will have your heart for the rest of your days. She will consume your dreams from the second you meet until the day you are wed."

Di'Ath raised a brow, but once again, the Queen of Zadanai continued before he could speak.

"Following your wedding," she said. "You will devote your every breath, every beat of your heart, to her health and happiness."

Di'Ath was not sure how to feel.

It was well known that the Tide favoured his mother. She was known across the land for her prophecies, for the futures that she could see in the water. Water was, she claimed, the perfect conductor for something as fluid and ever-changing as time.

There were many who travelled for days to seek an audience with her at the palace in an attempt to learn what the Tide had in store for them. And while her prophecies rang true, her family knew that she was just as likely to say that the Tide had told her something in order to elicit a desired outcome from her husband or children.

There had been a time when she had told Di'Ath's oldest broth-er—Di'Na—that the Tide had decreed that his hair would fall out if he kept stealing sweetcakes from the kitchens. Di'Na had never stolen a single cake since, but for the past eighteen years, he had developed an obsession with mirrors to ensure that not a single strand of hair was out of place.

Di'Ath could not imagine that Di'Na's wife found the practice endearing in any way.

Di'Ath wished that he could completely rule out the possibility that what his mother was telling him now was not like that. He wished that he could believe, without a shadow of a doubt, that the Tide truly had revealed that he would become devoted to the woman he was to marry the moment he saw her. Even though he had never seen marriage in the cards for himself until he was decades older, Di'Ath Adarhna had little interest in a loveless marriage.

His family, though large, had always been close, and he was not sure that he would survive an existence where he could not even say he loved his wife.

"I do not know what I am going to do without having you to turn to," Di'Ath admitted. "You have been my guiding star since I was born. Without you, I will be sailing blind. I will run aground and be stranded and…"

"Nonsense," his mother interrupted with a hum. "There is a time in every child's life when they must step out from their parent's reach. It is the flow of the river, the pull of the Tide. Water that stands still for too long becomes stagnant and a home for parasites. You will not become a home for parasites, my darling."

It was then that the Queen of Zadanai stood. Her jewellery chimed as she moved, the flowing layers of fabric whispering against one another as they shifted and fell into place.

Di'Ath took her in then—really, *truly* took her in.

Her shawl, blouse and skirt were the signature Zadanai blue, and embroidered in intricate, delicate goldwork. It was like looking out at the sea in the afternoon, with sunlight shimmering on the waves. The long, sleek black hair did nothing to diminish the image. If anything, it intensified it, just like those dark eyes did.

And the chains and jewels that were as delicate as the pointed ears they hung from…

Di'Ath's eyes watered once more. Oh, how he loved the fashions of his home. He loved how the women adorned themselves with lace, bells, and jewels, how they transformed dressing into an art form.

He loved how they would layer fragrances in the same way, leaving a man with the task of unravelling each note that graced his senses when she passed.

It was but another thing that he would miss after crossing the Zadanese

Sea. From the portrait of Calliope on his desk, he had already determined that the women of Ailiar did not know the art of dressing at all, and the pearls in her hair felt more like a hollow attempt at imitation than anything else.

The Queen bent to press her lips to Di'Ath's brow.

"I shall let you dress," she said. "If you hurry, we will have time for one last meal as a family before you go."

Di'Ath nodded.

His mother cupped his face for a moment longer before leaving him alone in his room for the last time in his life.

There was a special kind of torture in seeing something you wanted be so close and yet be just out of reach. Di'Ath decided that he would prefer to spend the rest of his days in the salt room, having the strength of his magic be constantly stifled as every last morsel of water was drawn out from air around him, than to endure the torment of knowing his home—his very world—would never be within his grasp again.

Perhaps he was desperate, but the young prince was seriously considering suggesting that very fate instead of climbing aboard the proud galleon moored at the bustling docks. Even though he and his family had made the slow, meandering journey through the streets from the palace all the way down to the docks, surely his parents would allow him to pull out of this arrangement. It was, in Di'Ath's opinion, the same torturous outcome.

His gaze flicked up to his father. The King of Zadanai was offering a small yet kind smile to the Zadanese people, who were waving and calling out to their monarchs. But Di'Ath knew Di'San well enough to notice the hard set of his jaw meant that he was not in the kind of mood Di'Ath would need the king to be in to broach the topic. Di'Ath would be foolish to so much as hint at the idea, lest he end up in a locked salt box and carried on board the ship regardless. There was no sense in doubling his discomfort when he had the opportunity to remain only mildly inconvenienced was still in the palm of his hand.

So instead, Di'Ath clenched his own jaw, and focused on the ship that had been chosen to carry him to his unwanted destiny.

The *Spirit,* though officially titled as a passenger ship on the necessary documents, was in truth a warship in everything but name. Di'Ath supposed it made sense—Di'San would not risk sending his son and daughter across the treacherous Zadanese Sea on any vessel that sported less than seventy cannons. Even for followers of the Tide, the Sea was a dangerous place. With pirates, seawyrms and other monstrous, unmentionable creatures lurking in the depths, those who thought that they could tame the Sea tended to find their lives cut short by it.

There were seventy cannons—two on the aft, thirty-six mounted on either side, and the rest below deck. He could not see them now, but Di'Ath imagined that some could be mounted upon swivel posts at strategic locations above deck as well.

He could not guess whether or not this sort of firepower would have any effect on sea creatures, and he could only hope that any pirates that they may come across would be in a much smaller ship. Perhaps a sloop. Though, he supposed, he could take down a sloop on his own. Surely, it was not delusional to believe that he would be able to cut through the hull of such a small ship with his magic, or that he could send would-be raiders to their watery graves.

Di'Ath was too busy imagining himself as the hero in a life-threatening situation to notice his father moving beside him. When King Di'San laid his heavy, warm hand on Di'Ath's shoulder, the young prince jumped.

"You, my son," the King's voice was low and gravelly. "Are making your country very proud. I understand that you are not entirely pleased with this arrangement, however I hope that when the Tide brings us back together, you will have come to see the wisdom of this decision. And, like your mother, I also hope that you are able to find some grain of happiness in what the future holds for you."

Di'Ath lowered his gaze to the paved path beneath his feet.

The small tiles had been arranged so beautifully, so artfully that it was as though he were walking on a field of brightly coloured flowers. What had he been so preoccupied with that Di'Ath had not taken the time to appreciate the artistry of the path? Why had he written off the docks as a place only to feel closer to the Tide and his magic? Why had he not—

King Di'San gave Di'Ath's shoulder a squeeze, pulling the young prince once more from his thoughts.

"You should go," he said. "Your sister is waiting for you."

And she was.

Sy'da stood by the very edge of the dock, as close as she could get without standing on the wood itself. She was bouncing on her heels, the gentle jingle of the bells around her ankle melting into the chatter, waves, and groaning ship around her.

"You take care of her," King Di'San said. "Keep her safe, and make sure the partner she chooses is kind to her."

"I promise," Di'Ath's voice near broke on his reply.

He nodded to reinforce his words and took a step away from his parents. Then another. And another, until finally, he was by Sy'da's side.

Do not look back, he told himself.

ELLE BROCKETT

Di'Ath knew that if he did look back too soon, he would never make it onto the *Spirit*, and the peace his pending nuptials had been designed to inspire would never be.

Sy'da lifted her hand and let it brush against Di'Ath's arm as he passed her. He could feel her follow him as his footsteps changed sound, becoming louder and almost hollow as he stepped onto the wood of the dock and made his way through the sailors making their preparations.

He did not slow when he came to the plank that bridged the gap between dock and deck. He did not acknowledge the cold fist that seemed to take hold of his heart the moment he felt the wood beneath his feet flex.

It was not until he was at the halfway point that Di'Ath stopped, pausing to look over the edge into the water below.

The dark, ever-shifting blue beckoned him. It seemed to call out, to promise him that if Di'Ath only dared jump, he could stay in the city forever. He would never have to leave Zadanai if he just stepped to the right instead of forward.

Yet, as much as he wished to do so, Di'Ath was unable to answer the water's call.

"Move on," Sy'da said as she poked him in the side with one of her perfectly manicured nails. "There is a line forming behind us, and I will not stop them if they decide to throw you overboard halfway through the voyage because you are being insufferable."

Di'Ath rolled his eyes and groaned, but he continued to ascend. When he was officially aboard the *Spirit*, he moved to the side to lean against the rich, carved wooden railing to look back towards his parents.

His father's arm was around his mother now, and Di'Ath felt a pang of guilt that he had been so focused on making sure that he did not turn coward and bring shame on his family that he had not stopped to give her one last hug.

King Di'San gave Di'Ath a nod, though whether of encouragement or approval, Di'Ath could not tell. Either way, he was where his father had planned him to be. Where, according to his mother, he was *supposed* to be.

So why did it feel so wrong?

If the Tide had revealed to his mother that he was going to fall completely in love with Calliope Ailiar, why was he not filled with excitement? If he was going to bring pride and glory to Zadanai, why did he feel like he was about to disappoint every citizen to have ever called Zadanai home?

Why was he so sure that he could forsake his fortune, his title, and even his name if it meant that he could stay here with his family?

There was a clang of wood against wood, and Di'Ath whipped his head around to see that the gangplank had been lifted and fitted against the hole to complete the railing.

It was too late.

Di'Ath could not back out. He had been lamenting his future for so long he had not taken the proper time to mourn the loss of his past.

Sails were released from their masts. The canvas flexed and snapped as magically-directed wind filled them. Sailors who wielded water magic stationed both at the aft and bow guided the *Spirit* away from the dock with such speed that Di'Ath was not prepared for how quickly his parents would appear to grow smaller.

He could still jump.

He could still throw himself overboard and into the water below. He could risk destroying himself just for the chance to swim home.

Come, come, come, the ship's wake seemed to call.

Di'Ath leaned forward. He looked over the railing to the white-capped wake below, imagining that each roll of the water was a hand waving, beckoning him to join them.

A hand closed around his forearm, soft, brown fingers tugging firmly on the brocade-covered limb.

Di'Ath looked up to find Sy'da by his side, still trying to pull him away from the railing.

"Come with me," she said.

Her face was split into a bright smile. The sunlight kissed the pointed top of her ears and added a glow to her thick black hair. Di'Ath did not want to acknowledge the reason why he did not like how happy and healthy she looked. He did not want to admit that she appeared so very much at home on the ship.

But even less than that, Di'Ath did not want to be the reason why that smile faded. So, he let go of the railing, and allowed Sy'da's hand to slide down from his forearm, where her delicate fingers slid in between his. He allowed her to tug him away from the aft of the ship and towards the bow, weaving in and out of the other sailors with nary a stumble, as if she had spent years working on a crowded ship.

Sy'da did not stop until they were at the bow, standing just to the left of the bowsprit.

She gestured to the expanse of glistening water with open arms, as if she were offering it all to Di'Ath.

As if the world and all it had to offer were ripe for his taking.

"Is this not the most beautiful sight you have ever seen?" Sy'da asked.

She sounded breathless, as though looking out over the sea was enough to take her breath away. Di'Ath wondered when—or rather *if*—he would find that kind of wonder and hope for what lay ahead.

"Yeah," he said finally. "It is."

FOURTEEN

AROS

LUVRAHN

SOMETHING HAD CHANGED WITHIN Dhuina the night of Aoife's story.

Aros couldn't quite put his finger on it, but he was certain that he had detected a determination that had seemed to set in while they had waited in their seats for the tavern to clear.

He hoped that she wasn't planning something stupid. She could return to Colosia if she liked, but he didn't want her to do it alone. Even with her wounds all but completely healed, it would be suicide.

What if she is determined to stay?

Aros dismissed the thought.

Whatever it was that he had seen, it seemed as though her fear she of elves had faded, even just a little.

They had spent the morning going over basic words and phrases in sign language in preparation for officially meeting Aoife that afternoon. Aros had introduced them to each other briefly following the story the night before, but he hadn't made time for anything more than that. He had been eager to get Dhuina home despite knowing that neither Aoife nor Palis would have accepted such a hurried introduction as legitimate.

Aros didn't want Dhuina to exert herself too much. He didn't want her to aggravate her healing wounds, and if that meant that they would have to visit the other two for dinner the following night, so be it.

To Dhuina's credit, she picked up the words he taught her quickly.

Aros felt pride swell in his chest as he watched her eagerly follow his example, and when he caught her practising out of the corner of his eye as he turned away for a moment to make them both something to eat for lunch.

It was odd, he thought, how quickly he had accepted the presence of the human in his home. For the first time since building his little cottage, Aros regretted having only planned for the one, open room.

If you had separate bedrooms, you wouldn't be able to see her at all hours of the day, a voice in his head said. *She would be able to hide, and you know you wouldn't survive that.*

Aros tried to push the thought away.

He was thinking like someone in love, and there was no way he had developed such feelings for her in such a short time. It had to be because he had found her in the Woods, or because he had effectively nursed her back to health after she had been on Di'Tyan's doorstep.

Gods.

He didn't even know how long she had been out there. He could guess it was longer than mere days. Weeks? A month? More?

He had watched over the past three weeks as the hollows of her cheeks slowly filled out, and how her arms no longer resembled thin, frail twigs. She had been wandering the Woods, alone, and had lost far too much weight. It was a miracle that she hadn't also been sick.

That was it.

That was why he felt such a connection to her. He would accept nothing else. And besides—what twenty-something-year-old human would want anything to do with a four-hundred-year-old elf?

Still, he hoped that she would stay in Luvrahn. Now that she was in his life, he wasn't sure what he would do if she were to leave it.

Like the night before, Dhuina had looped her arm through his as they walked.

The journey to the Reih household was silent. Aros watched as she took in the sights of Luvrahn. He wondered if her home looked like this, or if she came from some place larger. He couldn't imagine she hailed from the capital. She would not have crossed over the border if she had the chance to take refuge in another town.

Unless she was on the run. But from what could she have possibly be running?

He would ask her, he decided, after they returned home.

For now, he'd allow his friends to annoy her with questions.

Aros had barely knocked on the door to Aoife and Palis' home when the former swung it open. The short, plump female gave a warm, welcoming smile to Dhuina, bypassing Aros entirely.

Aros tried not to take it personally.

He took a step back, gesturing to Dhuina to say her greeting.

"*Hello, Aoife*" Dhuina said. She brought her hand up to her face, palm facing toward Aoife, and made a deliberate wave in the sign for *hello*. Then, she spelled out Aoife's name.

Delighted, Aoife clasped her hands together. She bounced on the balls of her feet before pulling Dhuina into a bone-crushing hug.

Aros stifled a laugh at the audible sound of air being forced out of Dhuina's lungs. She looked at him with wide, pleading eyes over Aoife's shoulder. Aros simply held up his hands as if to say *what do you expect me to do?*

Aoife pulled back and started signing rapidly. She was way too fast, and used too many words that Aros had not yet been able to teach Dhuina.

Dhuina turned pleading eyes on Aros once more, and this time, he obliged her.

"She said that she is happy to see you, and that you seem to be healing well. She has heard a lot about you, and hopes that you are settling in nicely."

"Oh!" Dhuina said. "Right, well... I..."

She bit her lip, and thought about what she was going to do next. Aros bit back a smile at the look of concentration on Dhuina's face.

"*Thank you*," Dhuina signed. "*I am welcome.*"

Aoife took Dhuina's hands in her own, patting them gently with a kind smile.

Dhuina's shoulders sagged. "I got it wrong, didn't I?" she asked.

"It's a work in progress," Aros chuckled. "You'll get there."

Dhuina pouted, and Aros chortled. He had never seen her pout before, and it was strangely endearing.

"Is that Dhuina?" Palis' voice came from the kitchen.

Aoife ushered Dhuina and Aros inside, closing the door behind them just as Palis emerged with a tray of cookies.

Aros could tell from the sight of the treats that they had not been made by Palis. They were not nearly burnt enough.

She was trying to look domestic in an attempt—Aros was sure—to make Dhuina like her more.

"Look at you!" Palis hummed. "You look so good! So healthy and fresh-faced. Aros must be adding more greens to your diet."

"She's the one adding the greens," Aros said, moving over towards Palis. "Dhuina has been cooking the last few days."

He reached to take a cookie from the tray, only for Palis to move it out of his reach. He frowned at her.

"Well, it's about time someone fed the two of you properly," Palis said. "How about we set this down, then Aros, you can help me get the pot of tea and cups?"

Aros' frown deepened. "Are you purposefully trying to keep me away from the cookies?" he asked.

"If I don't, they'll all be gone before the rest of us can get so much as get a whiff of them."

Palis carried the tray to a table decorated with a lace tablecloth and fresh-cut flowers before grabbing Aros' hand and pulling him towards the kitchen.

"She's looking well," Palis said.

"She is," Aros replied.

"How did she do last night?"

Aros shrugged, then took down four ceramic cups off their hooks under the cabinets. "She did alright, I guess. I think she liked the story about the Maiden."

"Everyone likes the story about the Maiden," Palis said. "It's a story about good triumphing over evil."

"It's a story about a woman thrust into a role she didn't want, all because she decided to run when faced with an equally unsavoury alternative," Aros replied.

"You need to be more romantic," Palis said. "Just because you're a grouch and a loner, that doesn't mean you can't see the world through a brighter lens."

Aros snorted. "There is nothing romantic about being forced into governing a country when you weren't raised to do so. It is a disaster waiting to happen."

Palis dismissed his words with a wave of her hand. She picked up the pot of tea with a thick towel before walking back out.

Aros followed, picking up the small container of sugar as he did.

As if drawn to her by some magic tether, Aros' eyes fell upon Dhuina immediately.

She was looking at an intricate, hand-crafted quilt that spilled over the edge of a basket by the hearth. Her fingers hovered over the stitching as though she ached to touch it.

Aros didn't understand why she didn't.

"It's beautiful, isn't it?"

Palis' voice made Dhuina jump backwards like a child caught doing something she shouldn't.

Aros bit back a laugh. Like the pout, the jump was endearing. Adorable.

"There is a lady here who makes the most wonderful quilts," Palis continued, setting down the pot of tea. "Her name is Deija. I will introduce the two of you one day. She has this one quilt on her wall that looks like a painting when you study it from the right angle. She didn't make that one, though."

Dhuina looked back at the quilt, a wistful expression on her face.

"I can't imagine that you are entertained in the barren wasteland that is Aros' hovel—*ow!* Sorry, Aros' *cottage*."

Palis rubbed her arm where Aoife her elbowed her, protesting her description of Aros' home.

"We have plenty of artisans that call Luvrahn home, and I am sure they would love to share their craft with you. Is there anything you would like to learn?"

Dhuina turned to Aros with an expression that suggested she was waiting for him to give her something before she answered. Was it permission she was seeking? Comfort?

She would never need to ask for the former.

For the latter?

You would burn yourself to keep her warm.

Clearing his throat awkwardly, Aros nodded.

"I…" Dhuina began, her shaking voice betraying her nerves. "I am actually a seamstress. Or I was a seamstress. I'm not sure if I can still call myself one when I don't have any tools of the trade anymore. But I love making clothes. I have really missed making them since I've been here. It helps clear my mind."

"Could you make me something?"

Palis' question earned her another reproachful elbow to the arm from her wife.

"You don't need any more clothes," Aros added. "And I'm sure that Aoife is just as tired as I am of telling you that just because you have discovered that someone has a talent, it doesn't mean that you need to ask them to make something for you."

"Oh, I am *so sorry* for supporting the arts," Palis said. "Not everyone likes to sit around in a boring, hollow cottage with only *furs* serving as decoration."

Aros sat down in a chair at the table.

"The furs are practical," he argued.

"So are quilts," Palis argued.

"They are unnecessarily fancy and require far too much time and effort when there are perfectly good substitutes that don't use as many resources."

The tips of Palis' ears burned red. Her nostrils flared, and her eyes narrowed—playing right into Aros' hand.

Aros loved riling Palis up. It was so easy, and she was falling for this particular trap *so* deliciously.

They had been friends since childhood and knew exactly to elicit certain desired reactions from the other. The decades that they had spent fighting side by side in the royal army had done nothing to dampen their playful, familial bond.

It certainly had done nothing to stop Palis from acting every bit the younger, annoying sister.

"Textiles are actually extremely important," Dhuina said, interrupting Aros' thoughts.

All three elves turned their attention to her, and her cheeks burned bright red.

Aros smiled at the sight, and he ignored the way Palis' gaze shifted between them.

"I mean, think about it," Dhuina continued. "Something as simple as a quilt can tell you a lot about the person who made it. The pattern will tell you where they came from. The fabrics and dyes will tell you how wealthy they are. Even the stitching can give you clues about their age and skill."

She chewed her lip and toyed with the flower pendant at her throat.

"And, if you know what you're looking at, it can tell you what region they were in when they learned to sew in the first place."

Palis turned a bright, *I-Told-You-So* smiled towards Aros. Aros sniffed in disregard, and reached for one of the still-steaming cookies. He sat down, looked at Dhuina and gestured towards the quilt with his chin.

"That quilt you were looking at earlier," he said. "What does that tell you?"

Dhuina met his gaze. Aros swore he could see the steel in it—the desire to lift her chin high and stand her ground against him.

Good, he thought.

"Well?" he asked.

Dhuina's gaze didn't waver.

"The colours are bright and strong," she said. "And the fibres are sturdy. Whoever dyed them had more than ample access to the plants they used, and the necessary mordant to achieve such a saturated hue. For them, dye isn't merely a hobby or passing interest. They had the time, money, and resources to do it properly. It is likely their profession."

Aros took a bite of his cookie.

Dhuina continued.

"So, that means that the fabric is expensive. Even if they were offcuts from another project, the person who bought the fabric did not spare any expense. The pieces are precise, and they fit together perfectly. The stitches are consistent, and the thread is also of high quality. Finally, the top is embroidered. Embroidery takes time and uses a lot of thread that could be saved for the structural stitches. Embroidery in itself is luxury. That's why you usually only see it on garments, or handkerchiefs if you want to show off that you have money."

Aros thought about the skirt she had worn when he found her. He remembered pausing over the embroidered flowers and swirls, the little, lovely hand-made stitches. Had she made it herself?

"Alright," Aros said, leaning back in his seat. The corner of his lips quirked up in a playful smirk. "You've told us that the quilt is expensive, but I don't see how that tells us anything about the person who made it."

"Doesn't it?" Dhuina asked.

An electric thrill ran through Aros' blood at the challenge in her voice.

"These clues tell me that the artist who made this quilt likely lived in a large city—either capital or merchant—and they were of high status. Whether they were commissioned to make this or whether they used their own funds, they didn't spare any expense. They had time to ensure that the seams lined up perfectly and that each stitch was the same length. On top of that, they had the time to embroider. The level of details has me thinking that even if they were paid to make it, the project was, primarily, one of love. It wouldn't have so much detail otherwise."

Aoife covered her smile with her hand. Palis snorted a laugh and took a deep drink of her tea.

Dhuina's gaze upon Aros did not falter.

"It would take months, at a minimum, and as there is no variation on fabrics of the same dye lot, this was not put away into storage and allowed to fade. This was done without interruption. The person who made this had little to no other responsibilities. They had a family or staff to take care of the household chores, and they were able to devote themselves to this project completely. I envy them for that."

Aros saw that hint of steel gleam brighter in Dhuina's eye. She lifted her chin defiantly, still refusing to look anywhere else other than him.

Did she like what she saw? Did she consider him to be remotely as interesting or beautiful as the quilt she had just talked about so intensely?

"So?"

Aros frowned.

"So what?" he asked.

"How did I do?"

"Her name is Moira," Aros said. "She is a seamstress in Balliach. Her father was a courtier, and she would help the Queen select the fabrics for her wardrobe. Moira was allowed to sample everything for herself. I'm assuming that that is where she got the fabrics for this quilt from."

Palis laughed. Aoife clapped her hands.

"You are never allowed to tell me that I can't collect any more pieces of art again," Palis said. "Oh, she is good."

Finally, Dhuina broke off the eye contact, and crossed over to sit down in the seat across from Aros. Palis reached for her guest's curls again, twirling them around her finger.

"Alright," Palis said. "The next time you're here, you're going to come early, and we are going to give this a good wash and a good braid, how does that sound?"

Dhuina's eyes flickered to Aros for a moment before she turned a smile towards Palis.

"I would love that."

FIFTEEN

DI'ATH

ZADANESE SEA

PRINCE DI'ATH HID HIGH amongst the rigging of one of the masts of the *Spirit*. It had been difficult to find any semblance of a quiet place amongst the two hundred men and women that manned the large merchant ship. He supposed he should be grateful. During the *Spirit's* prime as a warship, the deck would have been teeming with twice as many people.

Galleons such as this were known to carry well over four hundred souls when sailing into battle. Once peace had begun to become more of a normality, much of the Zadanese fleet had been converted into trade ships. They carried much, and the cannons provided a much-needed deterrent for any pirates or privateers that might seek to steal their fortune.

Alternatively, he could have been on a passenger ship, surrounded not only by people who were aboard to work, but those who would be interested in socialising, and discussing their plans for their arrival in Balliach two weeks from now.

As it was, if it was not his sister bursting in through the door of his cabin on the berth deck, demanding that they play a game or to cause whatever havoc she so desired—she had horrified many of the sailors with her pranks already—then it was his tutor, Re'Din, intent on making Di'Ath's last few days of freedom completely and utterly boring.

It didn't seem to matter that Di'Ath had spent months preparing for this trip, studying the ways and customs of Ailiar. It didn't matter if he had only spoken in the Ailian tongue with his tutors, forced to become near fluent in such a short time.

It certainly did not seem to mean a thing that Di'Ath was now able to recite several passages from their old, sacred texts off the top of his head.

And what passages they were—stories of cruel, horrid Gods that toyed with elves and humans alike, yet who still demanded reverence and worship. Of them all, Di'Ath's interest lay with Sonlien. The God of Rivers was as close to the Tide as Ailian Gods went.

Di'Ath had stayed up all night when he had first discovered Sonlien in one of the texts Re'Din had assigned for his reading. Sonlien was one of the first Gods to have come into contact with mortals. The god had slid down the side of Mount Wistra, the highest mountain point in Rupaburg, carving a path behind them. Water had followed the carved marks Sonlien left, creating the first river, and bringing fresh water to the parched elves at the base of the mountain.

Apparently, Sonlien wasn't much celebrated in Ailiar. They had become a minor God, standing alongside the likes of Bryha, Goddess of Sunshine. There were no holidays dedicated to them, no temples for devotees to worship them.

Perhaps Di'Ath could change that.

If he were expected to follow the Ailian texts and uphold the teachings of the Ailian Gods, then why shouldn't he push for the erection of temples to the God of Rivers? If he were expected to worship the deities of his bride's homeland, would it not make sense for him to adopt the God closest to his own faith?

Not that he would ever be able to turn his back on the Tide.

But now was not the time to dwell on such thoughts.

He still had two more weeks during which he would be able to proudly call himself Zadanese, and Di'Ath wanted nothing more than to hide away from the soul-crushing, mind-numbing lessons. He wanted to pretend that he was anyone other than the youngest Prince of Zadanai, or the next King of Ailiar.

So, he did what any self-indulgent prince did—he hid. He had made himself a cosy little haven amongst the rope and canvas, wedged in the place where sail yard met mast. He had found peace here, even as the yelling, laughing and swearing of the crew on deck floated up to him. He wasn't directly among the carcophony, and so it did not bother him.

Up here, it felt as though his soul had quieted. The same wind that filled the sails pulled strands of his dark curls from the leather tie at the nape of his neck. Salt coated his lips, and the sun warmed his face. Not for the first time, Di'Ath considered the merits of running away and joining the crew of ship just like this one.

He could jump overboard and use his magic to carry him to the next ship.

His power sang in his blood. The sea surrounding them seemed to call his name, beckoning him ever closer just as the water always did when he was near. It was dangerous to answer that call. He risked losing himself if he let the magic take over.

But he could do it.

It would be all too easy to walk to the end of the yard and simply dive into the waves below. The crew would likely hear the splash, but surely Di'Ath could hold his breath long enough that they would not see him. And then he would be free.

He would be able to construct a new identity for himself and follow a fate carved out all on his own.

It would be so very easy.

He stood and with shoeless feet, he started to walk along the horizontal length of wood that jutted out from the mast. When he made it to the end, he held tightly to a taut rope and leaned over the edge.

The water was beautiful. It was a blue as rich as the silk on his coat, and the depths unfathomable. It continued to call to him, to beckon. The waves seemed to be clamouring over themselves to reach up towards him like hands. His grip loosened on the rope, his hand sliding until he was holding on with only the curled tips of his fingers.

He could be one with the sea if only he would let go.

He could be one with the waves if only he dared jump. The water cared not for marriages and crowns. It did not bend to the whim of kings and queens. It knew no princes, no gods.

It was the Tide itself.

And it would take no more than one small decision for Di'Ath to fall into its depths, to where he belonged. He could be another dark shape, twisting and turning beneath the surface. He could—

Di'Ath frowned.

He was certain that there had not been such a dark shape beneath the water's surface when he had first leaned over to gaze longingly into the salt water. And the sea floor was far too deep for him to see the shadow cast by the ship onto the sand.

Even if the water were shallower, the shape did not behave like a shadow.

It moved independently of the *Spirit*, wriggling, writhing, and growing with each passing moment.

Realisation chilled the very blood in Di'Ath's veins. That was no shadow rising rapidly towards the surface. Shadows did not possess shimmering blue scales that reflected the light. They did not have fangs that glinted white beneath the water.

This was no shadow.

It was a seawyrm—a terrible, monstrous beast that had haunted Di'Ath's dreams as child.

Di'Ath swore. He turned his attention down to the busy deck below.

"*Biyar!*" he shouted the Zadanese name for the beast.

A sailor directly beneath him turned left, then right, trying to find the voice that had called.

"*Biyar!*" Di'Ath repeated. "Seawyrm, to the port side! Brace yourse—"

Di'Ath was interrupted as the ship with struck from beneath. Di'Ath lost his footing, and his body jolted to the side. He flung out his arms in a desperate attempt to grab hold of something—anything—to stop himself from landing painfully on the deck below.

You could land in the water.

Di'Ath grunted as he pulled himself back up on to the yard. He was too close to the mast to land in the water, even if he tried. Not that he should try. Between the beast and his magic, jumping into the water was sure to be his death.

Clinging to the yard, he looked down.

Below him, the crew had been spurred into action. They raced like ants in a frenzy, picking up weapons and securing loose cargo. Igdhraos and saldhraos pushed past their crewmates to get down to the gundeck.

As if cannons would be enough to break through the tough armour the seawyrms scales provided.

Di'Ath swung his body back and forth. Once he got enough movement, he launched himself towards the mast. He hit the wood hard, the breath violently forced from his lungs.

He needed to get down. He needed to get to Sy'da.

It was his fault that she was on this damned ship in the first place. If she died because of him...

He refused to finish that thought.

Sy'da would not die because of him. Even if it meant that she were the sole survivor of this entire ship, if *she* sailed into Balliach harbour without him.

Di'Ath repeated the mantra to himself over and over as he climbed down the mast:

Sy'da will not die because of me.

His limbs began to shake the moment he lost sight of the sea. Without being able to watch the water, he was unable to guess when and where the seawyrm would strike again.

Sy'da will not die because of me.

If he had thought the crew of the *Spirit* had been loud before, that was nothing compared to the cacophony emanating from them now. It was so deafening he couldn't hear the snap of rope beside him. The now unrestrained piece flew back, cracking across his face.

He slipped.

Sy'da will not die because of me.

Di'Ath looked down. It would take too long to continue climbing the rest of the way. He didn't have such time to waste.

He took a risk.

He jumped.

Pain shot through his knees. Di'Ath's body pitched forward, and he stumbled forward. He threw his hands out to catch himself. A male in too-worn boots tripped over Di'Ath's arms and went sprawling on the dark, solid wooden deck.

"I'm sorry," Di'Ath called, standing. "I'm so sorry."

He didn't waste any more time on the downed sailor though. He dove head first into the chaotic frenzy of frantic bodies.

"Sy'da!" he yelled over the clamour. "Sy'da!"

"Di'Ath!"

Di'Ath spun towards the sound of his name. It had come from behind him, he had been going the wrong way. If that decision led to the loss of his sister...

Sy'da will not die because of me.

Di'Ath pushed his way through the crowd and back to the mast. He climbed high enough to see over the heads of the sailors.

"Sy'da!" he yelled again.

"Di'Ath!"

He saw her then, pressed against the railing. She was trying to get to him, but as men and women passed her in their hurried attempts to get to battle stations, they kept pushing her back against the wood. Her eyes were wide with fear, her face unnaturally pale and she reached over their heads towards Di'Ath.

"Help!"

"I'm coming!" he called back to her.

He jumped down and pushed past sweaty bodies. He barely made it three-men-deep before a large shadow fell upon them.

Di'Ath looked up to see the seawyrms jewel-like tail above them. The sun highlighted the veins and bone in the fanned fins on the end, showing a complete spectrum of blue and cream.

It would have been beautiful if dread hadn't taken root within Di'Ath's gut.

He had heard far too many stories of seawyrms cleaving a ship in two. That sight above was often the last of sailors who had the misfortune of crossing paths with the beast.

His power bristled. It fought against the hold he had on it.

A strange, vibrating sort of feeling buzzed around Di'Ath's wrists his magic began to manifest. If he wasn't careful, he could seriously hurt the people pushing up against him.

If you are too careful, you will lose your sister forever.

Di'Ath clenched his jaw.

Sy'da will not die because of me.

"Move!" he bellowed.

He shoved aside the person in front of him. Then the next, and the next. He would push through the entire crew to get to Sy'da if he had to.

But the Tide was not in his favour.

The seawyrms tail came down in an ear-bursting *crash* on the side of the ship. Sailors screamed and the metallic smell of blood overpowered the smell of salt and sea. A young sailor doubled over and emptied the contents of his stomach on his comrade's shoes. Another began praying to the Tide.

Di'Ath continued pushing until he finally broke free.

It was not difficult to believe that seawyrms could cleave ships in twain when he beheld the destruction this one had wrought. A gaping hole stood where the banister had been. The wood of the deck stuck up at odd angles, shattered and cracked. The blood-soaked panels fell in on themselves. Pieces continued to break off and fall into the sea, the splash improbably loud, given the shrieks of pain and fear.

Di'Ath's heart leapt into his throat. How many people had they just lost?

The crew had cleared a large space around the damage, pulling dead and injured crewmates away from the crumbling deck, leaving thick trails of bright red blood.

Di'Ath swore he could taste the iron in the air.

He had been so distracted by the destruction that he had almost missed it—the thin, spider-web lines of ice sprouting from over the edge.

"Sy'da," he breathed.

He surged forward. Someone called his name. Someone called *Your Highness*. Someone reached for him and urged him to stop, but he did not listen. Those slivers of ice meant only one thing—his sister had gone overboard.

And he would not let her die because of him.

His feet slipped on the thick layers of blood. The still warm, sticky substance squelched up between his toes. Splinters of wood burrowed into the soft pads of his feet.

It did not deter him.

It barely slowed him.

"Sy'da!" he yelled.

"Di'Ath!" Sy'da called back.

Di'Ath made it to the shattered bannister and peered down. Sy'da gripped onto the lip of the cannon barrel, ice sprouting from her fingers. Her grip faltered, and she screamed.

"I'm coming!" Di'Ath said. "Hold on!"

"Hurry!"

Di'Ath looked behind him. A coil of rope lay just within reach, like a gift from the Tide. He grabbed it and started to lower it down towards Sy'da until he saw a now-familiar shadow moving beneath the surface of the water.

He lowered the rope quicker.

"Grab it!" he ordered.

Sy'da reached, but slipped. She screamed again, scrambling to grip the cannon with both hands again.

Di'Ath swore.

A mop of black hair poked out from the gunport. A dark hand reached towards Sy'da.

"Your Highness! Take my hand!"

Sy'da reached, straining. Their fingers brushed together just as the sea-wyrm crashed into the ship again. The force rocked the *Spirit* so fiercely it nearly listed.

But Di'Ath didn't care about that. He cared only that the force had sent Sy'da screaming on her way down to the raging waters below.

Di'Ath had no other choice.

The moment her fingers had lost grip on the cannon, Di'Ath knew what he must do. He did not so much as hesitate. With the crew rushing towards him in an attempt to balance the ship and stop it from capsizing, Di'Ath launched himself off the deck and into the sea after his sister.

The water welcomed Di'Ath with open arms.

For a moment that stretched into an eternity, he simply floated – weightless – held in the water's loving embrace. His magic hummed happily in his veins. It reached out to the water surrounding him, caressing the currents with tender affection.

The water seemed to sing in response.

If the fin of the seawyrm's tail had not brushed against him as it swam downward, Di'Ath likely would have been overcome by the overwhelming sensation of *home*.

His eyes flashed open. He twisted, he turned, searching the clear blue water for Sy'da.

Streaks of white caught his attention. He turned his attention downward and found her, beneath him, desperately trying to swim towards the surface. Shards of ice floated upward, passing Di'Ath as Sy'da's magic began to run wild.

She didn't have enough control over her magic yet to be able to control it with so much water surrounding her. Ice sprouted from her fingers. Her voiceless pleas escaped her lips in frozen bubbles.

She needed to stop. If she needed to reign in her magic. If she didn't, she risked not only killing the seawyrm, but herself and Di'Ath in the process.

She couldn't defend herself.

But Di'Ath could. Di'Ath could protect her, he could save her.

Sy'da will not die because of me.

He reoriented himself and swam downward. When he met with Sy'da, she clung to him desperately and tried to pull him toward the surface. But she knew as well as Di'Ath did that neither of them could swim fast enough to outpace the seawyrm.

Di'Ath looked down and saw the dark shape of the beast turning, preparing to propel itself toward them. He looked at Sy'da, then pulled her close and pressed his forehead to hers.

Her eyes widened and she shook her head.

He would not allow her to defy him though. Di'Ath pried her fingers off his coat and pushed her away. Before she could take hold of him again, he released his hold on his magic. The water answered gleefully, creating a current that carried Sy'da swiftly to the surface.

Di'Ath did not have long to relish the pure euphoria that came with releasing the leash he held on his magic until the dark, gaping maw of the seawyrm closed around him.

Sixteen

Calliope

Balliach

Calliope Ailiar was no stranger to being constantly followed everywhere she went. The Bloodmaids had been by her side since her birth—they had seen her take her first steps, heard her first words, and watched as she grew from tiny, writhing babe to the young woman on the verge of marriage and coming into her Affinity.

Unfortunately, Calliope had learned quickly over the course of the last week that being shadowed by someone who was always silent and being unable to get rid of someone who could not keep her mouth shut to save her life were two very different things. In the same vein, Calliope was learning very quickly that she did not possess the capacity for patience that she had once thought.

"They are absolutely fascinating, don't you agree?"

Calliope had already stopped paying attention to whatever nonsense that Lady Jaena Cu'Sar had been spouting. The dull girl had been prattling on ever since they had left Calliope's chambers earlier that afternoon, discussing every last detail of the tapestries that they passed, or the carvings in the seats along the hallway walls. Everything seemed to be of interest, and Calliope did not understand it. She didn't even seem to take a breath.

Perhaps I'll get lucky and she'll stop breathing all together.

Even so, the direct question had pulled Calliope unwillingly back into the conversation. She looked up from the book in her hands over to her blonde cousin, hoping that her displeasure wasn't translated onto her face.

Or maybe she did hope Jaena saw it. Would the other girl care to know that she was unwelcome company?

"I'm sorry?" she asked.

"The Bloodmaids," Jaena said, gesturing to the red-clad woman who stood just within earshot. "They are fascinating."

Perhaps if Calliope had been paying attention, she would have understood what babble of nonsense had led Jaena to such a declaration. But they had walked out here to take advantage of the last of summer's warmth. Calliope had wanted to do nothing thing afternoon other than sit among the flowers and forget all her troubles by reading about the woes of the fictitious.

And Jaena was ruining it.

She had come all the way from Rupaburg purely to ruin Calliope's last weeks of solitude before her betrothed arrived, filling her solitude and silence with useless jabber about fashion and gossip.

Perhaps Calliope should care about those things. Perhaps if she focused on these useless, trivial matters that other girls her age cared about, she wouldn't be so convinced that she had already failed her mother, her crown and her country before she was even old enough to come into her Affinity.

Or maybe, that's just another way you have failed.

Regardless, *fascinating* was not the word that Calliope would use to describe the Bloodmaids. *Annoying*, perhaps. Definitely *creepy*.

Despite having been accompanied by at least one of her mother's personal guard since birth, Calliope had truly been comfortable with the mask they wore. According to Oprianos, Meitranis knew each and every Bloodmaid by name, and was able to distinguish them all from one another.

And not just the twelve that had made it to true Bloodmaid status either—but their apprentices, and the initiates beneath them. There were over two hundred Saldhraos women that all covered their faces, leaving them unrecognizable, and somehow the Queen was able to name each one.

So weird, yes.

Famed and feared, definitely.

But not fascinating.

"Royal families of every country have dedicated guards," she said. "The Bloodmaids are no different."

Jaena rolled her large blue eyes.

"The royal guards in other countries aren't handpicked by the Queen, nor do they all have the same Affinity. It is more difficult to become a Bloodmaid than it is to become royalty if you weren't already born of noble blood. I've read that they are so renowned that they have inspired new religions in the smaller provinces of Ailiar and Rupaburg."

As though we don't have enough gods to pray to, Calliope thought.

"When I was little," Jaena continued. "I dreamed of becoming a great warrior. I loved watching tourneys and jousts, and I wanted nothing more than to be among them rather than simply watching and giving my favour. But in Rupaburg, women do not become soldiers or adventurers. It simply is not done. I thought that I would never see a woman in armour, let alone see one fight, slay beasts, or defend her homeland. Then, I stumbled across a book that mentioned the Bloodmaids."

Calliope focused on a leaf that had fallen onto the blanket they sat on.

It was the opposite for her. Calliope wanted a quiet life, one free of expectation, where she could fade into obscurity. Instead, she was fated to follow in the footsteps of the Queen who had won Ailiar their greatest victory.

"I became fixated," Jaena said. "I was certain that when I came into my Affinity on my 21st birthday, I would be a Saldhraos. I had planned to leave home—on foot if need be—to find the Blood Queen and prove that I deserved an apprenticeship with her Bloodmaids."

Calliope could not envision it.

This waif of a woman, whose ears were just as delicate as the rest of her, did not mesh well with the armour the Bloodmaids wore. She didn't believe that Jaena could so much as lift a sword to save her life.

And she certainly could not imagine Jaena being able to spend the rest of her days in silence.

"Alas," Jaena sighed. "I came into Air instead, and all such dreams were dashed."

Something akin to pity touched Calliope's heart.

For her, there was no doubt that she would come into her Affinity under Earth. All descendants of the Maiden did. It was the only bloodline that had a guaranteed Affinity.

Even the Adarnas spat out something other than a Visdhraos from time to time.

But the Ailian line would always produce a Saldhraos, no matter what Calliope might wish.

"But at least I still ended up here," Jaena said with a smile. "And I cannot think of anywhere else I would rather be."

SEVENTEEN

DI'ATH

ZADANESE SEA

THE TIDE TEACHES THAT death is oblivion.

There are no gilded halls and no endless parties with your ancestors to stretch into eternity. There is no rebirth, no second chance at life where you could right your wrongs and atone for your sins.

When you died under the Tide, there was only darkness and weightlessness as you became one with the water.

From where he currently stood—well, *floated*—Di'Ath Adarna was convinced that whichever prophet had shared this description of death and the ever-after had not actually experienced death in and of itself, but instead had simply been swallowed by a seawyrm. Because otherwise, it meant that Di'Ath was well and truly dead, and he would be well and truly pissed if his own personal ever-after was tainted by the stench of dead and rotting fish. He had not left his life of luxury, women, and gambling to only make it halfway towards Ailiar just to die by the fin of this wretched creature.

And if he was going to die? He was going to bring this beast to the bottom of the ocean with him.

The vibrating, buzzing sensation around his wrists grew stronger. Ropes of barbed water curled around them like Sy'da's bracelets, tearing and ripping into the cuffs of his billowy sleeves.

This is what he had kept such a strong hold on. This is why he had spent weeks in the salt room until he had been able to suppress it on his own. This hungry, needy physical manifestation of his magic that did not melt into the seawater and bile that surrounded him.

The seawyrm pitched downward, no doubt preparing to attack the *Spirit* again.

Di'Ath could not let that happen. He could not allow his efforts to save his sister to be in vain.

His magic sprouted from him like thick, barbed whips.

He had seen whips with sharp, metal spikes braided into the leather on display in his father's collection. It had been an old tool used for punishment, before the Adarna family rose to power by the previous royal family. His father had told him how the whip would shred the skin on a man's back as easily as a fork shreds chicken with each lash.

It was barbaric.

And Di'Ath's magic was no different.

The hungry barbed ropes stretched and lengthened.

They travelled up his arms like reaching fingers, shredding the fabric of his shirt as they climbed. They wriggled and writhed, sentient creatures of their own volition.

Di'Ath had kept it under his thumb for far too long.

He had kept his magic at bay, kept his power subdued and in that dark, quiet place of his soul where it was kept under lock and key. And yet, despite its imprisonment, his magic yearned to protect its master.

It yearned to bite into the muscled throat of the seawyrm that pulsated around Di'Ath. It yearned to rip into the pink, slimy flesh of the beast's innards.

It yearned.

And Di'Ath was no longer willing, nor able, to stop it.

He had already been under water long enough for his lungs to begin aching. There was no air even in the belly of this beast. He needed to act swiftly if he wanted to have any chance of surviving this encounter.

He gritted his teeth and rolled his shoulders in preparation for what was to come next.

Di'Ath Adarna flicked out his arms to his sides. The vicious ropes of water raced down his arms towards his hands, hanging from his grip in the form of ferocious, ravenous whips. The tips sliced into the sides of the seawyrm's throat, the crack echoing as clear in the water as a whale's call.

The creature roared in pain as the water surrounding Di'Ath turned tangy and metallic as blood flowed into it. The seawyrm thrashed, sending Di'Ath careening into the soft fleshy wall of its innards. He cried out, losing precious air.

He cracked his whips of water again. This time, it was not the tips that caught the creature's flesh. Di'Ath cut deep gouges inside the beast. Another earth-shattering, ear-bursting roar erupted around him. His ears rang, and his chest constricted. He needed to end this.

Di'Ath reached inward. He searched for that final restraint he held on to his magic like a glowing, golden rope. It was pulled taut, his power already taking more energy and more life force than was safe.

The problem with having such unique magic was that it tended to have a mind of its own. It behaved like a parasite, its survival contingent on the health of its host and yet too selfish to care for it.

And yet, Di'Ath had no other choice.

He severed that last restraint. The whips grew in length and width, the buzzing sound cutting through the water.

Di'Ath let out a death-defying roar and lashed out in a frenzied flurry of motion, cutting and slashing and tearing at the inner flesh of the seawyrm.

It became a dance, as elegant as dolphins twirling around each other in the wake made by passing ships.

He wielded his magic like a performer wielded ribbon, like a conductor waved a baton.

And, as though he were conducting an orchestra, the magic built to a wonderous, disastrous crescendo. Unable to be contained to mere whips anymore, it burst out of him. The force ripped apart the seawyrm. It sent shockwaves through the sea.

It shot Di'Ath to the surface and into the sky above.

Di'Ath's arms and legs flailed. He could do nothing as he climbed ever higher.

He could do nothing as, eventually, gravity took over and brought the prince down just as quickly as he had risen.

Di'Ath landed hard on the wooden deck of the *Spirit*.

If he'd had any air left in his lungs, it would have been forced out of him with the impact. Instead, he was left with nothing but searing, jarring pain in his spine as he stared up at the fluffy white clouds in the sky and gasped for air like a fish out of water.

People were muttering. He caught snippets of conversation in between the ringing—*dead, crazy, wild, dangerous.*

Monster.

Were they talking about the seawyrm? Or him?

His magic was unique, just as all Adarnan magic was. But while his mother could learn the future in waves, and while the second eldest brother could turn salt water fresh, there was nothing beautiful or helpful about Di'Ath's. It was pure and utter destruction.

He could not help his people in times of great need. He could not give them hope when all seemed to be lost.

He could only rip and tear and kill.

Di'Ath coughed. He rolled onto his side with a groan, stinky, slimy sea-wyrm entrails and dead fish slipping off him and landing with wet slaps onto the deck. The smell was horrendous.

Dozens of legs stepped backwards, away from him.

Di'Ath couldn't blame them. He would have to burn the remains of his clothes—there was no possible way that the stench could be washed out of them. Di'Ath coughed again. Saltwater and blood spewed from his lips onto the deck. They mixed with the innards of the beast as the ship rocked on the waves, swirling together in a putrid swirl of white, red, and yellow.

Di'Ath's stomach churned at the sight, and he rolled over again onto his back.

He had killed a seawyrm.

Not only that, but he had survived.

At least, he hoped he would survive. The pain had not subsided in his back, and he wasn't so sure that he could feel his feet. But there was air coming into his lungs now. It raked sharp, jagged fingers down his torn throat, but it was filling him. It was keeping him alive, even if it were only for the time being.

"Di'Ath!"

Di'Ath's head lolled to the right. His eyes shifted in and out of focus while he watched a blue blob break free from two dark brown blobs. It was only when Sy'da had fallen to her knees by his face and brushed his hair back with cold, soft hands that he truly saw her.

"Hi," he croaked.

"I thought you were dead," Sy'da's voice cracked.

Di'Ath made a sound that he hoped could be interpreted as a chuckle.

"If the Tide wants to kill me," he said. "It will have to try a lot harder than that."

Sy'da smacked him hard on the cheek. Though her hands were nearly frozen, the impact had brought painful heat blooming over the tender flesh.

"What was that for?" he managed.

"For taunting the Tide!" Sy'da hissed.

Di'Ath reached up to take her hand to comfort her, but Sy'da flinched away.

He frowned and followed where her eyes stared.

His magic was still circling his wrists. It was no longer the long, deadly whips that had killed the seawyrm, but it had not withdrawn completely. It twirled and twisted around his wrists, as possessive as it was dangerous.

He tried to call it back. He searched for that golden tether within him, desperate to restrain the power he had set free.

He could not find so much as a fibre

"Sy'da?" he asked with a tremor in his voice. "Sy'da, what do I do?"

Eighteen

Maida

Luvrahn

"How do you usually wear your hair, Dhuina?" Palis asked.

Her fingers combed through the wet curls on Maida's head, tugging more gently than Maida would have ever expected.

In the mirror, Maida watched as the water-darkened strands were pulled straight with each pass of Palis' hand, only to spring back into a coil once the elf let go. Maida wondered if anyone had ever had such a dark shade of auburn growing from their head. If she had the chance, she herself would jump at the opportunity to trade her bright orange for this deep, clay-red. Did elves possess some sort of magic that could make that a possibility? Was there some spell where she could have her hair appear perpetually wet to achieve the look she desired?

She still did not know what kind of magic the elves possessed. She was certain that they did have *something* though. The air was always crisp, the water always clean. The forge was always ready far sooner than she imagined could be possible without the aid of some supernatural interference.

But she had yet to see anything. She had yet to witness magic use with her own eyes, and she wasn't sure that she was brave enough yet to ask.

Perhaps she should. Then, she could ask if she could change her hair.

Or you could know what to expect when the time comes to run.

She shifted uncomfortably in her seat and met Palis' gaze in the mirror.

"I don't know," she said. "I just... pull it back. Sometimes it's with a ribbon, but usually it's with some piece of string or leather."

The expression on Palis' face was such a perfect blend of horror and disappointment that Maida felt heat rise to her cheeks. If Palis didn't have hold of her hair, Maida would have sunk down in her chair.

Maida had never imagined that she could feel shame for something as mundane as her hair. True, she had never worn elaborate styles. She had never learned how to twist and plait her hair in anything more complicated than a three-stranded braid down her back, but she kept it clean. Maida had always loved trying the new soap concoctions that the tavern-keeper's wife, Dana, would come up with.

She still remembered the last bar she had bought from Dana. It had been almost overpowering with the scent of lavender, and Maida had needed to steer clear of beehives to avoid having the darling, buzzing creatures trying to find a new home in her strands.

So why did she feel so embarrassed now?

Had she not done enough?

What else *could* she have done? Maida had no mother to teach her. The town was a two-hour walk away on a good day, and who had she even known well enough to broach the subject with?

It wasn't as though she could just knock on a door and ask the first woman she saw to teach her how to make her hair pretty.

Palis let go of her hair. She walked around and crouched in front of Maida, taking her hands in her own as she smiled kindly up at her. Maida's nose burned as it always did before her eyes started stinging with tears.

"Your hair is beautiful," Palis said gently. "And tying it back is a great way to keep it out of your face when you need to work. We can't have you accidentally stitching tunics with your hair, can we?"

Maida choked out a laugh, and Palis' smile warmed.

"If you like, we can put a few braids in your hair. If we place them just at the top, it will keep the hair from your face, and you can leave the back out. That way, it's practical, and you still get to keep this luscious length and volume. If we style it properly and sew it in with ribbons, it will hold for a while. And you'd look like a princess."

Maida sniffled. She nodded. It was a good plan, and she liked the image conjured in her mind.

But...

Traitorous tears fell. They streamed down her cheeks, wet and hot. Her breath hitched.

"Oh, Dhuina," Palis cooed.

She reached up and wiped away the tears with her thumb.

Maida was glad that Aros had left to run errands.

"What is it?" Palis asked. "What's wrong?"

"I don't know," Maida admitted. "I don't... I never had a mother. I don't know what it's like to have one. So why do I miss her? Why am I mourning all the things that she never got to show me? It's stupid, but right now, all I am thinking about is what she might have done with my hair. Would she have woven flowers into braids while we foraged in the woods for herbs and plants to make dye? Would she have encouraged the length, or would she be an advocate for a shorter style? Was her hair red and curly like mine? If not, where did this come from? My father had straight brown hair, I know it didn't come from him."

She looked down and lifted a damp curl between them. It glistened in the sunlight that streamed through the open window. It looked like luxurious lacquered wood in this light. Like the furniture in the mayor's house, adorned with pink velvet cushions.

"There were a few women with curly hair back home," she continued. "But none of them had hair quite as wild as me. I suppose that is partially my fault. I could have tried to figure out how to tame it on my own. And I have only ever seen one woman with hair close to my shade. I thought I was dreaming. It was the day before I... left... and it had only been in passing. The square was so busy. Everyone was preparing for our midsummer festival, and for a moment, I thought I had run into myself."

Maida laughed again, another harsh, barked tone.

"She wore a hood," she said. "As if trying to contain it, but I know just how impossible it is to hide such hair under something as powerless as a hood. Her curls poked out from underneath like vines in a cave, searching for sunlight."

Maida shook her head. She had never seen that woman before, and she never would again. Like the rest of the people she had ever known, the woman was probably dead. For all she knew, it was her arm that Maida had tripped over.

Maida shuddered. She could still feel the give of the flesh beneath her heel, like mud on a riverbank that had held on its own, but crumbled the moment a modicum of pressure was applied to it. Her stomach clenched, preparing for the fall that wouldn't come again. She lowered her shaking hand to her lap, clasping it with the other.

"Palis," Maida said. "I would be very grateful if you would braid my hair. The way you were planning, with the ribbons and the back out."

Palis pat Maida's knee and stood. She leaned forward and kissed Maida's brow before resuming her position behind Maida.

"This won't take as long as Aros' braids did," she said. "But if you need a break, let me know. Aoife is dying to give you some little berry pies she made."

As if on cue, Aoife rounded the corner with a mischievous look in her eye.

"*Pie time*?" she signed.

Maida's laugh was bright and genuine. She nodded, and Palis threw up her hands in mock defeat.

Palis had been right.

While it had taken two days for Aros' hair to be unwound, washed and re-braided, Maida's hair was done by the afternoon. Aros still had not returned from the errands he had needed to run, so Maida had braved the walk back home on her own.

Home.

It was odd to think of it that way, but it was better than calling it *Aros' Cottage* every time she thought about it. She supposed it was the same as Aros not wanting to call her *the human* and settling on *Dhuina* as a temporary name. That is what it was. Aros' cottage was not her home, but it would serve the same purpose until she could return to her true home.

As she walked from Palis and Aoife's house home, elves stopped in their conversations to turn and watch her. Maida supposed she couldn't blame them. If she had seen a stranger walking through her town alone for the first time, she would stop and stare too. But the attention was too much. She shoved her hands into her pants pockets and kept her head down as she hurried. Once she was home, she was fine. Once she was home, she could take the time to appreciate the crown of braids atop her head that Palis had secured with green and cream ribbons. She could appreciate how her hair now fell over her shoulders in a controlled manner and not as a wild, untameable mane.

Or you could be smart and plan your escape.

Her steps faltered.

Her escape. She needed to plan her escape. Time was getting away from her. She had already been here for nearly a month. That, plus the time she had spent wandering aimlessly in the woods...

Maida picked up her pace. If anyone tried to catch her attention, she didn't notice it. She kept walking, powering forward.

It should have been a relief to find that the cottage was empty.

Why did her heart sink when it discovered that Aros was not home yet?

She shook the thought from her head. At least if she was alone, she would have time to think. To plan.

She went to the small set of counters and hearth that constituted a kitchen. She pulled out flour and took water from the bucket Aros had brought in from the well that morning and set about mixing dough for bread.

It would keep her hands busy while her mind worked.

She thought about what she would need to survive the journey back: warm clothes, sturdy boots, and food. Her pack was propped up against the foot of the bed. If she could get her hands on a needle and some thread, she could mend the holes, and it would be sturdy enough to get back home.

She needed a waterskin. And probably some furs to keep away the worst of the chill.

She took a deep breath and poured her dough onto the counter. She began to knead.

Maida needed to find the tanner. No one would question why she wanted a new pair of boots. She was currently wearing an old pair of Palis', and they were too large. Maida needed to wear three pairs of socks just to keep them from slipping off her feet or causing her blisters.

It made sense that she would want a pair made to her size, whether she planned on staying here or not. And a waterskin? That was a necessity if she were expected to spend any time outdoors – and Palis seemed fairly adamant that she spend some time outdoors.

She continued kneading.

But once she got home, what would she do?

The town was gone. Everyone she knew was gone. Had her father survived? He hadn't been home when she woke that day, and she found no sign of any life in Silktide.

Not that she had stayed long to find out. Perhaps she had been too hasty and had left survivors behind.

Perhaps her father was out there, looking for her.

What if he's not? What if you leave here, go back, and find nothing? What then?

Could she stay here? Could she ever feel comfortable enough to live amongst elves?

The village wasn't that much different from what she had known growing up. She could hear birds singing, just like she had back in her cottage. It was a new thing to hear children playing outside, but perhaps she would move closer to town if she did go back.

If?

When had it become a matter of *if*?

She frowned and returned the dough to the bowl and covered it with a worn-through hand-towel, setting it aside to rise.

This was horrible. Palis, Aoife, and Aros were being too kind to her, and it was messing with her head. Elves were horrible, terrible creatures, and they were just waiting for their moment to strike.

The door opened violently, and Maida yelped. In her surprise, she lashed out with her arms. She hit the bowl hard, and she cried out in pain. She turned towards the door, pressing her back against the counter as she reached behind herself in search of something, anything, that she could use as a weapon to defend herself.

Her hand closed around a rolling pin just as Aros stepped inside, eyes wide. "Dhuina?" he asked.

His voice was laced with concern. It had Maida's stomach doing backflips and her heart skipping every third beat.

"Oh, thank Strea you're alright," Aros said. His shoulders were tight, even as his words seemed to hint at relief.

As though he had been worried about her.

"Hi," Maida said.

"Hi," Aros replied.

The two stared at each other for a long moment until finally, Maida broke eye contact to set aside the rolling pin. She rubbed her aching hand.

"I was just about to put on some water for tea," she said. "Would you like some?"

Aros nodded. He did not move from where he stood, and his eyes did not leave her for a second. Maida could feel the heat of his gaze with every move she made. She could hear how controlled his breathing was.

In for four counts, out for four counts.

In. Out.

Was he trying to calm himself?

Was he worried that she had hurt herself? That someone had gotten in and was hurting her?

Was he worried that she had left?

Maida pulled the smaller of the two cauldrons off the hook and set it on the ground. Then, she picked up the bucket and poured water into the cauldron. It was not until she had returned it to the hook over the coals that she realised that the fire was not lit, and as such, the water would not boil.

"I..." she said, colour rising to her cheeks again.

"It's okay," Aros said. "I'll get it started. I got you something."

Maida spun on her heel, the loose curls fanning out around her.

"You did?" she asked. "Why?"

Aros raised a brow and cocked his head to the side.

"Did you just ask me *why* I got you something?" he asked.

Maida looked down at her too-big boots and shrugged. "So, what if I did?"

Aros chuckled. The sound sent warmth spreading throughout Maida's entire being. If only she could boil water with the heat that his laugh brought to her body.

"I suppose there isn't really any argument to that," Aros said. "Anyway, it isn't much. I honestly didn't even really know what I needed to get or what you liked, but after finding out that you were a seamstress, I thought maybe you might appreciate this."

Aros handed the package out to her.

Maida hesitated before taking it. She carried it over to the dining table and sat down. It was wrapped in crinkling brown paper that not only bore the markings of measurements but had so many defined creases that it was certain to have been used many times over.

Careful not to be the one to destroy such a long-lived wrapping, Maida peeled back the paper while Aros crouched down and set about lighting the fire.

Disturbed by the movement, a bobbin of thread fell out of the package and rolled across the table. Maida lunged forward and grabbed it, barely stopping it from falling over the edge. She lifted it, turning the polished wood and cream-coloured thread over in her hand. It was the most beautiful bobbin she had ever seen, and the thread itself was of impeccable quality.

She set it down with a soft *thunk* and returned to the rest of the package.

A pair of shears and a plump pin cushion overflowing with pins and needles sat atop a piece of the softest linen she had ever held in her hands.

Her eyes watered.

"If there is anything else you need," Aros said, voice slightly muffled from being turned away from her. "Please let me know. As Palis said, there are plenty of artisans here in Luvrahn, and we can get our hands on most things. Deija said that this would be the safest bet until I knew what colours you liked. And she said that you could dye it anyway, that she had everything that you would need to do whatever you wanted with it but this would be a good start."

Aros was refusing to look at her. His back and shoulders were tense, and he was having more trouble than normal getting the fire started. Was he... nervous?

Was he worried that she wouldn't like the gift?

"She's right," Maida said. "I can dye it. I know how. I used to dye our fabric at home. And there's that field of dandelions out near the kapriae's paddock. If I harvest them before they die, I'll be able to dye the linen a lovely pale yellow. Plus, we can eat the leaves. Palis will be thrilled."

Aros snorted a laugh, but he still did not turn to face her.

She didn't know what possessed her to do so, but Maida stood. She moved around the table, returning to the kitchen to stand at his side. After a moment's hesitation, she bent down and wrapped her arms around his shoulders. The pine scent of him enveloped her again, and she buried her face against his freshly braided hair.

Aros reached up to hold her arm. He squeezed gently.

Just how was she supposed to run away now?

NINETEEN

AROS

LUVRAHN

THE WHIMPERS HAD BEEN soft at first.

They had begun so quietly that Aros had almost dismissed them entirely, all too eager to write them off as some creature outside that did not warrant his attention at such a late hour. The day had been long, spent chopping wood for the entire village in preparation for the coming winter. Tomorrow, he would carry bundles of the split wood to Dorsa's house, where Windra would use her Affinity over water to draw out the moisture before he distributed it amongst the townsfolk.

He was tired, and he wanted to rest as much as he could before the sun rose and he caught another early start.

Yet before he could settle to sleep, the soft whine that he could have believed had belonged to a mouse gave way to something far louder, and more desperate.

Before Aros could sit up, Dhuina's cry of terror filled his cottage. It felt thick, and tangible.

"Dhuina?" he called out to her.

Dhuina thrashed beneath the layers of fur on his bed. She wailed and begged. She pleaded for whatever horrors that plagued her in her dreams to end. Dhuina's breath came out in heaving, rasping sobs, and whatever was in her dreams did not allow her to hear Aros as he called out her name again.

It felt like moving through mud as Aros stood and crossed over to her bedside. No matter what he did, no matter how he reached out to his Affinity and tried to take control of the air, it would not clear. He couldn't understand it, and that scared him more than his inability to take control.

"No!" Dhuina said, her voice threaded with desperation.

Aros reached his hand out to her.

Dhuina tossed in her sleep again. The back of her hand slammed into his cheek with such force that he tasted blood. Aros bit back a curse before he took her by her shoulders and shook to wake her.

"Dhuina!" he said. "Dhuina, wake up! It's just a dream!"

He shook her again, and this time, Dhuina's eyes flung wide open. She stared through him, her chest heaving. Dhuina reached forward and gripped his shirt, closing in tight fists around the fabric. He leaned forward enough to ease the tension her grip created.

"Dhuina?" Aros asked.

Slowly, Dhuina's eyes focused. They darted from side to side, as though unsure which of Aros' to settle on. Tears streamed down her cheeks and her breath hitched.

"Okay, okay," he said. "It's going to be okay. I've got you."

"They're gone," Dhuina's voice cracked on the words, mirroring the cracking within Aros' heart. "They're all gone."

He had seen horrors beyond his wildest dreams, but Dhuina's distress had set a chill coursing through his blood and setting in his bones. He felt like a failure for not being able to protect her.

His brow furrowed.

He lifted her chin with his thumb and forefinger, coaxing her to look at him. Shining, evergreen eyes finally met his, and Aros was struck by how familiar they were. It was not just the fact that she had lived in his home for the better part of two months, nor was it the haunting gaze of the collateral of war—the look of those who had been left behind in all the death and destruction as those in power squabbled over Gods knew what. That moment, when Aros looked into Dhuina's eyes, he felt as though he had known her for centuries.

Her chin quivered in his hold.

"They're gone, Aros," she sobbed.

"Who's gone?" he asked.

"Everyone."

The admission seemed to shatter the dam, and Dhuina broke out in body-wracking sobs. Her breath became staggered heaves. She kept breathing in and in and in, seemingly unable to release the breath she held.

"Hey," Aros crooned, sliding his hand up from her chin to cradle her face. "Hey, listen to me, you have to breathe. Breathe with me, Dhuina. In, and out."

Dhuina still did not let go of her breaths. She opened her mouth, but no words or air came out. Her puffy eyes seemed to beg him for help.

Unsure what else to do, Aros did the only thing that he could think might help. He climbed onto the bed with her. Aros settled himself behind her, bracing himself against the cool wall. Wrapping his arms around her waist, he pulled Dhuina towards him and held her head against his chest.

"Focus on my breathing," he instructed.

Slowly, deliberately, he breathed in, held, and then breathed out.

After a few more shallow inhales, Dhuina finally exhaled. After a while, her breathing was as steady as his, save for the odd hitched breath. At least, that could be expected. At least that could be managed.

Aros stroked Dhuina's hair. Curls had come free of her braid, and he twirled them around his fingers in between gentle, careful pats of her head.

He held her silently, letting her take as much comfort as she needed.

He would not let go, he decided, until she was ready to pull away.

He counted time in heartbeats until those heartbeats stretched into minutes. He remained there, stroking her hair and letting her tears soak through his shirt like they had the night he had found her. How many more tears would his shirts endure before she lay in his arms without tears?

It doesn't matter, he told himself. *She could decide to never let me touch her again, and I would not complain.*

Aros was a male of honour. If he had anything left in this life of his, it was that. But even so, a secret part of him replied:

Liar.

By the time Dhuina moved, Aros had begun to think that she had fallen asleep. His hold on her loosened, expecting her to pull away. Instead, Dhuina pulled her knees to her chest and tucked herself against him.

"Are you alright?" Aros asked softly.

Dhuina shook her head.

"Did you want to talk about it?"

She was silent. Aros could hear the *click, click, click* of her picking at her nails. It was a habit that he wasn't sure she was aware she had, something that she did when her mind was racing. Unlike holding the pendant, which she seemed to hold when she was thinking—and those were two very different things.

"When you found me," Dhuina said eventually. "I had been running."

Aros frowned. That much was obvious. No one—whether human or elf—took off into the woods without the proper equipment unless they were running from something. But the way she worded it, he couldn't help but hear *I was on the run* instead.

"What were you running from?" he asked.

He rubbed her arm, both to warm and comfort her. Whatever it was, he would keep her safe.

"Home," Dhuina replied. "I guess. I suppose it's more like I ran from what happened."

"What happened?"

Aros' voice was soft, yet stern. He wanted her to feel comfortable enough to share this information with him, but by the same token, he was not about to stay unspoken between them. He was certain that whatever this secret was, whatever moment was haunting her, it was the key to understanding her.

To understanding why he felt so completely and utterly drawn to her.

Dhuina sniffed. She reached up and roughly wiped away the tears from her cheeks only for more to fall. Aros brushed the fresh tears away with his thumb until her cheeks were dry.

"I don't know exactly what happened," Dhuina said. "I don't know how it started or how everything just changed within a matter of hours. I don't know if it was an accident or by design. But the whole town—the *whole town*, Aros—was burnt to the ground."

Aros frowned. He didn't understand.

Villages, especially human ones, burned to the ground enough that it did not seem enough to warrant running. Migrating, perhaps, if the blaze was big enough and rebuilding seemed out of the question, but *running*? And on your own, into a country of beings that you had been conditioned to fear?

"I had always hated how Silktide smelled of fish and salt," Dhuina continued. "Whenever I went into town, I made sure to keep near the bakery, because the smell of the bread and pastries overpowered the fish when the wind was right. But I... now I cannot even conjure the memory of how horrible it had smelled before. Whenever I think about my home, all I can smell is..."

She trailed off. Her expression twisted into one of pain and despair.

"All I can smell is burning flesh. How is it I can have lived my whole life two hours from a town that reeked of fish and not remember the smell, and yet now, here I am, three months away from *one gods-damned day*, still plagued by the knowledge that charred human flesh smells like sweet, roasted meat?"

Dhuina had stopped picking at her nails. The lack of sound caught Aros' attention, and he looked down to see that she had gripped her legs. The long tunic she slept barely covered her knees while she sat as she did, and he could see her nails biting into the pale flesh of her shins. He gently took her hands in his, threading their fingers together. It was an effort to ignore the thrum of electricity that passed through them.

"Sometimes," he said softly. "Our mind decides to be cruel and will remember things that we would rather forget. I, for one, have many memories that I wish time would take from me. Unfortunately, we do not have control over what we keep in our minds and what we do not."

Dhuina's hands closed around Aros'. He felt the press of her nails in between his knuckles.

"You must think I'm a monster," Dhuina croaked. "For describing it that way. For calling it *sweet*.

Aros shook his head. He ran his thumb over the back of her hand.

"You are not a monster," he said.

Because if she was a monster, then he was one as well. War was never a pretty sight, and once you factored in the magical Affinities of the elves, it was all but guaranteed that one would experience finding the scent of burning flesh in the air. It had taken decades for Aros not to be caught off guard by the smell of meat on the battlefield.

"I was supposed to be in town that day," Dhuina said. "It was the day before our mid-summer festival. Eoin, the baker's son, had asked me if I would go with him. It was the first festival that I would ever attend with a boy."

She let out a short, mirthless laugh.

"Most girls my age would have spent time with a handful of boys already, but my father and I lived so far out of town that it wasn't something that was ever in the cards for me. Even if we lived in the town itself, or just closer, my father had always been a little overprotective on that front. He seemed to just get worse as I got older too, which I never understood. I thought fathers wanted their daughters to find suitable matches."

Aros' jaw tightened. He didn't understand the rage that was building within his chest as he imagined Dhuina being courted by another. Not only did he have no claim on her, but they had both had a life before meeting the other. He'd had his fair share of romances before leaving the capital. He had once loved a woman so deeply that he had sworn an oath to put down his life for her.

And he couldn't possibly love Dhuina. He barely knew her. You couldn't fall in love with someone in less than two months... could you?

Dhuina sniffed. She adjusted herself, tucking her head under Aros' chin.

He closed his eyes.

"Anyway," she continued. "I had planned on waking up early to meet Eoin and his family to help them set up their stalls for the festival. I wanted to make a good impression on his family, seeing as Eoin had made it clear that he intended to court me officially. I was so excited. I had so much energy and nowhere else to put it but into my work. So, I picked up a gown that I had been making for myself to wear on the last day of the festival. That was the day that Eoin was planning on asking my father for his permission to court me, and I wanted to look my best."

Another pang of jealousy pierced Aros' heart, just as inexplicable as the first. It wasn't as though she were here, in his bed, by choice. She was here merely from circumstance. When she had the chance, she would leave him.

She's had the chance, that secret part of him said.

"I stayed up well past sunset," Dhuina carried on, unaware of the Aros' internal conflict. "I burned far too many candles, and I had not even made it into bed. I fell asleep at the dining table, using the dress I was working on as a pillow. And my father... well, he was already in town. He was staying with friends that had commissioned work from him, so he was not there to remind me to go to bed that night, nor to wake me the next morning."

Her breath hitched again. Aros applied a little more pressure where he was rubbing his thumb on the back of her hand, and Dhuina's breathing evened out once more.

"So," she said, the word drawn out slightly, as if unwilling to continue her tale. "I didn't end up waking until close to noon. Once I did, I ran the whole way. It's so far, but I still wanted to help Eoin and his family. I didn't mean to sleep in, and I really didn't want to make a bad impression. But... by the time I got to Silktide, everything was gone. Not a single building remained. It was like a fire had been raging out of control for months, not just one night. I don't understand how it was possible. I was there the day before, and there wasn't even a hint of a fire. But the next day, Silktide was nothing but ash."

It was time for Aros' mind to race.

Theories were beginning to form in his mind, and he did not like that each one of them seemed to involve elves going on a rampage, hunting humans for sport. But what other explanation was there? Dhuina had been right—there was no way an entire town could be reduced to ash in one night. Significant damage, yes, but complete and utter destruction? No survivors?

It was like he had stepped back in time to before Meitranis had ascended to the throne. Before Meitranis, many elves had held the lives of humans in low regard. There were some who still thought that just because their lives were short, it meant their lives were expendable. Even in the Great War, the human armies were not taken seriously.

And the way the town had been effectively wiped from the map?

That sounded far too much like the work of a fire-wielding Rupaburgan elf that Aros was far too familiar with. A sadistic, immoral female who cared only for the opinion of one other—an equally dangerous male who thrived on death and destruction.

But it couldn't be them. Not with Meitranis on the throne and a Rupaburgan King by her side. Not even *they* would dare to break the peace brokered by the Blood Queen's union with their brethren.

There had to be some other explanation that he couldn't see yet.

"Your house wasn't burned," Aros said. "Why didn't you return there, then? Why did you run into the Edgeling Woods?"

Dhuina's laugh was dark and mirthless. It sent a chill down Aros' spine, and he shivered.

"And do what?" she asked. "Wait until death claimed me some other way? I know how to forage, and that would last me for a time. But I don't know how to hunt. I would have a season and a half to prepare for winter, and that is not something that I could do on my own. Besides, my father made me promise that if anything were to ever happen to him, I would run eastward. He said he had friends to the East that would recognise this—" She touched the pendant at her throat. "And they would help me. I thought that he was speaking nonsense, but still, he had not been home when I woke. And I couldn't find him in the ruins. So, I did as I was told. I got a little excited when Aoife had taken an interest in it, but it turned out to just be a dead end."

Aros didn't understand why Dhuina's father would send her east. If his memory served him correctly, Silktide was the easternmost settlement in Colosia and it was the closest to the border. Where had he thought he was sending her?

"Is that what you saw in your dream tonight?" he asked.

Dhuina nodded. "Yeah," she said. "Tonight, I saw it burning. It was like I was standing in the middle of the blaze, watching as everyone I ever knew burned to death, while I remained untouched. Sometimes, I just see it as I did that day—piles of ash and smouldering rubble. It doesn't really matter though. Every night, I trip over the same limb."

She sighed and shook her head. The friction between her hair and his stubble scratched the underside of his chin.

"But as though that weren't bad enough, my mind has decided to be a complete and utter dick and has added thunder to my dream."

Aros tensed beneath her. "Thunder?" he asked.

"Yeah," Dhuina said with a yawn. "And it doesn't make sense. It wasn't raining that day, or the night before. It had been dry for a week. Maybe it's just some weird way of my head trying to convince me that there wasn't anything that I could do to stop it, you know? Because thunder usually means rain, right? And rain would have stopped the fire. But there was no rain, in my dream or in real life, so... I don't know."

"What kind of thunder was it?" Aros asked.

"Hmm?"

"What kind of thunder? Was it rolling thunder, like a summer storm, or was it sudden, and violent?"

Dhuina thought about it for a moment before she answered. "The second one. It was almost like a cannon. But I know it wasn't a cannon. I don't know how to explain the difference. It was... sharper, almost."

Dhuina did not need to explain the difference. He knew it well enough to pray that he was wrong. He shifted to bury his face in the top of her hair. The rose-scented soaps Aoife had washed Dhuina's hair with filled his nose.

He didn't know how long he sat. He lost track of time before Dhuina's breathing began to slow.

"Dhuina?" he asked, voice muffled against her hair.

"Hmm?" she replied sleepily.

"How long were you in the Woods for?" he asked. "You said it's been almost three months since then. But you've been here just over two."

Dhuina yawned and pressed closer.

"Twenty-three days," she muttered, before sleep finally claimed her.

TWENTY

ANIAIJA

THE SEA BETWEEN SEAS

THE SEA BETWEEN SEAS did not seem to take heed of the seasons of the outside world.

It was a vast, barren wasteland that occupied the majority of the southern half of Ailiar. While it was theoretically traversable by foot or steed, it had been common practice to sail across the dunes with ships to shorten the journey and reduce the chances of coming across the subterranean monsters that lurked beneath the surface. Much like the true sea, the Between was home to a myriad of deadly creatures.

Sandwyrms in particular thrived in the harsh climates that the Between offered. These cousins of the sea- and swampwyrms spent the long summer months buried deep beneath the dunes, tunnelling beneath the sand and multiplying. As soon as the temperature turned and a chill took hold of the air, they began to rise to the surface, terrorizing anyone foolish enough to still be on their territory.

After ten long years, the crew of the *Mercy* still preferred the horror that came with watching the sands shift as one of the large creatures barrelled towards them just beneath the surface over the stifling heat.

It was autumn and they had passed close enough by the shore to see the trees turning their colours confirming what their calendar had already told them. The nights should not be anywhere near as hot as they were.

And yet, the crew spent their nights tossing and turning in their hammocks. Their sheets were regularly discarded in tangled heaps on the floor, making it impossible to identify which belonged to whom.

Not that it really mattered.

There was no chance that anyone still possessed the blanket that they had been issued when they had first come aboard, and everyone had accepted early on that it did not do to dwell on useless sentiments such as the ownership of linens.

There were far more important things to spend their time worrying about.

Like whether or not they were going to survive the coming winter.

As she lay sweating in her hammock, stripped down to nothing more than thin linen breeches and a tunic that had been half-sacrificed to make bandages so that it barely covered her breasts, Aniaija's mind was racing. They had lost another life. Their crew was dwindling, and she had heard the grumblings of dissent beginning.

She couldn't blame her crewmates.

They were never supposed to sail upon the Between. When Geomar sent out his recruitment flyers, every soul who had answered had been prepared to spend the next few decades sailing across the world, searching for adventure. Aniaija had planned on staying with them until they made land at Ters. Why? For the simple fact that she had never before stepped foot on Tersyk soil.

She had been born in a small farming village in Zadanai to a Zadanese mother and a Rupaburgan father. Her parents had decided to move their small family to Ailiar when Aniaija was too young to remember anything of her homeland. She had been raised in the capital of Ailiar, the city of blood itself, and returned to Zadanai shortly after she had come into her Affinity.

But Aniaija hadn't felt like she had returned home. She couldn't help feeling that the Tide itself had turned its back on it. Aniaija had spent months agonizing over whether it had been her Affinity that had caused her to feel so adrift from the religion of her forefathers.

So, she had returned to Balliach. She had barely stepped off the ship that had carried her across the Zadanese Sea when she had laid eyes on Reina, and then...

Well.

Aniaija didn't like to think about what happened next, but it had been enough for her to join the crew when Geomar had put out the call. After Reina, there was nothing to keep Aniaija tethered to Balliach.

She had stood on the deck, watching the elves on the dock waving towards their departing loved ones, unable to shed so much as a single tear for the city that had raised her.

Perhaps that was why she had been able to see it before anyone else. Perhaps that was why she had been the one to call upon her Affinity and redirect the cannonball that had been fired towards the *Mercy* from the bay's defence.

In the end, Aniaija supposed it didn't matter why she had been the one to stop that first cannon from sinking the *Mercy* right there in the bay. She had been able to redirect its trajectory so that it put a hole in the front of the ship.

Her cry had been enough to spur the others into action, and with the combined efforts of the near 800 crew and their families, they had been able to guide the *Mercy* south and onto the Between.

And now—now they were sweating their asses off, despite the breeze that the Aerdhraos were circulating through the sleeping cabin.

Now, Aniaija was staring up at the hammock above hers, wondering if this were to be their last season.

Unable to stand it any longer, she rolled out of her hammock. Feet bare, she weaved in and out of the maze of hammocks and piles of sheets until she found the stairs leading up to the deck. The air up on deck was no better than it was below, and she bit back a groan of frustration. She didn't know why she had dared hope for anything different. She knew better.

They all did.

Still, she stretched her arms above her head as she crossed over to the prow, gazing out over the horizon.

They were close enough to the westernmost edge of the Between that she could just make out the light of the moon glistening on the surface of the true sea.

Her heart ached to be so close, and yet so far. She longed to feel the roll of real waves beneath the *Mercy* again, instead of the slip and drag of the vessel through sand. She didn't care if it pushed her back down the rungs of the ladder again. She would gladly give up her position as Captain Geomar's second in command if it meant that they could dock again. She would walk into Di'Tyan's gilded halls with her head held high if it meant that her crew could stock their stores and get their hands on enough timber to mend the hole in the hull.

But it didn't matter what she wished, or what she would give.

Neither the *Mercy* nor its crew were welcome on Ailian soil, and without major repairs, they could not sail elsewhere.

For reasons beyond her comprehension, the very Queen who had gifted her former Admiral the flagship of her fleet had declared them traitors to the crown. Any attempt to sail into a desert port resulted in the near-death for them all.

A small group had once taken a lifeboat and rowed towards a shore with no town nor pier to speak of.

Aniaija still recalled their screams as they had been slaughtered by waiting soldiers.

They were stuck.

At least they had found the Oasis. The rocky outcropping in the centre of the Between had been a godsend. The tunnels provided protection from the elements and from monsters like the sandwyrms. It had been enough for those with families to find some relief. But it could not support them all. They could not grow crops there, and they relied on the *Mercy* to keep food and resources sufficiently stocked.

But the *Mercy* struggled to support those who lived aboard, let alone in the haven that housed its most precious cargo.

It had been months since they had come across a ship passing through the Between that had not borne the crimson sword of the Queen, and they would not risk attempting taking such a vessel. But tempers were wearing as thin as the clothes on the sailors' backs and Aniaija wondered, not for the first time, if she should have just let that cannonball hit its mark.

Her mind would certainly be calmer if they were at the bottom of Balliach harbour.

"You aren't moping, are you?"

Aniaija squeezed her eyes shut and tipped her face up towards the moon. Had she been so deep in thought that she hadn't heard Dapsa approaching? She never failed to notice when Dapsa was anywhere near her. Aniaija could pick out her footsteps in a crowd of thousands. She saw her smile in her dreams, and heard her laughter in every sunrise.

But this time, Dapsa had managed to sneak up on her.

Aniaija was determined to never let that happen again.

"You should be asleep, Dapsa," she said. "You have a busy day tomorrow."

Dapsa snorted. She leaned her back against the railing, standing beside Aniaija. A heady mix of plums and black powder enveloped her, and Aniaija drank it in greedily. How Dapsa managed to smell so nice while stuck on the same ship for more than a decade with limited bathing opportunities was beyond Aniaija. She would not question such a miracle, however, lest it cease.

"*We* have a busy day tomorrow," Dapsa corrected her. "Don't tell me you were trying to concoct some plan to get out of doing inventory with me."

Aniaija barked a laugh.

"Of course not," she said. "But I know that you cannot so much as count your own toes when you don't get enough sleep. I, on the other hand, am quite capable of functioning on next to none for weeks at a time."

The feat was entirely due to her golem, Tobie. Aniaija had spent the better part of a year collecting stones from different riverbeds and roadsides until she found the ones that were absolutely perfect. Then, she had spent weeks arranging them into the right configuration, including using shards of selenite in the place of whiskers.

Finally, Aniaija had spent three days funnelling energy into the cat-shaped mound of rocks and stones, until finally, it began to move. Tobie's first meow had frightened Aniaija so much that she had screamed.

Unfortunately, Saldhraos golems were inherently designed to protect their creators. Unable to understand that *she* had scared Aniaija, Tobie had leapt onto the girl's lap. The extreme use of magic and energy used to create the cursed thing had caused Aniaija to pass out. It had taken weeks for her to regain her full strength again as the golem fed on her energy, further establishing itself as a sentient being. Eventually, the golem was able to sustain itself, and shortly after that, it was able to perform its sole function:

To be a virtually limitless source of energy for its creator.

But Aniaija was trying to make a point, and she would not remind Dapsa of her unfair advantage.

Dapsa chuckled again. The sound was low in her throat, and it sent shivers down Aniaija's back despite the rivers of sweat coating her skin.

"Uh-huh," she said. "Whatever. What are you doing out here anyway?"

"Oh," Aniaija said with a careless wave of her hand. "You know, growing daisies."

Dapsa nudged Aniaija with her elbow. Aniaija opened her eyes and looked at her. The moonlight lit up the fraying edges of the scarf Dapsa wore to cover her hair. She looked every part a goddess, as they were captured by great artists. Even Dapsa's strong, proud nose was ethereal.

Dapsa was a Zadenese beauty.

And she should not be stuck here, trapped on a ship-shaped prison.

Dapsa's eyes softened.

"I'm being serious, Ani," she said softly. "What's wrong?"

Aniaija chewed the inside of her cheek before she sighed and slumped over the railing.

"I just... I don't know how much longer we can continue doing this. Our crew is breaking. It's been ten years since we have seen so much as a blade of grass, or held fresh, fertile soil in our hands. I know how close I am to giving up, and that terrifies me, because if I'm that close, what does that mean for everyone else?"

Hot tears fell onto already hot cheeks.

"Every time we go down to the sand, every time we bring back another crewmate, I feel myself unravelling just that little bit more. I feel like just one strong headwind will catch a loose thread and pull me undone completely. I was never supposed to become Geomar's First Mate. I was never supposed to be second in command. How can I lead our crew when I no longer know what direction I am facing? How can I assure them that we will one day be able to go home when I no longer believe that myself?"

Her breath hitched, and Dapsa rested a comforting hand on her arm.

Aniaija squeezed her eyes shut again at the contact, trying to ignore the heat of her touch. She wanted to shake it off. She wanted to grasp it in her own hands.

She did neither.

"We all know that you and Geomar do not have any more information than the rest of us," Dapsa said. "We know that neither of you possess some divine magic to tell us when all of this will be over. But we also know that neither of you will lead us astray, no matter how many storms we are ordered to sail into."

Aniaija opened her mouth to protest, but Dapsa put her finger over her lips.

"And when you do not have faith in yourself," Dapsa said. "Just know that I have enough of it for you."

Aniaija's tears flowed freely then. Dapsa pulled her into her arms, and for a glorious moment, all Aniaija knew was plums and black powder.

"How are we looking?"

Aniaija looked up past Dapsa to Geomar from her nest of crates and barrels. The two women had been hunkered down in the ship's stores for hours, after finally managing to fall asleep under the stars, propped up against one another. Despite the lacklustre sleep and the ache in their bodies from sleeping in such an odd position, they had woken just as the sun had appeared over the horizon.

After a quick breakfast of stew and biscuits, they had gotten to work sifting through the reserves of grain, fruit, and dried meat.

Skipping lunch, they had progressed to the stores of alcohol and medicine, which was where Geomar had found them.

If the food stores were poor, this was worse.

"Well, it's not great," Aniaija admitted.

"It's abysmal," Dapsa corrected. "We need to find another ship, and we need to find them soon. We can't return to the Oasis with this – it's barely enough to sustain the crew for more than a couple of months."

She pulled a face then added: "So long as we do not have another fever outbreak."

Geomar rubbed his beard. Sand dislodged from the wiry grey curls to fall to the floor, earning him a glare from Dapsa.

"We *just* cleaned," Dapsa grumbled.

Aniaija stifled a chuckle. As much as she enjoyed seeing Dapsa get testy with others, she wasn't going to risk having that ire directed towards her.

"We can tighten rations," Geomar said. "Stretch everything out a little further."

"Rations are already tight, Geomar," Aniaija said. "We've only been able to make what we have last this that long because we're already eating barely half of what we need. The crew won't accept further restrictions. They're tired and hungry."

"We are all tired and hungry," Geomar countered. "But we cannot refuse to do what needs to be done, just because we do not want to risk upsetting people. As my second, you of all people should know how important it is to focus on the needs of your crew, not their wants."

Aniaija unfurled herself from where she had been awkwardly seated. She set down the ledger and pointed towards the wall, gesturing towards the crew in general.

"They are at the end of their tether, Geomar," she said. "We are lucky we haven't already had a mutiny on our hands."

Geomar raised a brow.

"A mutiny?" he asked. "And where would they go once they took control of the ship, huh? Every single person aboard this ship knows that it is not just me who is being hunted down by Meitranis' men. It is the ship itself; it is the crew themselves. Let them overthrow us. Let them throw us in the brig. The worst that will happen is they will run out of rations and come crawling back for us to shoulder the responsibility and to make the hard choices."

Geomar stepped forward, and Aniaija swallowed hard.

"When I offered you your position," he said, voice dropping dangerously low. "I asked you if you could handle making the tough decisions. You promised me that you could."

"I can," Aniaija said.

"Good, now—Di'Tyan's hairy ball sack!"

Dapsa tried to stifle a laugh as Geomar jumped backwards, arms flailing. Tobie had jumped up on the crate next to Aniaija. Her deep, rumbling purr echoed in the too-bare storeroom.

Aniaija chuckled and reached out to scratch Tobie behind her ear.

Even after all these years, scratching something made of stone still felt odd. She could feel the grating of her nails in her very bones. The sensation shot right up her arm, straight to her teeth.

But despite her discomfort, she would not stop giving the feline all the love she deserved. She would not waste all the time sacrifice that had gone into the golem's creation, especially when success happened so rarely.

"I still have no idea how in the world that thing is so quiet," Geomar said. His chest rose and fell a little too heavily.

Aniaija couldn't ignore the pleasure she derived from seeing it.

"I think you're just losing your hearing in your old age," she said.

"I'm not that old," he grumbled.

"You were old when I first joined your crew. You're practically an Ancient One."

Geomar turned to Dapsa as if seeking her help. Instead of offering anything of the sort, Dapsa held up her hands in surrender.

She wasn't going to get involved in this.

"Bah," Geomar said, waving his hands dismissively. "You're both as bad as the other. And just so you know, missy, I still have a few leagues left in me yet before I become one with the sand and sea."

A dark emotion flittered behind his eyes. Aniaija chewed her lip while Geomar took a deep breath and cleared his throat.

She had seen that look before, when they burned their lost ones. She knew Geomar had always planned on being given to the sea when he died. She couldn't imagine what it must feel like to him, the old sea dog, to have something he had planned on doing for so long be so cruelly ripped from him.

"We will discuss the rations after dinner," he said. "Come up with something suitable. It will make the idea more palatable to the crew."

He nodded a goodbye to both Dapsa and Aniaija before turning and climbing out of the storeroom.

"I'll be back," Aniaija said.

She clambered over the crates, sacks and barrels and followed the captain outside. She caught him heading to the helm.

"Geomar?" she called out to him.

He looked at her through scraggly silver hair. His blue eyes looked pale and haunted.

"When it is your time," Aniaija continued. "I won't burn you. I won't let you burn like the others. I don't care if I have to steal a raft and drag your sorry ass all the way to the water on my own. I promise you on my very soul, that your final resting place will be the sea. It's where you belong."

Geomar's shoulders sagged. It was heart-wrenching, to see a man who had always been so proud brought so low.

Aniaija wondered if Geomar's mood had something to do with being so far away from his Affinity's element. She knew that she felt lost and untethered when she spent long stretches at sea. However, she had never gone a decade without being surrounded by her Affinity's element. Did Geomar feel untethered? Did he feel like he was walking through mud? Through swampland?

Did he feel like he had to fight for every breath?

"Thank you, Aija," he said.

Aniaija's heart ached at the rarely-used nickname.

"I truly do not know where we would be today if it had not been for you," Geomar continued. "You have saved us more times than I can count. I am eternally grateful to have you as a member of my crew."

"You would be dead," Aniaija said with a half-hearted grin. "And at the bottom of the ocean. Though I suppose that would make my promise redundant."

"You're not wrong there," Geomar chuckled.

He took a deep breath and straightened.

"There will be a ship crossing the Between after the Wishing," he said. "It should be carrying trade from the southern provinces to the mainland—the last before the ships stop for the winter. If we intercept it, we should have enough food to last us and the Oasis until spring."

Aniaija chewed her lip.

The Wishing was an Ailian holiday celebrating the goddess Oliantra. Oliantra was the goddess of pathways and revelations, and as autumn gave way to winter, the elves of Ailiar would pass on their gratitude for the year that had been alongside their wishes for the year that was to come.

The ships sailing through the Between after the Wishing would be carrying the last of the harvest for the year.

It was their last hope of any sort of chance of surviving the winter.

There was only one problem.

"That ship is going to belong to the Queen," she said. "It's going to have her soldiers on it."

"It's the only shot we have," Geomar said. "Our only other option is to accept certain death. I don't think the crew will go for it, though. Do you?"

Aniaija tried to rack her brain for an alternative. She tried to think of something—anything—that they could do instead of attempting to take on a royal ship.

Even if they could get away with it, even if, by some miracle, they survived, they would still need to tighten their rations between now and then. It was almost a full season until the Wishing.

She could only hope that they would come across something soon, and pray that the crew would view the potential prize as something worth even more sacrifice.

"And look at it this way," Geomar said, a devious grin twisting his mouth. "With the Wishing having just taken place, there will be no risk of Meitranis being on board. And no Meitranis means no Bloodmaids."

"*Fine*," Aniaija agreed through gritted teeth. "But we are not going in without the full support of the crew. And we are not going in without a plan."

Geomar's grin widened, and Aniaija felt regret sink its claws deep into her.

Twenty-One

Aros

Luvrahn

WHEN AROS C'ASAD HAD first found Dhuina in the Edgeling Woods, he had experienced the strange sensation of a weight settling in his gut.

It was not the weight of finding a lone stranger in the woods, days from certain death. It was not some anxious gnawing in his belly that could be linked to his years as a hunter, warning him to be careful of wounded creatures and the dangers they posed when cornered. Nor did it feel like the centuries he had spent leading the Queen's armies into battle.

The weight had felt like responsibility.

It had felt like oath if he were being honest. Like one of the many soul-binding oaths he had once sworn to Meitranis, Blood Queen of Ailiar.

Anyone could make a vow, but an oath?

Among elves, oaths held power. They held a special kind of magic of their own that was separate from the elements, unaffected by ones Affinity.

They were eternally binding, severed only in death.

Or if the pledgee willingly released the pledger.

I, Aros C'Asad, vow to always protect you, Meitranis Ailiar.

Aros had upheld this oath more often than any other. More than once, he had almost lost his own life in battles that he should have otherwise walked away from unharmed, simply because he had been bound to keep her alive.

He had tried to defy the pull of the oath only once.

It had ended with his cheeks stained with tears of blood and a twisted, wretched scar over his heart.

But Meitranis had remained unharmed, and Aros could still remember the feel of her pale, soft fingers smearing the blood over his cheeks as she looked upon him with such gratitude.

I, Aros C'Asad, vow to always serve the crown.

Once the words had left his lips, Aros no longer had control over his own mind when it came to matters of war and state.

If Ailiar declared war, Aros was powerless to refuse the fight.

If Meitranis had ever ordered him to marry for the sake of their country, he would not have been able to say no.

Aros always made sure to thank Oliantra for not leading him down that path and sparing him from such a fate.

I, Aros C'Asad, make this vow to the heir that I will guide her to her rightful place.

This oath had never come to fruition. The heir, Princess Calliope, had not been born until decades after Aros had been relieved of his duties and released from his vows.

Perhaps that was a good thing.

He could not imagine what the future of Ailiar would look like if he were responsible for preparing the heir to take the throne.

Aros could still hear the Queen's voice in his mind when he thought back to the day Meitranis had released him of all the oaths he had pledged to her.

"*I, Meitranis Ailiar, release you from the oaths that you have made both to myself, and to the crown,*" she had said.

The sudden lightness Aros had felt had made him feel giddy. He had been living with the weight and burden of responsibility that the oaths had placed on him for so long that to have them suddenly lifted was a stranger sensation than feeling them settle in the first place.

Aros hoped to never again feel that weight. It was why he had moved to the southern provinces which left him several weeks' travel from the capital. If he were any closer, he was sure to crawl back to the Queen's side.

And yet, when he had lifted Dhuina into his arms, the feeling that had settled in his gut and upon his shoulders had been so similar that he could have sworn he had just made another oath without realizing it.

It was probably nothing.

It had to be nothing.

He had been spending too much time thinking about Dhuina's wild, flame-coloured hair – a similarity, Aros had realised, that she shared with the elven Queen. His realisation must have played tricks on his mind. There was no other explanation – an elf could not make a binding oath with a human.

Still, the weight was uncomfortable, and Aros did not like how it seemed to pull him towards her whenever they were further than a few paces apart from one another.

And now, after she had revealed what horrors had led her to him, Aros was loathe to leave her alone. He wanted to turn around, return to his cottage, and climb back into that bed beside her. He wanted to hold her close to his chest. He wanted to keep her safe. He wanted to listen to her breathing slow as she fell asleep and feel her hand close around his tunic in her dreams.

But there was a voice in the back of his mind that kept insisting that there was more to this story, and Aros felt compelled to discover just what that was.

So after sharing a silent breakfast together, once Dhuina had set herself up at the table with her cloth and thread, Aros had walked out his door and down the path towards Aoife and Palis' house.

His feet hit the path too hard. His breathing was too loud. His teeth ground against each other in a way that made his head ache.

He needed to be told he was wrong. He needed to know that the sound that Dhuina had described (*like cannon fire, but sharper*) was not what he was imagining. And only Palis would be able to talk him down. Only Palis could make him see rationally.

Because surely, it couldn't be *him*.

Aros knocked on the door with unintended urgency. He shook his hand while he waited for the answer as though the movement could relieve some of the tension that had built within.

When the door swung open, he was greeted by a puzzled-looking Aoife.

"*Aros?*" she asked, signing his name.

"Hi Aoife," Aros' voice was breathy, his hands signing along with his words shakily. "Is Palis home?"

"*She is,*" Aoife replied. "*Are you alright?*"

Was he?

Of course, he was. It wasn't Aros who had been forced to flee his home upon finding it destroyed. It wasn't Aros who had no idea if there were any survivors. He had not spent the last few months reliving the horror of it all every time he closed his eyes.

So why did he feel this overwhelming sense of urgency? Why did he feel like Maida's dream had caused *him* to feel such worry?

"I am fine," he answered. "But I don't think Dhuina is."

Aoife pursed her full lips and nodded. She stepped back, gesturing for Aros to enter. Once Aros had crossed the threshold, she closed the door behind him. Aoife led him into the kitchen, past the hanging quilts that Dhuina had so admired.

Palis sat at the table, dressed in nothing more than a patchwork dressing gown secured with a tie around the waist. Her long fingers curled around a cup of steaming tea as she read from a small bound book.

Aoife walked over to the pot of water hanging over the hearth and set about making two more cups of tea.

"You are here rather early, C'Asad," Palis said, a teasing tone to her voice. "Have you come to tell me that you cannot handle our dear Dhuina anymore and beg me to take her in?"

She looked up from her book, and her smile fell immediately. Her brow knit together; her book fell to the table. She stood, eyes searching his face for answers.

"Aros," she breathed. "You look as though you've seen a ghost."

"I think Dhuina has," he said. "Or, rather, I think she has seen a ghost from *our* past. One we had both hoped we would never see again."

TWENTY-TWO

CALLIOPE

BALLIACH

THE SEAMSTRESS HAD ARRIVED early in the morning, shortly after Calliope had finished her breakfast of toast and bacon. It was customary for a new gown to be commissioned for the Wishing.

Moira and her assistants had brought bolt after bolt of exquisite fabrics in varying shades of red, green, and silver into Calliope's suite. Rolls of ribbon and lace of every colour imaginable were draped over every available surface, and Calliope was certain that every last inch of her body had been measured at least three times over.

She took some comfort in the fact that she was not the only one being subjected to such scrutiny. Beside her, a teenaged-looking assistant with mousey-brown hair measured the length of Lady Jaena's outstretched arms. In the past, Calliope would have had her measurements taken alongside her mother, but for now, she was subjected to less enjoyable company.

As Calliope had discovered was her usual way, her cousin was chatting unceasingly. How the seamstress' assistant kept a pleasant smile on her face the whole while was beyond Calliope.

Though, she supposed, at least the assistant is being paid to listen to the nonsensical ramblings.

"This," Lady Jaena said, continuing the one-sided conversation that Calliope managed to more or less ignore. "This is one of my favourite parts about parties and balls. You know what? I think that aside from the dancing, I might go so far as to say that it is *solely* my favourite thing about parties."

As Jaena sighed happily, Calliope cocked a brow.

"You enjoy being poked and prodded by pins and needles?" Calliope asked.

Crouched at her feet, Moira offered an apologetic smile up at her as she continued to push pins into the cream-coloured muslin. Calliope had not been pricked yet—today, at least—but she still tensed each time a new pin was added to the fabric.

The memory of the needles' sharp sting was still very present in her mind from the last time she had been visited by the seamstress.

"No," Jaena laughed, the sound carrying like chimes on the wind. "I love looking at the fabrics. I love wondering what kind of miracle the seamstress is going to perform. How can someone take a length of fabric and turn it into a ball gown?"

She gestured with a perfectly manicured hand to a bolt of fabric in a shade of the deepest forest green Calliope had ever seen. The colour would complement Jaena's complexion perfectly. Her hair would practically glow against the dark hue.

There would be no question of her turning heads at whatever function she wore it to. Perhaps such a gown would have men asking Oliantra for Jaena's hand as part of their wish for the new year.

"How can you look at this and know that if you cut it in just the right way and stitch the right stitches, it will be completely and utterly transformed into one of the most beautiful dresses the world has ever seen?" Jaena asked.

"It takes a lifetime of studying," Moira offered. "I spent my childhood watching my father cutting out what I thought were just simple shapes. But whenever he pinned them to the dress form, they always draped in such a beautiful and delicate manner that I swore his Affinity was some sort of thread magic."

Jaena's eyes widened at the thought.

"Could you imagine?" she asked. "Thread magic! Carpenters would not have the time to make anything other than wardrobes if thread magic existed."

Perhaps there would be an entirely new profession, Calliope thought. *Carpenters who specialized in creating only wardrobes.*

It was a novel thought. How many more people would have luxurious gowns, or tunics lavishly embroidered? It would become difficult to distinguish the rich from the poor if one could make beautiful garments with magic.

The cotton and flax fields would certainly be unable to meet the surge in demand. Sheep farms would be working themselves to the bone to breed enough sheep to be able to shear the required wool. Silk farms would certainly drive silkworms to extinction.

It was for the best, Calliope decided, that thread magic did *not* exist.

"Even so," Moira said. "There is still a certain kind of magic in knowing how different fibres behave. It may not be an Affinity, but it is no less magical. You also need to learn a lot about bodies. Each one is different, and no dress is going to sit on two people the same way. You must understand that to make any sort of garment that will truly complement the wearer."

The cousin and the seamstress continued their discussion, and Calliope deemed it acceptable to allow her mind to wander again, hoping it would do so aimlessly. Perhaps that she would stumble across memories of her childhood, when her mother would sit with her in the garden outside the Hall of Queens.

Instead, her mind decided to land upon thoughts of her betrothed.

What kind of clothes did *he* wear? The portrait she had of him showed him in royal regalia. The jacket was of a rich, ocean blue and intricately beaded. The collar appeared stiff, covered with delicate, metallic stitches that made up intricate golden swirls.

Did he wear similar things when going about his day-to-day? Would he think that her gowns, with the boned, conical bodice and heavy layered skirts, were too formal and stuffy? Would he prefer loose, airy gowns of chiffon and tulle, like those that Jaena wore?

And what did her mother think of the match?

Aside from the evening when she had been summoned to her father's study to be informed of the union, Calliope had not seen her mother at all. Calliope had turned to Meitranis and received a solitary answer:

The decision is final.

"Apologies for interrupting," Calliope blurted. "But Moira, have you seen my mother for her dress yet?"

The seamstress fell silent for a moment. She shared a glance with the mousey-haired assistant before turning a sad, tight smile toward Calliope.

Calliope wanted nothing more in that moment than to slap that pitying look off her face.

"I have, your Highness," Moira answered. "As you know, her Majesty plans her gowns well in advance. We began working on it the day after the Wishing last year. The final fitting was last week."

A cold weight settled in the pit of Calliope's stomach.

"You have been meeting with the Queen for a year?" she asked.

"I have met with the Queen every second week over the last year, yes," Moira said. "There was, of course, an extensive planning process. We made many versions of the gown to ensure that it truly reflected Her Majesty's vision."

Calliope's eyes stung.

She lifted her head, refusing to let the tears form, let alone fall. She had barely seen more than a glimpse of her mother in the past year and this woman, this *seamstress,* saw her regularly.

What had Calliope done?

Why did her mother no longer wish to see or speak with her? How could she have failed so miserably before she even had the chance to prove herself?

"Do you have enough to work on my gown elsewhere?" Calliope asked.

"I..." Moira looked first to Jaena, then to the Bloodmaid by the door. "Yes, your Highness. We are done for today. Are you sure you are happy with the fabric you chose?"

"It's fine," Calliope said. She held her arms out, and the seamstress' assistant worked quickly to take the muslin off her body. Once down to her undergarments, Jaena assisted her in redressing. At least having her cousin thrust upon her meant that Calliope didn't need to worry about other noblewomen being so close to her or within her private quarters.

It took too long for the seamstress to leave. There had been far too many people in Calliope's suite for far too long, and she was quickly becoming reduced to nothing more than a nervous ball of energy.

Once again fully clothed, Calliope perched on the bench seat beneath one of her windows, staring down into the bailey below. She picked at her nails as the yards of fabric, lace and ribbon were packed up.

She could not even remember which of the fabrics she had decided on. Perhaps she had chosen poorly, and Moira had been giving her a chance to change her mind.

Oh well, she thought. *It's too late now.*

She just wanted everyone to leave.

After a moment that felt like an age, Jaena plopped herself down like the damned fool she was.

"Are you not excited?" she asked. "I know it is still weeks away, but I love the Wishing. Will the prince be here in time?"

I sincerely hope not, Calliope thought.

Jaena did not give her enough time to answer.

"Isn't it so romantic?" she continued. "To celebrate the beginning of a new era with the one with whom you will be spending the rest of your life? You could wish upon the Star of Oliantra together."

Jaena smiled wistfully. Calliope rested her head against the cold pane of glass and closed her eyes.

It did sound romantic.

It was, perhaps, one of the most romantic things you could do with someone. Oliantra was, after all, unofficially the Goddess of Love. *Officially*, she was the Goddess of Paths, but her counsel was often sought out in romantic affairs, and new brides regularly visited her temple leading up to their wedding.

But as romantic as it may be, as worthy of all the love sonnets and poems, Calliope did not want to share her wish with the prince.

She did not want to stand beside anyone up on that balcony on the last day of autumn, save perhaps the Queen. But her mother had made her wishes alone since Calliope was eight years old, and with the growing distance between them, there was no indication that this would change any time soon.

Especially if the Zadanese prince were to arrive in time. It would be expected that Calliope and Di'Ath make their wishes together.

"Their ship is expected to arrive that very week," Calliope said quietly. "My father is certain that Prince Di'Ath will be in attendance. Father is planning on introducing him to court during the celebrations."

Jaena hummed as she sank into a mirror of Calliope's pose. Calliope stole a glance at her, and wondered if she looked even remotely as serene as Jaena did. Jaena looked like she needed only a frame to be one of the great masterpieces mounted upon the wall.

"I wonder what the prince will be like," Jaena mused. "He looks ever so handsome in his portrait. He looks brave and strong, with just the right amount of mischievousness."

Calliope frowned. She lifted her head off the window.

"You can see all of that in one portrait?" she asked.

Jaena grinned and twisted to reach for the portrait of Prince Di'Ath on Calliope's desk nearby. She brought it between them.

"Of course," she said. "The artist is really good. At first glance, it appears like any other royal portrait, doesn't it? The prince is sitting tall, he looks dignified. But there is a light in his eyes that betrays the jovialness that I am certain he carries."

Calliope took the small, framed portrait in her hands. It had been half covered in parchment and lace doilies before Jaena had pulled it from her desk. She inspected it closely, desperate to find that light that Jaena spoke of.

If she did, perhaps she would not think so poorly of this match.

Either Jaena was lying, or Calliope was blind.

"Regardless," Jaena continued. "I am certain that the two of you will fall madly in love the moment you meet, and the story of your union will carry on for eons after your passing."

Calliope could not disagree more.

Twenty-Three

Di'Ath

Port of Kei

It had taken days for Di'Ath to regain any semblance of control back over his magic. Even now, as the mysterious coral-guarded island state of Kei grew closer, Di'Ath could still feel damp rings around his wrists, like the blisters and scars left by iron shackles.

Di'Ath tugged his embroidered coat sleeve down again. He couldn't seem to bring them down far enough—as if the silk and cotton could hope to stand up to the power of his magic anyway.

He sighed and stared at the lush island ahead.

Di'Ath had only ever read the name of this place on a map. There were no books in the Zadanese library about the island, nor was it mentioned in any of the oral histories that he had heard. And yet, when Captain Py'Ques announced that they would be veering off course to repair the ship and re-plenish supplies at Kei, Di'Ath noticed that the faces of a concerning portion of the crew blanched. He had been curious, of course. However every time he asked someone about their impromptu transshipment port, he received some variation of the same:

"I can't spare time for ghost stories, prince."

"I have to get this rope down back."

"I have to relieve the crew below deck to keep the water out."

Di'Ath had wanted to scream. He wanted someone to just simply stop what they were doing and tell him what he wanted to know. He was a prince, after all. A prince shipped off to another country to fulfil his duty to his own, nonetheless—did this not afford him the luxury of being listened to whensoever he demanded it?

But no.

Not even Di'Ath the Dutyless could bring himself to throw a tantrum at being ignored. Not when it had taken the efforts of every soul on board to keep the *Spirit* afloat. Even then, they had almost ended up stranded when the water became too shallow, and the reef too treacherous. Every last Visdhraos, save for Di'Ath himself, had fed their magic into the ocean to raise the tide and bring the ship over the sharp, vicious coral and rock.

If they had not taken on so much water during the seawyrm attack, perhaps they would have made it over. As it was, by the time they had limped into port, the *Spirit* had taken on so much damage that the beam between the dock and the ship had no angle to it at all. Di'Ath eyed the level plank suspiciously before crossing it, a pack slung filled with the meagre remains of his possessions slung over his shoulder.

The seawyrm had gifted the rest to the sea.

The sound of his boots clunking on the wooden pier melted into the cacophony of the docks. Shouts of sailors aboard other ships rang through the salty air, the voices occasionally giving way to the lapping of the waves against the wooden pier and the cracking of the rigging of a nearby ship. Children called out to fathers returning on small fishing boats. Women in clusters wove nets on large crude frames. They leaned forward and whispered amongst themselves as they stared and pointed at the unexpected arrival.

None of this was out of the ordinary.

Di'Ath had spent enough time in the ports of Wylden to know that this was par for the course. Even the stares were expected. Any unknown ship brought the possibility of conflict or disease. Even in the busy trade season, Di'Ath had watched in fascination as the dockmaster had identified each vessel that had come into the harbour.

And besides, he would be likely to stare too if a ship with a great hole torn into the side of it arrived, towing the tail of a seawyrm behind them.

What did surprise him, however, was the mix of humans and elves. While one could expect to encounter maybe one or two humans in their lifetime, the population here seemed in balance to that of the elves. As Di'Ath waited for Sy'da to catch up with him, he noted that not only did the citizens seem mixed, but the families as well. Round-eared fathers picked up knife-eared sons. Elven youths coerced rambunctious giggles from human teens as they walked by.

Was this why the island state was so secretive? Was this what the crew had been so scared of?

Human and elf relationships were not forbidden by any means. Some older generations did not look too fondly upon the intermingling of the two races but it was not a common enough sentiment to warrant *paling* at the mention of the island, right?

Sy'da finally found him. She elbowed him, then gestured towards the end of the pier where Captain Py'Ques was deep in conversation with a much taller elf male. The two appeared to be engaged in an argument while trying to appear as though they weren't. Py'Ques twisted and gestured towards Di'Ath and Sy'da. The Keien elf narrowed his eyes at the Adarna siblings.

"I have a feeling we aren't exactly welcome here," Sy'da said.

"Maybe they just glare at you to tell you how ecstatic they are to see you," Di'Ath said with a shrug.

Sy'da snorted a laugh. "We might want to keep our sarcasm to ourselves if we want to survive our stay here," she said.

Di'Ath was inclined to agree. The stares that they had received earlier had turned colder the longer they stood on the pier. It sent shivers racing down Di'Ath's spine.

"The princess is right," said a sailor to Di'Ath's left.

He had long hair crusted with sea-salt and more than a few missing teeth. For the life of him, Di'Ath could not recall his name.

"The people here are a superstitious bunch," the sailor continued. "Every current, every wave means something to them. The fact that we are here when we aren't supposed to be might very well be interpreted as a portent of doom. So don't you two go wondering. Stay close to the crew. Too many people get lost on this island."

"When I asked around earlier, no one seemed to know anything about this place," Di'Ath said.

"Because they don't," the sailor replied. "Those that do, keep their mouth shut."

Di'Ath frowned. "Alright," he said. "You said they read the sea and the current. Do they follow the Tide?"

The sailor shook his head. He readjusted the sack slung over his shoulder.

"No," he said. "The people here follow their own gods. Neither the Tide nor the Ailian Ancient Ones have a single follower among those who call Kei home. But you keep that nose of yours out of places it don't belong. You're more likely to meet their gods than receive answers about them, if you catch my meaning."

The sailor nodded, and carried the sack down the pier, plopping it down unceremoniously by the captain and his companion.

Surely the sailor hadn't been serious. There were religions in the world that required such sacrifices, but Di'Ath had always found such beliefs to be rather stupid. How could a god expect to keep amassing worshippers if they just kept killing themselves?

"My prince!"

Di'Ath looked up to see Captain Py'Ques facing them again, waving him over.

He shot a look to Sy'da. His sister nodded.

"I'll be fine here," she said. "Can't be stolen to be a sacrifice surrounded by our own crew now, can I?"

Di'Ath shook his head and joined the captain and the Keian.

The Keian was an imposing man. He was taller than Captain Py'Ques and just as broad. Di'Ath felt like a child standing so close to him.

His magic thrummed in his blood, readying itself to jump out and cut the elf down to size if need be.

"This," Captain Py'Ques said, clapping Di'Ath on the shoulder. "Is the man that slew the beast that tried to send us down to the bottom of the ocean. If it were not for him, we would be one with the Tide right now."

Heat rose to Di'Ath's cheeks.

He hoped that it was not enough to burn through the complexion that the Tide had gifted him with. Standing more than a head shorter than the Keian man had been enough of a blow to Di'Ath's ego; he did not need to advertise his embarrassment.

The Keian man's eyes raked over Di'Ath appraisingly. Di'Ath focused his attention on the man's pierced, pointed ears and nose so strong it could almost be mistaken for Zadanese. To Di'Ath's disappointment, the Keian man's blue-black gaze gave away nothing to suggest whether he was satisfied with what he saw.

"It takes a man of great power to destroy a creature such as a wyrm," the man said with a voice as rough and raw as thunder rolling over the sea. "There are stories of such men, and how they use their power to either protect the world or destroy it. Which one are you, I wonder?"

A lump formed in Di'Ath's throat. His mouth was too dry. Di'Ath felt the need to avert his eyes in every fibre of his being. How was it so hard to hold this man's gaze?

"I did not take the life of the *biyar* lightly," Di'Ath admitted. "Given the opportunity, I would have preferred to let the creature live. Perhaps I would have let it kill the entire crew if it had not been for the fact my sister was aboard. Even when it had swallowed me whole, my only thought was to ensure it would not go after her."

Py'Ques shifted his weight beside him. Di'Ath wondered what that revelation had stirred within the captain. It can't be easy to know that the reason you still drew breath only made it so in order to save the life of another.

In the end, he supposed it didn't matter. Whatever reaction the captain was experiencing was his own responsibility.

The Keian man nodded at Di'Ath.

"Many men would brag about such an accomplishment. And yet here you are, lamenting a decision you were forced into making at a moment of certain death. I hope you will treat this second life you have earned with the reverence it deserves," he said.

After another moment of appraisal, he held out his hand.

"My name is Ilme," he said.

Di'Ath took the man's hand and shook it firmly.

"Di'Ath," he introduced himself. "I am sorry that we had to meet under such circumstances. As I am sure our captain has told you, we are in no shape to continue our voyage. We shall be as little an imposition as possible. We will pay handsomely for timber and any labour your people are willing to provide."

Py'Ques grumbled something Di'Ath did not catch. If Ilme had heard it, he ignored it. Ilme appeared to ignore him completely.

"Well met, Di'Ath," Ilme said. "I appreciate your apology, however if these were not the circumstances, then we would not have met."

Di'Ath's brow furrowed slightly. He was unsure what to make of the riddles in which Ilme seemed to speak. It was not as though the words were a lie. However, there was something about the way they had been said that did not sit comfortably with him. He couldn't place exactly what it was, and he would not stoop so low as to accuse a man of something he could not name. And yet Di'Ath could not shake the fact that there was something peculiar about his new acquaintance.

"Come," Ilme said, still addressing Di'Ath directly. "Your crew must be exhausted after navigating the reefs. Unfortunately, there will not be enough room at the Inn to accommodate everyone, so we will have to reach out to some of the residents to secure enough lodging."

"*My* crew are no strangers to roughing it," Captain Py'Ques said, emphasizing his ownership. "We will make camp if need be until we can be certain that we will not drown by sleeping aboard the ship."

Ilme raised his shoulders in a slight shrug. The sun glistened on the sweat that covered his tanned skin. "That may be the case," he said. "However I can tell you that the people of Kei would take offence if they felt their hospitality were to be found lacking."

The corner of Di'Ath's lips curled upward at the unspoken threat. How fortuitous that Di'Ath had been warned to be careful, yet the captain was on the verge of making a dangerous blunder that could threaten them all. While the captain was adept at traversing the sea, it was clear his diplomacy skills still needed work.

"We appreciate the hospitality, Ilme," Di'Ath said, hoping to smooth over whatever damage Py'Ques had caused. "And if there is anything we can do to assist the people of Kei while we are here, we are more than happy to help."

Ilme bowed his head to Di'Ath.

"It is appreciated," he said. "Now come. I will take you to the Inn."

Di'Ath returned the motion before he looked over his shoulder. When his eyes met Sy'da's, he motioned for her to join them. Sy'da pushed through the gathered, waiting crew and skipped over to them. Her smile was as bright as the sun, and she bowed her head respectfully to Ilme.

"Ilme," Di'Ath said. "This is my sister, Sy'da."

"It is an honour to meet you," Sy'da said. "Your island is beautiful."

Ilme dipped his head in return. "Thank you, Miss Sy'da. We do take great pride in our home. But let us get you settled. Perhaps then we can show you more of our island."

Sy'da beamed in delight. Di'Ath's brow rose. After the sailor's warning, Ilme's openness to share the sights of the island with them was unexpected.

You're more likely to meet their gods than receive answers about them, if you catch my meaning.

Would accepting a tour be subjecting themselves to an early grave?

Now was not the time to question the intentions of the elf whose mercy they were standing before. Now was the time to follow him as he led them off the pier, through the docks and towards a two-story Inn that overlooked the harbour.

Green paint peeled away from the swollen wood. Thick vines with vibrant pink flowers curled up cracked columns. Sand covered most of the first two steps leading up to the doorway. A bell rang as Ilme opened the door. The chime brought a smile to Di'Ath's face.

It felt cozy. Welcoming.

The longer he spent on this island, the less he understood the fearful faces of the sailors.

"Mr. Talts," Ilme said to an ancient, round-eared human behind the desk. "We have some guests that will be requiring room and board. What do we have available?"

Mr. Talts looked over Sy'da and Di'Ath in the same appraising manner that Ilme had looked over Di'Ath earlier. And, just like Ilme, Mr. Talts appeared to ignore the presence of Captain Py'Ques in favour of giving his attention to the former.

"We have six rooms available," Mr. Talts said. "How many were we hoping for?"

"We have a crew of a few hundred," Captain Py'Ques said.

Mr. Talts snorted. "We have a few cots that we could bring into the rooms. But you're only going to fit maybe eight to a room if they are comfortable sharing beds."

"We will give one room to the Prince and Princess," Ilme said. "The crew can discuss amongst themselves who will be staying in the rooms, who will stay downstairs by hearth, and who will be boarding with families."

Mr. Talts turned a frown in Ilme's direction, but he did not protest. Instead, he slid off his stool with a groan and reached for one of the keys that hung from the line of hooks behind him.

"You sort the rest," he said to Ilme. "I will take these two up to their room."

With a painful slowness that made Di'Ath want to dart forward and offer his own body for support, the human rounded the counter. His legs were bowed. The soles of his shoes were worn on an angle from years of walking in that stunted shuffle.

"I'll see you soon," Ilme said. "We will have dinner together, and discuss what is needed to have the ship repaired and ready to sail again."

"Thank you, Ilme," Di'Ath said, bowing his head.

Ilme nodded and turned to lead Captain Py'Ques back out of the Inn.

"Follow me," Mr. Talts said.

Di'Ath looked over to his sister, who merely shrugged. He reached out, and together they made the slow ascent to the second floor of the Inn behind the hobbling Innkeeper.

Twenty-Four

Di'Ath

Port of Kei

Di'Ath leaned out of the window of the small room he and Sy'da had been assigned. The air smelled of salt and fish, peppered with a rich floral note that he could not quite place. It wasn't necessarily unpleasant, but he would not be seeking out candle makers to recreate it any time soon.

The view, however, was one that he wished he could etch into his mind forever.

Their room was situated on the right-hand side of the Inn which was perfect for those who could not decide whether they wanted to watch the harbor in front or the jungle behind. Even from here, Di'Ath could see the kaleidoscope of colour that was the reef through the crystalline, clear waters. He could see the clusters of bright pinks and yellows beneath the water's surface, marred only by spots of blinding white as the slowly setting sun reflected off the crests of small waves and ripples.

Di'Ath had even convinced himself that he could see schools of fish from where he was, darting in and out of the coral and swimming away from small dinghies and swimmers.

Yet as beautiful as that sight was, Di'Ath's attention was drawn in the other direction. He had lost track of time while watching loud, colourful birds dart in and out of vibrant green tees. He could only imagine the strange and unusual beasts that were making the haunting, nightmarish calls from deep within, hiding behind vines and too-smooth tree trunks. Would there be giant cats, like the large saber-toothed centyen in Zadanai? Would there be small but ferocious monkeys, swinging from branch to branch?

His mind ran way with him, conjuring up dozens of questions that begged to be answered. And, although the sailor's warning still rang in his mind, Di'Ath found himself eager to search for those answers.

"How long do you think we'll have here?"

Sy'da's question pulled Di'Ath from his thoughts. He turned his back on the window to face her. His sister sat on the bed, brushing through her long black hair. She had changed when they'd first arrived, and her pink skirt and blouse fit in wonderfully with the flowers Di'Ath had seen blooming along the edge of the jungle.

She seemed to fit in wherever she was, Di'Ath realised.

He envied that. Envied how easily Sy'da seemed to be able to adapt to her surroundings while he had felt like a fish out of water the from moment he had turned twenty-one and come into his Affinity.

Perhaps that explained why the lure of water was so strong. Perhaps that was why Di'Ath was so eager to jump ship and hope that he would wash upon the shores of something *other* than what was in store for him.

Perhaps that was why he was considering running deep into the jungle and never returning.

"I don't know," Di'Ath replied. "I guess it depends on how much the locals are willing to help. They don't seem particularly pleased that we are here, so they may be motivated to supply any and all resources they have to get us off their island. By the same token, they may be just as likely to watch us struggle to fix it ourselves."

Sy'da sighed and threw herself backward onto the bed. The bedframe groaned in protest, and for a moment, her eyes widened in fear. Fortunately—or unfortunately, Di'Ath couldn't decide—the bed held firm and did not break.

"Do you think we'll make it to Ailiar in time for their Wishing festival?"

Di'Ath pondered the question.

They had set out to arrive in time to celebrate this odd festival with the Ailian royal family. He still wasn't sure what he thought about it.

Did the Ailian people really think that they could make demands of their gods?

Did the gods listen?

He supposed it wasn't so different from giving sacrifices to the Tide. But he had never asked the Tide to give him anything save for answers. Each offering he presented was in gratitude and reverence. To ask the Tide for anything seemed... improper. And yet the Ailians had an entire holiday dedicated to beseeching their gods for... what?

Riches?

Land?

Love?

The god and goddess of love had long fallen out of favour, replaced by the Goddess of Pathways and Revelations.

Di'Ath wasn't sure he would ever understand. Perhaps he would ask Calliope when he arrived. Maybe, if he had someone to sit him down and explain it from their perspective, he might be able to make sense of it.

"Not unless we encounter some miracle," he answered. "Our schedule was tight. We were due to arrive a week before the festivities."

"I still don't understand why we were sent over so early," Sy'da sighed. "She doesn't come into her Affinity until next year. The agreement is that you won't get married until then, right?"

Di'Ath crossed the room and sat on his own groaning bed. He rubbed his face with the palm of his sweaty hand before pushing back his hair.

How did the men in Ailiar style their hair?

"We are going over now as a kind of insurance policy," Di'Ath said. "The marriage is due to the rumours of Rupaburg amassing an army and making plans to start a war. The idea is that by entrusting our care to Queen Meitranis and King Oprianos, Zadanai is promising not to move against Ailiar. Thus, Ailiar should in turn protect Zadanai before I even marry the princess."

Sy'da's brown face paled. She tried to hide it beneath the fabric of her skirts, but Di'Ath saw her pick at her nails. Even if he hadn't known to look, he would have been tipped off by the soft jingle of her bangles and bracelets.

"I'm sorry," Di'Ath breathed.

Sy'da shook her head, still looking up at the ceiling from her prone position on the bed.

"I knew what I was getting into," she said. "Don't think for a second that I would make any other choices if I had the chance to go back in time. I'd rather face death by your side than know you were off in some strange land with bland food all on your own."

Di'Ath barked a laugh. It was good to see that his prediction of the food on offer in Ailiar had rubbed off on Sy'da.

"As long as you can teach their cooks how to make Zadanese sweets, I think we will be okay," he said.

"Oh, I will threaten to freeze every last one of them until they get it right," Sy'da replied with a grin.

Di'Ath had no doubt about that. He was about to voice as much when a soft, almost timid knock sounded on the door. He frowned and stood, walking over to open it. As soon as he did, he could hear chatter and laughter float up towards him.

On the other side of the doorway stood a gangly elf youth. His shoulders were hunched, his back arched, and his greasy, blonde hair fell into his eyes. He had an odd stench about him, as though he had gone stale. Di'Ath wasn't sure what to make of it.

He offered the boy a kind, diplomatic smile.

"Good evening," he said. "Can I help you?"

The youth cleared his throat. "I am sorry to disturb you," he said. "But dinner is ready, if you and the princess would like to come downstairs."

"Ah," Di'Ath said with a nod. "We will be right down."

The youth nodded but did not give any indication that he was going to leave. He simply stood, staring at Di'Ath with too-dull, sand-coloured eyes.

"Right," Di'Ath said.

He leaned back just enough to peer around the open door at Sy'da.

"Dinner, sister," he said.

Sy'da bounced off the bed and practically pranced over to stand beside Di'Ath. She beamed at the gangly youth and held out her hand.

"Good evening," she said. "My name is Sy'da. Who are you?"

"Eiv," the blonde said, ignoring Sy'da's offered hand. "Dinner is ready."

The youth turned and walked away. He stopped at the top of the staircase, turned, and stared back at them once more.

Sy'da's hand slipped into Di'Ath's, and she gave two quick, tight squeezes.

They would certainly be discussing this odd creature later.

"We're coming," Di'Ath said.

He pulled the door closed behind them and led Sy'da towards the stairs. He kept himself between Eiv and his sister, unsure if he could trust the boy.

Once Di'Ath and Sy'da joined him, Eiv led them down the stairs and through the reception room where they had met Mr. Talts and been given their keys. Di'Ath pulled Sy'da along with him as he followed the strange boy into a large hall toward the back. The ceiling was tall, and in the centre was a long, rectangular hearth with benches along either side.

The crew of the *Spirit* were gathered around the low fire, their hands cupped around wooden bowls filled with a rich-smelling stew.

"Your Highnesses," Captain Py'Ques called over the din of laughter and conversation. "I have saved you two a seat."

Di'Ath offered Eiv a nod of gratitude before pulling Sy'da through the throng of bodies towards the captain. Sy'da let go of his hand once they had reached Py'Ques, accepting a bowl of stew offered to her. She promptly sat and began eating, nearly moaning at the taste.

"I see you have met our host's son," Captain Py'Ques muttered to Di'Ath in a hushed tone.

Di'Ath frowned. "Eiv?"

Py'Ques nodded. "He is Talts' boy. I would suggest you say nothing but kind things about him."

"I wasn't planning on saying much at all about him," Di'Ath said.

Someone nudged his arm. Di'Ath looked down to see that the sailor who had stopped to warn him about Kei and it's locals earlier that day was holding a bowl out to him.

"It's good," the sailor said. "If we don't learn anything else about these people, at least we can swear that they know their food."

Di'Ath accepted the bowl and dipped his head in appreciation. The sailor didn't wait to see if Di'Ath agreed with his assessment before turning and disappearing into the crowd.

"So, what's happening?" Di'Ath asked Captain Py'Ques. "Did you have a chance to discuss our next steps with Ilme?"

Captain Py'Ques snorted a laugh.

"You mean your new best friend?" he asked. "Be careful getting too close to these people, prince."

Di'Ath's jaw clenched.

"What are our next steps?" he asked again.

Py'Ques tipped the remainder of his stew into his mouth. He wiped his face with the back of his hand before he answered.

"Starting first thing tomorrow, every free and able-bodied man on this island is going to be working on fixing the *Spirit*. Ilme predicts that it will take about two weeks before we are able to set sail again and that of course is contingent on good weather."

Two weeks.

They would miss the Wishing.

Out of the corner of his eye, Di'Ath caught Sy'da watching them intently.

"And how much is it costing us?" Di'Ath asked. "Do we have enough gold to cover repairs, labour, and accommodation?"

Py'Ques shook his head. "That's the thing," he said. "They don't want anything save for the seawyrm flesh."

Di'Ath shifted on his feet. "What?"

Py'Ques nodded. "My thoughts exactly. They don't care about the scales or teeth—they've actually said that they're going to harvest them for you as the Wyrmslayer. They just want the flesh. I've warned them that it was likely not fit for consumption seeing as you killed the beast two days ago. That did not seem to be a concern for them."

Di'Ath sighed and shook his head. "The more I learn about this place, the more confused I am," he said. "I don't get it."

He lifted the bowl to his lips and drank deeply of the rich, aromatic gravy. There were so many flavours that it was hard to pinpoint what exactly was in it. Even the chunks of meat and vegetables were unrecognizable. Although, he conceded, there was the possibility that he was eating something entirely foreign to him.

"Two weeks then, huh?" he asked. "I suppose we better make ourselves comfortable."

TWENTY-FIVE

MAIDA

LUVRAHN

MAIDA COULD NOT NAME the cold hand that closed around her heart as she stood by the dining table, watching Aros make the final adjustments to his pack. She had thought that she might be excited to no longer be under constant surveillance, but in truth, she was terrified.

After she had told him about the nightmares that plagued her – about what she had seen when she had fled her home – Aros had declared that he would return to Silktide in her stead. He would investigate on her behalf.

She had protested, naturally, but Aros had insisted that she remain behind for her own safety while he searched for some sign that someone, anyone, had survived.

A sign that, perhaps, her father still lived.

Maida toyed with the flower pendant at her throat. She rolled it between her thumb and forefinger so that the petals pressed into the calloused pads of her fingertips while Aros pulled the string of his pack tight, closing it around the stores of food, and clothing. Bloated waterskins hung off the side, the sloshing of the liquid within too loud.

"Are you sure you should go?" she blurted. "It's getting cold. What if you're not back before winter sets in?"

Why was she so worried about that?

She was sure that Aros had survived his fair share of harsh winters. He knew how to take care of himself. But if he perished on this expedition then it would be *her* fault, wouldn't it?

After all, he was only going because of her.

"I am sure," Aros said.

For a moment, Maida thought he might reach out to her and brush her hair back. She recalled how warm his body had been the night he had brought her out of her nightmare. His heartbeat had soothed her back to sleep, and he had still been wrapped around her when she woke the next morning.

But since then, they hadn't so much as brushed fingers against one another. It felt strange, like he had burrowed his way into her chest only to leave it hollow.

"You are in safe hands here," Aros continued. "I expect Palis will try to convince you to move in with her before I am even out of sight. I wouldn't be surprised if I come home to an empty cottage."

Maida's eyes stung with tears. She shook her head at the very idea of it, making the small silver beads in her new braids chime against one another.

"That isn't what I mean," she said, voice quiet and timid. "I... are *you* going to be safe?"

Maida saw the breath catch in Aros' throat. She saw how his chest rose yet did not fall as he held his breath at her concern. It was clear that he had been as unexpecting of this development as she. Maida was not sure which of them was more surprised than the other. Still, she could not shake the seed of worry that had burrowed itself deep within her heart when he had told her of his plan to travel to Silktide. Nor could she tear it out as it took root, growing stronger and hardier the fuller his pack became.

"I have survived far too much to not return to you," Aros said eventually. "I can handle this, Dhuina."

Unfathomably, Maida realised that she believed him. She couldn't understand how his simple words had convinced her that he would return, as though that simple fact was so rooted in truth it was etched in stone.

She nodded, returning his smile with a strained one of her own.

Aros swung the pack over his shoulder. The waterskins swung and sloshed.

He looked as though he were about to say something. She could see the thoughts flicker across his evergreen eyes. Whatever it had been, though, he had decided against speaking it. Instead, he lifted his hand and cupped her cheek.

Maida leaned into his warm touch.

Stay, she begged silently.

She shouldn't want him to stay. If he confirmed that there was nothing to return to, she could abandon her plans of running away. And yet, all it would take would be to breathe life into that single word.

"I should be home before The Wishing," he said.

Maida frowned. Aros chuckled.

"You should ask Palis about it. It's a festival marking the end of our year as autumn comes to a close. I'll be home before then, and we can go together."

Together. A festival, together, with a man.

Just as she was had meant to do back home.

"I'll hold you to it," Maida replied.

Aros nodded in agreement. Then, with a sigh, she passed her and stepped out of the cottage.

Maida moved over to the kitchen window.

She watched Aros walk up the hill towards the Edgeling Woods. Before long, he was joined by a small gaggle of children. They ran around him in circles, weaving in and out of each other as if they were decorating a maypole. Their laughter filled the air and floated back down to her in the crisp autumn air.

It was not until they were out of sight, swallowed by the crest of the hill, that Maida turned away from the window.

Since arriving in Luvrahn, Maida had not spent much time alone. Aros had embarked on errands now and then, but it had never lasted longer than a few hours. Even then, Palis or Aoife generally took it upon themselves to bring fresh baked rolls and cakes, or berries that Aoife had harvested on her walk.

Aros was not going to be home in a few hours. He was not even going to be home for a few days.

That hollow in her chest that she had blamed Aros for seemed to grow. How lonely she was already. She could run up the path, scream his name and beg him to stay.

But she needed him to go.

She needed to know if there was something to go home to. She needed to know if she was going to be spending her winter planning to leave or if she would be planning a new life here amongst the elves.

She needed him to go so that he would not cloud her judgement.

She just hadn't expected to feel this lonely.

Maida had never felt lonely in Silktide. She had never wished that she lived closer to town, never mourned the fact that she did not have friends to call her own. So why did the idea of not knowing when she would see someone again bear down on her with a crushing weight?

She wrung her hand.

Her eyes darted over the small cottage—the bed that had not been made that morning, the cups that still glistened with the remains of the tea that they'd shared, the torn tunic that Aros had decided against packing.

"That's it," she said, stepping forward and picking the tunic up off the back of the seat. "I'll sew."

She sank to her knees and pulled her new sewing basket out from under the bed where it now belonged. She brought both it and the tunic back to the table and set herself up in Aros' chair. She had barely threaded the needle, however, when she was interrupted by a knock at the door.

With a sigh of relief, Maida set her work aside. She stood, shook her hands in an attempt to disburse the nervous energy, and crossed over to the door. She turned the handle and pulled it open, expecting to see Palis with her sunshine smile on the other side.

But it was not Palis.

Standing on the other side of the door was the young blonde boy that Maida had seen chasing the girl in the tavern while Aoife had been telling her story. If she had to guess, Maida would have said that the boy was around eight. His grey eyes shone, and his gap-toothed smile was so wide it took up nearly half his face. His nose and the tops of his cheeks were red from playing out in the sun day in and day out.

Maida could see the beginning of a smattering of freckles.

"Hello?" she asked, head tilted to the side. "I would say that you are too late if you wanted to see Aros and say goodbye, but I am fairly certain that I watched you follow him up the hill."

The boy shook his head, the small points of his ears poking through his fluffy blonde hair.

"Nope!" he said brightly. "I'm not here for Aros. I'm here for you!"

Maida scrunched her nose.

"For me?" she asked.

"Uh-huh!" The boy nodded enthusiastically. "My mama and I are about to go to the meadow, and we wanted to see if you would join us."

Aros had mentioned the meadow once before. Apparently, it was where the village crafters gathered to work on their various projects while their children played around them. Aros had offered to take her there whenever she wished.

Maida felt a pang of regret at having never taken him up on the offer.

"I don't know," Maida said. "Aros said I'm not supposed to talk to strangers while he is gone. I don't think that he'll be happy if I go to the meadow with one."

The boy's smile widened even more.

"My name is Nanos," he said. "And now we're not strangers, are we? We're friends, and that means you've got to come to the meadow with me."

"Got to?" Maida laughed.

"Mmhmm," Nanos said. He rocked back and forth on his heels.

"Well," Maida said. "You've made a rather compelling argument. Should I bring anything with me? I was about to do some sewing."

"You can bring that!" Nanos replied eagerly. "Mama said that Aros brought you some pretty fabric. Everyone is going to want to see what you're making. Everyone loves seeing what everyone else is doing."

Maida chuckled. She opened the door the rest of the way and turned back to the table. She stuck her needle into the tunic and placed the tunic in the basket.

"Well, this isn't my big project," Maida said, looping her arm through the basket's handle. "But maybe I'll bring it next time. Aros has a few holes in his shirt, and I thought I would be nice and mend them while he's gone."

She returned to Nanos, a smile on her face.

She would put her plans of escape on hold until she knew whether they were worth going through with—the least she could do in the meantime was get to know her surroundings a bit more. And the elven inhabitants of Luvrahn were nothing if not a part of said surroundings.

"Shall we?" she asked, gesturing towards the path.

Nanos spun on his heel. Maida closed the door behind her before following him, checking that everything was sitting nestled nicely in her basket.

"Mama says you don't have a name," Nanos blurted as they walked. "Is that true?"

Maida chuckled at his openness. Were all children like this? Just asking whatever question came to their mind?

Had she been? She couldn't remember.

"Your mama is right," Maida said. "I don't have a name. But Aros, Aoife and Palis call me Dhuina."

Nanos' nose scrunched, bringing white lines across the pink skin.

"That's not a good name," he said.

Maida raised a brow. "Oh?" she asked. "Why not?"

"Because it means *human*," he said. "It's like calling a dog *Dog*, or a chicken *Chicken*. It's not a *name*."

"Alright then," Maida said. "Do you think you could come up with a better name?"

Nanos came to a stop so suddenly that dust clouds rose around his boots. Maida stopped and turned to see an expression of pure joy and amazement on his face.

"Can I really?!" he asked.

With that face, with that voice, Maida realised the error she had made. There was no way that she could say *no* to this boy now, not without shattering that precious little heart of his.

"So long as you don't name me after the Maiden," she said.

Nanos shook his head wildly, his curls fanning out around him.

"Noooo," he replied. "No one knows what her name was anymore anyway. But I promise that I will find a name that suits you. Just give me some time—I want to get to know you a bit better first."

Maida chuckled. "Alright," she said. "Then I hereby declare you head of the Name Dhuina Committee."

TWENTY-SIX

MAIDA

LUVRAHN

THE MEADOW WAS A sweeping expanse of shin-deep green grass and despite the season, it was smattered with wildflowers of every colour imaginable.

Maida had not been able to see it from Aros' cottage. It had not even been visible until she and Nanos had passed the well and the strange little shrine that leaned against it. She had followed the child through the town square and been brought to a stop at the beautiful scene before her.

Men and women sat on brightly coloured blankets while children disappeared over the soft crest of the hill. The children squealed with delight. Maida had not realised just how many children there were here. Other than Nanos, she couldn't spot any of the children that had followed Aros up the path. This small village was full of life, and promise.

And you're still thinking of leaving.

"Dhuina!"

Nanos had run forward to sit next to a stunning elf woman with long, honey-blonde hair kept back from her face in a single, thick braid. If she were human, Maida would have guessed that she was only ten or so years older than herself. But Maida did not know how to tell the age of an elf. She didn't even know how long elves lived for.

The stories that she had heard from back home said they were immortal. But those stories also said that they were heartless monsters that preyed on humans for entertainment, so Maida was not quite sure she was as ready to believe as easily as she once had.

The woman smiled and beckoned Maida over.

Nanos' shout had caught the attention of the other adults gathered there. They twisted towards her, gaze heavy. The air caught in Maida's throat. She swallowed hard around a sudden lump. The wicker of the basket creaked under her grip as it tightened.

She should have let Aros bring her here before he left. He would have told them all to look elsewhere and to leave Maida alone until she was able to adjust to the fact that she was now surrounded by dozens of elves.

Nanos unceremoniously pushed a basket overflowing with yarn away from him and pat the now-clear space beside him.

"Come on," he said. "I made a spot for you."

Colour and heat both rose to Maida's cheeks. She ducked her head and walked briskly over to Nanos and the woman he sat with.

"Dhuina, this is my mama," Nanos said, throwing his arms around the woman's neck. "Mama, this is Dhuina. But that's not her actual name. She said I could pick her real name though!"

The woman laughed. While it was honeyed and melodic, Maida felt a dark undercurrent beneath it. She recognised it as the laugh of someone who had lost something great. She recognised it as her own laugh—not the one she'd had before Silktide had burned, but the new one that she had found. The one that she had needed to be earn.

"My name is Thalia," Nanos' mother said. "I am glad that you have accepted our invitation and joined us. We have wanted to invite you before, but -"

"But Aros is a grumpy bastard and turned away anyone who so much as looked in your direction," interrupted a grey-haired elf woman.

Maida turned her attention to her. Her ears bore notches along both the top and bottom of the long points. Her teeth were yellowed, her lips were thin, and her bottom jaw seemed to jut out more than it should.

"Unless you're Palis," laughed a plump, smiling elf man. "But I suppose the only one powerful enough to stop her is Aoife."

"Even then, she'd be having a rough go of it," the notch-eared crone replied.

Thalia shook her head. She leaned over towards Maida.

"Don't worry about these people," she said. "They like to talk, but they're all harmless. And you're the first newcomer we've had in town in a decade."

"A decade?" Maida asked.

"We don't get many travellers out this way," Thalia said. "The southern provinces of Ailiar are fairly uninhabited. There are a few farms, usually ones that grow crops that aren't grown on the mainland, and a smattering of towns here and there. But Luvrahn is our own little haven, tucked away neatly against the border."

Maida frowned. The other elves were still discussing the merits of who and what could contain Palis should one need to, but Maida's mind was stuck on something that Thalia had said.

"I'm sorry," Maida said. "But what do you mean by *mainland*? We aren't an island. The continent is quite large, is it not?"

Nanos snorted a laugh beside her.

"Yeah, but the Sea Between Seas separates the southern provinces from the north, which is *huge*, so we call it the mainland," he explained.

Thalia pulled a face at her son.

"What have I told you about laughing at others?" she scolded.

To his credit, Nanos immediately looked down at the blanket in remorse.

"You said not to laugh at them unless they are intentionally being funny, because it can hurt their feelings," he muttered.

"That's right," Thalia said. "Now, what do we say to Dhuina?"

Nanos sighed so deeply that one would think he had been asked to do the most impossible, most embarrassing thing in the world.

"I'm sorry for laughing at you," Nanos said. "I didn't mean to. It was mean of me."

Maida bit back a laugh of her own.

"It's alright," she said. "I accept your apology. Thank you for explaining it to me."

Thalia ruffled her son's hair. "Why don't you go play, sweetheart?"

"But I want to sit with Dhuina," Nanos whined.

"You can sit with Dhuina later," Thalia said. "She isn't going anywhere. Go, go play."

Nanos turned pleading grey eyes to Maida. Maida gestured towards the other children with her chin.

"Go on," she said. "You know you'll think of a name faster if you're out there playing, right?"

Nanos gasped. He scrambled to his feet and ran off.

Maida watched him race through the grass and wildflowers, joining the throng of screaming, happy children.

"You don't have to accept whatever name he gives you," Thalia said.

Maida returned her attention in time to watch Thalia pull dried herbs from her basket, place them into a mortar and begin grinding them. The grating sound of the herbs against the stone had Maida gritting her teeth.

"I don't mind," Maida said. "It's not like I've had any luck coming up with one on my own. And I don't think I could handle anything Palis could conjure for me."

Thalia chuckled. "That's true," she said. "Still—if you don't like what he says, you can tell him."

"I don't want to upset him," Maida said.

"Boys need to learn that women can say no. Otherwise, they become men who are deaf to the word."

Thalia pressed the pestle down harder. Stone ground against stone. The fragrant scent of fennel and cumin wafted into the air. It made Maida's stomach grumble.

"Is that for your dinner?" Maida asked.

"Yes," Thalia said. "I am testing out a mixture to go with some roasted deer. If it goes well, I'll make it for the Wishing."

The Wishing.

Aros had mentioned the Wishing before he left.

"That is a festival, isn't it?" Maida asked.

Thalia smiled at her. "It is. It's our biggest celebration of the year. It is the last day of autumn. It is the one day of the year where we can commune with the gods without having to go to a temple."

Maida frowned.

"I don't understand," she said.

Thalia smiled kindly. Maida wondered if that's what a maternal smile looked like.

"Of course, we can pray to the gods whenever we please," Thalia said. "But on the Wishing, the Goddess of Paths and Revelations can be seen in the sky as her Star—the Star of Oliantra. Oliantra is one of the Ancient Ones, and she shines her Star so that we can give our thanks for the year that was, and make our requests for the year to come. Oliantra takes all of our wishes, and she delegates them to the relevant gods in order for them to fulfil them."

Maida sat with the explanation for a moment.

"Do people tend to go in pairs?" she asked.

"Why? You want to go with Aros?" Thalia teased.

Maida's cheeks burned, and she busied her hands by pulling the tunic onto her lap and picking up the needle.

"Couples do tend to make their wishes together," Thalia said. "But so do families. Sometimes, people sit with their friends and give their wishes to the gods that way. It depends on how you want to commune with them, and which relationships mean the most to you."

Maida wondered if Aros planned on giving his wishes to Oliantra with her by his side, or if he would just accompany Maida during whatever other festivities took place. Whatever his intentions, Maida found herself looking forward to it.

She spent the rest of the day in the meadow. Eventually, she joined the conversations of the other adults. The notch-eared woman turned out to be the one from whom Aros had bought the fabric, shears and thread. Maida expressed her gratitude, and earned herself promises of more fabric coming her way.

By the time she returned to Aros' cottage, Maida was exhausted. She fell into bed and was surprised to find herself looking forward to doing it all again tomorrow.

Twenty-Seven

Di'Ath

Port of Kei

Sleep continued to elude the prince.

In the week that they had spent on the island of Kei, Di'Ath had not slept through the night once.

Surely, there was a limit to how long one could go without proper rest, and yet Di'Ath could not surrender himself to unconsciousness. He couldn't even guess as to why he was having such trouble. Could it be the unseasonable heat that made each layer of fabric cling to him like a second skin?

He had stripped down to the barest minimum, wearing only a pair of loose pants that he had pushed up to sit just beneath his knees. The excess fabric bunched underneath him, but at least his lower legs were as bare as his chest. If he had not been sharing a room with his sister, Di'Ath would have had no qualms about sleeping in nothing at all.

But he was sharing with her, and as such he had resigned himself to merely banishing the sheets to the bottom of the bed and lying for untold hours doing nothing but staring at the ceiling. He had lost count of how many times he had traced the spider-webbing cracks in the paint above. He had lost track of how many spiders he had watched scurry above him, or how long he had tracked the moon's arc in the sky by watching how the soft light moved in through the gap in the curtains.

Sy'da, on the other hand, did not seem to have the same kind of trouble that he did. Her soft snores taunted him from the other end of the room and Di'Ath seriously considered flipping both her and her mattress over in retaliation.

He knew it was his exhaustion that was making him irritable. He knew it was making him unreasonable, but why should he suffer alone?

What had he done that had upset the flow of the Tide so completely that he was doomed to drive himself mad from a lack of sleep?

What a fitting end it would be—Di'Ath Adarna, Wyrmslayer, driven to insanity from being unable to simply close his eyes and dream.

After another hour of laying on his back and staring at the ceiling while rivulets of sweat trickled down his body, he finally conceded defeat. Di'Ath climbed out of bed and stretched his aching limbs before sinking to the floor on his knees. The wood was blissfully cool, and he considered trying to sleep on the floor after he was done.

Di'Ath reached under the bed for the chest he had stashed there a few days ago. It slid across the floor easily as Di'Ath pulled it towards him. He spread his legs, pulling the chest between his knees. The chest itself was rather simple. It had been made of dark wood and iron nails. The latch and hinges, however, were made of brass.

Di'Ath took a breath and flicked open the latch. He looked over his shoulder to make sure that the soft *click* of brass hitting brass didn't wake up his sister. She remained deep asleep, snoring away.

Satisfied, Di'Ath returned his attention to the chest. He lifted the lid, carefully guiding it backward until the chest was completely open. The moonlight seemed to redirect itself to the chest, glistening off the brilliant blue scales that lay within.

It had taken only two days for the locals to harvest and clean the scales from the remains of the seawyrm. As far as Di'Ath was aware, they were still working on the beast's fangs. What for, he did not know. A woman with white eyes had simply taken the basket of teeth and had smiled in such a way that it had sent chills down his spine.

Di'Ath scooped up a handful of the scales. They were as thick as steel lames, and roughly the same size. When the tanner had first pressed one into Di'Ath's hand, he had immediately been reminded of the armour of the Zadanese footmen. From there, the decision of what to do with them was clear—he would find an artisan in Balliach who could punch holes through the scales, and a seamstress with enough skill to transform them into a garment fit for battle and ball.

He doubted that the heir of Ailiar would dare wear Zadanai blue if she were ever to go into battle, but as Sy'da continued to remind him, it was the thought that counted. And what better way to say *I hope for a long life with you* than presenting something that could protect his bride from most weapons known to elf-kind?

He tilted his hand, letting the scales fall back into the chest.

They made a soft tinkling sound, not unlike coins.

They were beautiful. He could not deny the desire to keep them for himself. He could lean into being the Wyrmslayer if he wore armour made from their scales. Any number of men would do the same.

Many men would brag about such an accomplishment.

Ilme's words echoed in Di'Ath's mind.

I hope that you will treat this second life you have earned with the reverence it deserves.

He couldn't explain it, but Di'Ath was certain that by keeping the scales for himself, he would not be treating his life with the reverence he had apparently earned.

He sighed and closed the chest with another soft *click,* returning it to its place under the bed.

With a groan, he stood and rolled his shoulders in a vain attempt to work out the tension in his muscles. He pulled his arm across his chest, securing it with the other, trying to stretch it out. He didn't understand it, but Di'Ath could not shake the feeling that his body was tensed in anticipation of a blow he could not see coming.

His magic thrummed beneath the surface. It bubbled and flowed, begging to be set free. To be uncoiled. The sweat on his arms began to gather around his wrists, moving in slow circles like serpents.

Di'Ath shook his hands to banish the magic.

He needed to get out of this room. He was going mad, and if he lost his mind, who knew what his magic would do?

He checked on Sy'da before slipping out the door, not even bothering to pull on a tunic.

Silence greeted him as he stepped on the landing.

Di'Ath frowned. It had never been particularly boisterous in the Inn. The people of Kei did not seem to have the same taste for alcohol as the Zadanese sailors, and with the absence of drink, the volume in any place tended to be a little lower. Still, Di'Ath had become accustomed to hearing some sort of conversation drifting up from around the hearth.

Just the night before, Di'Ath had needed to keep his mouth firmly shut as he listened to a Keivan man tell wildly inaccurate and untrue stories about the Zadanese wilds. Di'Ath had stolen wide-eyed glances with his sister as the Keivan shared wild exaggerations and misconceptions.

He supposed that they were entertaining enough to keep from correcting the old man. While the stories didn't appear to offend any of the other Zadanese nationals listening, Di'Ath had not forgotten the warnings he'd received when they'd arrived.

But now, Di'Ath could not hear anything. He could hear no stories, no laughter, no indication of life at all. Perhaps it was later than he originally thought.

He could not even hear the song of cicadas.

Intrigued, he turned towards the staircase, only to be met by Mr. Talts boy, Eiv.

"Is everything alright, your Highness?" Eiv asked.

Di'Ath nodded and smiled awkwardly.

"Yes," he said. "Perfectly so. I'm just going to go downstairs."

"Why?"

Di'Ath frowned. "I'm sorry?"

"What is it that you need from downstairs?" Eiv asked. "Whatever it is, I can get it for you, but I'm afraid I need to ask you to return to your room."

"I... want to take a walk," Di'Ath said. "You can't bring a walk to my room. So now, if you'll excuse me."

Di'Ath tried to step around the boy, but Eiv moved to block his path.

"I am afraid you must wait until the morning," he said.

"You're afraid of a lot of things," Di'Ath muttered. "Why can I not go for a walk? I took one last night, and no one had any qualms. Why am I suddenly unable to do so now? Did I offend someone by leaving my room last night? If I did, I am sorry, but I think it should have been brought to my attention earlier."

Eiv offered what Di'Ath guessed was supposed to be an apologetic smile, but there was something so emotionless and doll-like in the rest of his face that it didn't exactly translate.

"I'm afraid that if you wish to go for a walk, you will need to wait until the morning," Eiv said.

"I do not want to walk in the morning," Di'Ath protested.

"Then you may go out tomorrow evening," Eiv said. "However, tonight is a holy night, and no one is allowed outside."

Di'Ath ears perked up at that.

"A holy night?" Di'Ath asked. "We weren't told that it was a holiday."

"I'm afraid I'm going to have to ask you to go back to bed," Eiv said.

The boy took a step forward, and despite himself, Di'Ath took a step backward.

"What kind of holiday is it?" Di'Ath asked. "Is it in celebration of something? Why does everyone have to stay inside?"

Eiv continued to walk, pushing Di'Ath backwards without laying so much as a hand on him. Di'Ath had no desire to return to his room. He didn't want to lay on the sweat-dampened mattress and stare at the ceiling. The very thought of it had him wanting to tear his hair out.

"Is there a ritual happening?" Di'Ath asked. "Are there offerings being made? Can we make an offering?"

He loved putting spices, flowers and coins on little boats made out of bark and leaves to send out to the Tide. Perhaps the people of Kei would be more trusting if he were to make an offering to their gods.

"No," Eiv said. "You cannot. You do not have to go to bed but you must go to your room."

It was not until Di'Ath stepped back and had felt the doorknob poke into his back that he realised the boy had effectively herded him back to his room. He shook his head in bewilderment.

"If I go into my room, will you tell me tomorrow?"

Eiv narrowed his eyes, before finally nodding.

Di'Ath would take that as confirmation enough. He raised a finger, pointing at Eiv.

"I am expecting a full explanation tomorrow. You will find time to explain to me what is happening tonight, where everyone is, and what's so important about it. Do we have a deal?"

Eiv nodded again.

"Alright," Di'Ath said. "Then I'll go to my room. I will see you tomorrow, Eiv Talts."

He reached for the doorknob and let himself back in.

Di'Ath closed the door behind him and looked down at the crack under the door, spying twin shadows that did not move. Di'Ath frowned.

How long would he have to wait for the kid to leave so he could sneak out?

He stayed by that door, staring at those shadows until his legs protested. Di'Ath moved to sit on the floor, propping himself up on the bed. Eiv still had not moved.

That was okay.

Di'Ath could be patient. He could wait.

He sat and stared for what felt like hours until his eyes grew heavy and his head began to loll to the side.

As he drifted off into long anticipated sleep, Di'Ath swore he felt the earth shudder.

Twenty-Eight

Di'Ath

Port of Kei

THE NIGHTS WITHOUT SLEEP had caught up to Di'Ath in such a manner that he slept well into the late morning. His dreams had been plagued with swirling flames and water, the two elements chasing each other around in ceaseless circles and creating a torrent of steam. While he had finally woken rested, Di'Ath had greeted the day with a sense of confusion that only seemed to grow as the sun followed its arc in the sky.

Sy'da had teased him mercilessly for sleeping through breakfast. She claimed that she had tried to rouse him from his slumber, but Di'Ath had never been a particularly deep sleeper. She denied any suggestion that she was lying, and Di'Ath found that he didn't care whether she had tried to wake him or not.

He had finally been able to sleep through the night. He was not about to question it, even if his stomach was protesting quite loudly.

Luckily, Di'Ath had woken in time for lunch.

He followed Sy'da downstairs and through to the hall where the crew of the *Spirit* were once again gathered around the hearth. The hall was not as packed as it was during evening meals, but it was still a task weaving through bodies to find their usual seat beside the captain.

"You decided to join the living," Captain Py'Ques said to Di'Ath, handing him a roll of bread and a cup of fragrant tea.

"Have you seen Eiv?" Di'Ath asked, ignoring the captain's remark.

Captain Py'Ques shook his head as he tore into a hunk of bread.

"Not for a second," the captain said. "Not that I was looking out for him. He isn't exactly the kind of person I tend to seek out though. Why?"

Di'Ath sniffed at the steaming tea in his cup with resignation. Why did it always have to be tea?

"I wanted to ask him about something," Di'Ath said. "He promised that he would take the time to speak with me today."

Captain Py'Ques barked a hoarse laugh. "He promised, did he? Well, I guess you better get to hunting, your Highness. Wouldn't want to let the young lad break his promise."

Sy'da pulled a face behind the captain's back. Clearly, she liked his response just as much as Di'Ath did – which was to say, not a lot at all. Though once again, Di'Ath could not pinpoint exactly what it was about Py'Ques words that rubbed him the wrong way. The captain's tone felt disrespectful, but not outwardly so. It wasn't quite the tone Di'Ath would use with the other high-born boys who tried to lie *to* women in order to lie *with* them, but it was in the same realm.

It simply did not sit well with him. Especially when he considered how much the people of Kei had been doing for them while they were here. They had fed and clothed the crew. They were repairing the ship, working from sunrise to sunset. Even if Di'Ath had not been warned against offending them, he would have been uncomfortable with how Py'Ques spoke about the locals.

"I suppose I better," Di'Ath said.

He ate his lunch quickly and began his search with Sy'da trailing behind him.

Mr. Talts had no answers. Di'Ath and Sy'da must have combed the entire beach and the township before the sun began to set, and they returned to the Inn.

The next day was the same—no sign of Eiv, no concern from his father.

Di'Ath didn't understand. How could the boy's father not be worried about the fact that he hadn't seen his son?

People go wandering, Mr. Talts had said.

That was it.

People go wandering.

On the third day, Di'Ath ran into the woman with the unsettling grin that had accepted the seawyrm's teeth.

She thrust a woven sea-grass basket into his hands, filled with corset busks, needles, hair pins and beads carved from the teeth and fangs. The beast must have had more teeth than he thought, but Di'Ath could not imagine how so many things had been carved from the strange material.

On the fourth day, Di'Ath's curiosity had given way to disappointment. He was treading water in a sea of unanswered questions. No one he encountered was willing to discuss the night he'd been forced to stay in. No one seemed to know to where Eiv had disappeared.

His unanswered questions took root deep within him. They carved out caverns and hollows for his unsated curiosity to fester—and Di'Ath was no stranger to how deadly such a thing could be if left unchecked.

By the sixth day, Di'Ath realised he was not going to get any answers. The *Spirit* had been fully repaired, and the crew spent the day carting crates, sacks and packs from the Inn to the ship.

On the seventh day, Di'Ath shook Ilme's hand and climbed aboard.

The sails opened with loud, ear-splitting *snaps* of the canvas, and the *Spirit* picked up speed as it pulled away from the port of Kei.

Beside him, Sy'da rambled about how happy she was to finally be back on the sea. Her voice melted into an unintelligible sound, mixing with the shouts of the crew and the creak of rigging as Di'Ath stared back at the strange little island. He still could not comprehend how the jungle beyond the beach was as green and lush as it was when they were so close to winter. He could not understand why the weather was so warm, or how the spray of sea water that showered him was not completely frigid.

There was much that Di'Ath still did not know about the island of Kei, but the one thing that he was sure would haunt him was that night he had been unable to leave his room.

Why had he been forced to stay inside?

What kind of rituals did the people of Kei participate in during the so-called holy night?

And what had happened to Eiv Talts?

Di'Ath sighed.

He was never going to get any answers. He would be lucky if he ever left Ailiar once he stepped foot on its soil. There was no chance that he would ever be able to return to Kei to find the answers he was looking for.

With resignation weighing heavy on his heart, he turned away from the stern of the ship.

A loud, thunderous *crack* erupted through the sky.

Di'Ath spun back around so quickly that he nearly threw himself overboard. Another *crack* joined the first. It sounded like a tree being felled after the arborists had successfully cut into the wood enough for the weight of the tree to take over – only louder. It was like the earth itself was being split in two.

With wild, darting eyes, Di'Ath searched the island for a hint of gaping ground. He expected to find the people of Kei to be scattering. He expected to see parents picking up their children and running. Instead, they stood on the beach as calm as they had been as they'd watched the crew load the ship.

The only difference now was that Di'Ath could see the fluid movements of the Visdhraos and the Aerdhraos calling on their magic, moving like kelp in water. The *Spirit* gained speed again, and Di'Ath realised that they were helping to move the ship out of their harbour.

But why?

The *Spirit* was already leaving. Why would they waste their energy pushing them through the reef quicker?

Sy'da gripped Di'Ath's arm and pressed herself against him. She had stopped her rambling, and Di'Ath could feel her tremble slightly.

"It's alright," he said. "They're just helping us get to sea."

A third mountain-cleaving *crack* rang out. Sy'da squealed. Di'Ath pulled her tighter against him, letting her bury her face against his chest. He rubbed her back, searching desperately for an answer to the sound.

The locals still did not run. They didn't appear afraid at all, yet he was certain that the sound was coming from the island itself. Was this a common occurrence? He could not imagine living in a place where such horrific, nightmarish sounds were regular enough that they no longer phased him.

"Let's go down to your cabin," Di'Ath said.

As much as his curiosity was compelling him to stay, it was clear that his sister was terrified. Sy'da sniffled as she nodded. She slipped her hand into his and tugged him to follow her as she pulled away.

Just as he was about to follow, a movement high in the mountain caught his attention.

Like a river flowing uphill, a crack formed in the mountainside. Boulders crashed through the jungle; birds took flight. There was a fourth shattering crack, and more fissures spiderwebbed over the mountain. It looked like an egg, though Di'Ath could only imagine what kind of monstrous creature would reside in an egg of that magnitude.

Whatever it was—Di'Ath would never learn the answer. The *Spirit* was moving far too swiftly, and all too soon the island and its mountain were obscured by rocks and fog.

TWENTY-NINE

MAIDA

LUVRAHN

TWO WEEKS HAD PASSED and Maida had settled into a routine that she found she quite enjoyed.

She woke with the dawn, starting her days with a breakfast of buttered bread that she had baked the day before. The kapriae's bleating no longer terrified her. Instead, she listened to the strange, strangled sound as she cupped her morning tea in her hands.

She generally had only an hour before there was someone knocking on her door. Usually, it was Nanos. Sometimes it was Palis. But every day since Aros had left, someone made sure to rap their knuckles against the dark stained wood. Maida would smile, gather her basket of sewing supplies, and carry it out the door and down to the meadow, listening to the incessant chatter of whomsoever had chosen to be her escort that day.

Once they arrived at that magical place where flowers still inexplicably grew despite the air that held such an intense chill that Maida had sown in one of the furs from the bed into her cloak, she would set herself down next to Thalia.

Deija—the notch-eared woman who made quilts—brought scraps of different coloured fabrics each day. Maida didn't know how the woman had amassed such a collection, or how she still managed to find a basketful of pieces to just hand over. But she wasn't going to complain. The colours were bright and vivid, and once she had finished patching Aros' shirt, she started putting the scrap pieces together. No two pieces of the same colour sat beside each other. No two patterns existed without a solid, plain piece in between.

Maida was not following a pattern but she had already done something similar before. The skirts she had worn when she ran from Silktide had also been a patchwork piece. The colours had been more muted, suiting the tastes and sensibilities of human fashion. The scraps of it still sat folded under the bed. Perhaps she could find a way to repurpose some of the tattered remains. Perhaps she could make pockets out of the pleated fabric that gathered at the waistband. It was the least damaged and though it wasn't a lot to work with. Still, Maida had not been able to bring herself to burn the remains. She was determined to find a way to keep it with her.

When she wasn't sewing while conversing with the adults, Maida had taken to chasing the children in the long grass that grew down the crest of the hill. She would run until her lungs ached and her legs felt like jelly before trudging back and plopping down next to Thalia.

"I hope you're aware that you can tell the children 'no' if you don't want to play with them," Thalia laughed. "They can survive an afternoon without you indulging them if you want a day to yourself."

Maida would have shaken her head if she could muster the energy.

"I know," she rasped through heaving breaths. "But I am happy to play with them. I just wish that they would wear out a little quicker. I don't think I was ever so energetic as a child."

Deija laughed, pulling shimmering golden thread through the quilt on her lap.

"I am firmly of the belief that with every generation, the children get more troublesome and unruly," she said. "Just so that parents are not able to use their own childhoods to their advantage."

A round of chuckles rose in agreement with the weaver,

"I recall when Nanos first started walking," Thalia said. "He tried to get into every drawer and cupboard he could reach. Once he figured out that he could use them to climb? Oh, Gods, I found him on the counter more times than the cat."

Maida's laughter mixed with the others. Nanos still had a habit of climbing things. She had watched how nimbly he clambered up trees, waiting for the most opportune moment to strike.

Maida had watched, hand over her mouth to keep herself from ruining the game by laughing, as unsuspecting elves passed beneath the tree's branches. The shrieks of surprise could be heard from streets away, and they had become so identifiable that a week ago, Maida found herself muttering *he's got another one* under her breath whenever she heard it.

"Whatever it is you got up to as a child," Deija continued, pointing her needle in Maida's direction. "You can bet that your children will be twice as crafty. Be prepared to keep yourself on your toes."

Maida's smile faltered.

She reached for her patchwork skirt and the new, buttery soft thread that Deija had gifted her. Perhaps, if she busied her hands with work, she would not dwell on the idea of having children or a family.

Because what chance of a family did she have, when she was the only human in the village?

What chance of a future did she have when her past had been burned to the ground?

Did it even matter what answers Aros brought back with him? If there had been survivors at Silktide, that didn't change the fact that she had never truly belonged there in the first place. Nor did it change the fact that she had run away. How could she trust that she would be forgiven and welcomed into the community now?

For the first time, Maida realised that she didn't want Aros to find anything.

If he didn't, maybe she could stay and make a life here. One full of creativity and light.

And besides, she didn't know whether humans and elves could be together or not. Perhaps there was a way to combat the monstrous differences between human and elven lifespans.

Perhaps she could ask the gods for an answer.

"Don't bother the poor girl about such things," Thalia said. "She does not need to be thinking about children now."

"Children between her and Aros would be a pretty sight," Deija said with a shrug.

Maida's cheeks burned bright red.

She bent her head over her work, determined to hide the blush. If she could focus for just a little longer, she would be able to move on to the next phase of her project—embroidery. She loved that part. She loved it when she could take a simple skirt, tunic or pair of trousers and truly make them unique. When she returned to the cottage, she would pull out her old skirt, and cut out the pieces she needed to make pockets. Once the embroidery was complete, the pockets inserted, and the lining stitched to the colourful patchwork, all she'd need to do would be to attach the waistband.

Then, she could get to making her underdress with the fabric Aros had gifted, the piece currently hanging on a line, drying from the latest dandelion dye bath.

Maida had just positioned herself to start the first stitch securing the lining to the top when Nanos appeared by her side.

The bottom of his blue tunic was turned up and bulging from whatever was being hidden within the fabric, leaving his white belly exposed.

Maida eyed him suspiciously.

"And just what do you have there?" she asked him.

"I found you more dandelions!" he declared proudly before he let go of the hem of his tunic.

A pile of bright yellow flowers rained down upon Maida and her project, bringing a laugh bubbling out of her.

Even though she had seen the wonder of the flowers that still bloomed in the meadow, Maida had been surprised to see so many dandelions flowering during the later months of autumn. She was accustomed to seeing them bloom for the first few weeks when the sun lost most of its power and gave way to cooler weather. But they were less than three weeks away from winter now. The children had spent the last two weeks gathering every dandelion they could find, eager to help Maida with her project.

It had been enough to dye the fabric that was currently drying, as well as a handful of spools of thread that she was planning on using to embroider both her underdress and her patchwork skirt.

Each day, she carried back overflowing baskets of the plant, thinking that they had surely found every last bloom.

Each day, she would have another pile of dandelions dumped unceremoniously on her lap by giggling, smiling children.

"Oh my goodness!" Maida breathed. "Where did you find all these?"

Nanos grinned and lifted his chin proudly.

"I'm not going to tell you my secrets!" he said.

Thalia let out the kind of sigh that Maida was now realizing was reserved only for mothers. Maida tried to hide the smile that was tugging on her lips.

"Alright then," she said. "Keep your secrets. But Nanos, I don't need so many dandelions at the moment. Would you want to join us and use them to make yourself a crown?"

Nanos' eyes went wide with wonder.

"Really?" he asked.

"Really," Maida smiled.

Nanos beamed with delight. He took hold of Maida's arm and lifted it. With his free hand, he pushed the dandelions off her lap then sat in it.

Thalia offered her a look that seemed to say, *you can tell him 'no' at any moment.*

But Maida did not want to say no. She enjoyed knowing that Nanos was comfortable enough to perch on her lap. It made her feel... normal. A part of the community of Luvrahn. She shook her head slightly before readjusting herself to begin stitching around him.

Nanos split the stems of the dandelions with his nail, threading the next one through the hole he created. He repeated this process until it was the size he deemed fit. Once he had the base, Nanos continued to thread and braid flowers into it, until every last stem he had collected had been used. By the time it was complete, he had created a crown fit for royalty. The dandelions were bright and proud, highlighted by the vibrant green of their leaves.

Satisfied, Nanos stood and turned to face Maida.

"Are you going to put the crown on now, Nanos?" she asked.

"Nope," he said, shaking his head. "I didn't make this for me."

"Oh?" Maida asked.

"I made it for you."

Then, with as much reverence as a priest crowning a monarch, Nanos lay the crown of dandelions upon Maida's head. Though the flowers themselves were light, Maida couldn't help but feel like a weight had settled upon her.

Nanos stood back to survey his work.

He titled his head, first to the left, then to the right. Suddenly, he clapped his hands loudly in front of him and exclaimed: "Oh!"

Maida jumped. She nearly lost the crown atop her head and shot her hand up to stop it from tumbling to the ground. Tiny yellow petals crumpled beneath her fingers as she readjusted it.

"Are you alright?" she asked Nanos.

"Yes!" he squealed. "I just have it!"

Maida frowned. "What do you mean?" she asked. "What do you have?"

"Your name! I have your name! I know what to call you!"

Maida's breath caught in her throat. She had forgotten that Nanos had charged himself with the task of naming her. Just as she had forgotten that she had given him her blessing to do so.

Around them, the elves of Luvrahn turned to listen eagerly to what it was Nanos had to say.

Maida's heart thundered with anticipation.

"Your new name," Nanos paused for dramatic effect. "Is Bryha."

Hushed murmurs washed over everyone. It felt like time had stopped, like they were all waiting for her to respond.

"That is the most beautiful name I have ever heard," Maida said. "Thank you, Nanos."

Nanos whooped with joy and threw his arms around her. Around them a round of cheers erupted. Palis beamed at her from across the other side of the blankets. Aoife signed *welcome Bryha*, and Maida caught dozens of voices testing out her new name on their tongues.

It seemed that everyone was happy that Maida had finally been named.

Everyone, save for the grey-eyed male who huffed and stormed back to the village.

THIRTY

AROS

SILKTIDE

AROS C'ASAD HAD SEEN war.

He had once been a soldier, after all. Perhaps simply calling himself *a soldier* was not putting a fine enough point on it. He had been one of Queen Meitranis' most trusted advisors. He had led her armies into battle. He had secured victories in her name for decades. He had fought beside her and her Bloodmaids more times than he could count, until finally she had secured peace for their people.

As such, he had seen famine of devastating proportions. He had seen death and murder committed for no reason other than the wickedness of men. He had watched as those who claimed to be fighting for the *greater good* commit atrocities beyond comprehension. And although it had been a good fifty years since he had carried the Queen's banner, or borne the likeness of the Maiden Sword, Aros C'Asad was neither so small minded nor gullible enough to believe that he would never see such atrocities again.

Elves lived far too long to harbour such useless hopes.

And yet, even after Dhuina had described everything that she had seen the last time she set foot in the human town of Silktide, Aros had needed a moment to compose himself before he pushed on.

A weaker male may have found himself doubled over and emptying the contents of his stomach on the ground at his feet. Decades of being surrounded by decay had thankfully hardened Aros' own constitution.

Aros stepped forward.

The three and a half months since the seaside town had been burned to ash had allowed for scavengers of all kinds. While many of the bodies had been eaten or dragged deep into the neighbouring woods – a small blessing, Aros conceded – the stench of burned and rotting flesh still hung heavy in the air. Not even the cloying scent of fish and seaweed could cover it, and no matter how much he reached for his magic to try and stir the air to clear the smell, he could not completely remove it from his nose.

He wondered if this space would ever be free of the reminder of what had happened here.

Perhaps this land would forever be doomed to remember. Perhaps the ghosts of those lost to the flames would haunt this space until time ceased to exist, and the world ended.

Either way, he was glad Dhuina had not tried to convince him to let her come.

He picked through the ruins, careful not to step on sun-bleached bone as he surveyed the damage.

Aros could understand why a young, human girl would turn and run at the sight before him. In honesty, he wouldn't begrudge many for turning tail. For it to still look so bad now, with grass growing between the cracks in the stone paths, and sickly-yellow vines choking the remaining posts and columns from the felled buildings...

Aros kept walking.

He wondered what this place looked like when Dhuina visited. Where was the bakery, where the human boy she was hoping to marry lived and worked? Did the fabric traders that she bought from set up where Aros now stood?

The deeper he went, the more guilt he felt for hoping that Dhuina had been exaggerating. Instead of twisting her memories into something scarier than they were, Dhuina's trauma appeared to have dulled them to make them more palatable.

Aros sighed.

He passed what once might have been an apothecary. He stopped and turned back to peer inside the pane-less remains of the shop window.

Puddles of glass in the debris-covered floor. The bottles and jars that had once lined over-flowing shelves had fallen, shattered, and been met with such heat that the glass had returned to a melted state before finally cooling in large, lumpy sheets. Charred herbs were immortalised within, never to be given the chance to decompose and return to the earth.

His heart fell to the pits of his stomach.

Even with the correct tools, no human would be able to create such a large fire that burned hot enough to melt glass this way while still being able to put it out overnight. Only Igdhraos could—and then, only an Igdhraos with incredible strength and control over their magic.

If they had the assistance of an Aerdhraos, he thought, *they would be able to destroy a town of this size in a matter of hours.*

He squeezed his eyes shut, trying to banish the image that came unbidden to his mind. Two faces – one, as dark and stern as his own, the other paler even than fair Dhuina. An Aerdhraos warlord and his faithful, unstable Igdhraos.

This could be their work. It was as swift and ruthless as they generally operated, with no regard for the lives they stripped away in the process.

But try as he might, Aros could not fathom why they would leave Rupaburg and traverse all of Ailiar just to set fire to human towns. Even if they were to go to the trouble of sowing discord and chaos in the human realm, would they not go to the capital? Why would anyone waste their time with border towns? It resulted in nothing but unrest, which could be quelled. If they wanted to declare war, all they had to do was sail further east.

Aros could not make sense of it.

Though he supposed that Kaidos and Leilara had never needed much of a reason to destroy anything. And it wasn't as though knowing if or why they had destroyed Silktide would be useful to Aros at the moment.

So, he continued onward.

He moved past the lost storefronts and the homes reduced to rubble. He moved past the barren flowerbeds and ignored the odd pile that looked too remarkably like a dog curled outside what should have been a door.

He followed the cracked path, coming to a stop at the edge of the town square.

Dhuina had said they were preparing for a festival. No – the largest festival of their year. This place was supposed to be full of colour and noise, not varying shades of grey and silence. He gazed out over the destruction. The rubble. The ruined remains of dozens, if not hundreds, of lives that had been brought to such a vicious end.

The fountain was supposed to be bubbling, not dry and cracked, with a misshapen lump hanging over the edge.

Aros frowned. From here, he could not confidently identify what that lump was. He stepped forward, each step too loud in his ears as his boots crunched on debris. But what was it?

It looked like a sack, thrown carelessly over the bottom-most pool of the fountain. Black and green strands stretched out from it. The stench of rot grew heavier.

Aros did not stop.

He closed the distance between himself and the fountain. He reached, and took the misshapen thing in his hands and pulled it up and out of the putrid water.

He should have known better.

He should have guessed that it was a body.

The human girl—young, he guessed, but he couldn't be sure—must have fallen over the edge of the fountain before the fire truly erupted. The parts of her that had been exposed to the elements had mostly rotted away or been eaten. But the half of her face that had been in the water was still bloated. The green- and blue-blotched skin began to tear away from the skull, sagging back towards the water it had been pulled from.

That was enough.

That was it.

That was the last thing Aros ever wanted to see of this place.

He set the corpse down on the ground beside the fountain. Let time and beast make short work of the poor girl's remains. She had spent enough time in the foul, stagnant water of the fountain.

Aros turned and made his way back to the main road of Silktide.

Before he left Luvrahn, Dhuina had written down how to find the path to her home. Aros had not expected that he would not need to refer to the notes she had given him. Her voice was clear in his mind, directing him as though she were there by his side.

He had not expected the hollow ache in his chest.

Instead of following the long road up the hill and past the farms, Aros wanted to return to Luvrahn. His feet seemed eager to oblige, and he found himself needing to consciously take each step forward lest they run away with him. He could not return to Dhuina without answers.

No matter how much he wanted to.

No matter how much he longed to lean against his kitchen counter, for-getting that there was stew cooking over the fire while he watched her sew at his dining room table.

No matter the fact that he didn't understand how she had such a hold on him.

He could not return until he got what he came for.

And so, even though he had been walking for two weeks, he walked for two hours more.

He understood how she had survived the attack on her hometown. This walk alone had been her salvation. The farms stretched out eastward rather than south, so he only passed two before all hints of life or dwellings ceased appearing.

Even if the attackers had considered exploring the path, the would have turned back an hour before glimpsing the house nestled in the woods.

Aros himself would have likely abandoned his search for Dhuina's home if she had not warned him of how long it would take. She may have lamented being so sheltered from the townsfolk and the life that ordinary humans lived, but this house had saved her. This house, with its overgrown gardens and dust-caked windows, stood unmarked and untouched by the horrors that had befallen Silktide.

Bright yellow dandelions poked through the dull brown of dead plants in the garden beds that had once been painted a pale blue. The sight of them brought a smile to Aros' lips. Back home, Dhuina had been eagerly watching the dandelions that grew in the fields from the window above the bed. They had begun to bloom the moment the weather had grown milder, much as they did in spring. Aros had never paid much attention to the lifecycle of the sun-like plant, but he had since learned that given the right circumstances, they would once again show their faces in autumn after giving way to the summer heat.

He wondered if Dhuina and her father would have allowed for the dandelions to grow in their flowerbed if they still lived here or whether they would have removed the bitter-tasting plant to make room for more intentional growth.

Regardless, and against all logic, the very sight of these hardy flowers would have been enough to convince Aros that this was Dhuina's home, with or without her directions.

From the moment he opened the door, Aros was overwhelmed with colour. Though muted under a layer of dust, it was still clear that the inhabitants had not been fond of bare walls or surfaces. How Dhuina managed to stay in his cottage with nothing for decoration astounded him. While his curtains were made of plain sackcloth, Dhuina's were made of patchwork, like the skirts he had found her in. The tablecloth was made of the same. Dye pots were stacked haphazardly by the fireplace. Flowers hung from the ceiling to dry.

This was where Dhuina belonged. He could not imagine her anywhere else.

Aros crossed over to the dining table and lifted the pile of fabric that had been left atop it. He turned it over in his hands and brought it to his face so that when he took in a deep breath, he would not be assaulted by dust.

His efforts were rewarded.

The piece—a gown, if he recalled her saying what she had been working on—still smelled like her. She had fallen asleep on it, and it still clung to the notes of honey and mint he had come to associate with her.

Still holding that gown close, he took another look around. Aros could imagine walking through that front door again and finding Dhuina asleep at the table, cushioned by the very fabric in his hands. He could imagine blowing out the candle that had melted itself onto the clay dish it sat on and carrying her to bed. She would curl into him, as she had the night he found her, and he would be loathe not to climb under the blankets beside her.

Aros cleared his throat and shook the image from his mind.

He was being stupid. She was clouding his judgement, and he needed to get her out of his head.

The sooner he did that, the sooner he could return to her.

He took a step back.

The floorboard creaked under his weight.

Aros paused.

He leaned forward, and the board creaked again. He rocked back, and the third creak of wood solidified his decision.

Aros returned the unfinished gown to the table before crouching down. It did not take long for him to pry up the loose board, and even less time for him to retrieve the aged piece of parchment hidden beneath it.

An all-too-familiar weight settled within his chest as he turned the parchment over to reveal the wax seal, and the sword emblem he knew like the back of his hand.

THIRTY-ONE

MAIDA

LUVRAHN

MAIDA HAD MADE A habit out of taking her evening meals with either Aoife and Palis, or Thalia and Nanos. She had not needed to cook herself a single meal since Aros' departure, save for the bread she ate with breakfast. It was an arrangement that she was not eager to have ended, for though she had defended Aros' penchant for meat and potatoes, she enjoyed the variety the two households provided.

Tonight's meal had been roasted poultry and a wide assortment of root vegetables, seasoned with more herbs and spices than Maida had ever seen. The bird had been dropped off by Dorsa that morning. Apparently, it was yet another meal that Thalia was planning on serving at the Wishing.

How Thalia planned on cooking so many meals on her own, Maida couldn't fathom, but the meal had been so good that Nanos had promptly fallen asleep once his plate was done.

"I suppose that means I'll be walking myself home," Maida laughed.

Usually, Nanos escorted her home, but she was not going to wake the poor boy.

"Are you sure?" Thalia asked. "I can walk you."

Maida shook her head and waved her hands in dismissal.

"I'm fine," she said. "And besides, I can't be the lost human girl forever, always escorted from place to place. I have a name now. It's time I start acting like it."

Thalia chuckled.

"Alright," she said. "But if Nanos asks, I walked you home, right to your door."

To Aros' door, Maida corrected mentally. Outwardly, she smiled.

"But take the lantern. You can return it tomorrow," Thalia added

Maida picked up her sewing basket in one hand, and the lantern in the other.

"I'll see you tomorrow, Thalia," she said.

"Tomorrow," Thalia nodded in agreement.

With that, Maida stepped out into the cool night.

She began to walk the now familiar path towards her home, humming under her breath as dirt crunched beneath her boots.

"There she is!"

Maida skidded to a stop, turning towards the slurred voice that had called out. She lifted her lantern to try and get a better look at the tall, lean figure leaning against the well in the centre of town. Even with the ten or so paces between them, she could smell the alcohol on his breath.

"Tell me, human," the male said, pushing off the well and striding towards her. "What makes you worthy of carrying the name of one of our gods?"

When he stepped into the light, Maida recognised the male for who he was. He had been with the hunting party that had found her in the woods. He had been sitting in the tavern during Aoife's story.

He had left the meadow when Nanos had named her.

Holsten.

"If you recall," Maida said, praying her voice did not waver. "It was not me who chose the name. If you have a problem with it, take it up with Nanos. I'm sure Thalia would love to let you interrogate her son."

Maida was certain that Thalia would be more likely to grind Holsten's *bits* in her mortar than to allow him anywhere near Nanos while he was in such a state. Still, the image conjured was rather satisfying.

"Now, if you'll excuse me, I'm going home."

She moved to step around him, but Holsten stepped into her path. His silver eyes reflected the lantern like smouldering embers in ash. They reminded her of her of Silktide, of the smoking, glowing remains of the homes and businesses that had been destroyed.

She didn't trust the look in his eyes. Maida may have grown to trust the people of Luvrahn, but that didn't mean she trusted all elves.

It certainly didn't mean she trusted this male who seemed ready to combust.

Maida lifted her arm to slide her basket from her hand to the crook of her elbow before transferring her lantern into that hand, leaving her right completely free. She rested her fingers atop the basket. Cool iron met her fingertips.

"You should go home," Holsten said. "You should leave here and never return. Ailiar is no place for you, *human*."

"If I could, I would," Maida replied. "And we both know that I now have a name, so if you're going to talk to me at all, use it. Otherwise, just close that festering trap you call a mouth and leave me be."

Holsten shot out his arm, catching her face.

His thumb and forefinger dug into her jaw as he forced her to stare at the shrine of flowers, toys, and candles around the well.

"We went to avenge him," Holsten hissed. "We went to hunt down that beast and bring it's head back for Fisa's mother. And Aros—that famed commander of Queen Meitranis' armies, that beloved brooding pit-stain of a male—came along to keep us inline. I knew the moment he agreed to join us that he would do everything in his power to stop us from killing that monster. And in the end, he killed it himself. For you. So, tell me *why*."

"I'll tell you why," Maida hissed. "When you tell me why it took two weeks of Aros' absence for you to grow the stones needed to confront me."

With a disgusted scoff, Holsten shoved her back. Maida stumbled but did not fall.

"You are nothing," Holsten spat. "They will get tired of their shiny new human toy soon enough. And then, you'll see."

He spat at her feet but turned and staggered away.

Despite her bravado, Maida's legs shook. She rushed back to the cottage, her fingers closed tightly around her shears. She did not sleep that night. Instead, she sat at the dining table with eyes glued to the door.

She was sure that Holsten had wandered off to pass out in some field, but she couldn't truly trust that he would leave her alone.

And so, when the sun finally rose, it found her still gripping her shears like a weapon and staring at that front door.

Thirty-Two

Aros

Luvrahn

WHETHER IT HAD BEEN the carnage or the discovery in Dhuina's home that weighed down upon him, Aros found the journey home to Luvrahn took him longer than it had to reach Silktide.

He was all too aware of the letter tucked neatly against his breast. Some days, he swore that he could feel it rustle and crease with each step. At night, he dreamt that it came to life and whispered untold secrets in his ear about the human girl he had found.

But that was preposterous.

It was nothing more than his mind running away with the dozens of questions and theories that chased each other around and around, denying him a moments peace or a restful sleep.

But finally, after well over a month of travelling, Aros was once again home. He was greeted by the scent of the sheep in the nearby fields, which came to him combined with the woodsmoke from the villagers' hearths.

Once again, bile rose in his throat.

How had Dhuina been able to stomach the smell of smoke or of roasting meat, when she had seen the ruins of Silktide when the embers had still been smouldering? At least Aros had his years of experience to harden him against such horrors. But her?

Aros pursed his lips together and pressed on, stopping at his cottage first.

It was, as he expected, empty.

It made sense for Dhuina to spend more time with Palis and Aoife than in his poor excuse for a home while he was gone, but he hadn't been able to shake the hope that he would find her sitting at his table just this once.

"Get yourself together," Aros grumbled under his breath.

There was no reason he should want her to be sitting in his home other than to know she was safe. Still, the hope and subsequent disappointment at his heart skipping beats and sinking within his chest.

Aros had barely taken two steps towards Palis and Aoife's home when he heard a scream.

His blood ran cold, and his heart stilled.

There was no logical reason to think that the scream had been Dhuina's, but his heart was not listening to his head. Aros dropped his pack and broke out into a run. His feet kicked up dust as he raced through the town, following the continuous scream as it grew louder and louder. Panic and rage fuelled his tired bones as he pushed through the exhaustion of his long journey to find the source.

He left the buildings behind and mounted the crest of a hill, where he nearly skidded to a stop.

It hadn't been a scream that he had heard but a squeal—and one of utter delight if the bright, radiant look on Dhuina's face was anything to go by.

Her wild red curls streamed behind her as she ran through waist-high grass, and another of those squeals broke free of her lips as a small creature leapt out of the grass to tackle her to the ground.

Aros' pulse jumped. He took a step forward, ready to go to her aid, if need be, but the human emerged again. When she did, Aros saw that the creature—now a squirming, thrashing thing tucked tightly under her arm—was Nanos.

His nerves calmed, even as more questions nagged at the edge of his mind.

"And the fearless hunter returns!"

Aros jumped, a curse falling from his mouth. How had he not heard Palis approach? Surely, he had not been so distracted by watching Dhuina that he would lower his guard.

"Palis," Aros muttered his greeting.

"Are you okay?" his friend asked, creases appearing on her smooth brow.

It took a moment for Aros to answer.

"She wasn't exaggerating," he said finally. "The place has all but been wiped off the map. If she had not survived, I would have put money on this being the work of Kaidos and his pet."

Kaidos was not known for his mercy, especially when it came to humans. But Dhuina *had* survived.

Aros was sure that not even Rupaburg would risk angering Meitranis by sending Kaidos into Colosia.

It felt like he was grasping at straws or as though the answers he sought were nothing but smoke, floating just out of his reach.

He felt the weight of Palis' hand on his shoulder. His eyes followed Dhuina as she continued to weave in and out of the grass, chasing after Thalia's boy. Her face was free of the fear and torment he had seen in her a mere month ago.

"Did you find out anything about who she is? What her name might have been?"

Aros shook his head in response. "No. Nothing. I found her home, but nothing with her name. I did find something else, though. Something that raises more questions than it answers."

Before Palis could ask, Aros reached into his breast pocket and pulled out the letter.

He watched as recognition settled on her face. He knew she was wrestling with the exact emotions he had felt when he first beheld the broken wax.

"That's *her* seal," Palis breathed. "Just who did you find in the woods, Aros?"

"I am not quite sure that I know," he admitted. "And I am starting to doubt that I was the only one who did."

THIRTY-THREE

MAIDA

LUVRAHN

As she had every day since Aros had left, Maida chased Nanos through the knee-high grass of the field below the meadow.

She'd opted for a pair of baggy, drop-crotched pants Aros had left behind, pulled tight around her waist with a braided cord she'd been gifted by Ualia, the young girl with ribbons in her hair that Nanos had been chasing through the tavern the night that Aoife had been telling her story. To keep the pants in check at her ankles, she had wrapped two thick strips of woven wool up to the widest part of her calf. If she had the right boots, she wouldn't need the leg-wraps. Boots were next on her list. The waterskin that she had traded the tanner two pairs of pants for swung wildly as she ran, undoubtedly leaving large green and purple bruises on her hip.

She didn't care.

She had recently adopted the ideology that life was not worth living if you spent each day unblemished. To sit idly and let the world pass you by was a life she no longer wanted.

True, she still wanted a peaceful life. That didn't mean it had to be bland, though.

She refused to wonder if this decision had at all been affected by Holsten cornering her all those weeks ago. She would not give him the satisfaction for having any hand in the way Maida decided to live her life. The bastard could

317

rot for all she cared.

Nanos made a hard right, and the bottom of Maida's borrowed boots slipped on the grass as she pitched herself to turn after him. She was going too fast and was nowhere near as nimble as the young boy who had become her constant companion in Aros' absence. So, instead of making the same hard turn as her prey, Maida Tailor ended up face down in the itchy grass.

Instead of crying or cursing herself, Maida laughed. She rolled onto her back and marvelled at just how blue the sky looked when framed by barely browning grass. Or, at least, she would have marveled at that if her vision had not been entirely taken up by the smiling, red face of Nanos.

"Are you okay?" he asked, barely containing his own laughter.

"I'm fine," Maida replied. "I just thought now would be a great time for a nap."

"Yeah, well, you thought wrong," Nanos said. "Now is a great time for chasing. Not napping."

Maida laughed again. With a groan, she pushed herself back up to her feet. She stretched her arms above her head and took a deep breath. She kept a watchful eye on Nanos the whole time, who, despite his laughter, seemed genuinely concerned that Maida may have hurt herself.

Maida decided to take advantage of it, and she lunged toward him with outstretched hands.

Nanos was too quick. He was too slippery and ducked out of her reach, bounding through the tall grass.

Maida swore under her breath and spun to race after him until something caught her attention out of the corner of her eye. She stopped and turned her full attention to the hill that overlooked the meadow and grassy fields.

Her mind must be playing tricks on her.

She had been thinking about Aros too much—*missing* Aros too much.

She had resorted to sleeping with the shirt she had mended the night before, having wanted something that still held his pine scent on it. It made sense for her mind to try to convince her that Aros was the man standing beside Palis watching her.

Because she *wanted* it to be him.

She wanted so badly for those dark fingers that brushed against the top of the grass to be the same that had cupped her cheek before he left that she had somehow convinced herself it was.

But...

Maida took a step forward. How that single step had done anything when there was such a stretch of ground between them, she would never understand, but it had done something. It had triggered something deep within her. It set her heart beating faster than a butterfly's wing. It constricted around her lungs, making her breath quick and shallow.

Because it *was* Aros.

He'd returned.

He'd come home.

Maida took another step forward, then another, making her way through the grass towards him. Her eyes watered inexplicably. Her lips felt too chapped. Her breath sounded too loud. The tender spots on her legs protested each movement, deeming now an appropriate time to make themselves known.

But Maida didn't stop.

She hiked up the hill with a determination she had never felt before. Aros was there, waiting for her. He had walked untold miles, all she had to do was walk up this hill.

"Aros!"

Nanos' voice rang out over the field.

319

Maida managed to tear her eyes away from Aros to watch the blur of boy run past her and up the steepest part of the hill. How he still had the stamina to *run* was beyond her. Perhaps, like she, Nanos had received a second wind. Perhaps his heart was pushing the blood through his veins and filling his young body with so much adrenaline that he had no choice but to surge forward.

Maida was unsure if it was her competitiveness or a strange sense of possession that overtook her when she picked up her own pace. By the time she reached the top of the hill, her face was flushed, and her chest was heaving. She stood, staring silently at Aros, save for the rasping of her breath as she tried to regain it.

He looked much the same as when he'd left, save for the short, thick beard that covered his jaw and the new growth of hair that Palis was already eyeing disapprovingly. But the angle of those cheeks was exactly as she remembered. He had neither lost nor gained weight on his journey. His eyes were just as green as ever, and she could not see a single scar or wound upon him.

Aros held Maida's gaze. She wanted to know what was going on in his head. Had he dreamed about her too? Had he been eager to see the break in the trees of the Edgeling Wood, desperate for a sign that he was almost home so that he could see her?

Was she foolish for having counted the days since he'd left, so that she might guess when he would return?

Distantly, Maida realised that Nanos was rambling on about his adventures. His voice was muted and muffled, as though the presence of Aros C'Asad dampened everything else.

Palis cleared her throat. Maida snapped her head towards the elf, whatever spell that had her transfixed by Aros broken. Nanos, too, fell quiet.

"I'm sorry, but it was getting a little awkward watching the two of you just stare at each other," she said.

Maida's cheeks burned, and she averted her eyes. It was amazing how instantly interesting the growth pattern of grass could be, or how invested one could become in how it fanned out beneath a boot.

"We weren't staring at each other," Aros said.

His voice.

Hearing Aros' voice felt like she had been starved for months only to be put into a great banquet hall. Her eyes fluttered, the grass blurred, and her breath caught in her throat.

"Uh huh," Palis said. "And I wipe the Queen's ass in my spare time. Look, I'm going to take Nanos back to the meadow, but first, I think he wants to introduce you."

"Introduce me?" Aros asked.

Nanos bounced on his heels, still filled with boundless energy.

"Yes, yes, yes!" he said, accentuating each word with a pumping of his fists.

Maida stole a look through her lashes. Aros was smiling. It was a lopsided smile and his eyes followed Nanos' bouncing, up and down.

"Alright," Aros said. "Just who do you have to introduce me to?"

Nanos turned toward Maida and gestured with wide arms and open hands.

"Mr. Aros C'Asad," he declared. "It is my pleasure to introduce you to Miss Bryha of Luvrahn!"

Maida felt the weight of Aros' eyes on her, and once again, she found the ground completely and utterly enthralling. Out of the corner of her eye, she saw the calloused pads of his fingertips enter her field of vision. He was holding his hand out to her, palm up.

Slowly, she slipped her own pale hand into his. She held her breath as Aros lifted it to his lips and pressed a gentle kiss to her knuckles.

"It is a pleasure to meet you, Bryha of Luvrahn."

Maida's insides twisted. Her legs turned to jelly.

The baker's son had never made her feel this way, not even when discussing marriage.

"And with that," Palis said. "You and I are going to go back to your mother."

Nanos groaned and whined in protest, but Palis ushered the child away, leaving Maida alone with Aros.

Silence fell between them, much like it had before. It was heavy, yet not entirely uncomfortable. After a long moment, Maida realised that her hand was still in Aros'. She cleared her throat and pulled her hand free, picking at her nail with her other hand.

"So," Aros said, his voice was warm and sweet as honey. "You have chosen the name 'Bryha.'"

"Technically," Maida said. "Nanos chose the name Bryha. He made me a crown of dandelions, put it on my head, and then seemed to have an epiphany. Apparently, it's the name of some goddess of yours."

She could still smell the mead on Holsten's breath as he leaned over her. She could still feel the cool iron of the shears in her hand as she pressed the point of them against his gut.

"Sort of," Aros said. "I mean, it depends on who you ask. Technically speaking, she is the daughter of an Ancient One, not an Ancient One herself. Her father is Rynhan, the God of the Sky, and Bryha is the goddess of the Sun. She gave the Earth all the yellow flowers, and she is the source of all warmth and light. Legend says she fell in love with the moon, and now they spend eternity chasing one another through the cosmos."

"That sounds rather tragic," Maida said.

"It's one of the great love stories of our people," Aros said. "Nanos chose well though. You shine like the sun, and I can see that you're regaining your warmth."

Maida's breath came out as an airy, weightless thing. She let out a tight, nervous laugh.

"Well," she managed. "I don't know about that."

Silence fell over them again. She chewed her lip, feeling the flaking, dry skin catch beneath her teeth.

"Did you... did you find anyone?"

Aros' smile faded. Maida didn't need him to confirm what that meant.

Her eyes watered.

Aros stepped forward but she kept the distance between them mirroring his movement. She held up her hand to stop him.

"I'm sorry," he said.

Sorry.

He was sorry. For what? He hadn't burned down her home. He hadn't stolen the life she had planned for herself. He had merely been the one to confirm that dark, dreaded thought that had been haunting her for months now—there was nothing to go back to. Should she still want to leave Luvahn, she had nothing.

She supposed it was good that she hadn't thought of leaving for a while now.

"What are you going to do?" Aros asked.

She met his eyes again, and that's where she saw it—the knowledge that she had planned to leave. It was as clear in his eyes as a hole in fabric. He had known, and still, he had left to bring her answers.

Maida reached for the pendant at her throat, pressing the metal petals into her fingertips.

"I suppose you're stuck with me," she said. "At least for winter. In the spring, if you're up for it, you could help me build a house."

Thirty-Four

Maida

Luvrahn

Aros C'Asad had been true to his word.

He had arrived two days before the festival. Unfortunately, this meant that Palis arrived with the dawn on both days, bearing a list of things that the village needed help with to get ready. Maida had listened to Aros' half-hearted protests. She had watched him engage in the friendly, familial banter with Palis as he questioned what she would have done if he hadn't come home in time.

Palis had merely responded that she knew he would, turning to Maida reinforcements. Maida had kept her mouth shut, keeping the promises Aros had made her to herself.

I have survived far too much not to return to you.

I will be home before the Wishing.

He had kept his word, and because of that, Maida was not about to use it against him.

The morning of the Wishing had been bright and clear. There was not so much as a hint of a cloud in the sky as Maida joined Thalia and Nanos in stringing the last of the garlands between houses and wrapping them around tree branches. After a lunch of sandwiches and fruit, Maida was finally ushered back home.

Aros was not there when she returned, and despite having come home to an empty cottage every day for the past month, Maida felt her heart sink like an anchor. It was becoming increasingly difficult to ignore that she felt something for him, just as it was becoming increasingly *easy* to forget that he was an elf, and she was not.

As Maida stripped off her pants and tunic, she wondered if he felt the same. Perhaps tonight would be the perfect time to ask him. It was a celebration, after all—the time of year when elves gave thanks to their gods for blessings bestowed. Despite everything she had lost, Maida could see herself thanking the Ancient Ones for Aros.

At the very least, she could thank *him* for giving her the beautiful, soft fabric she had transformed into the flowing chemise she pulled over her head. Using the dandelions, Maida had been able to colour the fabric a soft, buttery yellow. And though it had taken hours, the collar was gathered with hundreds of tiny, embroidered smocking stitches. It was a detail she would never omit from one of her creations if she had the chance to include it. Smocking allowed for a certain stretch at those crucial points where one would otherwise need to add draw cord or toggles. It was less bulky and looked finer, in her opinion.

She loved it so much that she had added it to the cuffs of the chemise sleeve. It added to the volume of the ruffles around her wrist, and there was something so utterly enjoyable about the gentle firmness of the fabric as it hugged her.

Once the chemise was in place, Maida pulled her new patchwork skirt over her head. It slipped smoothly over the underlayer and, once secured with the bone toggles at the back, sat snugly at her waist. She twirled, making the fabric fan out in a kaleidoscope of colour. She had embroidered flowers and swirls onto the bright colours, and Aleicia—Luvrahn's resident spinner—had crocheted a scalloped border for the hem.

It was just similar to the one she had made in Silktide, only brighter and richer in colour.

Then again, Maida supposed that *she* was brighter now too.

Satisfied that the patchwork skirt and the dandelion chemise complemented each other enough and were sitting correctly, she pulled on her final layer. The bodice made of brown, tightly woven linen, was given structure by the kapriae hair sandwiched within.

Dorsa had told her how the gambesons were constructed similarly, but with more layers of linen, each soaked in glue to make them firmer and more impenetrable. Maida had wondered what was used in Colosia, where kapriae did not exist.

She laced up the bodice at the front with a thin strip of the fabric she'd used for the chemise, bringing the garment tight and snug around herself.

She wished she had a mirror.

She wished Aros would come back.

Maida toyed with her pendant, running it back and forth along the chain. It was the only thing she had left of Silktide, the only thing she had ever had to remind her of the mother she had never met.

What would she think of Maida's current situation? What would she think of Maida's decision to stay?

A familiar knock rapped on the door, and Maida let the flower-shaped pendant drop back against her chest. She turned towards the door, waiting for it to open.

She didn't need to wait long. Palis Reih rarely waited for an invitation before letting herself in. It was a habit that Maida had been forced to become accustomed to quickly. This time, Palis crossed the threshold wearing a skirt of her own, foregoing her standard pants and tunic attire.

Flowers of all shapes, colours and fragrances were piled into the basket hanging from her arm, though Maida did not miss the sheer number of dandelions that made up the bulk of it.

"You're dressed!" Palis said. "Good. Once I've finished with your hair, we can go down to the meadow. The festivities are about to begin."

Palis ushered Maida to sit at the table. She set down the basket and pulled free a brush and comb.

Maida barely had time to get comfortable before Palis was brushing through her hair and twisting braids into it.

"Where's Aros?" Maida asked.

Behind her, Palis chuckled.

"Did you miss him that badly?" she replied.

"Didn't you?" Maida returned. "You two are close. You've known each other for years, right?"

Palis continued to braid Maida's hair, but her speed faltered.

"Try nearly two centuries," she said. "We knew each other as children. We were as close as siblings, even when Meitranis came along."

"Meitranis?" Maida asked. "Isn't that your Queen?"

"Your Queen now," Palis said. "You live here, so she's your Queen, too. But yes, that Meitranis. Aros fell in love with her the moment he saw her. Most people did, I suppose. She was beautiful, bright, happy, and carefree. She didn't really want to rule, but the heir of Ailiar does not get to decide their fate."

Maida frowned. "Surely that is the same for all monarchs, though," she said. "The first born is the heir in most countries, right?"

"Usually," Palis replied. "But in Ailiar, it's different. The monarchy is bound by magic—only the first-born daughter of the first-born daughter can take power. Only the true heir can wield bloodstone and the Maiden Sword."

328

Maida still wasn't quite sure she understood.

"What if the royal family is overthrown? Aros used to be a soldier, so I know you have wars. If the royal family is overthrown and a usurper takes power, what then?"

"Then the world will descend into chaos," Palis said. "Though we aren't exactly sure what that chaos will entail, we can imagine that it would be unending war, famine, plague, and disastrous natural phenomena beyond our imagination. Only Rupaburg has been stupid enough to wage war against us and risk killing the last in line. And now, to keep the peace, one of their own is married to her. We have not been engaged in any form of combat since."

Palis continued to braid Maida's hair until it was twisted into a crown atop her head, threaded with flowers and ribbons.

Then, she reached for a small hand mirror in the basket and handed it to Maida.

Maida's breath caught. Her cheeks had filled out, and her freckles stood proudly amongst the slightest tan imaginable. Her eyes seemed to shine with life, and her hair burned with a lustre never before seen.

"Oh my," she breathed.

"You, my dear," Palis said, fixing an errant curl. "Are stunning. Aros won't know what to do with you."

Maida's cheeks burned with the heat of a thousand suns. She set the mirror down, unable to stomach looking at herself any longer.

"Come," Palis said. "Let's go celebrate."

Maida looped her arm through Palis' and allowed her friend to lead her out of the cottage and down the path. It didn't take long for the sound of music and laughter to catch up to them. The sun was already beginning to set over the horizon, and the days were already far too short. Lanterns hung from trees and lined the paths, flames flickering joyously within their confines.

The smell of roasting meats and caramelised sugar was carried on a gentle breeze towards them.

Even though she was still sated from her lunch, Maida's stomach growled. She decided the first thing that she would do would be to grab something to eat, but as soon as they rounded the corner and saw the meadow laid out all in front of them, that idea vanished.

The entire township of Luvrahn had gathered here. Whether they stood in clusters chatting or danced in either pairs or groups, or whether they sat on one of the many blankets under the stars, they had one thing in common. There was something about the quality of the excitement radiating off them all that Maida had never experienced before. Was this what celebrations were supposed to be like? Was the bubbling excitement within her something to be expected from such festivals?

She had never attended any festival in Silktide. The mid-summer festival was supposed to be her first. And so, she had no way to prepare herself for the way the music seemed to enter her body and encourage her to move.

A male elf with dark brown hair and kind amber eyes took her hand and pulled her over to a group that was already well into a dance. Before she knew it, she was being spun around.

Laughter bubbled from her lips as she danced and twirled. She was passed from partner to partner, the dance never ending. For a fleeting moment, she wondered if this was where the tales of elves forcing humans to dance until their feet were worn down to nubs came from. She spun and spun, dancing in the arms of men, women and children alike.

It seemed as though every last elf in Luvrahn wanted to dance with their human—every elf, except for Holsten. But Maida would not lament that fact. If she never saw that horrid man again, would be all the happier for it.

The dancing seemed never ending until finally she was handed off to a set of familiar arms.

Maida did not need to look up to know who the firm chest belonged to, but she smiled up into Aros' face all the same.

And oh, was he a beautiful man.

If his complexion had reminded her of the night sky when she first saw him, now she was certain that he had stepped out of the cosmos. She could imagine the star-lit heavens parting to reveal this god of slumber, of revel-ry—of all things that took place on moonless nights.

The silver piercings along the long points of his ears only served to cement this idea in her mind as they reflected lanternlight like shimmering stars.

"You look beautiful tonight," Aros said. He twirled her on the dancefloor.

Maida's felt warmth colour her cheeks and prayed that the light was poor enough that he wouldn't notice.

The smile that tugged on the corner of his mouth said otherwise, however, and she only blushed more fiercely.

"You dance differently than the others," Maida said.

Immediately, she cursed herself for saying so completely and utterly stu-pid.

"Well, you know we all have varying histories," Aros said. "Mine involved ballrooms and dance lessons."

Maida's brow furrowed, earning her a chuckle from her dance partner.

"What? Don't believe me?"

"Actually," Maida said. "Out of all the people that live here in Luvrahn, you are the last person I would expect to have grown up anywhere near ballrooms."

They were pressed so close to one another that Aros' laugh reverberated through her. She was keenly aware of his hand spanning her lower back, his breath on her neck as he tucked her close for yet another spin.

Gods above and below.

Surprise graced her when she realised that she had leaned on the elven plea, but if she were being honest—there was no human equivalent. Every point of contact between her and the elf felt as though it had been set alight, and the only thing she could think of to grant her any kind of help or clarity was the gods themselves.

Maida let him sweep her in graceful arcs around the makeshift dancefloor, unaware that the other villagers had ceased their dancing to stand back and watch. For all she knew, she and Aros were the only two souls left in the world.

The illusion of solitude was short-lived. Aros slowed their steps to a gradual stop, letting go of Maida's waist to brush back rogue curls that had fallen from her thick braid.

His fingers traced her jaw, coming to rest under her chin.

This was it. Maida Tailor was about to be kissed by an elf. Her traitorous heart pounded in her chest, and her eyes fell onto Aros' lips.

"It's time."

Palis' voice had never been more unwelcome.

Aros stepped back. The absence of his skin on hers was more prominent than his touch had been. Determined not to show her disappointment, Maida turned to face Palis.

"Are you ready to send your wish to the gods?" Palis asked.

The truthful answer would be a resounding 'no'.

Despite Palis' attempts to convince her otherwise, Maida was still not entirely certain that the elven gods would be interested in listening to a human's wishes or dreams. And if they were not interested in hearing them, how could she possibly imagine that they would deign to grant them?

Surely it was a fool's hope to even dare to dream that the Ancient Ones would take their time to listen to what she wished for.

Surely, they would do nothing more than laugh at the desires that had taken root in her heart.

But Maida did not voice such sentiments. Instead, she smiled and nodded.

She allowed her friend to take her hand and tug her away from the makeshift dancefloor to the blankets that covered the ground just before the crest.

Maida had been too distracted dancing with Aros to notice that many had already migrated this way. Thalia sat with Nanos on her lap, pointing up at a bright star in the sky that had not been there before. On the blanket beside her sat Deija, holding a candle reverently before her.

Everyone, it seemed, focused their attention on that impossibly bright star that had appeared out of nowhere.

Maida stared up at it in awe herself. How had she not noticed it before? Surely, the star did not just show up out of the blue. Or... maybe it did.

Palis let go of Maida's hand and sat on the left blanket with Aoife. Maida wondered what to do only momentarily before she felt Aros' warm hand rest on the small of her back, guiding he to the blanket on the right.

Together, they sat.

Aros leaned back on his elbows and stretched out his legs in a display of comfort and relaxation that Maida had never seen in him before. If she had thought the star beautiful, it was nothing compared to the man beside her.

"What now?" she asked in a hushed whisper.

"Now," Aros said, equally as quiet. "You look upon the Star of Oliantra and talk to the gods. You tell them your fears, your hopes and your dreams. You thank them for the good things that came this year, and then you ask that they grant you your desires for the year to come."

Maida chewed her lip as she returned her attention to the silver, glittering star.

A mere month ago, she would not have anything to thank the gods for. A month ago, she would have begged the gods to show her a way home.

Now, though, her desires had completely and utterly changed.

She looked up to that star and silently begged with everything that she had, desperate for the stars to hear her.

THIRTY-FIVE

CALLIOPE

BALLIACH

THROUGH THEIR REFLECTIONS IN the gilded mirror, Calliope watched Lady Jaena Cu'Sar hum as she twisted Calliope's hair into intricate braids atop her head. Ever since her cousin had arrived from Rupaburg, she had taken over most of Calliope's grooming and dressing. Calliope had protested, but the maids previously responsible for the job seemed all too enthusiastic about handing over this particular set of duties to someone else.

Calliope shoved away the sensation of abandonment that had come with that.

"I am so excited," Jaena said.

Her smile was so wide that Calliope swore she could see every one of those bright, white teeth. They looked remarkably smooth, like the pearls she was sewing into Calliope's hair.

Was there ever a time that Jaena did not smile? What would it take to wipe that joy from her face?

How cruel was Calliope, that she was fantasising about destroying the hope and happiness of someone who had done her no wrong?

"Do they celebrate the Wishing in Rupaburg?" Calliope asked.

Jaena shook her head.

"No," she said. "We share some gods, but Oliantra is not one of them. And Rupaburgans don't really spend much time worrying about silly things such as wishes. They tend to make their own luck."

Calliope wondered if Jaena felt as lost and adrift as she did. She spoke of Rupaburg as if she didn't belong there, as if she hadn't been born and raised amongst the famously frigid mountains.

Jaena slid the last pin in place in Calliope's hair.

"There!" she declared triumphantly. "All done!"

Calliope took a moment to admire Jaena's work. As much as she disliked her cousin's constant chatter, she had to admit that Jaena knew what she was doing when it came to the matter of hair styling. It looked like Calliope had defiant curls determined to break free of the braids, rather than the limp, straight locks she actually possessed.

Her eyes were painted with a light dusting of red and gold, which complemented the dark crimson gown she wore. The candlelight glinted off the beads embroidered on the stiff bodice, giving the illusion of living, flowing blood.

For perhaps the first time in her life, Calliope Ailiar felt like the future Queen.

"Shall we?" Jaena asked.

Calliope took one last moment to admire herself in the mirror before nodding at her cousin.

Together, with a Bloodmaid in tow, the two wandered through the twisted halls of Balliach castle. The sound of music grew louder the closer they got to the Great Hall.

And the closer they got to the Great Hall, the more Calliope's heart pounded. By the time they reached the heavy doors, it was thundering in her ears.

"Are you ready?" Jaena asked.

Calliope wanted to yell at her.

Of course, she wasn't ready. The fragile confidence she had found looking at her reflection was now gone, shattered beyond repair. She wanted nothing more than to turn tail and run back to her room. Perhaps she would lock the door and stay isolated and alone until she starved to death.

Instead, Calliope took a deep breath and nodded.

Taking that as the order, the guards stationed outside the Great Hall opened the doors, revealing the revelry within.

Aside from the Hall of Queens and the Maiden's Garden, Balliach's Great Hall was one of the most glorious places in all the land. It stood two stories tall, and the strategic placement of gold-framed mirrors and opulent chandeliers bathed the space in a warm, golden light. The accents of bloodstone running through the walls and floor like the veins within marble seemed to glow of their own accord, pulsing in time with the music that flowed from the orchestra on the balcony above.

Stationed atop platforms that had been brought in and set up throughout, performers of all types showed off their skills. Igdhraos had their flames dancing around each other like ribbons. Saldhraos had strings of stone moving through the air as weightless as feathers, shaping and reshaping them into various animals to the delight of all in attendance. Visdhraos showered the noblemen and women with glittering bubbles that landed atop their heads and stuck in their hair.

Calliope's breath was stuck in her throat as she took in the majesty of it all. While her eyes darted from performer to performer, she could almost forget that her mother had refused to see her. Was this the way she was going to spend the rest of her life, distracting herself from the sheer fact that her own mother did not care for her?

Perhaps she was simply busy, Jaena had said.

Perhaps.

Or, perhaps Meitranis had been made privy to information that Calliope had not, leading her to the decision not to waste any more time on her only daughter.

Calliope took a shaking breath and lifted her chin.

"Her Royal Highness, Calliope Ailiar. Descendant of the Maiden, First Daughter of the First Daughter, Heir to the Throne and the next Bearer of the Sword," the herald announced.

Heat rose to Calliope's cheeks as the gathered nobles paused both their dancing and their conversations to look toward the door. She clenched her jaw and kept her eyes forward, refusing to meet the gaze of anyone as they bent at either waist or knee in deference to her.

Just within the confines of her periphery, Calliope caught sight of Jaena dipping into a curtsey as well.

"And accompanying her, Lady Jaena Cu'Sar."

There was a whisper of dozens of dresses brushing against one another as the noblewomen lowered their curtsies ever so slightly in acknowledgement of Calliope's companion. Some of the lords snuck looks at Jaena before clearing their throats and returning their attention to the stone floor.

Calliope swallowed the lump in her own throat.

They aren't bowing lower for her, she told herself. *They're already bowing, and simply don't want to look rude.*

That was it. It had to be. Who in their right mind would show more deference to the cousin of the Blood Heir than to the heir herself?

And besides—Calliope didn't care about *them.* She did, however, care about the woman sitting at the other end of the Great Hall, to the left of her father.

Calliope's mother, Meitranis, sat with her back ramrod straight. Her blazing hair was styled in a way that mimicked a waterfall, braids pinned atop her head with long, flowing strands cascading downwards.

She looked as though a river of fire flowed from the crown atop her head.

She looked fierce.

She looked... right through Calliope.

That lump returned to her throat.

It was as though Meitranis did not register that her daughter had entered, or that she even recognised her.

Calliope's eyes stung with traitorous tears. But now was not the time to mourn the gaping rift between herself and her mother. She lifted her chin, steeled her gaze, and stepped forward.

She did not care who was in her way. She was Calliope Ailiar, daughter of the Blood Queen, descendant of the Maiden, and heir to the Ailian throne.

They could move, or she could walk over them.

Like a great sea parting, the crowd made way for her and her cousin.

Hesitantly, as though they fearful of being reprimanded, the orchestra struck up again.

By the time Calliope and Jaena reached the long table at the end, standing across from the Queen and King, the music had swelled back to its fullest. The guests began dancing again, though they gave Calliope a wide berth.

Jaena dropped into a low curtsey. Oprianos responded with a nod and kind smile.

Meitranis, however, simply continued to stare.

She was dressed in Ailiar red—as usual. Her bloodstone crown only served to cement the image of a lake of fire in Calliope's mind. Her cheeks were more drawn than Calliope remembered, the high cheek bones too prominent, her skin too pale. Her wide eyes were too sunken, and the shades of light brown and shimmering gold did nothing to hide that fact.

She looked... not like herself.

And she was still wearing that godsdamned black stone about her throat.

Calliope could not remember when her mother had first started wearing the garish necklace of twisted iron, but once she had begun wearing it, Meitranis had not taken it off. It was disgusting, and it suited neither Meitranis nor her wardrobe.

Calliope didn't understand why she continued to wear it.

"Your Majesty," Calliope said, dipping her head in respect to her mother.

Still, Meitranis did not move. She did not speak. She did not so much as hint that she knew who was standing in front of her.

Oprianos leaned over and whispered in her ear.

Meitranis' lips curled into a smile.

"Calliope," she said. "You look beautiful. Please, sit. Enjoy your evening."

Calliope's eyes stung once more with fresh hot tears. She turned to her father, who simply offered a warm, kind smile and gestured to the seats waiting for Calliope and Jaena.

She sniffed and lifted her chin.

She would not let tears fall.

With a final bow of her head, she turned and made her way to her seat.

The moment she and Jaena were seated, servants filled their waiting goblets with wine.

Calliope reached for her cup, drinking perhaps a little too deeply.

For the first time since Jaena had arrived, Calliope was grateful for the mindless prattle that she devolved into. Though she didn't pay attention to the remarks on gowns or gossip, the sound was enough to distract herself from the strangeness her mother had exhibited.

Was she sick?

Was her mother dying?

Was that why she hadn't seen her for so long?

Would she make it until Calliope came into her Affinity and could rule?

Her mind was plagued with questions. She allowed Jaena's babbling to drown most of them out, until suddenly Jaena leaned back in her seat a little too quickly. The expression of disgust on her face appeared only briefly before it was once again schooled into the perfectly approachable smile that Calliope was used to. Calliope supposed she would soon learn the answer to the question that she had been thinking earlier—what would it take to wipe that smile from Jaena's face?

"Are you alright?" Calliope asked.

Jaena did not have time to respond as Councillor Sancor leaned his gnarled hands on the red and gold brocade tablecloth. The cloying stench of dust and mildew threatened to overtake the warm, honey and vanilla scent of Calliope's perfume in as much the same way the dark fabric of Sancor's sleeve threatened to swallow all the colour and opulence around it. Calliope would concede that there was something to be said about how easily Councillor Sancor could ruin a moment.

At least now she knew what had Jaena's smile faltering. She couldn't begrudge her cousin's visceral reaction to the wretched man. She could only hope that she'd exhibited as much mastery over her own that Councillor Sancor would not find some way of punishing her for it later.

"Your Highness," Councillor Sancor said. He swayed a little on his feet, and the rich, tart notes of the wine were carried on his breath. "I am so terribly sorry to hear that your betrothed could not be present for such a wonderful occasion."

Calliope pursed her lips together. He was drunk. Calliope had never seen him drunk before.

"Thank you," she said cautiously. "I cannot say that I am unconcerned for the prince's safety and wellbeing, but I will admit that I am grateful for the chance to celebrate our most holy day with my family one last time before I must share it with my future husband."

Councillor Sancor made an odd noise in the back of his throat. Calliope could not tell if it was one of approval or derision, but the guttural sound had her muscles tensing, ready to flee.

"Once could argue that the prince is now a part of your family," he said. "That is, after all, how marriage works. You leave your family to join another."

He offered a smile that was far too large to be genuine. It was wolfish, predatory. It was a smile that Calliope expected to find on a dark, hooded figure down the end of an alleyway, not on the face of a man beloved by the king and granted the high position of tutoring the crown princess.

"Perhaps the prince will not want to partake in our customs," Calliope said. "And I cannot say I relish the idea of forcing him to do so. As much as the Wishing means to me, I would not want it marred by the presence of someone who does not appreciate its significance, or who does not wish to be a part of it."

And besides, she thought. *He will not be considered a part of this family until we have said our vows.*

If he ever feels like family at all.

Calliope returned his predatory smile with a sweet one of her own. It hurt her cheeks. It strained her lips to the point she worried they would crack.

But Councillor Sancor seemed to have accepted defeat.

He nodded and straightened, withdrawing those old, musty sleeves from the beautiful brocade tablecloth.

Jaena shifted her weight in her seat.

"Enjoy the festivities, Councillor," Calliope said.

"And you, Your Highness."

Councillor Sancor bowed low, his stench seeping into Calliope's nose.

It took every ounce of self-control that she had not to curl it in disgust. Finally, Councillor Sancor took his leave, stalking back to his seat.

Jaena snorted a laugh. She brought a napkin to her face to hide her unladylike display.

"I'm glad *someone* found that encounter funny," Calliope said under her breath. "But I will remind you who froze when he first made an appearance."

"I do so hope you get rid of him when you are Queen," Jaena said, reaching for her goblet of wine. "His very presence makes me feel unwell. I don't understand how you put up with him."

Calliope turned to look at her cousin. How did she have the courage to voice the thoughts that Calliope only dared think? She could not deny how liberating it felt to have someone to share in the misery that Councillor Sancor spread amongst all those he met. Was this what friendship felt like? Bonding over a mutual disdain for someone truly horrendous?

She chuckled, earning herself a surprised yet kind smile from Jaena.

"If you like," Jaena said. "I would be honoured to be by your side when you make your Wish to Oliantra."

Calliope paused.

Making your Wish to Oliantra was a personal thing. It was something shared with family, friends and loved ones. Technically, Jaena was family, so Calliope supposed that meant she *should* allow Jaena to stand beside her while she made her Wish.

She opened her mouth to reject the offer, but the words that came out surprised her:

"I would be honoured to accept."

Jaena smiled.

Confused at the betrayal of her own voice, Calliope spent the rest of the celebration feeling untethered.

She saw the plates of roasted meats being brought to the table. She tasted the rich sauces and the crisp potatoes. She knew that she stood and danced, but it was as though she were experiencing it all from outside of herself.

It was not until a loud, ancient bell tolled, signalling the time for everyone to make their way outside to gaze upon the Star of Oliantra, that she seemed to snap back into her body.

"Are we ready?" Jaena asked, looping her arm through Calliope's.

Calliope forced a smile, then looked over her shoulder at her parents.

Her father led Meitranis toward a spiral staircase tucked at the back of the Great Hall. The staircase was usually closed off, the archway hidden by stone manipulated by skilled Saldhraos. Now, however, a golden glow emanated from it, and the Queen and King began their ascent, followed by four Bloodmaids.

Calliope took a deep breath and followed.

The Bloodmaid assigned to her for the evening kept close behind her as the royal family climbed the winding staircase to a small balcony that overlooked the gardens. The Bloodmaids remained in the stairwell in single file, leaving the limited space outside for Meitranis, Oprianos, Calliope and Jaena.

The balcony had been built specifically for the Wishing. It was the perfect spot for gazing upon Oliantra's Star and offered for those below the perfect view of the royal family.

Calliope gazed down at her people gathered below.

What would they wish for? What would they be thankful for?

Meitranis looked up at the Star, reaching to touch the strange black stone around her throat.

Calliope still didn't understand why she had chosen such a necklace. It did not compliment her outfit at all—it was too bulky, too plain. She wore it every day.

Clearly, Meitranis had not given up on her appearances—her dress and hair were far too fine for that. But that necklace...

"Look how beautiful it is," Jaena whispered.

Calliope looked up to the sky.

The Star of Oliantra was indeed beautiful. It shone brightly, glittering like a diamond against the dark sky.

What are you going to wish for?

What *could* she wish for? She had everything she could ever want, except...

Calliope stole one last look at her mother before she turned pleading eyes back to the Star of Oliantra and made her fervent wish.

Thirty-Six

Aniaija

The Sea Between Seas

"How do you think they're going to take the news?"

Aniaija drummed her fingers atop the half-empty crate of apples while she considered her answer to Dapsa's question. The apples were on the verge of being too rotten to eat, despite the efforts of herself and the other Saldhraos to slow the effect of decay.

She doubted the crew's reaction to the news that they would not be able to let as loose as they were used to would be a positive one. The Wishing was the biggest celebration on the Ailian calendar. Grumbled complaints had rippled through the crowd like a stone dropped into a lake when it had been announced that they would not be returning to the Oasis to the celebrate the holiday with their loved ones. It had taken the better part of an hour to remind them that returning to the Oasis empty-handed was not the solution and that they risked missing their last chance of looting enough stock for the winter.

A small pocket of the crew didn't seem to share the same wisdom, and Aniaija didn't miss the harsh looks sent her way. Nor did she miss the fact that those same looks had not been cast in Geomar's direction. She feared she would never understand what some people hated most about her. In a crew made up almost completely of Ailian citizens, it didn't make sense for her gender to have played a part in the way people doubted her. With a matriarchal royal family that stretched back millennia, hatred towards women was blissfully uncommon. Perhaps it was the barely detectable Zadanese accent, peppered with a smattering of Rupaburgan inflections that she could never shake despite her best attempts. It could even be that a Saldhraos had risen throughout the ranks and become the second in command aboard a ship built for the sea—a position traditionally only held by a Visdhraos or Aerdhraos.

She felt a weight press against her leg and looked down to find Tobie rubbing against her.

That, she thought. *That is probably why they hate me so much.*

"I don't know," Aniaija admitted, her voice quiet. "Actually, I don't think they'll take it well at all. But I don't understand—we do inventory regularly; we keep on top of what we have. We ration everything down to the last crumb. Did we really miscount so poorly that we thought we had a whole other crate?"

Dapsa closed the distance between them, the heels of her boots clicking loudly on the floor. She cupped Aniaija's face in her hands and forced her to look into her eyes.

Not for the first time, Aniaija wondered just how irreparably she would damage their friendship if she were to just lean forward and steal a kiss from her.

"This is not the time to spiral," Dapsa said firmly. "And I know it is very tempting to let yourself break down right now, but your crew needs you. *I* need you. Now, we will take this crate up to the deck and we will let them have as many apples as they want tonight alongside their regular rations. They're just going to have to do without alcohol this year."

Aniaija whined like a child being told they could not have any more sweets. A ship's crew without alcohol was probably worse than a crew without food. If they weren't already considering a mutiny, she was sure they would once it was announced that they would not be allowed to drink during the celebrations.

"They're going to tie me up and drag me behind the ship as sandwyrm bait," Aniaija protested.

"Not if I have anything to say about it," Dapsa said. She patted Aniaija's cheek affectionately before letting go of her face. "Come on, let's get this up there and deliver the news. The sooner we start, the sooner it's over, and the sooner you can hide in the crow's nest like the brooding little beetle you are."

Aniaija curled her nose and furrowed her brow.

"A *beetle*?" she asked, dumbfounded. "Did you seriously just call me a *beetle*?"

"What if I did?" Dapsa asked. "What are you going to do about it, beetle?" She walked around the crate to the other side with a dazzling smile on her face.

"Are you going to help me lift this or not?" she asked.

Aniaija considered the merits of making Dapsa carry the crate upstairs alone, but ultimately decided against it. Though both women were strong enough to lift the crate on their own, they had always shared the load whenever they could. And besides, Aniaija had been called worse than a *beetle* before.

Together, the two women carried the crate of apples up to the deck. Dapsa whistled to grab the attention of the crew, and Aniaija waited for the chatter to die down.

"Now," Aniaija began. "We all know that this year has been our most difficult. We have had to restrict rations more every day. And I know that the Wishing is usually the time of year when we relax those restrictions a little and really enjoy ourselves during the holiday."

Murmurs rippled throughout the crew.

"Unfortunately, we cannot be quite as frivolous as we have been this year. We don't have enough alcohol for everyone, and we don't have enough rations to put on a feast."

"First, you're stopping us from seeing our families, and now you're taking away our food?" a voice called.

Aniaija searched the crowd for the owner of the voice but couldn't find them.

Geomar should be taking care of this, she thought bitterly.

"No," Aniaija said. "We aren't taking anything away. I know it's not much, but unfortunately, all we have to spare is this crate of apples. Everyone can eat as much as they want, but we have nothing else to offer."

"We can't even drink?"

"We don't have enough alcohol for everyone, so we've decided that no one should be drinking tonight," Aniaija said.

Timidly, Nori raised his hand.

Aniaija frowned. "Yes, Nori?"

"I... might be able to solve that problem."

Dapsa crossed her arms. "What do you mean?"

"I..." Nori said, looking like a child about to receive a reprimand. "I have been distilling wine from cacti. And I have enough for everyone, so..."

Aniaija's jaw dropped open. A million and one questions raced through her mind at once:

How long has Nori been distilling cactus wine?

How had no one noticed that he was distilling cactus wine?

If he had enough for everyone, where the Tide had he been hiding it?

"Alright..." Aniaija said. "I suppose, if you're willing to share, then we see no objections."

To her surprise, a cheer rose from the crew.

Nori's cactus wine was strong.

Within a few hours, the *Mercy's* deck was covered with snoring sailors, carried off to the land of dreams on the wings of alcohol. The cloying, sickeningly sweet scent that accompanied the drink seeped from the sailors' pores and tainted the desert air. Aniaija felt as though she were walking through a forest of cacti, as thick and luscious as the jungles in Zadanai, as she carefully picked her way through the sleeping bodies.

She had tried to go to sleep herself, but the single cup of cactus wine had not been enough to lure her into the same deep state of unconsciousness as her peers. When those around her started dozing off propped up against crates and barrels, she had disappeared below deck to curl up on her hammock. Then, when sleep remained elusive, driven away by snores and drunken ramblings of those who carried on conversations in their sleep, she decided that she couldn't take staring at the cracked ceiling any longer.

Instead, she stood at the bow of the *Mercy*, and stared up at the Star of Oliantra.

The Star still shone brighter than any other around it. Aniaija had never been able to wrap her mind around the phenomenon of a star appearing only one night of the year.

She grew up following the teachings of the Tide. She was a sailor, accustomed to using stars for guidance and navigation. This had led to her feeling more than just a little uncomfortable with the idea of something as constant and unchanging as the stars just... vanishing.

That discomfort had been why, after so many years surrounded by Ailians who still worshipped the Ancient Ones, Aniaija had never before partaken in the festivities. Sure, she'd have a drink and chat when approached, but more often than not, Aniaija holed herself away in the crow's nest. She told herself that it was for security, that she was merely keeping an eye out in case the Royal Navy decided to take advantage of the crew's distraction, or if a sandwyrm decided to start their annual surfacing the moment the seasons changed. No matter how hard she tried, or how many times she repeated that same, tired excuse to herself, Aniaija could not ignore the real reason she separated herself from the crew during the holiday.

The truth was, Aniaija did not feel like she belonged.

True, her quick thinking and decisive action had saved their lives. She had sailed under Geomar before. Tide, she had even engaged in an impromptu friendly wager with the captain regarding just how many women they could coax to their beds. But a Saldhraos didn't belong on the sea. Aside from working with the Igdhraos to create cannonballs, there was nothing really that a Saldhraos could contribute other than menial labour.

She had spent her earliest years in Zadanai, until her parents had decided that Ailiar would afford them more opportunities. Instead, Ailiar had been their death, and if it hadn't been for Geomar, it would have been Aniaija's as well.

The soft, steady *thump-thump-thump*s of Tobie's steps alerted Aniaija to the cat's decision to follow her out. She would not have been surprised if it had not been for how much the crew had played with the stone beast in their drunken revelry. Aniaija had expected Tobie to sleep like, well... a rock. But apparently, the crew had not worn Tobie out well enough, and Aniaija's movements had garnered some level of excitement.

"You are going to be useless if we find rodents on the ship tomorrow," Aniaija said to the golem.

Tobie rumbled in response. The golem wove in and out of her legs before jumping up onto the railing and pressing its stone body against Aniaija.

Aniaija chuckled and returned her attention to the Star.

She didn't understand the tradition of offering your wishes to the gods. Offering them all to only *one* god was even less understandable, especially if one also expected this deity to delegate wishes accordingly. How could anyone truly believe that there was a deity so benevolent that they would listen to whatever it was you had to ask them?

The Tide was easier to understand.

It did not listen to prayers or wishes—it simply carried you to where you needed to be. The Tide knew what you were destined for, and so it would ensure that you ended up in just the right spot to be able to fulfil said destiny.

Though, in all honesty, Aniaija had found herself uncertain of the Tide's plans for her. She could not imagine that the Tide would have intended for her to end up so far away from any ocean, river, or stream. Even as a Saldhraos, Aniaija was certain that she was not supposed to be stuck in the middle of a desert, with *hundreds* of souls dependent on her for their survival.

She felt so strongly that she should be in a small yet busy seaside town, working on the docks and returning home to a smiling wife. She dreamed about walking in through a front door with hinges just a little too loose that one had to lift the door as they opened it to avoid a horrific shriek, only to find her wife curled up on an overstuffed and over-patched chair under the window. She wouldn't care if she came home to an empty plate, or if the hearth had been left unattended for so long that the fire had gone out, so long as her wife's face brightened when she realised Aniaija was home.

Her eyes stung with tears while she grieved a life she had never lived.

The Star seemed to be winking at her, and for the first time ever, Aniaija felt herself compelled to ask something of it.

"I know that I am a stranger to you," she said, her voice shaking. "I know that I am probably too late, that dawn is too close and that you have likely ceased holding court for those of us here so far below you. I know that I should have spoken to you earlier, when my friends and my crew were doing so, but you should know more than anyone that I have never felt like you were for me."

Tobie headbutted Aniaija's shoulder before turning her face up to the sky in a mirror of her elven companion.

"I did not grow up hearing stories about you," Aniaija continued. "My mother was determined that I would hold onto the beliefs of her home, and my father was all too willing to let her. I have spent most of my life in these lands. I have spent a decade in this desert, and still I know little about your histories. I know nothing about the other Ancient Ones. I have never stepped foot in a temple or prayed for guidance or pity."

A tear rolled down her cheek. It followed the curve to the corner of her mouth so that when she spoke again, salt touched her tongue.

"But I am praying to you now," Aniaija said. "I am begging you now. We need a fair wind and I do not foresee a change in the Tide, so *please*. I do not know how much longer we can survive on the Between. If you have any will left at all to bargain for a stranger, I beg of you to please ask the Gods to grant us a reprieve. Send something our way so that we can go home. Point us in some direction so that we can begin anew with our families."

Tobie made a choked, garbled sound that was akin to a meow, as if to second Aniaija's words.

But the Star just kept winking down at them, and Aniaija could discern no difference in the world around her. Had the goddess Oliantra been listening? Would she bother passing Aniaija's wishes along?

"You can leave me here," Aniaija added, unwilling to acknowledge the desperation in her voice. "You can let me die here, in the sand, just please let the rest of them go home."

Thirty-Seven

Aros

Luvrahn

FOR THE FIRST TIME in more than half a century, Aros C'Asad felt as though his wish had been heard by the Goddess of Blessings and Revelations.

He looked down at the redhead walking beside him as they slowly meandered back up the path towards his home. The corners of his mouth lifted into that warm, genuine smile that had become so easy since he had returned to Luvrahn.

Since she had hiked up her skirts and run up the hillside to greet him once she had caught sight of him.

At first, Aros had not been sure of the name that Nanos had chosen for her in his absence. However, as Aros had watched Bryha play with the children and dance with the villagers, he realised that the child had been right. Bryha may as well be the living embodiment of the Ancient One, reincarnated so that she might shine her light on the villagers of Luvrahn following the devastating loss of Fisa.

The crown of dandelions and sprigs of winter greens on her head had sold the whole package. Who would have thought some weeds and leaves could have looked so regal, braided into that wild red mane she called her hair.

Surely, she should be among the stars, not gazing up at them.

And as for the gazing, Aros might have mistaken her for a life-long devotee if not for the roundness of her ears. Bryha's eyes had shone with tears as she tipped her face towards the bright Star of Oliantra. She had looked upon the Star with such longing and reverence that Aros had nearly forgotten to offer his wishes to Oliantra himself.

He had been too entranced with how the moonlight had bathed her in a soft, silvery glow, or how the dandelion-dyed gown she had made seemed to shimmer as though made from starlight itself. The curls that had fallen free of the braids had framed her face. Her brow had been creased as she seemed to plead with the elven goddess.

Would the Ancient Ones listen to a human? she had asked.

While he had answered in the affirmative, Aros had not been certain. And yet, as he had watched her pray, he could not imagine a realm in which a god of any kind would ignore such an earnest, genuine prayer.

Whatever it was that she had asked the Goddess for, Aros hoped that she would receive it.

Even if it takes her away from you?

He tore his gaze away from her. He would let her leave if she so chose, even if the very idea of it had his heart splitting in two and devouring itself in his chest.

He would be honourable.

Aros did not realise that he had reached for Bryha's hand until their fingers laced together. He looked down at their joined hands and wondered if she was just as surprised about their contact as he was.

Bryha hummed. She swung their hands back and forth between them.

The smile on Aros' face grew.

"What did you wish for?"

Her voice was slow and thick with exhaustion. The poor thing had been pushing herself far too much while preparing for the celebration. Aros made a silent promise to make sure she rested for the next couple of days. It would not do for her to get sick as they went into winter.

"I'm sorry?" Aros asked.

"What—" Bryha yawned. "What did you wish for? You did wish, didn't you? It is called *The Wishing* after all."

Aros chuckled. Bryha leaned against him, and he could feel her warmth seep in through the layers of their cloaks. Perhaps, if she were an elf, she would be an Igdhraos. The Affinity would suit her—resilient, passionate, and the potential to be something brilliant and devastating with the right attention.

And as far as he knew, air was the best thing to stoke a flame with.

"I did make a wish, yes," he answered her.

Bryha hummed again, this time in triumph. She squeezed his hand.

"Then tell me," she said. "What did you wish for?"

"We really should not share what we wish for, little stitcher," Aros said.

Warmth bloomed in his chest as he earned another pleased sound from her.

Yes, he decided. If Bryha had been an elf, she would most certainly be an Igdhraos.

"Why not?" Bryha asked.

"Because," Aros explained patiently, albeit with that chuckle colouring his tone. "Our wishes are between us and the gods. They are to remain only between us and them until the day they are granted."

Bryha giggled. It bubbled out of her in that infectious manner of laughter borne of too much cider and mead.

"What's so funny?" Aros asked, trying to tame his own laughter.

"What if you forget?" Bryha asked. "What if you forget what you wished for, and the gods grant it, and you don't even know they granted it? Or, what if you forget, and the gods decide that there is no point in granting your wish, because you forgot?"

Bryha's steps became slower and shorter the closer they got to their cottage. Aros breathed in the scent of linen, honey and mint.

His sheets all smelled of her now.

He could not find a reason to complain about that.

"I do not think anyone would forget what they asked of the gods," Aros replied.

"People forget important things all the time," Bryha countered. "How can you tell me that you would not forget a wish that you never spoke of out loud?"

Aros tugged her towards their cottage. She followed without complaint or resistance, though the movement had her body leaving his for the briefest of moments. He used his hold on her hand to pull her back to him, and she returned to his side with enough force to elicit an *oof* from her.

She laughed and rested her cheek against his shoulder.

Aros lifted the latch. The door opened with a quiet creak, and together, elf and human crossed over the threshold.

"Home," Bryha murmured happily.

She dropped Aros' hand and crossed over to the bed.

Aros turned his back to close the door behind them. He heard the clink of brass as Bryha undid the clasps of her cloak and a heavy *whoosh* of the fabric as it dropped to the floor. His hand tightened around the iron knob of the door.

Don't turn around, he told himself. *Don't turn around.*

Behind him, Bryha lifted the blankets. The rustle of fabric and fur was louder than it should be. Why else would he be able to hear it over the thundering of his heartbeat in his ears?

He did not move. He did not let go of the door handle until all sounds of movement stopped.

Aros let out a breath and began to remove the layers of his clothing. He draped his cloak over the table. He took off the woollen overtunic and untied his breeches. He kicked his boots off and pushed them underneath the table with his foot. He pulled off his breeches and lay them along with his cloak and overtunic on the table, keeping his undertunic on.

He ran his fingers along the side seam, where Bryha had mended the hole.

"So," Bryha said, yawning wider now that she was curled up under the blankets. "What happens if you forget?"

"I am sure that the gods will not hold it against me if I do forget what I asked of them," Aros replied. "I do not believe that they would be so petty and cruel."

"But are you willing to risk it?" Bryha asked.

Aros had risked far more than the wrath of the gods, but he was not willing to share that part of himself with this girl. She did not need to know what horrors he had both endured and committed in the name of his Queen and country.

"I suppose if they were," Aros considered. "Then I would be glad for them to ignore my request. I do not want to ask for anything of a being that would hold something beyond my control against me. But I suppose, if you insist, I can tell you what it is that I wished for."

Aros paused, waiting for Bryha to respond. If she truly wanted to know, she could ask him again.

When no response came his way, Aros turned to face her. He smiled again, his cheeks beginning to ache from the expression.

Bryha was already asleep. The exhaustion had finally taken its toll. She had not even removed the flowers from her head or changed out of her dress. She lay facing him, as though she had planned to continue the conversation. Her nose was buried in the thick pile of one of the furs, but her eyes would have been on him.

Aros swallowed hard.

He walked over and perched on the edge of the bed. Gently, he touched her soft cheek.

Your heart is not made to love a thing as fragile as she.

But was Bryha truly so fragile?

She had survived the destruction of her town. She had spent weeks travelling on her own with no food, no water, and no way of knowing what might lie ahead of her. Over the past few months, she had fought to regain strength in her legs, and had forged relationships with the people she had been taught to fear.

And then, there was the matter of the letter. If nothing else, the order to bring her to the Ailian capital of Balliach meant *something*, and it was not lost on him that the orders were to present her before her twenty-first birthday.

The time—if she were an elf—that she would come into her Affinity.

No.

Bryha did not seem fragile in the slightest. Perhaps, once the mystery of who she truly was had been solved, Aros would allow his heart to be soft. He would allow for Palis' warnings to be in vain, and he would throw caution to the wind and allow himself truly to fall in love again after so long.

But for now, Aros C'Asad would be content himself with gently picking the flowers out of Bryha's braid and continuing to make silent wishes to the gods to keep her in his life.

Thirty-Eight

Maida

Luvrahn

Maida was no stranger to coastal storms.

Silktide, a trade town on the Colosian coast, had its fair share of destructive winds, rolling thunder, and wild waves. She had seen the river near her home overflow more times than she could count. She had watched the young village men helping the baker re-thatch his roof. She'd experienced week-long stretches where she'd had to wear the hem of her skirts tucked into her belt so that she didn't drag them through the deep puddles of mud surrounding the fountain in the town square.

But this?

She had never seen a storm like this.

The crack of thunder cleaved the sky above in two. But there was no lightning preceding it, and the ground was as dry as the bones she sometimes stumbled across in the forest. The sun had abandoned her, although it was close to noon, leaving only black, grey and red to stain the once-blue sky.

She was in the town square. The town was still and serene, with not a hint of movement or life. The fountain bubbled, but the water looked too thick. It moved too wrong.

Her boots made no sound on the stone path as she neared the fountain. She leaned over the edge of the feature, resting her hands on the outermost boundary to peer into the waters below. It was too dark. She could not see the glint and glimmer of the coins and talismans that had been tossed into it over the years.

Maida frowned and pulled back, wiping the warm, sticky liquid from her hands onto her skirt.

Another thunderous boom, this one chased by the sound of horrific screams. She spun around, and still saw no one. The screams grew louder, the booming growing closer. Still, she saw no life, and still no lightning or rain fell from the heavens.

The first hint of smoke curled around her, poking and prodding at her sense of smell.

Maida continued to twist and turn, searching for someone—anyone—in the empty streets. Where had they gone? She could hear them. They were so loud. She should be able to reach out and touch the panicked voices.

But she was alone.

Run.

Maida froze. Her father. That was her father's voice. She nearly twisted an ankle with how quickly she spun. Still, she saw nothing and no one.

Run, his voice insisted again.

Why was he telling her to run? What was happening? Why couldn't she find him?

"Dad?" she called.

Run.

His voice was insistent. Desperate.

"Why?" she asked. "What's happening?"

RUN!

Maida lifted her skirts and obeyed. She ran towards the entrance of the town, towards the path that led home. She had barely made it past the cobbler's hut before she skidded to a halt, stopped by a figure in the middle of the path.

The figure lifted a hood from her head, revealing a mane of wild red hair, *just like hers. She grinned a wicked, twisted grin.*

"*Who are you?*" *Maida demanded.* "*What do you want?*"

The woman did not answer. Instead, she took a step forward, and lifted a flaming hand. A thunderous boom cracked overhead, and Maida screamed.

THIRTY-NINE

MAIDA

LUVRAHN

THE SCREAM DID NOT amount to anything more than a muffled jumble of sound, stifled by a large, warm hand covering her mouth. Maida struggled beneath the weight above her. She clawed at the hand. Her nails caught on flesh. Layers of skin lodged beneath them and the nailbed. She grasped at the wrist, pulling and pushing, trying everything her sleep-addled brain could think of just to get the assailant off her.

Despite her efforts, the grip over her mouth only tightened. Fingers dug into the bone of her jaw, and Maida's muffled cries for help devolved into pained whimpers.

"Hush!"

Warm breath washed over her ear. The tone was harsh, but Maida recognised the whispered voice. Aros. Aros was holding her, keeping her quiet.

Hurting her.

Why was he hurting her?

"You need to be quiet," Aros continued in that harsh, hushed tone. "And you need to listen to everything I tell you without question. Both of our lives depend on it."

Maida stilled beneath him. Finally, her sight adjusted to the dark just enough that he was staring down at her with an intensity that terrified her to her very soul. Perhaps this was all still a dream. She'd had those sorts of dreams before. They were the kind of dreams that made her think she'd woken up only to find herself startling awake. Surely, this was another such dream.

Otherwise, why would she still hear the roar of a fire in the distance? Why would she hear screaming?

Why were lights dancing on the ceiling of the cottage as though a blaze raged outside?

And what else could she do if this were a dream but cooperate?

She nodded as best as she could, wincing as the movement brought more pain from Aros' hold on her.

Slowly, as if he didn't believe her, Aros loosened his grip. The chill of the night air rushed to fill the space between Maida and Aros' hand as he pulled away.

Maida pushed herself up. A crushed flower tumbled out of her hair and over her shoulder, falling into her lap. Her eyes tracked Aros as he left her side and picked up two packs that were so stuffed the seams were close to bursting. She would scold him for risking popping seams later. For now, she simply asked:

"What's happening?"

"There's no time to explain," Aros said. "We need to—"

His words were cut short by a loud, sky-shattering *boom* that cleaved the sky in twain and rattled the glass in the windows. Dust fell from the rafters, shaken free by the violent vibrations outside. She felt the colour drain from her face as the fear from her nightmare was tossed aside and replaced by something much more primal.

She watched the dust fall, landing on the blankets she lay under and sticking to her sweat-slicked arm. She saw how it didn't simply cover her in a layer of dust but added to the layer already there.

This had not been the first clap of thunder. She had heard it in her dreams. It sounded the same, like cannon fire, only sharper.

Her muscles tightened.

Her breathing became shallower, and her eyes widened.

Some part of her, deep within, was screaming at her to remember what this sound really was. Because it wasn't thunder. No lightning preceded it. It signalled no rain.

"We need to go," Aros said.

He picked up her cloak from where she had abandoned it earlier that night and held it out to her. On shaking legs, Maida clambered out of the bed. Her foot caught in twisted blankets, and she pitched forward. The only thing that saved her from landing flat on her face on the hard wooden floor was Aros' hand.

He caught her.

He freed her foot from the tangled blankets and steadied her on her feet. Then, he thrust her cloak into her hands, readjusted the packs on his shoulders, and moved to the door.

Maida pulled the cloak around her shoulders, grateful for having been so tired that she had not changed out of her clothes from the Wishing. She pulled the woollen fabric tight around her while Aros slowly pulled open the door just enough to peer out. Maida could feel her heartbeat in her throat as she watched him.

She reached up and gripped her flower pendant tightly.

Finally, Aros seemed satisfied with what he saw outside. He returned to her and gripped her tightly by the arm.

"Stay quiet," he repeated. "Stay close. Do *exactly* as I say."

"What is happening?" Maida asked him again, her voice catching.

Again, Aros did not answer.

Instead, he pulled her out of the cottage, and turned right towards the fields and the kapriae's paddock. But as much as Maida had planned on doing exactly as she was hold, a sound caught her attention and she stopped, looking over her shoulder down the path she had walked so many times in the last three months, towards the town square of Luvrahn.

She was not dreaming. The sounds of screaming men, women and children were real, and they were being carried through the air from a burning Luvrahn.

Her heart faltered.

At least in Silktide, she had only seen the aftermath of the destruction. Now, she was witnessing it first-hand.

Now, the acrid smell of burning hair mixed with that of burning flesh.

Her legs turned to jelly and gave out under her. Aros did not quite catch her this time, and dimly, Maida heard him swear as her body hung awkwardly and painfully between the ground and his hand while she stared in horror at the flames reaching cruel fingers into the night sky.

Bile rose in her throat. Flames licked the stars. Her heartbeat thundered in her ears. Sparks jumped from one thatched roof to the next.

Plumes of dark smoke rose and grew as Visdhraos tried desperately to extinguish the fire with their magic. But it was useless. Once the fire was out, another one, larger and wilder, one took root and blazed with revenge-worthy intensity.

"Come on," Aros grunted. He bent, and gripped Maida's other arm, pulling her back to her feet. "We have to go. *Now.*"

When Maida did not immediately cooperate, Aros began dragging her alongside him. Her knees and bootless feet scraped against rock, and all at once Maida was once again running through the Edgeling Woods, fleeing the charred remains of her home.

Except this time, it was not a dream. It was not even a memory. And yet, she was once again fleeing an unknown, unseen danger.

What a cruel, heartless twist of fate that she would lose another home, just as she had declared that she would stand her ground to protect it.

"Bryha!" Aros hissed.

Suppressing a sob, Maida scrambled to right herself beside Aros. He pulled her along and let go of her arm only when they reached the fence that kept Jon the kapriae in his paddock. Aros climbed over the fence, his movements smooth and sure. Maida was more unsteady. Her foot slipped on the rung as she leaned over the top railing and she pitched forward violently.

With a curse under his breath, Aros caught her and righted her once again. How many more times would he do that before he decided that she wasn't worth the time and effort? How long before Aros left her behind to fend for herself?

Desperate to ensure that did not happen, Maida followed him across the paddock. They kept low to the ground over the flat expanse of grass until they came across Jon.

The beast snorted when it noticed it had company. He reached out with his snout to sniff Aros' head. Its lips moved over the braids like fingers, tracing the intricate twists of hair, before it turned those soul-piercing eyes on her.

Maida swallowed hard and took a step back.

"I'm going to boost you up," Aros said. "Then, I'm going to hand you the packs and mount behind you."

The packs made a *thumping* sound as Aros dropped first one, then the other onto the grass. When Maida turned to him, he was holding his hand out to her.

"What?" she breathed.

He wanted *her* to *get on* that thing? It had been *him* who told her about the time Jon had eaten a deer that had jumped the fence and made the mistake of wandering too close, and now he wanted her to get on the beast's back?

"We don't have time for this," Aros growled. "Get on the kapriae now, Bryha!"

"Bryha!"

Maida spun on her heel towards the second voice that had called her name.

At first, she could not see who it was. It was too dark, and the only light come from the burning village. Just as she was about to give up, a burst of fire flared in the town square, and Maida could make out the dark silhouette of a small child running towards them.

She did not need to see the details of the child's face to recognise the child who had given her the name she now shared with an elven demigod. She had spent so many hours watching him run that she could recognise him from the sound of his gait alone.

"Nanos!" Maida called into the chaos.

Aros cursed behind her as Maida surged forward, running back towards the boy and the burning village. Maida felt the brush of Aros' fingers along her shoulder in his attempt to stop her, but she had moved too quickly. Like the Maiden fleeing the tyrant King Thar, Maida was just out of reach of her pursuer.

Her cloak billowed out behind her as she raced over the field. Her footing was more sure than it had ever been before, as though by having no choice but to trust that each step of hers would land in the right place, her feet would not fail her.

Aros could be as mad as he wanted to be with her. He could mount the kapriae and leave her behind, but Maida would never be able to live with herself if anything happened to this child when she could have done something to stop it.

She may be fleeing again, but she would not leave this child to the mercy of whatever horrors were unfolding in her adopted home.

Smoke burned her lungs. It clawed at her throat, punishing her for every breath she took.

She called out Nanos' name in answer to every time he called out hers in a heart-wrenching call and response punctuated by the screams of burning elves.

Another flash of fire rose from the village in a golden explosion of light. More screams filled the air. Maida swore that she could taste sizzling, melting skin on her tongue. But that was not what finally had her faltering.

The light had cast a new silhouette.

Maida could not make out much, but it was clear enough that the figure was walking towards her, following Nanos. Their pace was as steady as their shoulders were broad. Some dormant, ancient part of Maida cowered in fear at the very sight of them.

She couldn't place exactly how she knew that this figure was responsible for the death and destruction currently happening in her home, but the certainty was there.

"Nanos!" she yelled. "Hurry!"

Her voice broke on the last word, but Nanos was close enough now that she could hear the boy's sobs as he ran. It would not be long now before Maida would be able to pick him up and carry him back to Aros.

If Aros hadn't left.

Nanos stumbled on roots and rocks, but he kept running. He kept calling out *Bryha*, even as each recitation of her name became more and more unintelligible through his tears.

Maida tried to keep her eyes on him. She wanted him to know that she was here, that she would save him and that she would get him away from all this horror.

But the approaching figure lifted his arms, and for the first time, Maida realised that Palis had been right—she *had* seen Aros use his magic. The way that this figure lifted his arms was a more exaggerated version of the small flicks of Aros' hands as he coaxed air into the fireplace or at Dorsa's forge.

Dread weighed her down as the realisation sank in.

The figure was calling on their power, and she doubted that what they would unleash would be something as harmless as a gentle breeze.

She pushed herself through the bone-chilling terror, forcing her legs to run faster than she ever thought possible.

The distance was closing between her and Nanos. She could see his sandy hair, illuminated like a halo by the raging fires behind him. She could see the shape of his nose, the terror in his eyes.

She reached; fingers outstretched.

Just one more step. One more step and she would be able to snatch him up in her arms and race back to Aros and Jon.

One more step, and she could run away without guilt.

The sharp, cracking thunder exploded again. This time, it did not sound as though it was coming from a distance. It erupted just in front of her, shattering the air. The force of it flung her backwards, lifting her off her feet in a way she never thought possible. She landed hard on the packed earth, crying out in pain.

She rolled onto her side, coughing and gasping, trying to breathe, trying to do anything to stop the pain that gripped every fibre of her being.

"Nanos?" she croaked, only to realise she could not hear herself.

She could not hear anything save for a loud, constant buzzing in both her ears. She looked up at the sky, at the Star of Oliantra that continued to wink down at her as though still waiting to hear Maida's wish.

Useless Gods, Maida thought.

Pain arced throughout her body as Maida pushed herself to sit up. She felt the vibrations of the groans in her throat. She felt the screaming of each muscle in her body as they protested every minute movement she made. She lifted a hand to rub her eyes. She had barely touched them before they began to sting so horribly that she thought they were burning.

Maida held her hand up, peering through squinted eyes as best as she could to inspect it. Her face blanched when she realised it was covered in a warm, sticky liquid.

It shined, reflecting the light of the distant fire and the stars above.

And even in the dark, Maida could see it was red.

Her mind warned her against what she was about to do. Still, Maida turned to gaze toward the spot where Nanos had stood. There was no longer a boy there, with his hand outstretched and pure, unadulterated terror in his eyes.

In the place he had been, the grass glistened with a thick layer of blood and littered with chunks of flesh and bone. She screamed again, crawling on her hands and knees to the splattered remains of the young boy. Something soft and wet gave way beneath her hand. She lifted it to get a better look but dropped it as she was lifted from the ground by the back of her cloak.

She did not even fight. Maida became nothing more than a sack of bones as she was roughly manoeuvred onto the back of a foul-smelling beast. The scent of pine enveloped her, and she realised she was pressed against Aros' body.

This simple fact that he was here and hadn't left her stopped Maida's mind from shattering entirely.

She realised she was bracketed between him and the two large, curled horns of the kapriae. Aros took her hands and directed them to the longer fleece along the beast's neck. He forced her fingers to close tightly around it before spurring the beast into a gallop.

Aros was yelling at her. Maida could feel the vibrations of his chest against her back, but her ears still refused to work.

She should look back.

She told herself that she owed it to the people she was leaving behind to turn and bear witness to their last hours while she did nothing to fight against being pulled away.

But she didn't.

Maida did not have enough decency, even while yet another home burned as she fled.

She was the coward she'd always known she was.

FORTY

DI'ATH

BALLIACH

THE SECOND LEG OF their voyage was far less entertaining than the first.

Di'Ath felt guilty for wishing that another seawyrm would attack the ship, just so he had something to break the monotony, but when he had endured a week and a half of wandering the ship, all but twiddling his thumbs because all help he offered was rejected, he couldn't help but hope for some distraction, however devastating it may be. He hated that the crew didn't let him help. He had tried over and over to convince them to forget that he was a prince. He tried to insert himself into the daily chores to prove himself, only to be told to leave.

It isn't your blood that has them refusing you, the captain had told him one afternoon as Di'Ath had stood slumped over the railing and stared toward the horizon. *It is that you saved us from that beast.*

If I had done nothing, Di'Ath asked in reply. *Then they would let me join them?*

Di'Ath hadn't accepted the captain's response in the affirmative. He didn't understand how killing the seawyrm had brought about such a reverence from the crew. Any one of them would have done the same—every one of them had tried. But because his Affinity had manifested in the way that it had, because it had been his sister in the water with the creature, he was being cast aside?

373

Not cast aside, the captain said. *Absolved of any duty for the remainder of your voyage.*

Di'Ath hated it. He hated that he woke up to the same rocking of the ship that he fell asleep to, with nothing meaningful with which to fill the time between. Perhaps he wasn't cut out for the life of a sailor after all.

Di'Ath had even found himself searching for Sy'da. He sat with her in her cabin, playing cards with her until even that had ceased to provide any hint of entertainment. He had been about to give in and allow his sister to braid his beard when he heard the calling of gulls. In his excitement, Di'Ath knocked the whole deck of cards to the floor of the cabin as he rushed out.

Sy'da called after him, calling him all sorts of unsavoury names that would have made courtiers faint.

But Di'Ath didn't care.

He heard the gulls, and gulls meant land.

He raced up the stairs to the deck. He darted around sailors as he rushed to the prow and searched the horizon for a sight of something other than the flat, never-ending expanse of water.

Nothing.

He could see nothing but glistening blue. And while that made his magic sing within his veins, it did nothing to soothe his heart.

Determined to catch a glimpse of this famed land, Di'Ath found himself climbing the masts again. He could not stop himself from searching the water below for any dangers that might lurk beneath the surface, despite his daydreams.

He lifted his hand to his brow, shading his eyes from the sun. Even though they were in the first days of winter and the air was turning cooler, the sun still shined with the brightness of a summer's day. Still, Di'Ath could see nothing. He leaned forward, hoping that if he were just that little bit closer, he would be able to spy the city that was to become their home.

Moments turned into minutes, and just as he was about to abandon all hope, he was rewarded.

Di'Ath saw the castle first, mounted upon a hill with spires piercing the sky like lances. The sun's light glanced off the walls, like the shimmer atop a wave.

The *Spirit* sailed closer.

Di'Ath wondered if the sailors had been spurred by the excitement of learning that land was so close. It seemed as though everyone aboard had been called to action and were using their Affinities to make the ship move as quickly as possible.

Slowly, the rest of the city of Balliach became visible.

For a moment, Di'Ath considered the possibility that he had been at sea for too long. His eyes must be playing tricks on him. The castle couldn't be *red*. Surely not.

He had read that the capital of Ailiar had been rebuilt out of bloodstone over the centuries, but he had thought it an exaggeration. Surely, the Queens of Ailiar had not lowered themselves thus in order to transform their city. But the closer the ship came to shore, the brighter the castle was.

And it was red, glistening and shimmering like crystalline blood.

But it was not just the castle.

Pooling down the hill and covering seemingly every building, home and structure below, stretching all the way to the docks, was bloodstone. No wonder there had been no attempt to overthrow the Ailian line. No intruder would make it one step onto the pier before the Queen crushed them like a bug.

His own magic purred in delight at the thought of such overwhelming power.

Would Calliope have control over bloodstone the moment she came into her Affinity, or was it something that she would have to learn? Di'Ath's barbed whips had manifested immediately, just as Sy'da's ice had. But they'd both needed additional time to learn how to control their powers. Surely, it would be the same for the heir of Ailiar.

Did that not make it dangerous to have the city built from the red stone?

After defeating the seawyrm, Di'Ath had started to believe he was on the verge of indestructibility, but would he be able to defend himself if Calliope or her mother turned on him?

Would he be able to save Sy'da should his betrothed lose her temper, or control?

A new anxiety awakened within him. It had nothing to do with being unhappy with the current that the Tide had chosen for him but the uncertainty of whether he could keep Sy'da safe. Just how much bloodstone was in the walls of the keep? Would he be able to sleep without fearing that his soon-to-be wife would decide to end his life while he lay vulnerable beside her?

"Di'Ath!"

The voice startled him, and he nearly lost his grip on the mast.

Di'Ath looked and saw his sister waving up at him. He waved back and, with a sigh, began to climb down to join her. When his feet were once again on the solid wood deck, Sy'da bounced on her heels in excitement. The bells around her ankle chimed, mixing with the creaking of rope and wood and the rush of the waves as the *Spirit* sailed through the water.

Di'Ath chuckled.

"Your tassels are going to get tangled," he said. "And then you will look unpresentable for the Queen. How foolish will you feel then?"

Sy'da elbowed her brother playfully, her grin as bright as the sun.

"Not as foolish as you if you don't get rid of that fluff on your face," she said.

Sy'da reached and tugged on Di'Ath's beard.

"You look like an old man with this raggedy thing. If you're going to grow a beard, at least keep it trimmed."

"I like looking like an old man," Di'Ath replied, batting away Sy'da's hand. "But I will shave once we are settled."

Sy'da pursed her lips.

She didn't look like she had spent the last month either on the sea or stranded on an island. Sy'da looked refreshed, with shiny hair and smooth cheeks. Her blouse and skirt did not have a single wrinkle in the billowy fabric.

Di'Ath did not know how she managed it.

His lips curled into a devilish grin.

"You know," he said, taking a step closer to her. "If you didn't look so well put together, I wouldn't look so dishevelled."

Sy'da's eyes narrowed. The bells on her anklet chimed as she took a step back. She lifted her hand, frost forming around the rings on her fingers as she called on her Affinity.

"If you put so much as one strand of my hair out of place, I will freeze you where you stand and your betrothed will be forced to marry you right here on this deck."

Di'Ath held up his hands in surrender. His power buzzed, ready to rise to the challenge Sy'da was offering. He could cut through the ice she was prepared to anchor him with no matter how thick it may be.

"Fine," he said. "I won't mess you up. Let everyone see what a Zadanese royal should look like."

Sy'da smirked. She tossed her hair over her shoulder and walked to the railing, turning her attention toward the city. Ice branched out beneath her hold, the wood cracking as it froze.

Di'Ath tightened his jaw. Hopefully they would be able to find someone here with enough knowledge to help Sy'da control her power. He wondered if the royal family of Ailiar also had a salt room.

Perhaps they just entombed anyone who lacked control in bloodstone.

"Why is it so... *red?*" Sy'da asked.

Di'Ath shook his head. "I thought that it was some... lie or trick," he said. "I didn't think that the city would actually be made of the stuff. I don't know whether to be impressed or disgusted."

"If it is the latter," came the tutor's voice. "Then I would keep it to yourself. The people of Balliach have welcomed the changes and improvements that the Queens have made over the years. Bloodstone is virtually indestructible, and civilian property loss here is significantly lower than in other countries since the Queens began to lend their powers to construction."

It was Sy'da's turn to shake her head this time.

"I still don't understand why a Queen would take interest in construction," she said. "Surely their magic works like everyone else's—wouldn't it be tiring? Do they not have other, more pressing issues than making sure the local apothecary can stand the test of time?"

"You used to spend your days among our people back home," Di'Ath reminded her. "Is this not the same?"

"I didn't use my affinity," Sy'da countered. "I didn't exhaust myself. Handing out food or spending hours with the local children isn't the same as building homes and businesses out of ice. That would have me drained and unable to function for Tide knows how long."

She had a point, Di'Ath conceded.

Di'Ath could call the water from the air to pool into his palm and feel nothing. He could make waves in a tub or small pool with nothing more than the twitch of his finger.

But the barbed ropes of water he had used to kill the seawyrm?

Di'Ath had been glad for the days stranded at Kei which had allowed him to regain his strength. His father had told him that magic was like a muscle—the more he used it the easier it would become to wield it.

But by the same token, he cautioned against getting lost in his Affinity.

Sometimes, his father had warned. *An elf's magic can be so strong that it pulls them down into their own destruction.*

Di'Ath swore he had felt the beckoning call when he had plunged into the sea. It had been his magic coaxing him to the depths of his own end.

"It would be a small price to pay," the tutor said. "To have so much of the element you control protecting you and yours. Imagine if you were to try and take this place. The moment the Queen heard of your intentions you would be unable to scratch your own nose without forfeiting your life."

"There must be something that could penetrate bloodstone," Sy'da said. "It can't be completely indestructible. Nothing ever is."

She turned to face Di'Ath. "I wonder if it can withstand your water," she said.

"Did you not hear what he just said?" Di'Ath asked. "I would surely be executed for so much as entertaining such a thought."

Sy'da shrugged. "Even the largest, most sturdy mountain bows to the water eventually."

Di'Ath did not remind her that it took centuries for water to carve its marks into mountainsides. Instead, he nudged her with his elbow, and offered a small smirk.

Sy'da replied with a grin.

Together, the young royals watched as the city of Balliach drew ever closer.

They watched still as the *Spirit* docked, and the crew began to unload the ship of the crates and barrels. Di'Ath paid particular attention to a carriage that had arrived shortly after the first rope had tethered the *Spirit* to the dock. All four horses were the same beautiful, ash grey, with red plumes spouting from their bridles.

Escorting them were silver-clad knights, a sword emblazoned on their chest. A handful of frill-necked nobles sat astride their own fancy steeds as they waited nearby, chatting to one another as they stared at the ship.

Sy'da pulled away from him, skipping down the gangplank and along the pier to meet the welcoming party.

Di'Ath did not understand her enthusiasm to greet them, nor did he share it. It was, however, entertaining to see the expression of confusion and concern that was passed from Ailian to Ailian at the sight of Sy'da.

He wondered if it was her sunny countenance or her exposed midriff that caught their attention the most. He could not see a single other woman showing nearly as much skin as his sister. Since it was the early days of winter, he supposed he could not blame them.

Even he could feel the chill in the air, and he was wearing a coat over his tunic.

"My Lord?"

Di'Ath sighed and patted his tutor on the shoulder.

"I know," he said. "I'm going."

And with that, he followed his overly eager sister off the *Spirit* to the waiting carriage, and towards the beginning of the rest of his life.

FORTY-ONE

MAIDA

TEIVAN FOREST

BY THE TIME MAIDA and Aros stopped for anything longer than to relieve themselves as they fled the carnage and destruction of Luvrahn, the sun was already beginning to set on the following day. Even so, the stops to relieve themselves had been so few and far between that Maida had grown thankful for the dryness of her lips. Once they cracked and she could taste blood when she licked them, she knew that there was nothing else left in her to expel.

Her legs were stiff and sore.

Her entire body ached.

Maida had never so much as ridden a pony before and she had just spent hours astride a beast wider than the broadest draft horses she had ever seen.

She winced as Aros lifted her off the kapriae and lowered her to the ground. She had no trust left in herself not to fall ass over tit if she were to take a step. So, instead, she simply stood where she had been placed and stared at a singular amber leaf on the ground in the hopes that it would keep her steady.

Aros led Jon the kapriae to a low-hanging branch and secured him to the tree by his reins before turning to unburden the beast of the packs it carried, which he then set down next to Maida.

He continued to move around her as he gathered sticks and dry leaves to build a fire.

She should help.

Maida knew that she should help. But she could not move. She could not speak.

She kept quiet, continuing to stare at that godsdamned leaf. Not even the hungry crackling of a newly lit fire, fuelled by some unfelt gust of wind, broke Maida free of her trance.

She registered that Aros had left. She didn't know how long, or how far he had gone. All she knew was that he had wandered off and that sometime later he had returned.

Maida still did not speak when she realised that in his hands, he carried their waterskins. They were now full, the water sloshing within and making her dry throat feel like a desert. That must mean that there was a stream nearby. She could not hear it.

True, she could not hear much over the snapping fire and the ringing in her ears, which was insistent and unceasing. Would it ever go away or was she cursed to suffer it drowning out the sound of all life around her for the rest of her days?

Aros caught her attention with a wave of his hand.

"*Sit,*" he signed.

Maida nodded and obeyed.

If she had permanently damaged her hearing, at least she knew how to communicate without words.

Her eyes focused on Aros' hands. Along with filling the waterskins, he had brought moss from the riverbank. He knelt before her and pulled away the tattered remains of the hem of her patchwork skirt.

If Maida's heart could break any further than it already had, this sight would have shattered it.

It had taken weeks to remake the skirt—a brighter, stronger version of what she had been wearing when she fled her first home. And now, it had suffered the same fate as she fled her second.

And her legs...

Her poor legs, which had taken so long to heal, were once again littered with bloody gashes.

There was no telling whose blood coated her legs more—hers or Nanos'.

Unbidden, the memory of Nanos running toward her, hand outstretched, tears streaming down his face and glistening in the moonlight rushed to the forefront of her mind. She could still see the whites of his eyes in the darkness.

She had been so close. If she had only reached out a little further. She swore she had felt his finger-tips brush against her own.

Searing pain bloomed in her leg, and Maida hissed.

Her eyes refocused on Aros. He had wiped away some of the blood on her left leg and had been probing around one of the more serious open wounds.

"I know this is easier said than done," he said, tone low and even. "But you cannot let yourself dwell on what happened. You cannot let it consume you."

But he's gone, Maida wanted to scream.

Her lips betrayed her, refusing to part. Her tongue refused to move, and her voice refused to give life to the words that raged inside her mind.

"If you allow it to consume you," Aros continued. "Then your survival will be for nothing. You will not be able to avenge them or live a life worthy of their sacrifice."

Why didn't Aros seem to understand?

They were his friends, too. He had lived there for half a century and he had built Luvrahn from the ground up. Why was he not screaming? Why was he not breaking down and cursing his gods for allowing his home and his family to be destroyed on the most holy of nights?

If Maida could move, she would be screaming.

She would break every branch she saw, throw every rock, and curse every last Ancient One whose name she knew.

I couldn't save him, she thought.

He asked me for help.

I couldn't save him.

She hissed in pain again as Aros dug deeper into that open wound. She was about to shove him away when he picked something white from the bloody gash.

It glistened in the waning sunlight, and the blood covering it reflected the flickering flames of the fire.

She didn't recognise the shape of it at first, the smooth curve, the flat edge at one end, and the hard, pointed roots on the other. It looked odd, out of place, and yet so damn familiar.

Recognition hit her all at once.

She felt cold take over her as her face blanched.

She barely had enough time to twist to the side before she vomited. The acidic bile splashed onto the tattered remains of her skirt.

Aros rested his hand on her shoulder, giving a squeeze that could only be interpreted as having intended to be comforting.

But how had Maida not felt a *tooth* slicing into her flesh and becoming embedded?

Had it been the shock? Had it been the heat of the moment?

Slowly, she turned back to Aros.

She didn't know what possessed her to do so, but she held out her hand.

Aros hesitated, but he dropped the tooth into her palm and returned to his work of tending to her wounds.

Maida stared at that tooth while he worked. It was one of Nanos' front teeth. Maida had seen it countless times as Nanos laughed, smiled, or told one of those wild stories children loved to tell.

And now it was here, in her hand, perhaps the only tangible proof that he had ever existed at all.

The shaking began with her hands.

Maida closed her fingers tightly around the tooth to keep from dropping it. The roots dug into her palm, but she didn't care. Not when the shaking took over her entire body, and her breath turned too shallow to be of any real use.

A pathetic, high-pitched whine escaped her lips.

Aros stopped what he was doing and pulled her onto his lap. He curled around her. He brushed her hair back out of her face, and rocked her gently, hushing her as she broke down in his arms.

FORTY-TWO

AROS

TEIVAN FOREST

AROS HELD BRYHA UNTIL her sobs subsided.

The fire had burned low, and he would need to tend to it to avoid needing to light it again.

But Bryha showed no intention of leaving his embrace.

How tragically poetic, he thought.

Only a night ago, Aros had been steeling himself to tell Bryha how he felt about her. He had been mustering the confidence to ask her to stay with him, rather than to search for a plot where she could build her own house. Only a night ago, he had been pulling flowers out of her braids and looking forward to the sunrise.

But now, she was in his arms, as he wanted, but she was bloodied, wounded, and peppered with shards of tooth and bone.

There was only one person he knew who was capable of such a thing. And even though it confirmed all of Aros' feelings, it brought more questions to the surface.

What was Kaidos doing in the southern provinces? What had he been doing in Colosia?

Who was he working for, and what was the end goal?

"Why did we just leave them?" Bryha's hoarse voice cut through his thoughts.

Her voice was so raw. It must hurt terribly for her to talk.

Aros swallowed a lump in his throat. He should have expected the question. He knew she wouldn't like the answer. Even he didn't like it, but the actions they had taken had been planned for longer than she had been alive.

"We left because we had to," he said. "They will manage."

They will manage.

As if they had simply lost the tavern due to a fallen candle on a haybale. But they hadn't. They had lost *everything*. Kaidos and his twisted, merciless sidekick Leilara had done to the village what they had done to armies for decades.

They had destroyed it.

Shame settled deep within him. The seed took root in the very core of his being.

Aros had run.

It didn't matter that this had always been the plan in the event of such a tragedy. They had still run, and Aros felt like a coward. He should have stood against Kaidos. He should have done everything in his power to bring him down.

Even if it meant his own life.

It would have meant hers.

If Aros had stood against Kaidos and lost, it would have certainly meant Bryha's death. The idea of such a thing had his heart twisting and turning, choking itself with its own veins and arteries. He could not let her die. Even if he had not been predetermined to race across Ailiar at the barest hint of danger, he would have dragged her onto that kapriae anyway, and run for her life. He would sooner be seen as a coward than have her corpse added to the pyre.

If Kaidos bothered to dispose of the bodies, that is.

"I don't understand," Bryha said quietly. "Something terrible is happening back there and we just ran. Why? Palis once said that you could take out an entire army yourself, so why did we run? Why did we leave them behind?"

Aros took a deep breath to steady himself.

"There was a plan," he said.

Maida looked up at him with a frown. The sweat and mud caked upon her brow cracked with the movement.

"What do you mean, a plan?" she asked.

Aros turned his face toward the sky. He could not bring himself to look at her.

Not when she was looking at him with such an accusatory gaze.

"Everyone at Luvrahn—save for the children—came from elsewhere. We call it the city of the lost. Some of us are fugitives. Some of us were escaping unjust persecution, abuse, hardship…"

He sighed.

"Others," he continued. "Are retired."

"Retired?" Maida asked.

Aros nodded. "Myself, Aoife and Palis, we all worked for the Queen. Aoife was a spy. Palis was an emissary. I controlled Queen Meitranis' armies. I was the Lord Marshall of Ailiar. But I had seen enough bloodshed. I earned my retirement during the last war. I moved as far away from Balliach as I could so that it would be inconvenient for Meitranis to try and bring me back to Court."

That was a half-truth. Aros had wanted it to be inconvenient for *him* to return, not for Meitranis. Aros knew himself well enough to accept that if he were within a day's ride or less, he would be back at Meitranis' side at the barest hint of her needing him.

Living on the other side of the country wouldn't have been enough. So, he had crossed the Sea Between Seas and settled near the Colosian border.

"When we founded Luvrahn," he continued. "We knew there might come a time when the life we had carved out for ourselves would be threatened. Every soul in Luvrahn knew what to do and where to go in the event of an attack like this. My job had always been to ride out and inform the Queen. But the scouts we usually have out were hungover or still drunk from last night's revelries and we were taken by surprise. The male who orchestrated this waited for the Wishing and for us to lower our guard. Not even he would be so stupid as to attack without having the advantage of surprise."

Bryha fell silent for a moment. She appeared to be weighing his words, though Aros could not tell if she was searching for truth or judging the part he had played.

A tear rolled down his cheek.

"So," Bryha said after a long stretch of silence. "You had a plan, and everyone knew what to do. There is a chance that some people survived?"

Aros stared blankly at the dull stars above.

"Palis and Aoife will lead everyone they can through tunnels and out into the woods," he said. "Once it is safe to do so, they will either rebuild or travel to the rendezvous point. Once we make it to the capital and inform the Queen of what is happening, we will go searching for them."

Maida tucked her head under his chin. He could feel how weary she was.

Aros rubbed her back in gentle circles, wary of the bruising she must have from being flung backward with the force of Kaidos' magic.

"Why didn't you leave me behind?" Maida asked.

Horror seeped into Aros' very pores at such a thought.

"Because," he said, choking on his words a little. "You are human. The moment Kaidos knew you were here in elven lands, despite the laws protecting you and your kind, he wouldn't hesitate to take you. And, once he had you, you would wish for the same fate as Nanos."

Maida took a shuddering breath.

"What do you mean? Who's Kaidos?"

"Kaidos," Aros sighed. "Hails from Rupaburg. They're not as... forgiving of humans as Ailiar is. They never liked that Ailiar gave humans enough land to build their own country. Some of their people have adapted to more modern ideologies, but Kaidos isn't one of them. Kaidos would have taken you and put you to work in a mine or some other labour-intensive job, providing you with barely enough food and water to survive. You'd be there until the day you died."

Maida curled up tighter on his lap.

Aros squeezed his eyes shut as though he could block out the terrible truth of his next words.

"He is also my brother."

FORTY-THREE

CALLIOPE

BALLIACH

WHEN COUNCILLOR SANCOR HAD arrived to tell Calliope that the ship from Zadanai had been spotted on the horizon a week following the Wishing, she was forced to come to terms with the fact that she truly had begun to hope that it had found its resting place on the sea floor.

She had even dreamed of the prince and his crew joining the ghosts of sailors past, floating beside the creatures of the deep for the rest of eternity. She had seen his face surrounded by fish more times than she had seen his portrait.

She had not shared these thoughts or dreams with anyone. As far as they were concerned, she had developed a habit of wringing her hands since the day of the Feast out of concern for the prince's well-being.

"Your father has requested that you and Lady Jaena stay in your rooms when the prince arrives," Sancor said.

Calliope lowered her needlepoint with a frown.

"Why?" she asked.

"He wishes to introduce you at dinner," Sancor explained. "Consider it a blessing, your Highness. The prince has been travelling for weeks – allow him to make the best of himself before the two of you meet."

"I would not be so sure," Lady Jaena said, nudging Calliope with her elbow. "Every good romance book I have read says that men look their best when they are at their most rugged."

Calliope tried to ignore her cousin, but she was unable to stop herself from considering the idea of Prince Di'Ath bursting into her room. In her mind, he would make a beeline for her and capture her mouth with his own. She would still be able to taste the salt on his lips, and the perfectly pressed skirts of her dress would become crumpled as he showed her what thoughts kept him occupied on his voyage.

She sucked in a breath of cold air.

Stupid girl, she thought. *You wanted him dead moments ago.*

"I hear that the men in Zadanai know how to treat a woman well," Jaena sighed dreamily. "They shower their wives with jewels and clothes. They throw festivals to declare their love. Oh, how romantic."

"All the prince needs to know is his place," Sancor said with a sneer. "He is expected to uphold our traditions and provide support for our princess."

Jaena was cowed immediately. The dreamy, loving look on her face disappeared, and she was suddenly extremely interested in a spot on the floor.

Something unfamiliar twisted in Calliope's gut. True, she still did not like nor trust her new lady's maid, but she did not feel any satisfaction from the reaction Sancor had elicited from her.

"The prince has been sighted, and we will remain here until dinner," Calliope said. "Now, is there anything else, or can we be left to ourselves, Councillor?"

Sancor dropped into a low bow. "That is all, your Highness. I will see you this evening."

As the door closed behind the wretched old man, Calliope felt she could finally breathe again. She would never trust that man. She didn't understand why her father did, or how Sancor had wormed his way into such a privileged position.

Once again, she found herself determined to ensure that he would find himself preoccupied elsewhere the moment she took the throne. It was the only thing that could get her through interactions with him, the only way she could stomach the way his mere presence made her skin crawl.

Jaena took a little longer to recover. She returned to her own needlepoint silently.

"Shall I keep an eye out for rugged lords for you then?" Calliope offered.

Jaena's porcelain cheeks flushed bloodstone red.

"Perhaps," Jaena said. "Though in truth, what I hope for most in a husband is that he is kind. I can look past an ugly exterior if the heart is pure, but it is much more difficult to appreciate a beautiful face if the man wearing it is cruel."

Then you should not be looking for a nobleman, Calliope thought.

Despite not keeping close confidences with the noblewomen of court, Calliope still heard much. The beautiful lords were regularly found to be arrogant and unfaithful. The ugly ones tended to believe they were beautiful, doubly so if their wives were pleasant to look upon.

She voiced neither her opinion nor her observations, however,

Instead, she offered what was perhaps the first true smile that she had ever given Jaena.

"I will endeavour to find you a kind match, then," she said.

"Thank you," Jaena beamed.

The two women fell back into their routine,

Calliope had begun dozing in her chair by the fire when she heard Jaena exclaim, "He has arrived, your Highness!"

Calliope had not even noticed that Jaena had left her seat to stand at the window, nor had she heard the hoofbeats of approaching horses.

"What do you see?" Calliope asked.

"He is quite handsome," Jaena said, that wistful tone back in her voice. "He holds himself tall."

Calliope had to bite the inside of her cheek to stop herself from suggesting that Jaena marry the prince in her stead. By some miracle, she managed to keep her tongue in check.

"That does not tell me much at all," she said instead.

Calliope set her needlepoint aside and crossed over to stand beside Jaena. The window was wide enough for both young women to look down into the courtyard to watch as the new arrivals into Balliach drew their horses to a stop.

There were ten in total—all dressed in Zadanai blue—sitting astride sturdy brown horses with thick, flowing manes.

Calliope opened her mouth to ask Jaena which one she believed to be the prince, but then she found him. The portrait she had been given had done him no justice.

He was the most beautiful man she had ever seen.

His black hair fell over his shoulders in wild curls, and his jaw was covered in such a length of scruff that Calliope wondered if he always kept a beard, or if it had been a result of his journey. She hoped it was the former—of all the books she had read, she'd preferred the ones where the dashing knight had been ruggedly handsome.

Perhaps that was why she had initially been so uninspired by the portrait she had received.

In the portrait, he was clean-shaven, his hair braided back away from his face.

Perhaps this marriage would not be such an unhappy one after all.

Calliope leaned closer to the window, pressing her hand against the sun-warmed glass.

The woman sitting astride the horse beside him must be his sister. Her hair was longer, the ends brushing against the saddle she sat upon. She was here for the same reason Lady Jaena was—to find an Ailian husband and start a new life in a kingdom far from her place of birth. If Calliope had not been the first-born daughter of the Blood Queen, if she had not been the only child of the King and Queen of Ailiar, perhaps she too would have been sent across the world in search of a husband.

But that was not the fate the Gods had set, and her betrothed had been forced to travel to her.

She watched as her father stepped out into the courtyard and greeted their guests. King Oprianos bowed, and she supposed he was making some excuse for her mother—the Queen—being absent.

Whether they were too tired or their own customs did not lead them to expect her presence to begin with, their Zadanai guests did not seem to mind.

A man to Prince Di'Ath's right spoke with the King, and soon, the party dismounted their horses.

The prince was graceful in his movements, and Calliope was watching so unashamedly that she did not have the presence of mind to move away from the window as the prince looked up—directly at her window.

As he looked up, Calliope swore that he smiled at her.

FORTY-FOUR

DI'ATH

BALLIACH

AFTER BEING INTRODUCED TO King Oprianos, Di'Ath and Sy'da were led through Balliach castle to their suite of rooms. With each twist and turn of the never-ending hallways, Di'Ath hoped that he would catch a glimpse of the princess that had been looking down at him in the courtyard.

The portrait had not done her justice. Even from the distance the three floors had put between them, Di'Ath had seen curiosity on that pale face. It had ignited something within him that he had not expected to feel. Was this the *instant connection* his mother had spoken of?

It didn't feel as all-consuming as he had expected. Perhaps if he were to see her without a pane of coloured glass between them, he would feel it more keenly. Perhaps, if he were to see her directly before him, he would feel said connection snap into place, like a cosmic tether between them. There were stories about such things in Zadanai. He had never believed them possible, but if his mother was sure that he would fall in love with his intended so completely and so thoroughly, perhaps she had been right.

Or, more likely, he was simply trying to convince himself that the journey, near-death experience, and the strange happenings in Kei were all worth it.

"This is your suite, your Highness," said a small, mousey attendant. "And your Highness, Princess Sy'da, you are directly across the hall."

Di'Ath frowned.

He had been so lost in thought, so concerned with whether he would see the princess, that he had not bothered to take note on how to get to his rooms. He would need to pay better attention later, lest he get lost within the labyrinthine castle. The castle in the Zadanese capital of Wylden was far more straight-forward in its design. It made sense. Living quarters were grouped together, barracks were assigned to their own sector, and the kitchens were in just the right place for all royal children to sneak a snack in the middle of the night without wandering too far from their beds.

But here?

Di'Ath could not even hazard a guess as where the main foyer was, or how to find food should he grow hungry in between meals.

"A bath has been drawn for the both of you," the attendant said. "And I will return in an hour to escort you to the dining hall for dinner, where you will dine with the Queen, King and Princess."

Di'Ath looked the attendant over. The boy was young, and the points of his ears poked out from beneath thick, brown curls. His cheeks and nose carried a hint of sunburn on otherwise pale skin.

He appeared to drown in the Ailian red ruffles.

"Thank you," Di'Ath said. "We will ensure that we are both ready for dinner."

The attendant smiled and nodded, offering a bow to both Di'Ath and Sy'da before scurrying off down the hall.

"Do they not deem us worth being guarded?" Sy'da asked, gesturing to the empty spots beside the door.

Di'Ath was not oblivious to the fact she had chosen to speak in Zadanese, despite the exchange Di'Ath had shared with the attendant in Common. He wondered if that meant she was more scared or uncomfortable than she looked.

As much as he wanted to ease her discomfort, he was also—at his core—her older brother. So, when he responded in their mother tongue, his words unravelled any assurance their language attempted to give.

"Perhaps they are setting us up to assassinate us more easily," he said.

He chuckled and nudged her with his elbow. "Come," he said. "Let us be clean and pleasant smelling for when they come to slit our throats."

Sy'da glared at him before pushing the doors to her suite open.

Di'Ath watched her go with a frown.

He would need to sit her down and speak with her about what had happened aboard *the Spirit* and with the seawyrm. In truth, he should have done so much earlier, but he had been too preoccupied first with regaining control over his magic, then with the mysteries of Kei. Now, he had to worry about making a good enough impression on his future bride so as to not destroy the peace agreement that had been reached between the two countries. It was up to him to ensure that Zadanai remained protected should the rumours of Rupaburg's gathering army have any merit.

Sy'da would have to wait.

Di'Ath sighed and pushed his way into his room.

Immediately, his nose curled in disgust at the lacklustre furnishings. Where were the cushions? Where were the rugs and blankets? Why could he still see cold grey stone between the sparse tapestries on the walls? Did Ailians not believe in comfort and colour?

He stalked over to the bed and pulled back the covers, layer by layer. First, a thick, downy blanket in a dull maroon. That was fine, he supposed. The second blanket was a plain cream, boiled wool blanket with a simple stitch on the edge. Practical, yet wholly unappealing to the eye.

Di'Ath nearly blanched when he realised that beneath those two blankets lay the white linen sheets.

"How do they survive with only two blankets?" he asked himself, before dropping the covers and turning to the pillows.

There were four in total, set up in two stacks of two. He pressed down on the stack closest to him and sighed. They were certainly not stuffed to his liking.

Tomorrow, he would need to take his sister into town and search for better bedding options. Too few of his belongings had survived the seawyrm attack to furnish this suite to his liking, and seeing as he and the princess would not be wed until she came into her Affinity, he could see no reason why he shouldn't make himself more comfortable.

He turned away from the bed and followed the scent of florals in warm water through an open door.

A copper bathtub, lined with white linen, stood in the centre of the bathroom. Steam still rose from the water, bringing forth the heady scent of rose and lavender. Candlelight reflected off the surface, glimmering and glinting like sunlight off the sea.

Eagerly, Di'Ath shed himself of the clothes he had worn up from the docks, leaving them in piles on the floor. He would deal with those later – or someone else would. For now, the only thing Di'Ath both wanted and cared for was climbing into that bath.

Once freed of the confining silk, leather, and linen, Di'Ath submerged himself into the blissfully hot water. He sighed with relief as the warmth seeped into his muscle and bone, relaxing them after the weeks of travel.

In the grand scheme of things, this particular bath definitely paled in comparison to the baths of his home. At least now, though, Di'Ath was not plagued with the knowledge that he would be immediately sticky with sweat once more, as he had in Kei. Here, the seasons made sense, and the air was as cool as one would expect in the early days of winter.

Di'Ath would, however, endeavour to find a vendor for the oils and flowers he preferred in his baths. The rose petals and lavender soap were not quite rich enough for his tastes, and the water did not leave his skin feeling as silken and smooth as he was accustomed.

Still, he had taken the better part of the hour allotted simply revelling in the comfort and luxury of a proper bath once more. He did manage to save himself enough time to set himself up before a mirror and shave the weeks of growth along his jaw. He hated how it felt to look at his shaven face and see a boy who seemed years younger than he felt.

And Tide, Di'Ath wasn't even old. By elven standards, he was still barely a child. Oh, how the weight of duty and fear of imminent death aged you.

Unable to stomach looking at himself anymore, he focused on dressing, grateful that his trunks had been brought up while he bathed.

He pulled a blue and gold brocade coat on over a soft linen tunic, and secured it closed with a silk sash around his waist. Just as he slipped his feet into his embroidered court shoes, he heard a knock at the door.

"Come in," he called out in Common.

The door opened, and Di'Ath sighed with relief when he saw his tutor, Wes'Pin, rather than the Ailian attendant enter.

"Are you ready, your Highness?" Wes'Pin asked.

"Could this not have waited until tomorrow?" Di'Ath replied, switching back to Zadanese lest guards had been set out by the door. "We have only just arrived, surely we deserve some time to recuperate properly before being subjected to stuffy, awkward dinners."

Wes'Pin frowned at Di'Ath.

"The Queen and King of Ailiar have welcomed you graciously to their home," he said. "If they wish for you to show your face at dinner, you will do so without complaint. Until you are married to the princess, you are nothing more than a guest in a foreign court, do you understand me?"

Di'Ath snorted. "Do you mean the Queen who could not so much as show me the courtesy of greeting me upon my arrival?"

Wes'Pin closed the distance between them with a speed that Di'Ath did not think him capable of. Before he knew it, the wizened old man's wrinkled finger was in Di'Ath's face, pointed in warning.

"You will take care to keep *that* kind of talk to a minimum in these walls," Wes'Pin hissed. "You are not yet married, and this alliance can still fall to pieces in a moment if you are not careful. Remember why we are here. Remember who you are and what you represent."

Di'Ath swallowed hard. He had never once felt scared of his tutor. The man was so short and so old that the very idea had never crossed his mind. But the sheer fury on his face was enough to chill the blood pumping through his veins and have him believe that he'd rather face a seawyrm again rather than find out what venom lay hidden within Wes'Pin.

"You're right," Di'Ath said with a nod. "I'm sorry."

Wes'Pin grunted with what Di'Ath hoped was approval before turning back towards the door. "Now come. We do not want to keep the Ailians waiting."

Di'Ath followed his tutor out the door. He was relieved to see Sy'da waiting in the hallway, freshly bathed, and dressed in her usual beautiful, embroidered skirt and blouse.

He wondered how long it would take for her to adopt Ailian fashion.

His sister was flanked by two palace guards in silver plate. He noted the sword emblazoned on the cuirass.

Curious that they lean so heavily into the mythology of their line, he thought.

Did they truly believe they were the descendants of a woman so blessed by the gods that they not only spared her from a horrific death, but allowed her to draw some fantastical sword that one could only expect to find in fairytales? Perhaps it was an intimidation tactic, meant to strike fear into the hearts of their enemies.

Because who wouldn't fear going against someone who was blessed by gods?

"Is it too late to get back on a ship to Zadanai?" Sy'da asked in Zadanese. "I was just getting used to not being followed around everywhere I went."

"First you complain about not having guards stationed outside your door, and now you're complaining about having them. Make up your mind," Di'Ath teased, nudging her with his elbow. "But if you think for one second that you are going to be allowed to leave my side now, you are sorely mistaken. You're trapped, forever. My companion for the rest of my days."

Sy'da groaned and looped her arm through Di'Ath's.

"At least I'm not the only one with a tail," she said, gesturing with her chin.

Di'Ath turned his head, and barely suppressed a groan.

Another two guards had been stationed outside his door as well.

Great, he thought. *How am I going to sneak around now?*

"If you would kindly follow me, your Highness."

Di'Ath hadn't even noticed the attendant. He jumped when he spoke, earning a quiet snicker from his sister.

"Right this way."

The attendant bowed, then turned, heading back through the maze-like hallways. Di'Ath tried to remember each twist and turn this time, but there were so many that quickly he lost track. Forget the guards, sneaking through the layout of this bloody place would be Di'Ath's greatest struggle.

After what seemed like an age, they arrived at a set of heavy wooden doors.

"Ready?" Sy'da asked.

"Never," Di'Ath replied.

The attendant lay his hands on the doors and threw his whole weight into opening them.

Di'Ath had hoped, perhaps foolishly, that he would be introduced to the Princess of Ailiar in a small, intimate gathering. He had expected that they would be accompanied only by her parents, his sister, his tutor, and the palace guards. Instead, Di'Ath was greeted by the sight of a filled dining hall. Dozens of nobles sat at tables along either side of a wide aisle that opened to an empty space before the table where the royal family sat.

It was a strange configuration. It reminded Di'Ath of a horseshoe, with the Queen and King in the centremost part, while the princess and a blonde woman sat on the right arm of the horseshoe. The left arm was empty, presumably reserved for Di'Ath and Sy'da.

"His Royal Highness," the attendant called out, voice much louder and clearer than Di'Ath had expected of such a small man. "Prince Di'Ath of Zadanai, and Her Royal Highness, Princess Sy'da of Zadanai."

Di'Ath winced at the horrific mispronunciation of both their names. He wasn't *Die'Uth*, he was *Dee'Ah-th*. And it was *Psy-Duh*, not *See'Duh*. Still, he bowed his head in greeting to the room while the seated nobles dipped their own.

The attendant made a sweeping gesture with his arm towards the aisle, indicating that they should step forward. After taking a steadying breath, Di'Ath straightened, and walked down the aisle with Sy'da by his side.

Once they reached the table where the Ailian royal family sat, he bowed at the waist. Sy'da dropped into a curtsey, the bells and beads on her skirt tinkling pleasantly with the movement.

Neither Queen Meitranis nor King Oprianos bothered to stand from their seats. Di'Ath clenched his jaw to hold back his frustration at the disrespect.

"Your Highnesses," King Oprianos said. "I am please to present to you my daughter, Calliope Ailiar. First Born of Meitranis Ailiar, Descendant of the Maiden, Blood Heir to the Ailian throne and Crown princess."

Di'Ath turned towards the princess and bowed again.

Princess Calliope, at least, seemed to be questioning her decision to remain seated. Each muscle appeared tensed, ready to move at a moment's notice. Her dark eyes darted between him and her parents, unsure of what she was supposed to do.

At least we have that in common, he thought.

"It is a pleasure to meet you," Di'Ath said. "I apologise for the delay in our arrival. We came across some... unforeseen events that I will bore you with another time."

"I'm sure you will not bore her," King Oprianos said before the princess had the chance to so much as open her mouth. "Now, young prince, if you and Princess Sy'da would take your seats, dinner is about to be served."

Di'Ath frowned.

This felt... wrong. This did not feel like how an introduction between two young royals destined to be wed should go. The princess had not even uttered a single word, and already he was being ushered to his seat?

He looked at Sy'da. She could offer no more than a slight shrug of her shoulders.

Di'Ath returned his attention to the wide-eyed princess who seemed so unsure of everything going on around her. He would make sure she had the time and space to speak her mind, he decided. If that was all he could offer in this union, he would be glad of it.

For now, however, he would find his seat, and he would wait.

FORTY-FIVE

CALLIOPE

BALLIACH

SO HE HAD DECIDED to shave.

Calliope was surprised to realise she thought this was a shame. At least, she thought, it was not entirely a disappointment. Prince Di'Ath's jaw was strong and angled, and there was a dimple in his cheek when he smiled that she would surely have missed if it were to be covered in hair. That she was to be wed to a man that looked just as handsome both with and without a beard was something to be grateful for, she supposed. Perhaps one day, she could work up the courage to convince him to grow it out again, just so she could see how it felt beneath her fingers.

"Your Highness," Lady Jaena whispered in her ear. "You are staring."

Calliope quickly averted her eyes. Her cheeks burned while Lady Jaena stifled a giggle by her side. Calliope swallowed the hard, dry lump in her throat before she nudged her cousin under the table with her knee.

She hoped that the smirk she saw out of the corner of her eye had been a trick of the mind, and that the prince had not borne witness to her childish antics. She couldn't bear it if she learned that her betrothed had seen her acting so unladylike on their first night of meeting one another. As it was, she could not even remember what had been said during his formal introduction when he had entered the hall with his sister.

Calliope had been transfixed on the man from the moment he had stepped through those heavy wooden doors. She was certain that she had never seen a man walk with such confidence without exuding an air of self-importance. She was sure that she had never seen a man bow in such a fluid motion, nor one that did not seem to harbour some hidden resentment towards the need to do so before a woman.

But her hope that she had gone unnoticed was shattered when she stole a glance upward and found her betrothed grinning openly and unabashedly at her.

The warmth spread higher, extending from her cheeks and reaching the very tops of her ears.

Calliope regretted the braids that kept her hair off her neck and away from her face. She wished she had opted for a more relaxed hairstyle, so that her hair might afford some protection from those bright, mischievous eyes.

Not that it would have been an issue if their seating hadn't been so artfully arranged for Di'Ath to have a direct line of sight. As it was, he sat directly opposite her on the other arm of the horseshoe styled table. If the table at the end of the hall had been left in one long line, the prince would have to lean either forward or back to get a glimpse of her, and Calliope could have simply leaned the other way.

As it was, Calliope had nowhere to hide. She could not even engage Councillor Sancor in conversation to shield herself from the curious gaze of the prince across the way. Nor was she able to hide the fact that *she* was staring at *him*.

Calliope tried to distract herself by looking at someone else—anyone else. Her mother and father sat beside each other at the main part of the table. Meitranis was closest, and her long red curls were styled into an elegant up-do that resembled a beehive. Strands of hair cascaded from it like twisting vines, and ropes of glistening freshwater pearls had been draped artfully over the entire thing.

Calliope studied the pleasant, yet unsubstantial smile of her mother for only a moment.

When was the last time she had seen her mother smile honestly?

Why hadn't Prince Di'Ath's arrival brought her some joy or pride? Why hadn't she at least given some indication that she was happy with the way things were turning out?

Because she's not happy, that horrid, internal voice told her. *She's too disappointed in you to ever truly be happy. She knows that you will be the downfall of Ailiar, and the destruction of the Maiden's line.*

Calliope reached for a bloodstone goblet with shaking fingers. She brought it to her lips. Wine heavy with notes of berry and pepper flowed over her tongue. She hoped that her dislike of it was not apparent. Aside from the childish display earlier, she didn't want to appear immature for not liking something so universally loved as wine.

As she set the goblet back down, Calliope found that the conversation around her seemed to blur. Notes and words fell over themselves until they became nothing more than a giant tangle of noise that she could not make sense of. Her heart thundered in her chest. Her breath came too quick and too shallow.

The first course was laid out in front of her—a light soup with a greenish hue and a watery texture. It may have had chicken in it, but Calliope was all too focused on making sure she did not make a fool of herself while she ate to really take note.

The second course had a tiny roasted bird upon a nest of greens. When she cut into it, she found the creature stuffed with breading and pomegranate seeds.

Distantly, she could hear Lady Jaena rambling on about something of little importance beside her while they ate. Calliope was too lost in the tangle of sound that only seemed to grow in volume and unintelligibility. The air was getting thicker, making it harder for her to take it into her lungs.

Was an Aerdhraos toying with her?

She didn't want to give them the satisfaction of knowing that she was struggling if they were. And besides, it didn't seem like anyone else was having problems breathing. The Aerdhraos would need to be particularly skilled in their craft to target only one person in a dining hall as great as this.

If they are so skilled, she thought through the haze in her mind. *Then let them kill me.*

The third course had roasted vegetables and fragrant slices of roast kapriae, drizzled with a rich, thick gravy. It was strange to think that something as

Finally, the fourth and final meal arrived. It was a selection of figs, kapriae cheese, salted crackers and other assorted sweetmeats. Usually, this would have been Calliope's favourite course. But she still felt as though she were watching herself from a distance.

It was not until an unfamiliar, feminine voice cut through the fog in her mind that Calliope truly came into herself again.

"That was lovely, thank you."

She leaned forward, searching for the source of the warm, cheerful voice. She found Princess Sy'da smiling up at the servant clearing her plate. The servant looked rightly confused. He stumbled over some words that Calliope did not catch, and that only served to make Princess Sy'da smile more brightly as she placed her cutlery atop the plate he held.

Strange, Calliope thought.

She would have considered questioning the princess' actions if it were not for the figure that came to stand before her, hand outstretched. The embroidery on the jacket cuff was exquisite. Glass beadwork caught the light of the chandeliers, giving the illusion of containing their own flames.

Calliope lifted her gaze and found herself staring into an ocean. At least, that was the colour of Di'Ath Adarna's eyes. Calliope could fall overboard into them and drown without complaint.

She swallowed hard again, fidgeting with her napkin under the table.

"Your Highness," Prince Di'Ath said. "I know that this is not a ball, and I apologise for any impropriety on my part, but the musicians are playing beautifully, and I cannot allow their skill to go unaccompanied by dance. Will you do me the honour of dancing with me, Princess Calliope of Ailiar?"

Calliope looked toward her mother.

Queen Meitranis had clearly been watching the encounter, but she did not so much as blink in response to Calliope's silent request. Did she truly care so little about her daughter that she would not offer counsel in this moment of need? Calliope's next move would reflect not only on herself but on the crown. She didn't understand why her mother wasn't giving her a sign of what she could do.

Oprianos gestured with both a hand and a dip of his head to signal that Calliope should accept Di'Ath's offered hand.

She looked back up at the prince, her heart caught in her throat.

His smile was warm, and Calliope could imagine that it shined only for her as she stood from her chair and rounded the table to join him. That smile only burned brighter when she slid her pale hand into his.

He tugged gently and led her to the empty dance floor. He began to lead Calliope in a dance that she was not quite sure she had ever learned, but to whose steps she somehow knew. Di'Ath's hand found a home on the small of her back so effortlessly that she was certain that this was what love was like.

Easy, effortless, a dance that no one ever taught you, but that you instinctively knew.

Warmth bloomed from the place where Di'Ath's hand rested, even through the layers of fabric and stays. His other hand kept a firm yet gentle grip on her own as he led the dance. Calliope followed, looking up into those ocean eyes. It felt as though his mere presence was keeping her tethered to a world that seemed so indifferent to whether she even existed.

If she were a smarter woman, perhaps she would have used that time to ask him questions. Perhaps she would have inquired about the delay in his arrival or how he found Balliach so far.

But she had never claimed to be a smart woman, and so instead, spent the rest of the evening staring at the face of her betrothed, certain only that up until this moment, she had been completely and utterly wrong about everything.

"I must say, the two of you looked positively perfect together," Lady Jaena said. There was a wistful hum in her voice, not unlike when she spoke of the latest 'brushing of fingertips' scene in one of her romance stories.

Calliope watched her in the mirror as she worked diligently to remove the jewels and pins from the braids in her hair. It was odd, but for once, Calliope did not find herself wanting to shrink away from the blonde's hands, nor comparing herself to Jaena's beauty. Instead, Calliope found comfort in Jaena's presence.

Had Di'Ath's arrival been enough to invoke this change?

Surely not. Surely one dance had not been enough to alter Calliope's perception not only of her cousin but of herself.

Still, instead of fighting some snark remark on the tip of her tongue,

Calliope found herself smiling. She dipped her head and felt her cheeks warm.

"The way he held you when you were dancing – oh, it was as though the two of you were already in love!"

Had not Calliope thought that being in his arms must be what love felt like? Had she not come to the decision that she had been wrong about their union being empty and loveless?

"I think this is an absolutely wonderful match," Jaena continued. "And, not to mention, your babies will be so beautiful! Can you imagine them inheriting his thick curls?"

Calliope's smile faltered.

What if their children had hair as pin-straight as her own? What if they did not inherit their father's rich skin, his strong jaw and kind gaze? What if they looked like her, pale and plain, with dull hair and duller eyes?

"His sister is a great beauty as well," Jaena continued, oblivious to Calliope's inner turmoil. "Do you think that I could pull off Zadanese fashions? Perhaps I am too fair for the richness of colour, but the silhouette is stunning. And the embroidery! I have no doubt that they use real gold for those edgings, but for the life of me, I cannot comprehend how the fabric appeared so weightless with all those embellishments!"

"Perhaps she is an Aerdhraos, like you," Calliope said.

Lady Jaena shook her head.

"No," she said. "I've done my research. Princess Sy'da is a Visdhraos, like her brother and the rest of her family line. And, like her brother and the rest of her family line, her magic is heightened and specialized. On top of generic water manipulation, she can also create and control ice."

"I guess that must have been useful in Zadanai," Calliope mused.

It was well known that Zadanai had mild winters and harsh summers.

411

Calliope wondered how Di'Ath and Sy'da would fare in Ailiar, where the summers were only warm, and the winter brought snow that smothered everything. There had been years where the frost had been so vindictive that it had killed even the hardiest of crops.

Perhaps they would adjust as well as her father had, though she supposed that coming from a land that only saw a single season without snowfall each year was easier than coming from a land that saw no snow at all.

"Do you know what Di'Ath's specialty is?" Calliope asked.

Jaena shook her head as she set the last of the pins on the vanity and began to untwist the braids in Calliope's hair.

"No," she said. "That has been rather quiet. There are rumours, of course. Apparently the Zadanese royal family have what they call a 'Salt Room'. It's where they put Visdhraos that struggle with controlling their magic because salt draws out water. Apparently, the prince spent some time in there. Whatever it is, it's strong."

Calliope chewed her lip.

"What if I can't match him for strength?" she asked.

Lady Jaena dismissed the thought with a scoff and a wave of her hand.

"You're the heir to the Ailian throne," she said. "No one in the world is going to be stronger than you once you come into your Affinity. Honestly, I'm a little jealous. Only the Blood Heir knows for certain what Affinity they will come into before they come into it."

But did she? Calliope had been plagued with the idea that she was not going to come into the correct Affinity for as long as she could remember. All heirs to the Ailian throne were Saldhraos, wielding power over earth and specialising in the control of bloodstone. It was all but certain that she would follow the trend.

But still, she had never been able to sit comfortably in that certainty. It had chafed her, taunted her, and she had wondered over and over what would happen if she did not.

"I wonder how Princess Sy'da gets her hair so long," Jaena mused, still brushing out Calliope's hair. "Do you think I could convince her to share her secrets with me? I would love to have hair that fell to my knees like hers."

"Perhaps," Calliope said tentatively. "We could invite Princess Sy'da to join us the next time we go to the gardens."

Lady Jaena's face lit up with excitement at the idea. It was, surprisingly, infectious. Calliope felt warmth and excitement bubble within her as well, and she smiled once again.

"I think that would be wonderful, Callie," Jaena beamed.

Calliope stared dumbly at Jaena's reflection.

Callie.

No one had ever called Calliope *Callie*. No one ever called her anything other than *Your Highness*, or *Princess*.

And she didn't know how felt about it.

FORTY-SIX

MAIDA

TEIVAN FOREST

ALTHOUGH MAIDA WAS NO stranger to sleeping on the ground, she did not sleep well. She jolted awake every few minutes as images of Nanos' exploding body plagued her dreams and kept her from getting any semblance of rest. Even with Aros' arms wrapped tightly around her, sleep remained elusive. It was a small consolation to discover that Aros had also failed to rest.

At an unholy hour in the morning, when the sky was still black and the stars still winked down at them, Maida looked up to see him staring at the fire. She watched the flames dance in the reflection of his eyes. She distracted herself from her grief and her nightmares by focusing on the way the light cast shadows on his face.

Even now, amongst everything that had happened the night before, Maida marvelled at how beautiful Aros was. If he noticed her staring, he didn't show it. He didn't move or speak, and eventually Maida tucked her face back against his chest and tried once more to go to sleep.

After several more hours of waking with a scream caught in her throat, the sky lightened, and the sun began its ascent.

"We need to get going," Aros said as he pulled away from Maida. "We still have a long way to travel."

Tears stung Maida's eyes. She didn't understand how she had any more tears left to cry. Surely, she had shed them all already; surely they'd all fallen for Nanos, Palis, Aoife, Thalia, and the other villagers. If she hadn't cried them all already, had she even mourned them properly?

Maida pushed herself up to sit. Every muscle in her body burned. Her limbs screamed with every movement; her legs begged to be let out of their misery.

She pulled out a scrap of fabric from her pocket and carefully unwrapped it to reveal Nanos' tooth to ensure it was safe. She didn't understand the impulse to keep it. Perhaps it was simply a reminder of the young boy himself. Perhaps there was no logical reason to hold on to it, but it felt wrong to discard of what may be the only remains of the boy who had given her a name and helped her feel like she could belong in Luvrahn.

Well… the only remains that weren't slivers of bone too small to keep hold of, yet sharp enough to slice into flesh.

"Get changed," Aros said, dropping one of the packs in front of her.

Maida looked down at herself. A second patchwork skirt destroyed. An underdress that she had painstakingly gathered dandelions to dye it, stained. The bodice, riddled with tears and embedded with more pieces of white bone.

She had been so happy to put the whole thing together, and so excited to see Aros' reaction…

And now it was as good as gone.

She sighed and rewrapped the tooth in its protective rag before tucking it into a pocket of the pack. Then, she pulled out a pair of loose pants, a wool tunic, and a pair of orange wool leg wraps.

Aros wandered back to the river. Maida presumed that he was once again filling the waterskins, and she took advantage of his absence to change.

The pants were designed to trap the wearer's body heat within them. After she pulled them on and tied the leg wraps around her shins, she stood. The black fabric billowed over the top of the leg wraps like the top of fluffy muffins.

They'd be warmer than her skirt, and more comfortable to ride in.

Maida's shoulders sagged with the realisation that *getting moving* meant once again climbing upon the kapriae. Her thighs had not ceased aching from the day before, and the cuts along her shins had not stopped stinging since Aros had removed the bits of bone and rock. She was not convinced she would be able to command enough control of her own legs to keep herself mounted on the wide beast, despite being bracketed between Aros' legs.

As if he knew what Maida was thinking, Jon the kapriae watched her with those unnerving, vertical-slitted eyes. Maida could not tell whether it was sympathising with her or planning on turning her into its next snack.

When she had first arrived in Luvrahn, Aros had told her that they ate meat. Though she had never seen Jon each meat herself, she had no reason to not believe what Aros had said.

And besides, the creature had all but stripped the tree it was tethered to of its bark, and still looked ravenous.

Leaves crunched and twigs cracked behind her. Maida turned to see Aros returning with the filled waterskins. He added them and the packs onto Jon's saddle. Then, he pulled out a leather belt and held it to Maida.

"Here," Aros said.

The belt was long, studded with brass, and was home to both a pouch and a dagger. Maida hesitated before reaching out and taking it. It wrapped around her twice, but the weight of it was comforting.

"The next time we stop," Aros said, pointing to the dagger now hanging from Maida's waist. "I will teach you how to use that thing. If you find you need to use it in the meantime, bury the point of it into whoever or whatever is coming at you as many times as you can to ensure that they will not follow you when you run."

Maida swallowed hard.

She looked down at the dagger, feeling the weight of it on her hip suddenly increase tenfold. She did not feel as though she were capable of stabbing someone until they could no longer pursue her.

But then again, she had also not felt that she would have ever found a home amongst elves, and yet here she was, mourning the loss of it.

"Okay," she said, her voice barely a croak.

It hurt to speak. It hurt to breathe.

It hurts just to still be alive, she thought to herself.

"We should go," Aros said.

He did not wait for Maida's agreement before he lifted her onto the back of the kapriae. Maida winced as the pain shot up through her legs before scooting forward on the beasts back and taking hold of the coarse mane. Aros mounted behind her, his thighs pressing against hers.

With a silent nudge of the beast with his heel, Maida and Aros were once again on the move, putting ever more distance between them and Luvrahn.

Taking Maida ever deeper into the land of elves – ever further from the land of men.

FORTY-SEVEN

MAIDA

TEIVAN FOREST

MAIDA AND AROS SPENT the two weeks travelling from sunrise to sunset. They didn't see so much as a hint of another person, elf or otherwise, as they rode Jon the kapriae through the thick woodland known as the Teivan Forest. There was, however, plenty of small game that Aros shot from his mounted position, field dressed, and then cooked once they made camp for the night.

Maida missed Thalia's cooking. She missed the freshly baked bread that Aoife insisted on making for her. She missed the smell of the stew in the tavern carried toward her on the wind while she stitched in the meadow. Without anything more than salt to season the rabbit roasting over the fire, Maida longed for the complex herbs and spices that was rubbed into every bite of meat back in Luvrahn. Then, just as her mouth began to water at the memory, guilt slammed into her, like Holsten pinning her back against the wall.

She shouldn't be worrying about food when they were all gone. Like Silktide, Luvrahn was most assuredly completely burned to the ground. How could she be mourning the loss of food when she was still pulling bits of Nanos' bones out of her hair?

Thankfully, it was usually around the time that the guilt truly set in that Aros would nudge her with his boot and gesture with his chin for her to stand. For about an hour, he would run her through simple drills with a dagger so that she would be able to defend herself.

The first night he had attempted to train her had been a complete and utter failure. Every time she missed her mark in her attempts to stab Aros, she broke out in tears. It took three days before she stopped tearing up, and as time passed, her blade made contact more often than not. Still, she was not convinced that she would be good at defending herself should the need arise.

"Remember," Aros said, chest heaving after a particularly tiresome training session. "This is only a last resort. Your first option must always be to run. Especially in Ailiar, where you will face with people far older, stronger, and more powerful than you. Remember, we have magic. You don't."

"Why have you never shown me your magic?" Maida asked.

Aros averted his eyes, inspecting his dagger for burrs and other potential damage.

"Aros?" Maida pressed.

"I don't use it very often," he said. "I don't like using it."

"Why? Is it... is it like Kaidos'?"

Aros shook his head. His braids had been pulled back into a bun at the top of his head, but the beads still clinked against one another with the movement.

"No," he said. "We are both Aerdhraos, but that is the extent of our similarities on the magical front."

Once again, Maida saw the devastation of Nanos exploding right in front of her, as Kaidos' magic all but sent a cannonball of air through him.

"Mine is... a little more subtle than Kaidos'," Aros continued. "I can make it so that instead of pure air, you are breathing in poison or smoke. I can also make it so that when you breathe in, the air goes straight to your head, and you become so euphoric and low in inhibitions that you might think that you had drowned your sorrows in an entire cask of wine."

Maida looked down at the grass beneath her feet. She and Aros had trained for long enough that their boots had brought moisture to the surface, creating a muddy patch around the struggling, browning blades of grass.

For the first time, the silence that fell between them was uncomfortable. Even when Maida had been terrified of him, the silence had never chafed quite like this. She couldn't put her finger on why this particular silence felt so... wrong.

Was it because he had revealed the nature of his power? She was one step closer to knowing *him*, and yet she felt she knew less than she ever had.

Aros returned to the fire, sitting down by its bright orange flames.

"Get some rest," Aros said, patting the space beside him. "We'll hit town tomorrow. We'll stay there until we secure passage on a ship."

Maida lay down, tucking her arm under her head in lieu of a pillow. A ship meant that they were close to a coast. She wondered if seeing a port would make her feel homesick for Silktide. Would the smell of fish and salt bring her to tears again? Would her grief over the loss of her father be renewed?

"We're that close?" she asked, vainly fighting back a yawn.

"We are," Aros said. He reached down and brushed stray curls out of her face. "Tomorrow, we will enter the port town of Do'Meirah. We should get a night or two in an inn before we can get on a ship."

Maida sighed wistfully. She could sleep in a bed again. Even if it were only for a night before she was reduced to sleeping in whatever arrangements were commonplace on a ship. Would she have to sleep in a hammock? On the floor? With whatever livestock the ship may be transporting?

Whatever it was, at least it was not outside on the damp ground with only Aros and a campfire to keep away the winter chill.

"Tomorrow," she said, yawning again as exhaustion took hold of her. "Tomorrow, we see the sea."

They had woken early the next morning.

Maida sat straighter upon the kapriae's back, earning joyful bleats from the beast as they continued to travel through the never-ending Tievan forest. Maida was tired of the too-tall, too-bare trees and the lack of undergrowth. She was tired of seeing bare roots and moss-less rocks. She wondered how they had been so fortunate to come across enough animals to keep themselves fed when it didn't look like there was anywhere for them to live.

It was only the knowledge that soon they would be free of this place and would see a vast expanse of blue that she could gaze out at while they waited for a ship to carry them to the northern provinces of Ailiar that kept her moving forward.

As the hours wore on, the tree growth thinned. Slowly, Maida could see pathways forming. They grew thicker, more worn, and eventually met with a road.

In the distance, she could make out the tops of buildings and see carts being drawn by kapriae towards them.

She frowned.

"I thought you said we would be reaching a port town today," she said to Aros, twisting to look at Aros.

Aros nodded, keeping his attention on the path ahead.

"I did. That's it—Do'Meirah."

Maida's frown deepened. She could feel her brow creasing over itself, feel the wind-chapped skin cracking with the movement.

"You do realise I grew up in a seaside town," she said. "I know the sea when I see it, and I am certain we are nowhere near it. There are no gulls in the sky; the wind is not strong, nor do I smell fish. This isn't a port town. Either you're lying, or we're lost."

Aros chuckled behind her. His chest rumbled against her back. Maida leaned further into him, eager to feel the comfort of his mirth despite both their losses and his apparent ineptitude.

"You do not want to put money on either of those guesses," he said. "You do not know every sea in the world—not all of them are made of water."

Maida scoffed.

Being *made of water* was the very basis of a sea. It was the basis of an ocean as well, though she would not claim to know much about oceans. She did not really understand the difference between *sea* and *ocean*, but the distinction did not matter at this moment.

What did matter was that *seas* were large bodies of water, and she could see no evidence of such a thing. Even as they drew closer, with the sun inching towards the horizon, Maida failed to see anything to suggest that they were about to reach a port town. She could not even see masts or flags of ships waiting in the bay or at the docks.

Once they reached the town limits and Aros dismounted the kapriae to lead the still-mounted Maida through the streets, Maida became increasingly certain that Aros was either lying or wrong.

The air was full of dust, not salt. Sure, people milled about the wide, busy streets, bringing more noise and chaos than there had ever been in Silktide, but it was certainly not a port town.

She craned her neck, looking down every street from her perched position to try and catch a glimpse of blue as Aros led her through the crowded streets.

All she saw were crates, carts, and children weaving in and out of the crowd.

Finally, Aros came to a stop outside an inn.

He handed Maida Jon's reigns and leaned against her leg.

"Stay here," he said. "I'm going to see if they have a room. If something happens and you need to run –"

"Then I run," Maida said. "I know."

Aros nodded. He pulled away, patted her thigh, then disappeared inside.

Once more, Maida twisted atop the animal as it shifted from foot to foot beneath her.

The roads in Do'Meirah were much older than those found in Luvrahn and Silktide. Maida watched carriage wheels fall into neglected holes, and women with long skirts and cloaks lift their garments almost to their knees in a vain attempt to keep the hems free of dirt and grime. Men wore boots so caked in light brown dirt that Maida couldn't even imagine what colour the leather originally was.

Everything was just... brown.

She lost track of how long she had been left alone, watching the people mill about in their dirt-clad life, when Aros finally returned, followed by a young boy with sandy blonde hair and eyes far too small for his round face.

"There's a room," Aros said. "The boy here will stable Jon, and we will get some rest. Tomorrow, we'll enquire about a ship."

Maida nodded.

She gratefully accepted Aros' help dismounting, still finding difficulty with it after all this time. It felt good to have solid ground beneath her feet and even better to have Aros slip his hand into hers and tug her inside, slinging their packs over his shoulder in the process.

The ground floor of the inn was as busy as the street. It stank of stale beer, old gravy, and sweat. Maida curled her nose and pressed herself against Aros.

At least Aros' sweat was something she was used to, something that she had grown accustomed to and could ignore for the most part. But the air stank of the sweat of drunk strangers and weary travellers, and neither was something Maida could pretend didn't exist.

She wondered if Aros' magic could dispel the horrid stench. Perhaps it was too far engrained in the wood tables and benches. Perhaps it had been stamped into the cracked stone floor too often and become part of the very structure itself for any sort of magic to remotely be of help.

Maida trusted Aros to manoeuvre her where needed and followed his directions blindly until they were at the bar, greeted by a bald innkeeper who looked like a withered grape.

"Good evening, young miss," the innkeeper said to her. "Now, if the two of you will follow me, I will lead you up to your room."

He set down the glass and rag he had been using to polish it and stepped out from behind the bar. His once-white pants were stained with hundreds of spills and resembled a rainbow of browns, reds and greens.

Brown was quickly becoming one of Maida's least favourite colours.

She squeezed Aros' hand tightly as they followed the innkeeper up the creaking staircase to the floor above. They followed him down the narrow hallway, pressing against a wall of peeling paint to allow another patron to pass through before finally coming to a stop at a half-rotten door.

"Here we are," the innkeeper said, shoving a key through the lock and swinging the door open to reveal a tiny room with a simple bed and a barrel tucked against it, acting as a side-table.

"I thought you said that it would sleep two," Aros said, a frustrated edge in his voice.

"It'll sleep two," the innkeeper said. "I've seen larger folk than you and your lady friend fit in this very bed. Though if you're really not that happy with it, you can try the inn down the road. I hear they sleep *eight* people to one bed there."

Maida could feel the muscles in Aros' tighten. Wanting to avoid any potential conflict, she took a step forward.

"This is perfect," she said. "Thank you so much for your hospitality."

The innkeeper looked her up and down. Maida didn't like how he focused on her rounded ears, like being human once again put her in danger.

"Good," the innkeeper said, thrusting the key into her hand. "I will ensure that there are bowls of stew and some bread waiting for the two of you when you come down. You look half-starved, and I won't have people thinking that it's because we don't feed our guests enough."

Maida forced a polite smile in return and stepped out of the innkeeper's way as he left her and Aros alone.

It wasn't until she could hear him begin the descent down the staircase that she let loose some of the tension in her shoulders.

Aros let go of her hand and deposited the packs in the corner on the floor. His face looked drawn. His eyes were haunted.

Guilt clawed its way into her chest once more as she realised that she had been far too focused on what *she* had been feeling that she had not considered asking how *he* was faring after the loss of his friends.

Of his home.

He was just about to open her mouth to offer her apology and condolence when he cut her off.

"I'll take the floor," he announced.

Maida's mouth dropped open.

"I beg your pardon?" she asked.

"I'll take the floor," Aros repeated. "And you can take the bed."

Maida was suddenly all too aware of the weeks that he had slept on the bench at his kitchen table while she slept in the bed since he found her, and the lengths he had gone to so that she might have answers about her home. And yet here he was, once again offering to sleep on the floor when a bed was readily available, after two weeks of sleeping in each other's arms?

She snorted.

"No," Maida said firmly. "That is not going to happen. You will take the bed."

"Bryha..."

Aros' voice was heavy and thick with the weight of all he had to carry. He did not appear to have it in him to argue with her. How had she not seen how weary he was until now?

It only hardened her resolve.

"You will sleep in the bed," Maida said firmly. "I insist. And if you insist on *me* sleeping in the bed, then I suppose we are just going to have to share. It is big enough to fit the two of us, and it is not as though we are not accustomed to lying beside one another for heat. I am not going to argue with you about this."

Aros sighed, but he did not press the subject. His tired eyes looked even a little grateful for her insistence. Maida offered him a smile that she hoped was comforting before the two of them used the water in a bucket by the door for a quick wash to clean away the worst of the muck before heading downstairs.

True to his word, the innkeeper had a steaming bowl of stew and bread waiting for them. The bread was not as soft and fresh as the loaves Maida had become accustomed to, but it was welcome after a week of eating only game and hard tack.

The smell hadn't lessened, however, and the sound had only grown worse as more elves filed in searching for their next flagon of ale or mead.

The inn would have been charming if it had been looked after properly. The large hearth had a beautiful mosaic framing it, and impressive wooden beams crossed the ceiling. But everything was covered in a layer of grease, alcohol and grime.

Thankfully, they didn't need to spend much time in the filthy place. With their bellies full and a warm bed waiting for them, neither Aros nor Maida were inclined to stay amongst the boisterous patrons. They quickly gave their thanks to the innkeeper as they returned the bowls and cups, and returned upstairs to their room.

Once there, Maida perched on the side of the bed. She unwound the strips of wool from her leg and stepped out of her pants. She kept the tunic as she slid in between the blankets, her back turned away from Aros as he, too, undressed.

It was only when she felt the dip of the lumpy mattress as he climbed in beside her that she rolled over towards the warmth that emanated from his body. She could barely make out the shape of him in the darkness since he had blown out the candle they'd used for light, but still she knew deep in her bones that they were holding each other's gaze.

She wanted to reach out to him. She wanted him to hold her as he had done out in the wilderness.

"Aros?" she asked, her voice shaking.

"Yes, Bryha?" Aros replied.

A lump formed in Maida's throat. *Bryha*.

It was both her name and not her name. It was a symbol of kindness, love and acceptance from a community that had welcomed her a one of their own. It was the first feeling of belonging that Nanos had given her.

And now... it felt like more of a lie than ever.

Could she continue travelling with Aros without him knowing her true name?

Could she continue falling in love with him?

"Maida," she corrected him in a whisper.

Aros' breath caught. Maida felt the very moment his lungs stopped pulling in air, the second the blanket stopped rising and falling with his breath.

Her heart thundered in her ears. What if she had made a mistake? What if she had been right to keep her name from him?

What if he hated her for lying?

Deciding that it was too late to change her mind now, she cleared her throat and spoke again, her voice steadier this time.

"My name is Maida," she repeated. "And I don't want to travel any further with you without you knowing that."

Silence fell over them. It made her skin itch.

But finally, Aros broke it with a voice so quiet, it was as though he were testing the weight of her name on his tongue.

"Your name is Maida."

He lifted a hand and gently brushed her hair back before cupping her face. Maida pressed her cheek into the palm of his hand, closing her eyes.

"Your name is Maida," Aros repeated, making her feel that, despite everything that had happened, they would be okay.

FORTY-EIGHT

DI'ATH

BALLIACH

When Di'Ath had decided that he wanted to acquire more lotions and perfumes to make his rooms more aromatic, he certainly was not using Balliach castle gardens as an example. The air was pungent, despite the 'interesting' Ailian ritual of welcoming winter and the new year by making demands of their gods – something he was grateful to have missed—the flowers that lined the stone pathways were still in full bloom.

Di'Ath was not sure he would ever get used to it, just as he was not sure that whoever had designed and planted this garden knew what they were doing.

He was not unaccustomed to strong perfumes or odours—there were plenty of gardens in Zadanai. He had spent many hours lying in the flowerbeds, watching the clouds rolling in the sky above him. They had all possessed strong scents too, but there was just something about the flowers of Ailiar that simply assaulted his senses. It was far too heady and far too sweet. Not one scent complimented the next, and it left his head pounding.

Perhaps he was simply just not used to the types of plants that Ailiar had to offer. Perhaps it was nerves that were playing a part, making him feel things more keenly than he otherwise would have. He was, after all, walking side by side with his future wife, and it would make sense for all of his senses to be heightened as the twinge of anxiety urged his heart to beat faster

Behind them trailed not only his tutor and the palace guards that had been stationed outside his suite, but two women dressed head-to-toe in Ailian red. He had been entranced when he had first seen them, with the mask that covered the top half of their faces and the veil that covered their hair. He was intrigued by the fact that their mouths were left exposed, knowing that neither them nor their acolytes spoke.

At least, the Bloodmaids did not speak with words. They spoke with their hands, communicating silently in a way that he admired. Perhaps he would find someone to teach him—he was sure these women had many stories to share.

But as interesting as they were and as much as he wished to learn more about these famed warriors, neither of them were the woman he was supposed to be talking to. They were not the ones he should be engaging with, desperate to learn more about, eager to devour all the knowledge that they held.

No. The woman he was supposed to be interested in was the one by his side, who held her back mast-straight and her chin high. The corner of his mouth twitched up in a smile. The movement caught the princess's eye, and she turned her face towards him. Her eyes widened, and the tops of her cheeks were tinged pink.

No portrait could have ever caught such a thing and done it justice.

"My Lord?" she asked.

"No," Di'Ath's brow pulled down into a frown even as his smile widened. "No, do not call me that. Please, we are to be wed, and I would feel like a failure of a husband to have my wife call me *my Lord*."

Those rose-bud-pink lips pursed, and she looked both confused and frustrated. But there was no one here that she could turn to for permission now, not like she had at dinner the night before.

He had wondered if she would have danced with him without her father there to urge her to do so. True, it had been rather unorthodox to ask the princess to dance when no one else was. But he was determined to encourage her to speak her mind more often, and to feel free to act however she wished in his presence.

He could see that curiosity within her—and he had determined that he would coax it out of her.

"Then what shall I call you?" the Princess asked.

"Di'Ath," Di'Ath replied with a cocky smile. "For now. Until you can no longer contain yourself and find that you are overcome with the desire to call me your love. At such a time, I will also accept *my light*, or *my guiding star on the endless seas*."

He had gently taken her arm as he'd spoken, looping it through his own so they walked connected to one another. Calliope looked down at their entwined arms and his brown hand covering her pale one. Di'Ath could see a thousand thoughts flashing behind those eyes. She thought much and said little—the moment they had shared while they danced the night before had said as much. But what did she think about his words? He knew they were borderline arrogant, but such exaggerations had won the affections of many women back in Zadanai.

Perhaps you need a different approach with the princess, he thought.

Truthfully, he had not expected her to agree to promenade around the gardens with him. He had paced in his suite—alone, Sy'da had locked herself away in her own rooms—waiting for the attendant to return with Calliope's response.

Perhaps he needed to tread a little more carefully. The desired outcome was indeed different this time. He wanted more than a few nights warming her bed.

Needed more.

"Tell me," he said, voice softening. "What is your mind telling you?"

"My mind is asking me if this is appropriate," Calliope said.

Di'Ath could tell that she was choosing her words very carefully.

"Are you uncomfortable?"

The princess quieted while she thought about her answer. For a moment, Di'Ath thought that she was going to pull away from him. But instead, she gave him an answer that soothed and quieted his own doubts.

"No," she said. "I am not."

Di'Ath smiled.

"Good," he said. "Neither am I. And, my Lady-"

"If I am not to call you *my Lord*, then you are not to call me *my Lady*," Calliope interrupted.

Di'Ath's eyes widened in surprise. Her words had been quick, and there was a hint of a smile pulling at the corner of the princess' lips as she spoke. He vowed then that he would dedicate his life to making her smile so brightly that it eclipsed the sun.

As her husband, it would be his duty, after all.

"Then," he asked, voice low and conspiratorial as he leaned closer to her. "What shall I call you?"

The space around her eyes wrinkled slightly as that ghost of a smile grew. And oh, how her eyes shined when she smiled.

"You shall call me Calliope," she said. "Or... Callie. Until you can no longer bear the weight of not calling me *my dear*, or *my heart*, or *my light in the dark*."

Di'Ath's lips split into a wide grin.

Perhaps this wasn't going to be all bad after all.

FORTY-NINE

AROS

DO'MEIRAH

IT HAD BEEN DECADES since Aros C'Asad had woken with someone else in bed beside him. He had not taken a since the settlement of Luvrahn, and before that, he had all but lost interest in having someone warm his sheets. Aros had loved before. He had loved dearly, and so completely that it had nearly destroyed him when it was unreciprocated.

But that was what happened when one fell in love with a Queen.

Queens did not marry soldiers.

On the night of the Wishing, Aros had found himself hoping that perhaps Bryha—no, *Maida*—would be willing to consider the possibility of spending the rest of her life with him. He supposed the gods thought they were funny, giving him what he wanted after so cruelly taking everything else away.

Perhaps they were cruel and petty, despite his claims to the contrary.

But Luvrahn had been attacked, besieged by the very male Aros had tried so desperately to convince himself was not involved in the burning of Silktide, and Maida was pressed against him, under the same sheets.

Her head was on his chest. It rose and fell with each breath Aros took, and Aros found himself trying to take shallower breaths in an attempt not to disturb her. She deserved some peace.

They deserved some peace.

Maida's hair had begun to free itself from the tight braids that it had been

433

woven into the night of the Wishing. It stuck up, wild and rebellious, after not being tended to for weeks. Aros attempted to smooth it down to no avail. The locks of hair sprung outwards, fierce and free the moment his fingers left them.

He let out a soft chuckle before remembering that he was trying to let her sleep.

Aros brushed his fingertips across her cheek.

Maida.

The name seemed to tug at some foggy, unwilling memory in the back of his mind. It sounded familiar, almost as though it could have been elven.

Almost as though it could have been *Ailian.*

But why would a human bear an elven name? He couldn't make sense of it, and yet here a human lay asleep, soundly nestled against him. A human that, if he was correct, had borne *two* elven names. Was it possible that the name only seemed familiar because *she* was now familiar to him?

If that was the case, why was there a persistent, niggling voice in his mind that pointed towards some uncooperative memory? Why did it demand that Aros take not of it? What had he forgotten so thoroughly that he could not even name what it was?

His attempts to discover whatever had been forgotten were thwarted by the stirring of Maida in his arms.

She groaned. She buried her face in his chest as if to block out the very world. If the world did not appear to be crashing and crumbling around them, Aros may have found it within himself to simply lay there and let her rest.

"Maida," he whispered softly.

Maida groaned again.

This time, she rolled over and away from him. The cold patch left in her absence sent cracks through his heart.

He sat up and looked down at her. There were deep indents on her cheek and temple from the folds of his shirt. She must have slept on his chest for a while before he woke up. That mended most of the hollow ache that her rolling away had caused.

"Come on, Maida," he whispered again. "We have to get up. We have to talk to a someone about a ship"

"No."

The corner of Aros' lip curled upward.

"No?" he asked.

"No," Maida repeated.

"I'll drag you out of this bed," he warned.

"And I will show you how well you taught me to use that dagger."

Maida opened her eyes and glared at the ceiling. The hard look in those evergreen eyes did not last long before it gave way to glistening tears.

Aros sighed and climbed out of the bed.

"Come on," he said. "Let's get something to eat and secure our passage on the next ship out. After that, we can crawl back into bed and waste the day away. How does that sound?"

They should be wasting the day away.

There was more that needed to be done other than securing passage. They needed to sell Jon. They needed to buy food and other provisions. They needed to take stock of what they already had and make sure it was enough to survive a winter trekking over Ailiar. But if the promise of being able to crawl back under the covers later would help get Maida out of them now, he would make it.

His efforts were rewarded.

Maida threw back the sheets and climbed out of bed. She sniffled as she sought out the cleanest set of clothes that she owned and pulled it on. They would need to bring up a few buckets of water before the day was out, Aros decided, so that they could both bathe and freshen their clothes. Two weeks on the Between was enough to have anyone feeling dirty. It would be nothing but a disservice to themselves if they did not try to clean their clothes even a little before boarding a ship.

Once they were both dressed, Aros led Maida back down to the tavern beneath the public house. He left her rubbing her eyes at a table while he went to the bar and ordered a hot bowl of stew for them both. Like their dinner the night before, the meal was accompanied by two hunks of bread.

Instead of spiced mead, he ordered steaming cups of tea and carried it all back to her on a tray.

Maida accepted her breakfast without complaint, but Aros could see a hollowness in her eyes. She poked at her food so slowly that it was cold before she could finish it.

"You need to keep your strength up," Aros said. "I know it's hard, but you're helping no one if you don't eat."

"I had eaten plenty that night," she reminded him. "And we were of no help to anyone."

"Maida, we are—"

"We're following the plan," Maida cut him off. "I know. That doesn't make it feel any better. That doesn't change the fact that we left them to suffer. To die. What is the point of warning the Queen of what is happening if everyone we know is dead?"

Aros looked down at his own empty bowl. He titled it, watching how the remnants of the stew's gravy ran along the lines carved over the years by hundreds of scraping spoons.

"If we do not warn the Queen," he said, voice measured. "Then their deaths will be for nothing. Nanos' death will be for nothing."

Maida's nose scrunched, and her lip curled into a vicious snarl.

She looked purely elven at that moment.

"Nanos' death *was* for nothing," she hissed. "No child's death is worth whatever cause you might conjure. You cannot spin what happened to him into some legend or story about bravery or good overcoming evil. I won't allow it."

Aros stilled.

Even though Maida had been growing stronger and braver each day since he'd found her, he had never known her to speak in such a way. He didn't blame her. He couldn't.

But he wished she could understand.

She was still young—so young—and she would never live as long as he had. She would never see the death he'd seen. He knew he sounded callous. He knew that he might even look a villain in his eagerness to shut out the pain he felt when he thought about those he had left behind.

Because the truth of the matter was, it did not matter how well they had planned for any eventuality. Even the best laid plans were set askew when the right player entered the field. And Kaidos?

Kaidos C'Asad was the one player you never wanted to see on the other side.

"Once we are done with our business in Balliach," Aros said. "I will take you back to Colosia. Silktide is gone, but we can use the Queen's contacts in Kingskeep to get you settled there."

Maida looked up at him at the mention of the Colosian capital. Her brow was still knit together in a frown, but the anger had shifted to disbelief.

"You're sending me away?" she asked.

"You should be with your people," Aros said. "And if things continue to get worse in Ailiar, then you can't stay. I'm just trying to keep you safe."

His gut twisted at the thought of sending her anywhere he was not, but he had not lied. She would be safer in Colosia. If Meitranis could broker an agreement with the human King, perhaps Maida might even find a place at Court if she so wished.

Not that he could imagine her at Court.

Maida belonged in a small village, where she knew every neighbour, and where she could run with the children in grass that grew to her armpits. She belonged in a small, close community where she could dye fabric spun and woven by the local women who she drank tea with.

She belonged in a small, quiet cottage.

She belongs with you.

He cleared his throat and stood, reaching for her bowl.

Maida thrust it into his hand. She was upset with him. It didn't matter. In the end, how either of them felt about anything didn't matter at all.

She turned her face away, watching the fire dance in the hearth.

Aros sighed and carried the empty bowls and cups back to the counter.

"Where can I book passage to the north?" he asked.

"You'll be hard-pressed to find passage before the routes close for winter," the haggard barkeep said. "But down at the docks is an office. Tell 'em Drewda sent you, and you might get lucky."

"Thank you," Aros said.

He returned to the table and beckoned Maida to follow.

Maida stood, and Aros led her out to the busy street outside.

Do'Meirah was the busiest land-port town in the southern provinces of Ailiar. It was where most of the trade between north and south flowed through, and even in early winter, the streets were packed with elves.

Aros reached behind him to grasp Maida's hand as he wove through the traffic, pulling her towards the docks.

So close to the Sea Between Seas, there had not been enough rain to dampen the dirt roads. Dust and grime, kicked up by hundreds of pairs of feet, covered everything. By the time they passed the trader shops, the grocers and the butchers to finally arrive at the trade offices, Aros and Maida's boots were a light brown rather than the dark, rich earthen hue the leather had been stained with.

Aros pushed open the door. A bell rang overhead, and he led Maida to the back of a short line before the desks.

The dust and dirt had also made home here.

He couldn't imagine living in such a place. He might prefer the outdoors and minimal comforts, but he always preferred being *clean*.

Perhaps a Saldhraos would find it comforting.

Good thing he wasn't a Saldhraos.

Behind the counter, a white-haired, hunch-backed stick of a man sat and listened to the requests of the party before him. Aros tapped his foot on the wooden floor until Maida squeezed his hand.

He looked down at her, and she forced a smile up at him.

Aros sighed and squeezed her hand back.

The party at the table finished their business and left. As they passed, their toddler daughter waved at Maida. Maida smiled and waved back, but the moment the door had closed behind them, that smile disappeared.

She leaned against Aros.

"I can't wait for all the errands to be run," she sighed. "Then we can go back to bed."

Aros nodded in agreement.

The next party moved forward. Aros moved along, turning to look out the window. Outside, he could see the docks.

Land-ports had always fascinated him. They looked so much like regular ports that it was difficult to imagine that ships had been made to travel over anything other than sand dunes. The piers were raised wooden platforms accessed by ramps and staircases so that sailors and travellers could board via the upper deck. Lower platforms allowed stewards and handlers to load stock and provisions on below deck.

There was a ship at port now. He couldn't see too well from here, but it looked like the crew were checking the rigging.

"Next!" the steward called.

Aros hadn't even noticed the party before them clear the way to the desk.

"Good morning," Aros said as he approached. "I'm hoping you can help me. We want to book passage on the next ship to the north. For the both of us."

"The Ancient Ones favour you," the tired steward sighed. "The final ship to cross the Between leaves in two days. Other than that, you'd have to wait until spring, or brave the journey on foot."

"The journey on foot would take months," Aros said. "We don't have that kind of time."

"Not to mention that it's across a *desert*," Maida muttered at his elbow.

Aros did not bother to mention that the fact it was a desert was the least of their worries. The creatures and beasts that lived in the sands were the real concerns.

"Then I guess you better get on this one," the steward said. "So, two?"

Aros nodded.

"That'll be two gold crowns."

Aros frowned. "Two gold crowns?" he asked. "That's a bit steep, don't you think?"

The steward met Aros' eye. Aros could not see a single spark of life behind that gaze.

"You want to book last minute passage through the Between on the last ship going through. The rate is going to be steep. Again, you can always wait, or you can walk."

Aros shook his head, but he pulled two gold crowns from his pocket and placed them on the desk. The steward gave an affirmative huff, before he stamped a thick piece of parchment and slid it over.

"Next!" he called.

"What now?" Maida asked as Aros led her back to the door.

"Now, we need to see if we can find anyone in need of a kapriae."

FIFTY

MAIDA

DO'MEIRAH

ALTHOUGH SHE COULD NOT say in good faith that she had learned to trust nor even truly *like* the large, nightmarish beast that had carried her across the southern provinces of Ailiar, Maida's eyes still pricked with tears as she said good-bye. She scratched his nose while her lip wobbled, and she choked back sobs.

After she and Aros had found an old man and his wife willing to purchase Jon for their farm about an hour out of town, Maida tried to convince Aros that they would need Jon themselves once they reached the other side of the Sea Between Seas. Unfortunately, her pleas fell on deaf ears, and so she was reduced to the indignity of a runny nose and stinging eyes.

"I promise you that he is in very good hand, miss," the old man said.

His smile was as kind as his back was bent. She could see nothing that would suggest that he could not be trusted to keep his word.

"Old Jon here will not have much work to do at all and will spend most of his days grazing the fields and keeping out pests. Plus, my wife will likely feed him so much that he will grow fat and lazy."

Maida sniffled and nodded.

Aros wrapped his arm around her shoulder. "Come on," he said. "Let Jon go to his new home. We have a ship to board."

As if on cue, a loud, ear-piercing whistle rang out, signalling a warning for all those who wished to board the docked vessel.

She gave Jon one more scratch on his nose before turning away and tucking herself under Aros' arm. Aros thanked the man and turned Maida towards the docks. It wasn't until they were out of sight, having turned down a street, that Jon let out a mournful bleat. Maida let out a choked sob, her tears finally free to flow down her face.

Aros readjusted his hold on his pack before giving her shoulder a squeeze.

"He'll be alright," he said. "And maybe when this is over, we can come back and see him."

They would never come back.

She didn't understand why she felt so strongly that this was a fact, but she felt it in the very marrow of her bones. She would never set foot in Do'Meirah again. She would nevermore see the beast that had saved her life.

Maida wiped her eyes and gripped the strap of her bag tightly as Aros continued to lead her to the docks.

She could not focus on anything more than putting one foot in front of the other. She took notice of nothing, save for the moment the dusty ground gave way beneath her boots to the wood of a creaking staircase that led up to a raised dock. Maida snapped back into herself to peer over the edge.

If she fell, she would certainly have a moment to reflect on all the decisions that that had led to this moment. Would she see her father, too? Would she see Nanos, and Aoife, and Palis?

Would she mourn never again feeling the warmth of Aros' hand?

"For two," Aros said beside her.

"Your tickets?" came an unfamiliar voice.

Maida didn't turn to look. She merely presumed that Aros presented their tickets. He tugged her away from the edge and escorted her across the plank. Their steps sounded hollow on the wood, and even more so when they stepped onto the deck.

Sailors and passengers alike wove in and out of each other as the crew prepared to sail.

Once again, the shrieking whistle sounded.

"We leave in ten minutes!" a voice rang over the din.

"We should find our quarters," Aros said.

Maida did not answer. Aros led her over the deck and down below to the sleeping quarters, deep in the belly of the ship. Maida struggled to see where they were going in the dim lighting, but Aros appeared to have no problems at all. Eventually, they found their room, and Aros pushed open the door.

There was a closet to store their things, a small desk, and two beds. They would be able to sleep comfortably, though they would be apart from each other.

"This isn't as bad as I thought," Maida said. "I was sure that we'd be sleeping with the livestock."

"Not for two gold crowns," Aros muttered.

He opened the closet and set their packs inside.

"Do you want to watch the departure?" he asked.

Maida shook her head. "No," she said. "I just want to rest. Is that okay?"

Aros offered her a smile.

"I'll leave you be then," he said. "I'll come back and check on you shortly."

He tucked her hair behind her ear before letting himself out and closing the cabin door behind him.

Maida's whole body felt heavy. Though they had slept at the inn, it was as though the exhaustion from the last two weeks was finally catching up to her. She chose the bed to the left, diving under the blankets and pulling them up to her chin before promptly falling asleep.

She didn't wake until midday the following day. As if divined by fate, Aros walked in just as she was sitting upright and rubbing her eyes. He led her to the galley, where she got a plate of food, then up to the deck, where she ate it under the warm sun.

Maida wasn't able to bring herself to do much more. After lunch, she returned to their cabin and back asleep once more. The second day on board was much the same.

Her third day on the Between, Maida felt stronger. She carried her cup of tea up to the deck. She leaned against the railing, looking out at the vast expanse of sand.

She still didn't understand how any of this was possible, magic or no magic. Still, she was aboard a ship that was sailing through a desert. The rolling red dunes looked like waves, especially when the wind whipped up the sand like sea spray.

She heard Aros' familiar footsteps come up behind her. She felt the heat radiate off his body once he reached her side.

His very presence made her feel calmer.

"How much longer?" Maida asked.

"Two weeks," Aros told her.

Two weeks.

It seemed as though half of her life could be summed up in two-week increments. Sure, it had taken her over three to be found in the Edgeling Woods after she left her home, but if she had known where she was going, it would have been closer to two—just as it had taken Aros two weeks to get to Silktide. Then, it had taken two weeks to reach Do'Meirah after they fled Luvrahn. Now, they would spend the next two weeks on the Sea Between Seas.

"And after that?" she asked.

"A month," he said. "Give or take."

"What if we're too late?"

Maida looked up at Aros. Some unspoken worry flitted across his eyes, and she realised he had already considered this possibility. If they were too late, then it surely meant pain and destruction.

"I don't know," Aros said. "I can't work out Kaidos' motives. I don't know if he's working of his own volition or if Rupaburg is behind this. Either way, the Queen needs to know so that she can act accordingly."

Maida sipped her tea.

"Do you know the Queen?" she asked. "Personally?"

The corner of Aros' lips curled upward ever so slightly.

"I did," he said. "We were friends."

"What is she like?"

Aros was quiet for a moment, considering his next words.

"Kind," he said. "Meitranis always had time for anyone and everyone. Before she became queen, she spent most of her time in the city amongst her people. She loved music. She loved dancing. The Wishing was her favourite holiday, and we would spend hours dancing and drinking and enjoying ourselves while Oliantra watched from above."

Maida's gut twisted. She shouldn't feel the growing resentment festering within her at the thought of Aros dancing with someone else. He was hundreds of years old, and she not even a year over twenty. It was useless to feel jealous about a time long gone.

"Unfortunately," Aros continued. "Both war and marriage change people. When her mother died in battle, Meitranis was forced to take on a role she never wanted. To end the war, she was forced to marry a man she did not choose. She still celebrated the Wishing in lavish style but lost her light."

Maida was suddenly embarrassed by the jealousy she had felt. She had lost so much and seen such terrible things, but surely, they did not come close to the horrors that this elven queen had endured.

"Do you think she will be happy to see you?" Maida asked.

"I don't know," Aros admitted. "She always told me I would be welcome back in her court whenever I wished. But it has been fifty years since I've so much as seen Balliach."

Maida sighed and leaned against him.

He still smelled of pine, despite their travelling. At least now there was nothing for them to do, save rest and wait.

Maida continued to watch the dunes as they sailed through the Between when something caught her attention out of the corner of her eye. She leaned forward, looking around Aros to watch the crest of a dune intently. Perhaps it had been a trick of her imagination, but something deep within her gut warned her that it wasn't.

She kept her eyes on the dune while Aros tried to get her attention.

Then, as though the Ailian gods had listened to her silent plea, the dune split into two, and another ship was revealed.

"Shit," Aros swore, pushing Maida behind him.

"What's that?" Maida asked dumbly.

"Go!" Aros commanded. "Go, find the captain. Tell them we're being chased."

Chased? She thought. *How? By whom? It was just another ship.*

And then, a sound far too close to the familiar destructive boom of Kaidos' magic, rang out across the Between. Maida nearly lost her footing as a cannon ball slammed into the mast above. She screamed as splinters of wood rained down upon her.

"Go!" Aros commanded again.

And this time, Maida did not question him.

FIFTY-ONE

ANIAIJA

THE SEA BETWEEN SEAS

ANIAIJA BAHRA HAD RAIDED more than her fair share of ships in her lifetime.

It came with the territory of being stuck on a desert with no other way of sustaining the lives aboard your ship. Despite this, anxiety and doubt both took root deep within her chest.

It was worse when she found herself questioning their decision to leave the ships they raided intact.

They would not have been stuck on the Between for the last decade if they had been ruthless enough to take the timber needed to repair the gaping hole in the *Mercy's* hull. They could have even commandeered another ship and sailed off the Between and returned to the true sea. They could have found themselves a safe haven, a place to grow and thrive.

Yet, in the early days of their impromptu exile, they had all decided that it was against their moral code to risk the lives of the sailors of the ships they raided. It would make them no better than the corrupt Queen who had promised them freedom, only to try and kill them all.

This was not supposed to be their life.

When Aniaija first joined Geomar' crew, she had been looking forward to a life of adventure and honour.

There was no honour in what she was doing now. Even though it was the only way she could ensure that her crew and their families survived, guilt gnawed at her very soul as she kept her eyes on the mast of the ship sailing ahead of them. They had caught sight of it leaving Do'Meirah three days ago. They had kept their distance, following them deep enough into the Between that they could not turn and run, nor would they receive help in time.

What were they transporting?

It was already three weeks into winter. The cargo had to be desperately needed somewhere for the crew to risk sailing now that the sandwyrms were active.

Were there passengers aboard? Would they have enough food to keep the *Mercy* and the Oasis fed until the spring ships began sailing?

She felt Fredericks step up beside her. He did not appear to have the same moral conundrum she was struggling with. He bounced on the balls of his feet, his barely contained energy radiating from him like heat.

His magic called out to her own, coaxing it to the surface, ready to bend the earth around them to their will.

"You seem eager," Aniaija said. "Do you miss having a black eye?"

Fredricks snorted.

"No," he said. "Though I don't mind the attention that comes with it."

Aniaija shook her head.

The last time they had raided a ship, Federicks had taken an elbow to the face. He had walked back aboard the *Mercy* with a bleeding nose and swollen, black and blue bruises around both eyes. He was right though—the single and non-monogamous women had all fawned around him, offering sympathy and comfort.

Some of the men, too.

"Nah," Fredericks said, leaning against the railing. "Perhaps I'm just eager for revenge."

Aniaija sighed.

"It is not revenge if it is not exacted upon the one who caused you the grievance," she chided. "It is merely violence."

"Save me your Tide bullshit," Fredricks said. "It is because of the crown that you and I are stuck on this gods-forsaken desert. *That* ship is carrying goods for the crown. Keeping whatever supplies it has on board meant for the northern provinces will hurt Balliach. Therefore, by targeting *it*, I still targeting the bitch that caused me my grievance."

Aniaija readjusted the belt that held her sabre at her waist.

"You can justify any atrocity if you twist it like that," she muttered.

"You signed off on this," Fredricks reminded her.

"What are our other options? We have no supplies. Our people need to see their families. If we go back to them empty handed, it'll doom us all. This decision was not made lightly."

"But the decision *was made*," Fredricks said. "And you do not have the right to dictate how other people react to it just because you feel uncomfortable about the part you played in making it a reality."

Aniaija clenched her jaw.

She hated the truth that rang out in his words. She wanted to argue with him, to defend her choices.

But they did not have the luxury of the time it would take to debate their side. They were closing in on the ship; it was just over that dune. Soon enough, Aniaija would have no time to worry about whether what she was doing was moral or not.

"Are you ready?" Aniaija asked, a new steeled tone to her voice.

"Oh," Fredricks said with a wolfish grin. "I was born ready."

Together, they reached out with their magic, taking hold of the sand in the dune that separated them from their prey. In perfect unison, they tore the dune in two, and the *Mercy* burst through with the rage and magnificence of a god.

Beside them, Saldhraos and an Igdhraos prepared the cannon, and soon the thunderous boom of cannon fire rang out.

Screams erupted from the ship ahead as the cannon ball struck the centre mast. Canvas fluttered as they fell, covering passengers and sailors alike.

As though something foreign had taken over her, a feral grin curled Aniaija's face.

With one of the sails gone, the ship would be unable to outrun the *Mercy*.

Still, Aniaija and Fredricks focused their magic on the sand directly in front of the ship, stopping the Saldhraos on board from splitting it.

Whoever they were up against was weak. They weren't anticipating coming across someone else on this voyage.

This would be easy.

Within a few minutes, the *Mercy* was alongside the other ship. Aniaija had caught sight of the name and smirked to herself.

The *Fleeting Lady*.

How ironic.

With war cries to rival those of the fiercest armies, the crew of *the Mercy* made their way onto the *Fleeting Lady*.

Fire, water and stone flew through the air as both crews fought against one another, but the crew of *the Fleeting Lady* stood no chance.

The skirmish was over in minutes, and the crew and passengers of the other ship were subdued and bound. Aniaija rolled her neck, pacing back and forth as she kept an eye on the prisoners.

Around her, the *Mercy's* crew liberated every crate and barrel they could find. She heard alcohol slosh against wood, smelled smoked meats, and saw fine fabrics spill over the top of containers.

Some of the trepidation she had felt over raiding the ship in the first place lifted. Aniaija sighed in relief.

They had supplies now. They could survive the winter, and the people aboard the *Fleeting Lady* could return to Do'Meirah with nothing more than wounded pride.

She coughed.

The air felt... strange. It stung her throat, like smoke clawing at her from the inside.

She coughed again, doubling over.

What is this? What's happening?

"Enough!"

Captain Geomar's voice rang out, clear and commanding. It was followed by the sound of crashing waves. Suddenly, the air in her throat was clear again.

Aniaija turned and saw that one of the prisoners was dripping wet.

His skin was as dark as night. His eyes glistened like stars as he stared dumbfounded at Geomar. Beside him, a pale human with bright red hair looked horrified.

Geomar stared at the two for a long moment before huffing and turning his back, heading back towards the *Mercy*.

"Bring those two aboard," Geomar said.

Aniaija scoffed. She ran after Geomar, moving to stand in his way.

"Are you mad?" she hissed. "We don't take prisoners. We can't feed them."

Over Geomar's shoulder, she saw the human grow even paler.

Perhaps she should have chosen a more... diplomatic phrasing.

"That is an order, Bahra," Geomar said.

His old, weary eyes held hers until Aniaija broke away.

"Fine," she said. "Fredricks! Get those two on board and in the brig. Now."

Fifty-Two

Maida

The Sea Between Seas

Iron shackles weighed cold and heavy on Maida's wrists. No matter what she did or how she sat, Maida could not relieve the discomfort. On the contrary—every attempt to relieve the pain or make herself more comfortable did the opposite.

"Stop moving," Aros said. "We will be out of this soon enough."

"Out of this?"

In stark contrast to that of her companion's, Maida's voice was panicked.

"I am not sure if you have noticed, but we are currently sitting in *chains* in the *brig* of a *giant pirate ship.*"

Aros rolled his shoulders and leaned back against the wall of the cell. He was far too calm and appeared far too comfortable for Maida's liking.

How could he look so peaceful while they were chained? Where was the rage that she had seen when the pirates had first fallen upon them? Where was the cunning hunter that had ensured her safety when intruders had destroyed yet another one of her homes and burned it to the ground?

"It is not a pirate ship," Aros said simply, as if she were a child, and he was telling her something obvious.

Maida scoffed.

"Is it not?" she asked. "We were set upon by pirates, and we are now aboard the ship they were sailing on when they did so. I would hazard a guess that this is, in fact, a pirate ship."

The corner of Aros' mouth tipped upward, stoking the flames of Maida's frustration.

"How is it that you can just sit there so calmly as if we are not about to lose our lives? As if everything we have lost trying to get to your Queen is about to be for nothing?"

"We are closer to the Queen than you can imagine."

And there was that tone, that playful underlying note to his voice that he used whenever Palis was close to figuring something out and yet could not see it.

"What do you mean, we are closer to—"

Maida's question was cut off by footsteps. It was not one set that she could hear descending the wooden stairs towards them, but two. Two pirates coming their way, meaning Maida did not have time to deal with whatever madness Aros was spewing.

If the calm, collected hunter had been driven mad by the sun, it would be up to her to get them out of this mess.

Maida bared her teeth as the pirates came into view, recognising the woman as the elf that had ordered she and Aros be brought aboard. The pirate had been smiling then; her lips curled into a feral grin as her crewmates wrangled Aros into submission. Maida had seen no alternative but to be more cooperative.

After all, how would she, a human of twenty, be able to fight against a crew of elves?

But the pirate was not smiling now.

She looked down her aquiline nose at Maida, completely undeterred by the pitiful snarling that came from Maida's mouth.

Maida could not decide which expression she preferred.

"Well, well."

Maida's attention snapped towards the other pirate. He was far older than his companion. His skin was wrinkled and leathery, his beard grey and wiry like a scrubbing brush. He looked as though he belonged on the water, not sailing the sand of the Sea Between Seas.

"Slap my ass and call me a sandwyrm," He barked a laugh so rough it all but confirmed Maida's suspicions about him belonging on the sea. "If it isn't Aros C'Asad."

Aros' laughter echoed off the iron walls of the cell. Maida shot him an accusatory look, but he did not remove his attention from the old pirate.

"I see that Di'Tyan spat you back out, Geomar," Aros teased. "What happened? Did you annoy the God of the Dead with your off-key shanties and your shitty breath?"

Maida's eyes widened at the insult, but Geomar, as Aros called him, simply barked out another full-bellied laugh. At least the woman by his side appeared to be suitably annoyed by the interaction.

"Come now, C'Asad," Geomar said. "We all know that you missed me singin'. I would place coin on you crying yourself to sleep every night, wishin' I could sing you another lullaby."

Aros snorted.

"I cry myself to sleep every night mourning the damage you did to my ears on a daily basis. They still bleed whenever I think of you, and I would cut them off if I were not so sure that I would be cursed to still hear you wailing in my head and be left with no way to drown you out."

The pirate let out another rumbling laugh. Maida was getting rather sick of the sound.

"Everyone thought you were dead!" Geomar said. "No one has seen you in... well... in-"

"In half a century," Aros supplied. "Yes, I know. Now, my dear friend, as much as I am loving our little reunion, could you please let my friend and I out of these chains? I am sure that she would be more appreciative of our encounter if she was able to see that we are not your prisoners."

"*She* is right here," Maida muttered.

Now was not the time to be offended that they were talking about her like she wasn't there while she was, very clearly, sitting right beside them, but she could not keep a lid on her agitation.

"But of course, Lord C'Asad," Geomar said with a half-hearted bow. "Aniaija, would you do the honours?"

Geomar gestured towards the door of the cell and the woman, Aniaija, sighed as she pulled a ring of keys from her belt.

Maida watched as she picked out a key without so much as considering whether it was the right one.

The heavy lock popped, and the door groaned as Aniaija pushed it inwards. The pirate crossed over the threshold, and freed Aros before bending to undo the shackles on Maida's wrists. Her scent washed over Maida, reminding her of black tea and freshly cut grass.

It made Maida homesick in a way that she had not expected, and she leaned closer to hold on to the scent as much as possible.

The irons fell away from Maida's wrists and landed on the floor with a heavy thud.

Maida looked up to find Aniaija watching her with a puzzled look. Her dark brows were furrowed, and her nose scrunched to one side, as though trying to better understand what Maida was.

She gave a slight shake of her head before returning to Geomar's side.

"Thank you, Aniaija," Geomar said.

Aros and Maida stood, but while Aros found his footing on the rocking ship easily, Maida struggled to remain upright. She stumbled, her legs nearly giving out beneath her, until something firm and solid placed itself under her arm.

Maida was surprised to find Aniaija propping her up.

She had not even seen the woman moving, and yet now the pirate's arm was around her waist, preventing her from falling. How had she moved so quickly? And why, after looking so disgusted with Maida's presence, was she helping her?

"Don't worry," Aniaija said. "You will get your sand-legs soon enough."

Maida could not find the words to respond. How was Aniaija's voice so smooth? Why did she smell like home? What kind of magic did she possess that had Maida considering lowering her guard?

Her thoughts were interrupted by Geomar's laugh, and she vowed that she would stuff the first thing she could find into that man's mouth if it meant he would shut up.

"You best be careful with that one, C'Asad," he told Aros. "She will steal your little girlfriend before you can say *beach gnat*."

"Pay him no mind," Aniaija said. "He is just jealous that I get more on the docks than he does. And I get repeat visitors."

Get more... oh.

Maida wished she had missed the wink the pirate gave her as her cheeks burned.

"Bah!" Geomar waved his hand in frustrated dismissal. "That was one time, and it was unfair conditions. You can recover quicker than I."

"I suppose you also think it is unfair that I got four in one go?" Aniaija continued to tease.

Maida shifted her weight uncomfortably. She looked to Aros, who offered a kind, though ultimately unhelpful, smile.

To her relief, Geomar decided to change the topic of his own accord.

"We can continue this conversation later. We have much more pressing matters to discuss. Such as—why in the world are you on the Between, C'Asad?"

Aros clapped Geomar on the shoulder.

"Let us go somewhere more comfortable, and we will tell you everything you need to know."

FIFTY-THREE

AROS

THE SEA BETWEEN SEAS

ALTHOUGH HE HAD NOT been keen on letting Maida out of his sight, Aros had relented and allowed her to be whisked away by the Zadanese girl. He reasoned that if he trusted the old sea dog despite the years that stretched between now and the last time they had seen each other, he should extend that trust to Geomar's second in command as well.

Regardless, he had questions to ask, and he was not entirely sure he wanted Maida to hear such answers just yet. So, while the girls embarked on a tour of the *Mercy*, Aros remained with Geomar in his cabin.

He eyed the former Admiral, arms crossed over his chest.

"What brings you out to the Sea Between Seas, Geomar?" Aros asked. "What business could Meitranis possibly have out here? And just how much did she pay to convince you to get off the water?"

Geomar had been reaching for a bottle of rum when Aros had spoken. The captain paused, and his hand was so tight around the neck of the bottle that Aros could see the whites of his knuckles.

The captain set his jaw, closed his eyes, and took two deliberate breaths before setting the bottle back down.

"The Blood Queen did not send me here, my friend," he said.

Aros' brow furrowed. He uncrossed his arms and pushed off from the cabin wall, certain that he had misheard Geomar.

"I'm sorry?" he asked. "What do you mean? Why are you here, if not on Meitranis' orders?"

Geomar picked up the bottle again and poured them both a drink. He sat down heavily in the chair behind his desk before he answering

"After you left," he began. "Things... changed. Her Majesty started makin' decisions that weren't like her. Of course, it didn't happen all at once. There were a few small things here and there, minor changes to staff that seemed inconsequential. Then, she went away for a year. Before she left, she claimed it was for developin' relations and maintaining peace with Colosia. When she came back, she said she had been followin' the will of the gods and had been communin' with them."

Aros finally lowered into a seat of his own.

"Meitranis does not put stock in any of the gods but Oliantra," he said.

"You think I do not know that?" Geomar asked, exasperated. "If she were indeed communin' with the gods, then she did not like what they told her. She came back and appeared to have lost her very reason for livin'. It was after then that Oprianos started making decisions."

Geomar stared off into some unshared past, his eyes glistening with tears.

"I had been spendin' most of my days down at the docks. I did not notice how bad things were until it was too late. When I finally noticed that somethin' was amiss, I did what I thought you would do."

"Me?" Aros asked.

"Yes. You were always her closest and most trusted friend. I thought that if I could figure out how you would handle things, I could take care of things. Though if you were still here, I doubt she would have even stepped away in the first place."

Aros turned his attention to his rum.

He had spent countless nights lying awake, wondering if he had made the right choice in leaving Balliach. But to see Meitranis—his Queen, his best friend, the woman he loved—marry his *uncle* for nothing more than a political alliance...

He had not been able to bear watching her wither under a loveless marriage.

He had been the worst kind of coward.

"When I realised what was happenin'," Geomar continued. "I confronted her Majesty and questioned why Oprianos was decidin' anythin' at all. She told me that he was well within his right as a monarch to make such decisions."

Aros scoffed. "That is not how things work in Ailiar."

"That's what I told her. She's the Queen, the Blood Heir, the *Blood Queen*. Only *she* can make decisions because only *she* is gods-chosen."

Geomar sighed and took a deep swig of his drink.

"Of course, she did not listen to me. And instead, I prepared for my retirement."

Aros raised an eye. "Retirement? But you are on-"

Geomar held up a hand. "Le' me finish," he said. "It was not a voluntary retirement. Her Majesty gifted me the *Mercy*. She said that as we were now at peace, we would no longer need the flagship. She said, she knew how much I loved the ship, and as a thank you for all me years of service, she wanted to gift it to me."

The muscle in Geomar's jaw tightened.

"She told me that I was welcome to take any crew that wished to follow me into retirement. So, I did. I took the ship. I went to my crew, and I asked every one of them if they wanted to spend the rest of their days sailin' with me. I went so far as to let them bring their families with them. After all, if I were no longer the Admiral of the Queen's Fleet, what incentive did I have to return to Balliach?"

Aros understood his reasoning. Had he not himself severed every connection he had just to keep himself from returning to the same city?

The gods must be laughing at him.

"It took two months, but I had my crew—all 900 souls that had decided to lift anchor and abandon their home for a chance of a lifetime of adventure on the sea. It was, admittedly, a larger crew than I had anticipated. Space was a little tight, but seein' as my sailors brought their families, it was fair t' assume that some would drop off at ports along the way, so I wasn't concerned."

Geomar exhaled loudly.

"We did not even make it out of port before the first shots were fired. The dockside cannons were aimed at us. We thought it was a mistake, that someone just being stupid and setting them off by accident. But that is when the hull got busted, and why we are on the Between. If it weren't for Aniaija, we'd be on the sea floor by now."

Aros shook his head.

"I don't understand," he said. "Why?"

"We didn't find out until we tried to pull into a port to fix the hole and get our bearin's. We were told that we'd been branded as traitors to the crown and that there was a warrant out for my arrest. Apparently, I stole the *Mercy*, abandoned my post, and threatened the Queen's life, so the King wants my head."

Aros felt his heart break for his friend. To go through so much for his Queen and country, only to be on the run... It was horrific. He couldn't imagine a worse sense of betrayal.

It didn't sound like Meitranis in the slightest.

"We will take you to Dei'Nach," Geomar said. "As promised. But Aros... I fear you will not find the answers you so desperately seek in Balliach. I fear that what we have both left behind no longer exists."

Fifty-Four

Calliope

Balliach

Calliope pretended to focus on the dusty tome before her as she tracked the movements of Councillor Sancor through her periphery, wondering why she had said those words to Di'Ath in the gardens. *Until you can no longer bear the weight of not calling me my dear, or my heart, or my light in the dark.* Where did she think she was? In a romance novel?

The old man paced back and forth while he droned on about some battle that had been waged long before Ailiar's written history. Calliope had once asked why anyone would bother learning something that predated the written word—Sancor's response had been to assign her a list of readings so long that Calliope had missed out on every informal social engagement during her thirteenth summer.

Sometimes, she tried to convince herself that this punishment had led to her lack of friends. Thirteen was a foundational age for any young woman. Whatever transpired between their thirteenth birthday and the day they turned fourteen would mark them forever. It was a year when girls were both overly sensitive and overly cruel. It was a time where true friendships were solidified, and lifelong rivalries took root.

Calliope had not had the chance to make friend or foe, so now—barely half-way through her nineteenth year—she had no one save for the silent Bloodmaids and Jaena.

You wouldn't have any friends anyway, a dark, twisted part of herself said. *No one would ever want to waste their time with someone like you. You're nothing. Your own mother can't be bothered to send so much as a smile in your direction.*

When Di'Ath had arrived, Councillor Sancor had cancelled their lessons.

Unfortunately, it appeared that his leniency relating to her studies now that the prince was here had only been temporary. He had sent a messenger to her rooms early in the morning to remind her that she was expected to meet him, and that her schedule had returned to normal. While there was not much that seemed at all enticing about becoming Queen, the idea that she could replace Sancor the moment she was crowned was one that Calliope clung to desperately. Once she was Queen, there would be nothing keeping her from expelling the wretched old man from the keep. Perhaps she could go so far as to expel him from the city itself, or—if she dared—Ailiar.

A knock on the door caught her attention, and she lifted her face towards it.

The young guard who stood in the doorway looked familiar. It took but a moment for Calliope to recall that it was he that had led her through the halls to her father's study when Jaena had arrived.

His armour fit better now.

That was good.

"Apologies, Councillor," the guard said with a low bow. "But the King has requested your presence."

Blue eyes met Calliope's. Her brow furrowed. There was something familiar in that look. She wasn't sure exactly what it was that glittered and glistened there, other than a promise that the trajectory of her day was about to change completely.

"What is this concerning, boy?" Sancor asked.

"I am afraid I was not privy to the information, Councillor," the guard said. "But the King did stress that it was important you meet him in his study now."

Calliope bit the inside of her cheek to keep herself from smiling. The insolent tone in the guard's voice was so minute, she wondered if Sancor heard it at all. Whatever this guard had been up to since Jaena's arrival, he had certainly grown more confident in himself.

Perhaps having a properly fitted suit of armour helped with that.

"I see," Sancor said. "But I am in the middle of something with the princess. Can he not wait?"

"No, Councillor," the guard said. "The King wishes that you go to him immediately. He seemed in a rather foul mood, if I'm honest. He instructed me to escort the princess back to her quarters once I informed you."

Sancor's jaw clenched. Calliope's shoulders tightened and her breath caught as she watched the wretched old man flex and close his hand once, then twice.

After taking a moment to compose himself, he turned towards Calliope.

"Enjoy the rest of your day, Your Highness," he said. "We will resume tomorrow."

Calliope dipped her head. With a dramatic sigh unbecoming of someone his age, Sancor swept out of the room, nearly bumping into the guard on his way.

The guard leaned back, watching Sancor. When he was satisfied, he returned his attention to Calliope with a beaming smile.

"Enjoy the rest of your day, Your Highness," he said, mimicking Sancor.

Then, he left her alone.

Confused, Calliope closed the tome and stood. She smoothed out her skirts and walked out the door, turning to the right without so much as glancing in the opposite direction. She didn't want to tempt fate and risk running into Sancor, even though he was surely many hallways away now.

She didn't even know where she would go.

The guard had mentioned escorting her back to her rooms, but he had just left her there. She simply did not understand.

"Your Highness!"

Calliope looked up to see Lady Jaena waving at her from down the hall.

She could feel the grimace settling in on her features. She tried to transform it into a genuine smile, yet Calliope could not help but feel that she had been cheated. She had been gifted an unexpected reprieve from Councillor Sancor, only to be saddled with her cousin's inevitable non-stop chatter.

Though she had recently decided that Jaena was not completely unbearable, she didn't want to waste this rare opportunity for solitude.

She should turn around.

She could still turn around.

Even though Jaena had noticed her and called out, Calliope could still concoct some lie about being distracted. She could claim to not have heard Jaena, or not to have noticed her.

But the brief moment of plausible deniability slipped through her fingers as Calliope met Jaena's direct gaze.

Lady Jaena's sunshine-bright countenance seemed to brighten even more at the slight nod that Calliope offered in acknowledgement. She picked up her pace, sending the pastel-blue skirts of her dress flowing around her like water. Calliope suspected Jaena might be using her Affinity to make the fabric move the way it did, and she tucked the accusation away in her mind to ruminate on later. For now, though, the princess would focus on how Jaena was approaching her entirely too quickly, and how brief her taste of freedom had been.

"I am so happy to have run into you," Lady Jaena said as she approached. "You have absolutely no idea."

"I am sure I do no-"

Calliope was unable to finish her sentence as Jaena slipped her hand into Calliope's. The blonde did not stop walking, however, and quickly Calliope felt the tug of the movement. Just as she made the decision to try and pull herself free, someone looped their arm through Calliope's on the other side.

Together, Jaena and the stranger spun the crown princess of Ailiar around until she was facing the way that she had come. Jaena dropped Calliope's hand to clasp both of her own before her. She looked far too pleased with herself, and if Calliope did not have some stranger still holding onto her, she swore that she would have slapped that look right off her face.

"What is the meaning of this?" Calliope asked.

"We thought you could use an afternoon off."

The voice, deep and melodious, had come from somewhere behind Jaena.

In her confusion and anger at the Rupaburgan Lady, Calliope had not noticed Prince Di'Ath of Zadanai leaning against the wall. A mischievous grin split his face from ear to ear, and beside him stood the young guard that had been her salvation mere moments before.

The guard shifted his weight from one foot to the other nervously, but the expression on his face was one of pride.

Once Calliope had taken a good look at the three faces before her, she turned her attention to the one by her side.

Sy'da's grin matched that of her brother. She pat Calliope's arm twice before pulling away and moving to join Jaena.

"I cannot believe that this worked quite as well as it did," Sy'da said with a laugh.

"I thought that Sancor would see right through me," the guard said.

Di'Ath pushed off the wall. He patted the guard on the shoulder in an encouraging manner, and offered him a bright smile.

"No way," he said. "You were very convincing, Gregory. Even I wondered if the King had requested him after we had set all of this up."

The pointed tips Gregory's ears burned bright red. He cleared his throat and lifted his chin in a vain attempt to hide his embarrassment.

"Th-thank-you, my Lord," he said.

Di'Ath made a noise that Calliope thought may have been faint annoyance. She wondered if he had asked Gregory to call him by name as well. He would have more luck getting one of the Bloodmaids to speak than to convince a guard or member of staff to address a royal by their given name.

"So," Jaena said, tearing Calliope's attention away from Di'Ath. "Now that we have sprung you from your torture, I think that Sy'da, Gregory and I will go and wreak havoc elsewhere."

Gregory snorted, inspiring a giggle from Sy'da.

Calliope frowned. "You concocted a plan to get me out of my studies just to abandon me?" she asked.

"Oh, no, your Highness," Jaena said with an airy, dismissive wave of her hand. "I would not call this abandonment. Not when you will have the dashing Prince Di'Ath to keep you company."

Calliope almost missed Lady Jaena's wink when her eyes met Di'Ath's gaze once more.

His eyes were so warm, so inviting, and oh how Calliope wanted to fall into them.

"I..." Calliope stammered. "But... chaperones..."

"You have your Bloodmaids," Gregory said. "They count, unless you go to the Hall of Queens."

"And you two are engaged to be wed," Sy'da chimed in. "Back home, no one would bat an eye at a young couple spending time together before the wedding."

"It sounds so much better than Rupaburg," Lady Jaena muttered. "Where you're kept apart until the vows."

"Of course," Di'Ath said, catching Calliope's full attention. "I will not force my company upon you, my Lady. That being said, I do so hope you agree to spend the afternoon with me."

With four sets of eyes on her, Calliope felt her heart begin to race. She weighed every argument – every reason why she should not spend the afternoon with the handsome, charming prince.

And every reason why she should.

She felt the corner of her lip curl up into a smile before she realised she had even settled on a decision.

"On one condition," Calliope said.

"Anything," Di'Ath offered.

"You must call me Callie."

Despite the fact that Lady Jaena had outright declared that she, Sy'da and the guard Gregory would be heading off on their own little adventure, Calliope had not expected them to actually leave her alone with the prince.

Of course, she was not truly alone. The sound was faint and familiar enough to her that she could almost pretend that she could not hear the rustling of the Bloodmaid's skirts behind them. But with the heat of her betrothed searing through the fabric of both their sleeves, Calliope found that her senses were heightened.

"I must admit," Di'Ath said, breaking through Calliope's thoughts. "I did not pick Lady Jaena for the type to entertain such trickery. Not that I am complaining. I am very happy with the results of her scheming, but she has put me to shame."

Calliope looked up at him, trusting that he would manoeuvre the both of them out of the way of any obstacles as they wandered the halls of the keep.

There was a darkening around his jaw, the tell-tale sign that the beard she had first seen him sporting was hiding just beneath the surface. Her fingers ached to reach up and touch it.

"What do you mean?" she asked instead.

"Well," Di'Ath said. "This morning, I had a knock on my door. I was expecting Sy'da, but when I opened it, your Lady Jaena was standing there with a gleam in her eyes that I have not seen in anyone other than my sister when she has devised something devious. Usually, that kind of look gets me into trouble, but I decided to give her the benefit of the doubt."

A chill ran down Calliope's spine.

"Lady Jaena went to your room?" she asked.

Di'Ath nodded. "She said that you had been called to studies with a horrid tutor, and that you would benefit from being liberated. She came up with the whole thing—the story, which guard we should choose, giving us some time alone. It was all her idea. You have a good friend in her, Callie."

Calliope wanted to savour the way *Callie* sounded falling from the prince's tongue, but a lump was forming in her throat. Jaena had gone to the prince's room. She had walked right up to his door and she had knocked. She had gone to him. She—

"Callie?"

Di'Ath had pulled the two of them to a stop, and looked at her with concern. "Are you alright? Did I say something? Are you feeling alright?"

"I..." Calliope began. "I am fine, truly. I just got distracted, I think."

"Distracted?" Di'Ath asked.

"Yes," Calliope said with an overly enthusiastic nod. "You see, I was thinking about what the guard – what *Gregory* said."

Di'Ath tilted his head. "What did he say?"

Calliope considered her next move for a moment more before she settled on it.

"You set up this surprise for me," she said. "Can I surprise you?"

"My Lady," Di'Ath said, voice low and teasing. "Are you about to reveal to me that you too have a devious side?"

Calliope beamed at him, her smile bright and unrestrained for the first time she could remember. Without another word, she began pulling Di'Ath down the hall. It did not take long for the two to start running. Their laughter bounced off the stone walls as prince followed princess through the twists and turns of the keep. Courtiers jumped out of the way, and for the first time, Calliope Ailiar did not pay attention to the words that fell from their lips.

By the time they arrived at her intended destination, the pair were breathless and panting. Through heaving breaths, they laughed. They held each other up, keeping one another from falling to the ground as they doubled over with rib-straining mirth.

"Where," Di'Ath finally managed. "Where are we?"

Calliope let out one last laugh, before she pushed open a set of heavy wooden doors and pulled him through. Just as the doors closed behind them, Calliope caught sight of a frustrated Bloodmaid.

Di'Ath's hand slipped free from Calliope's as he wandered further into the room which she had led them to.

No. Not room. *Hall*.

The Hall of Queens.

The only place, as Gregory had reminded her, that they could be truly alone.

Calliope turned her back to the door and watched as the prince slowly moved from portrait to portrait. He took his time with each of the former queens as if he were getting to know each one before he moved on to the next.

It felt respectful.

Reverent, almost.

"This leads to one of the most sacred places in our country."

Calliope's voice had been soft, yet it still felt too loud in this space.

She lowered her haze to the plush carpet in apology to the long-dead queens.

"Leads to?" Di'Ath asked. "It feels like this hall should be one of the most sacred places. In the teachings of the Tide, we become a part of it when we die. It feels like these queens reflected in these portraits are truly part of this space."

Calliope returned her attention to the prince. He had paused before the portrait of the Maiden. He lifted his hand, fingers outstretched. She expected him to touch the worn nameplate, just like so many had done throughout history.

Instead, Di'Ath frowned and pulled his hand back.

"What was her name?" he asked.

Calliope closed the distance between them. She stood by her prince's side and looked up at the Maiden.

"We do not know," she admitted. "Our scholars have been searching for her name for centuries. There are theories that Queen Deirma removed all record of the Maiden's name during her rule, but there is no evidence of such a decree. And besides, her reign was so short, it does not make any sense for her to have been able to do so."

Calliope tensed for a brief moment as Di'Ath's fingers once again nestled between hers. He tugged gently until she followed him as he searched for the mad queen. They found her in the middle of the hall, looking off to the side rather than directly at the viewer of the portrait.

Calliope swallowed a lump in her throat.

"Tell me about her," Di'Ath said. "Please."

"Deirma was the only Queen of Ailiar to have reigned for only a year," Calliope began. "Her mother, Queen Cheimaten, did not abdicate the crown willingly, as is tradition, and Deirma's daughter had already come into her Affinity by the time Deirma was crowned. I think the assassination of Deirma was the only successful one in our history."

Di'Ath turned towards her. In her periphery, Calliope could see that his brow was furrowed. She could feel the slight tightening of his hand on hers.

"Well, it was the only assassination to have been conducted by our own line," Calliope continued. "My mother's predecessor, Fetreina, was assassinated as well. We were already at war, but Rupaburg believed that if they removed Fetreina from the equation, they could defeat Meitranis. At the time, it had only been a year since my mother had come into her Affinity, so she was still young and inexperienced."

It was Calliope's turn to pull Di'Ath away and lead him to another portrait. This time, they came to stand before her mother. Queen Meitranis Ailiar looked down at them with a commanding, authoritative air. Her jaw was set, and her eyes blazed with fiery resolution.

Here, she was every inch the Blood Queen.

For the first time, Calliope did not feel ashamed to be standing before this image of Meitranis.

"But what they did consider was how much my mother loved her people. She was the kind of princess who spent her days in the city working with the peasants and getting to know them all by name. Fetreina had been so focused on fighting her war that she did not have time to so much as visit the orphanages. My mother did not want to be that kind of ruler, and yet..."

Calliope's breath caught.

Di'Ath's hand left hers, and just as Calliope was about to protest, his arm slipped around her waist and pulled her close to him.

"My mother," she continued. "Was forced to join the war she did not want any part of to save the people she loved. As retribution for this, she became the most ruthless, merciless soldier on the battlefield. There are so many accounts of her standing atop piles of corpses that she had slain herself, covered in blood and entrails, goading the next line of soldiers to try their luck at her hand. After a hundred years of fighting, the King of Rupaburg finally answered her call to meet her face-to-face on the battlefield and to fight for his country like a true King."

Di'Ath remained silent, staring up at the portrait of Meitranis while Calliope spoke.

"King Einos," Calliope said. "Did not survive his encounter with my mother. Much like the Maiden, Meitranis severed his head and presented it to his men with a sneer on her face and a curse on his line. She told the men that Ailiar would not kill another Rupaburgan soul, unless provoked, until the next King was crowned. Then, she would sit down with the new King to discuss peace."

"Was this where the marriage between your mother and father was brokered?" Di'Ath asked.

Calliope let out a laugh.

"No," she replied. "Rupaburg went through three more kings before they settled on Jeiros. Each one had thought themselves stronger and smarter than the one before, and each one had their heads severed from their shoulders. Jeiros was the only one who met with my mother in her own city. He was the only one who did not let his pride get in the way of progress. Together, they came to an agreement. The war would officially be over, and both nations could finally begin to heal. On one condition."

Di'Ath snorted. The unprincely behaviour brought a smile to Calliope's lips.

"That the two nations be united in marriage to prevent any further conflict," he said.

Calliope nodded, and finally rested her head on his shoulder. It was the most comfortable she had ever felt.

"My father is the nephew of King Jeiros," she said. "At the time, Jeiros did not have any children. He was not even wed. So, he offered his nephew, and my mother agreed. There would be a period of five years to allow for the rebuilding of the two countries to begin before the wedding. Since then, there has been no fighting. It has been peace for the last two decades."

"We will maintain that peace," Di'Ath promised her. "We will ensure that your realm flourishes."

Calliope shook her head.

"No. Not my realm. *Our* realm."

FIFTY-FIVE

MAIDA

THE SEA BETWEEN SEAS

WHILE AROS HAD DECIDED that he would sleep above deck and under the stars, Aniaija had insisted that Maida sleep in a hammock beside her with the crew.

Unlike trying to stand or walk, Maida found sleeping on a ship to be easy and calming. Though she supposed that sailing on an actual sea might be different, sailing on the Sea Between Seas meant that the hammock swayed from side to side lulling her into a quick and dreamless sleep. Of course, she couldn't discount the effect of the past two and a half weeks would have had on her body. Sleeping on cold, hard ground in the early weeks of winter had not been kind, and even if she had not been plagued by nightmares of Nanos' death and the destruction of Luvrahn, her sleep had suffered greatly.

However, in the early hours of the morning, Maida jolted awake as something hard and heavy landed on her legs. She lifted her head to try and see what it was, but the cabin was still too dark, and her eyes still too crusted with sleep to make anything out. The heavy thing—a creature, she surmised—started walking up her legs. From within it emanated a deep rumbling sound, like rocks vibrating against one another in a bowl.

Maida's breath caught in her throat as the thing continued to climb up her body. Whatever the creature was, it seemed uncaring that each step led to small, localised points of pain as its weight was centred on the small feet.

Slowly, Maida reached under her pillow for the blade Aros had given her. Her fingers wrapped around the hilt just as the creature stepped into the single sliver of pale moonlight that streamed in through the port hole. Large green, luminous eyes reflected the light, and they were staring directly at Maida.

Maida screamed. In her attempt to get away from the odd, bumpy creature atop her, she tossed so wildly that she overturned the hammock and landed on the hard, wooden floor below.

The creature hit the ground as well. Despite its small stature, the heavy *thunk* it made when it landed reminded her of the time she had accidentally dropped an entire trunk of clothes.

At least the low rumbling had stopped.

Still, Maida tried scrambling away from it. The creature appeared unperturbed at her frantic attempts to create distance between them. It stretched, bowing down on its front legs and arching its back like a cat before it began to walk towards her again.

"Get away, get away, get away," Maida whined.

With the hiss of a new-born flame, a candle flared to life. It illuminated Aniaija's concerned face, highlighting the sharpness of her nose and the deep set of her brow. Groans of protest rippled through the sleeping crew at the sudden light.

"What is it?" Aniaija asked. "What's wrong?"

"What is *that*?!" Maida nearly shrieked, pointing to the creature.

In the candlelight, she was able to see it more clearly. Unfortunately, being able to see the beast made everything worse.

What she had thought was a creature made of flesh and bone looked more like a pile of rocks that had been possessed by some dark magic to move of its own accord. It had stopped advancing on her—for now—and had taken to sitting. Its thin, rocky tail flicked up and down, creating a *thunk*, *thunk* sound on the planks of wood with each downstroke.

"Do you mean Tobie?" Aniaija asked. The corners of her lips lifted slightly, and her eyes shone with mirth as she appeared to be fighting off the urge to smile. "She's the ship cat. Tobie takes care of any pesky rodents or other pests that might find their way on board. You might not think so, but rats are extremely common on the Between. We were all shocked to learn that when we first started sailing sand."

Maida's mouth gaped like a fish.

"*Cat*?" Maida asked, incredulous. "I may not have seen much in my life, but I have seen enough to know that *that* is not a cat. Cats are not made of rocks and stones! They have fur, and whiskers! They're like dogs, and deer, and bears!"

Aniaija stared blankly at Maida as though she were stupid for a long moment. Just as Maida felt the heat of embarrassment and indignation rise to her cheeks, Aniaija broke out into a fit of laughter.

More protests rose from the crew. Some of them went so far as to yell at the two women to *shut the fuck up* – but Aniaija did not stop laughing until tears streamed down her face.

Maida's cheeks burned hotter. She clenched her jaw and refused to look at either Aniaija or the strange stone cat that had started its odd rumbling again.

"Oh, by the Tide," Aniaija said breathlessly. "I'm sorry. I forgot that not everyone knows what a golem is."

Maida watched in equal parts disgust and fascination as Aniaija scratched the stone cat behind one of its rounded ears. How did it feel to scratch stone? She couldn't imagine it would be pleasant. Maida had needed to claw at the riverbank as she fled Silktide and had felt her nails scrape against the rocks embedded in the mud. The sensation had sent shivers up her arm and down her spine. She had felt it in not only her bones, but in her teeth. She could not imagine willingly scratching stone to show such a creation affection.

"What exactly *is* a golem?" Maida asked tentatively.

Tobie abandoned Aniaija and crossed over to Maida, rubbing against her leg. Maida recoiled from the unnatural feeling of living stone pressing against her. Tobie either didn't notice or didn't care.

"Well," Aniaija said. "You know how people with the same Affinity can have different specialties and skills?"

Maida chewed her lip. She knew that Kaidos had special abilities. She knew that he used his magic to send a cannonball of air hurtling at such speed that it obliterated the target on impact. But other than that, she didn't understand much of it at all.

So, she shook her head.

"Oh," Aniaija said, her brow furrowing. "Well, this is going to be a bit more difficult to explain than I thought. But basically, a person's magic will fall under one of the four elements."

"I know that much," Maida said.

Aniaija held up a finger, asking her to be quiet.

"For many," she continued. "Their magic extends only to the simple control and manipulation over their respective elements. Aerdhraos can summon a gust of wind, Igdhraos can fan a flame, Saldhraos can encourage crop growth and Visdhraos can influence the flow of water. Some people are stronger, and can summon storms, create fire from nothing, or move boulders without lifting a finger. But there are a few who are even stronger than that and have an additional power that corresponds with their Affinity. For example, Queen Meitranis is a Saldhraos. She has power over earth. She can control rock, stone, and mineral, but she can also control what is known as bloodstone."

Maida frowned.

"Do you mean, like the stone that was created when the Maiden slew King Thar?" she asked.

Aniaija nodded. "The very same. And with nothing more than a single thought, the Queen can make anything out of bloodstone. Weapons, clothing, furniture. Her personal guards wear clothes embroidered with thread spun from bloodstone. The city itself is a cache of unending power for her because so much of it is constructed of bloodstone. But I'm getting off topic. You asked about golems."

Maida flinched as Tobie gave a gravelly meow.

"So," Aniaija said. "Some Saldhraos can breathe life into stone. There is a whole process to it. You have to pick the right type of stones, put them in the right order, pick out what animal you wish to replicate... And then, the ritual itself leaves you completely drained. However, after that initial stage, the golem helps to generate energy, which in turn, makes you stronger. Magic isn't an infinite resource. It's dependent on your own strength and endurance. A golem allows a Saldhraos to draw on energy outside of themselves."

Maida looked down at the stone beast still rubbing against her leg. It seemed to be demanding love and attention from her, but Maida was not quite ready for that.

"So, they're a part of you?" Maida asked.

Aniaija nodded. "There is a theory that to create a golem, you must split your soul in two and put it in the stones. Because of this, it's considered taboo in a lot of circles. It was y outlawed in Ailiar for a while. It's perfectly legal now, but there are still some very religious circles who believe that Di'Tyan won't accept you into his Hall if you've split your soul."

Aniaija reached out and toyed with the length of Tobie's tail. Maida could not fathom how the creature didn't lose any of the pebbles that made up the tail when there was nothing to secure them together.

Nothing, she thought, *but magic.*

"Do you actually give a part of your soul to a golem when you create it?" Maida asked.

Aniaija's smile disappeared.

"I don't know," she admitted. "But I have seen what happens when someone loses their golem, and I can only guess that such a thing is what spawned the idea in the first place."

Tentatively, Maida reached out to scratch Tobie under the chin. That same unpleasant shiver ran up her arm as her nails scraped against rock. How Aniaija was so comfortable with patting it, she did not know.

"What happens?" she asked, against her better judgment. "When you lose a golem?"

Aniaija swallowed hard.

"Well," she said. "The short version is that it drives the person insane. The one that I saw… her screams were some of the worst I've ever heard, and I've seen more than my fair share of death and war. It sounded like the entire world was being cleaved in two. She completely broke and lost the will to fight. That was just the immediate effect. Over the next few weeks, she refused to eat or drink or sleep. She looked like a walking skeleton. Once we finally convinced her to start looking after herself again, she became fanatic about discovering a way to bring her golem back from the dead. She spent every waking moment poring over those books. She sifted through the sands where they had been fighting, where her golem had been killed. She looked at every single grain of sand, trying to decide whether it had been a part of her golem or not… Obviously, we were all concerned, but she wouldn't listen to reason, and we figured that she wasn't hurting anyone else. That is… until she stole a child, and she…"

Aniaija's breath caught, and the moment before she spoke again stretched long enough for Maida to seriously regret her curiosity.

"After trying to recreate her golem with her own magic and failing, she believed that the life of a child would have enough energy to do the job."

Maida felt bile rise in her throat. Sacrificing a *child*.

"There's death, there's murder, there's collateral damage in war, but killing a child is by far the worst thing I have ever seen in my life."

"You… you saw it?"

"I did," Aniaija said. "I tried to stop her. It's how I got this."

Ani twisted and lifted her shirt, a jagged scar along her spine.

"I couldn't move, and I had to watch her…"

Maida did not want to hear what Aniaija had seen, but she didn't shy away from the story. It wasn't something Aniaija had the luxury of deciding not to know, so Maida wanted to carry as much of that burden as she could.

To her relief, Aniaija didn't elaborate.

"Obviously, not everyone reacts that way when they lose a golem, but you know what people are like. They'll make a connection between two things and decide that Thing One always results in Thing Two. Once that connection is made, it's difficult to destroy it. Ideas are born easily, and are damn near impossible to kill."

That was certainly true. Maida thought about a ship that had once pulled into Silktide. It had been stranded at sea for weeks without wind to fill its sails, and by the time the sailors had finally made port, they all were sun-crazed. A handful of the men aboard had hurt the villagers, believing them to be demons and illusions. Still, the people of Silktide had blamed the entire crew, and sent them back out to sea without letting them replenish their supplies.

Maida had always wondered if anyone else had noticed how for the following month, there had been no wind once the ship disappeared over the horizon.

And besides—hadn't she herself believed that elves were horrible, evil creatures that wanted to enslave and eat her? She was no better than the other citizens of Silktide, unwilling to acknowledge that the dismal actions of a few did not necessarily represent the entire group. She couldn't honestly say that if she had been born and raised in Ailiar that she too wouldn't have fallen prey to the idea that creating golems should be outlawed.

She looked down at Tobie again. This time, when she tried to pet her, she used the pads of her fingers instead of her nails. This felt much better, and it made the creature rumble louder.

"You're going to be exhausted tomorrow," Aniaija said. "You should try to get back to sleep. I can take Tobie if you want."

Maida shook her head. "No," she said. "Don't worry. She can sleep with me if she wants."

FIFTY-SIX

MAIDA

THE SEA BETWEEN SEAS

OVER THE COURSE OF the week and a half that Maida and Aros sailed across the Between upon the *Mercy*, Maida had been forced to learn very quickly that Aniaija was not the type of person to rest. Even when their assigned chores had been completed, Aniaija had always ensued Maida was never idle.

Maida was still undecided whether or not she enjoyed the fact that when there were no more decks to swab and no more inventory to count, or that Aniaija all but forced her to partake in the pirate's favourite activity—sparring.

She did enjoy watching, however. Maida sat atop a barrel, wind whipping her hair and sand scratching her cheeks while she followed the arc of blades through the air.

Maida had once caught part of a play in Silktide, where the actors danced across the stage with carefully choreographed steps and swings of their blunted swords. She had watched the children of Luvrahn chase each other with wooden replicas of axes, and war hammers, and blades of various sizes. But nothing compared to watching two elves go at each other, showing no mercy and giving no quarter.

If the blades had not been blunted by the magic of a Saldhraos sailor, limbs surely would have been severed. As it was, Maida watched as mottled bruises were added to an already large collection on the arms and thighs of the *Mercy's* crew.

The first day that Maida had been brought along to participate in the 'fun'—as Aniaija called it—she swiftly discovered that the training that Aros had provided her with as they travelled through the Tievan Woods was limited. That first night, she had laid in the hammock, praying that whimpers of pain that escaped with each shift of her weight went unheard. Suffice it to say that Tobie's arrival that night had not been welcome in the slightest.

Now, at least, Maida was able to block a handful of blows before she caught a solid *thwack* to her side with the flat of a sabre. She had even managed to hit a male elf by the name of Nori. He had laughed as her blade made contact with his skin; the burrs caused by the constant hit of steel-on-steel cutting into the topmost layers of his skin. Maida had apologised profusely as bright red blood beaded on the surface, only to have Nori ruffle her hair as though she were a child.

Maida would need years of training to even dream of coming anywhere near the skill of the two women sparring before her.

Aniaija's movements were quick, sharp, and decisive. There was no hesitation. The moment Aniaija began to move, she followed through with her blows. Even when her opponent—this time, the Aerdhraos Dapsa—moved to block the oncoming attack, Aniaija changed course seemingly without thought.

This time, though, Maida was certain that Aniaija was going to lose.

Dapsa lifted her blade over her head and brought it down. It was sure to land on Aniaija's unprotected skull, should Dapsa choose not to pull her blow at the last moment. But Aniaija swung her own sabre up. Steel clashed against steel, and sparks arced away from the kissing weapons as Aniaija pushed Dapsa's sword up and away. It was a technique Dapsa had been trying to teach Maida—use the momentum of the attack to deflect it rather than simply trying to stop it. Not only did it prevent jarring in your arms, but it also threw your opponent off for a fraction of a moment. This split second of a distraction allowed Aniaija to bring her blade back up to *thwack* firmly into Dapsa's side.

Aniaija's grin was as wide as Dapsa's eyes.

"And you're dead," Aniaija practically purred as she slowly drew the sword across Dapsa's middle.

Dapsa laughed and shook her head before stepping back in resignation.

"I can't believe you beat me again," she said with a laugh.

"Believe it," Aniaija said with a chuckle. "Because it's going to happen again. And again. And again. Maybe you need a little more motivation. What if I were to pay you twenty gold crowns if you bested me?"

Maida nearly choked. It had cost Aros two gold crowns to secure passage for the both of them across the Between, and Aniaija was offering *twenty*?

Dapsa raised a brow. "Crowns mean nothing on the Between, Ani," she said. "Why would twenty of them sway me?"

Aniaija shrugged. "Maybe you want to stash them away for some pretty scarves when we can finally set foot on proper land again."

Dapsa rolled her eyes. "Fine. What are the terms?"

Aniaija's grin grew more wicked. A sense of foreboding washed over Maida at the feral, predatory sight.

"Any time. Anywhere. Blades only. I do not want to be shot with an arrow while trying to move the ship. And you cannot hurt anyone else. Other than that, everything is fair game. You win when you have a blade to my throat or at my heart."

The two women shook hands in agreement, and what happened next happened so quickly that Maida nearly missed it—Dapsa had pulled Aniaija forward and brought her sword up, aiming for her ribs. Unlike the inexperienced Maida, Aniaija appeared to have been expecting this.

There was a *clang* of metal on metal as she pushed Dapsa's blade out of the way, flourishing her weapon and ending with her blade kissing Dapsa's throat.

Maida's breath caught at the sight.

"It was worth a try," Dapsa panted.

Maida had no idea how the woman was still grinning with a sword at her throat, or why it seemed as though Aniaija was seriously considering kissing Dapsa.

"It was a good try," Aniaija admitted. "Just not quite good enough."

The two disengaged, and Dapsa dipped her head to Aniaija before sheathing her weapon. She walked over to the crates and barrels where Maida was sitting, picked up a waterskin, and drank deeply.

Aniaija pointed her blade at Maida.

"You," she said. "Your turn. Up."

"I really don't fee—"

"Don't you even think about talking back to me," Aniaija said. "I don't know what your story is, or where it will take you, but I do know that a sword is one of the few companions that can help you in any situation, so while you are aboard my ship, I will ensure that you know how to use one."

Maida groaned. Reluctantly, she stood and trudged over to Aniaija. She picked up the heavy arming sword that Aniaija had assigned her when they first started.

"I hate how heavy this is," she grumbled.

"You'll get used to the weight," Aniaija said. "Now, let's get work on that speed of yours."

To Maida's displeasure, Aniaija worked her for hours, until the sun had nearly completely disappeared beyond the horizon.

By then, Maida was so thoroughly worn out that she was unable to muster more than an exhausted half-smile when Aros arrived. Captain Geomar, who had followed Aros, chuckled when he saw Maida bent over, desperate for breath, and dripping a lake's worth of sweat onto the deck. Her pendant swung back and forth from her neck.

"What have you done to her?" Geomar asked.

"Just some training," Aniaija shrugged. "Nothing too bad."

"Well, I hope she'll be right to disembark tomorrow," Geomar said. "We should reach Do'Meirah just after noon."

Maida looked up at Aros. Sweat dripped into her eyes, the salt stinging.

"From Do'Meirah," Aros said. "It should be about a month on foot to Balliach. I'm hoping we can find a kapriae along the way to make it quicker."

"So long?" Maida asked.

Aros nodded, no hint of the smile she had come to dream about in Lu-vrahn.

"It's the best option we have," he said with a sigh. "I just hope that we aren't too late."

FIFTY-SEVEN

CALLIOPE

BALLIACH

THE DECISION TO VISIT the temple of Oliantra had been a surprise.

It was a tradition in Ailiar for prospective brides and women in love to reach out to a devotee of the Goddess of Blessings and Revelations to determine whether the person courting them was *the one*. There was little evidence to support the practice before the time of the Maiden, but in the centuries that followed, women had flocked to the temple to ensure that they were about to enter into a loving and fruitful marriage.

Calliope had never seen much point in it. Not for her, at least.

Despite being blessed by the Gods, the heir of Ailiar would never have a choice in their husband.

Calliope was not sure if there was anything the priestess could reveal that would stop any pending nuptials, short of a plot to take the country over and destroy Ailiar from within. In the end, the queens and heirs of Ailiar were still subject to politics and the petty needs of their neighbours.

Up until that morning, Calliope had not intended to visit the temple at all, regardless of the expectation. She had been resigned to accepting her fate and whatever it held, good or bad, as it came to her.

She did not see the point in knowing what was to come if she did not have the power to change it. What good would it do to know that your future was damned? How could a person go on waking each morning knowing how many days they had left? How could someone hold so much as a smidgen of hope for happiness if they knew they were destined for pain?

But that morning, Calliope had woken with one single desire—to visit the temple and ask the priestesses what Oliantra saw for her future with Prince Di'Ath.

She could not tell what the driving factor behind the change in her mind had been.

Perhaps it was the walk in the garden.

Calliope could still feel the ghost of Di'Ath's arm around her waist. That night, she had dreamed of running through the flowers with him, their laughter ringing out for all to hear. Perhaps it was the fact that Di'Ath had seemed so insistent that the two of them would fall in love with one another that had convinced her to follow the tradition.

Until you can no longer contain yourself and find that you are overcome with the desire to call me your love, your light, your guiding star on the endless seas.

As if the moment one was in love, they lost themselves to it. As though, when someone's heart belonged to another, they would cease adhering to all polite social practices.

As though romance stories were true.

Prince Di'Ath was as charming and handsome as any good romance hero was. And like in those stories, he smelled divine. Calliope had found herself looking forward to the day when she could wake up in sheets that smelled of him. She imagined it would be difficult to climb out of a bed that smelled of sea salt and amber.

Even now, as she pulled around her shoulders a deep green cloak that had never been in his presence, she swore she caught a whiff of his scent in the way the air moved. Salt, and citrus, and vanilla.

She pulled the fabric of the cloak up to her face, burying her nose in it and breathed in deeply. But the scent of him was not there; instead all she could smell was rose, honey, and jasmine.

The door opened so quickly that she jumped, the fabric falling from her hand.

Gregory gave her an apologetic look before Lady Jaena stepped into the room.

"Good morning," Lady Jaena said with a grin and the most perfect curtsey one could imagine.

Her sky-blue eyes focused for a moment on the cloak before settling on Calliope's face.

"Are we going somewhere?"

Calliope bit back the retort that danced on the tip of her tongue. She hadn't wanted company at the temple. She didn't even know if it was more common for brides to take their friends with them or if it were expected that she would go alone. But still, there was something about talking with a priestess about one's pending nuptials that suggested a need for privacy.

"I am going into the city," she said. "I have some errands to run. You may stay here; you do not need to accompany me.

Jaena's brow creased.

"You are not going into the city on your own," she declared. "I will come with you. Whatever errands you have to run, we can run them together. We could stop at a tea shop on the way, or on the way back, whichever you prefer."

Calliope gestured to the red-clad woman standing by the door. She took far too much satisfaction from the way Gregory's face paled the moment he noticed the Bloodmaid. She recalled the first time Gregory had come to her rooms and how quickly he'd paled then too.

Funny. It had been months since Gregory had come to take her to her father. Months, and Calliope had still not cleaned the blood from her project.

"I am never alone," Calliope said. "So please, take today to yourself."

"You wish me to spend today however I choose?" Jaena asked with a polite smile.

"Yes," Calliope said, fastening the closures of her cloak. "You may do whatever it is your heart desires."

"Then I choose to spend it with you."

Calliope paused. She replayed the conversation over in her head, again and again, and she couldn't believe how easily she had played into Jaena's hands. *No, I want you to stay at the castle*, is what she should have said. Instead, Calliope had talked herself into a position where she could not make Jaena stay behind without risking offending Jaena's family and whatever arrangement was struck to bring her here.

From the corner of her eye, Calliope swore she saw the Bloodmaid smirk.

"I am only following your wishes, your Highness," Jaena continued.

If she were a lesser woman, Calliope would have huffed. She would have yelled and screamed and stamped her foot and demanded that Jaena leave her alone.

But Calliope was not a lesser woman, and she could not simply throw a tantrum to get her way.

"Fine," she muttered. "But keep up. I have no intention of dawdling."

"I will go fetch my cloak," Jaena said with a grin.

"Where are we going?"

Calliope pursed her lips the moment Jaena spoke. Could the woman not keep her mouth shut for five minutes? Must she always be asking questions? What did she have to gain from being so inquisitive?

She could take a lesson from the Bloodmaids and keep quiet. Perhaps Calliope could suggest that Jaena play pretend. After all, she had admitted that it had been her dream to join their famed ranks.

But you wanted friends, she thought. *And friends talked to each other.*

Talked to, perhaps. But more often than not, Calliope felt like she was being talked *at*.

Calliope may have softened towards her cousin, but she still had not come to terms with exactly how talkative Jaena truly was. And now, as they wandered through the sickeningly nicknamed *Lovers District*, it was more difficult for Calliope to pretend she wasn't bothered by it.

"*I*," Calliope corrected sternly as she desperately tried to keep out of the eyesight of vendors selling perfumes guaranteed to make men fall head over heels. "Am going to the temple of Oliantra."

"Why?" Jaena asked.

Calliope clenched her jaw so tightly that it ached. She continued to weave through the throng of people, heading toward a building at the end of the street with a black stone roof. Why were there so many people? There were no holidays around the corner, nothing special or out of the ordinary where one would be expected to buy a gift for a lover.

Were the streets of Balliach always this crowded, or had the arrival of Di'Ath and Sy'da brought people to the capital?

There was still over a year before the royal wedding.

Calliope couldn't make heads or tails of it.

"It's a tradition," Calliope explained. "With the help of her priestesses, I am going to ask Oliantra what lies ahead for me if I marry Di'Ath."

They were nearing the temple now. The crowd did not seem to be thinning at all.

"If?" Jaena asked. "What do you mean *if*? You're set to marry him. I thought you liked him, Callie."

Calliope turned to her. She opened her mouth to say that she did like Di'Ath, but another voice responded in her stead.

"The princess simply wishes to know what path she is on, and what other paths may be open to her."

Calliope spun on her heel, only to come face-to-face with a priestess dressed in robes so black they swallowed the light around them. She wore a shimmering powder on her tan cheeks, which shone like stars when she moved.

The priestess' voice was warm and inviting, like tea with honey. How she had found them in this crowd, Calliope wasn't sure she wanted to know. The gods worked in ways neither elves nor humans were designed to understand, and their priests and priestesses were not far removed.

"And," the priestess continued, smiling at Jaena. "I am afraid she must discover such a path on her own. I will have to ask you to wait here with the Bloodmaid. Your princess is in good hands, and this will not take long."

Wait here with the Bloodmaid.

Calliope had lost count of how many times she had wished the Blood-maids would leave her be, and now she was expected to step into a strange place without one. She had expected the Bloodmaid to at least follow her in.

Maybe this was a bad idea.

It wasn't too late to back out. Jaena was right. Calliope was set to marry Di'Ath. She liked Di'Ath. She could imagine being happy with him. Nothing that this priestess or any god could say would change her mind on the matter.

A weight settled on Calliope's arm.

She looked down to find the priestess' tan hand on her. She was still so unaccustomed to people touching her that the contact threw her off guard. She swallowed hard, forcing down the realisation that she wanted to be touched.

"Come, princess," the priestess said. "We have been waiting for you."

With a final look over her shoulder to Jaena and the Bloodmaid, Calliope followed the priestess into the temple. They walked through a winding, twisting series of hallways eerily lit from the sun straining to break through the black stone ceiling.

They had turned in so many directions that Calliope had no hope of finding her way out on her own. How long had it taken for the priestesses to learn their way through this temple? And why was this path, in the Goddess of Pathway's vey temple, so confusing?

Calliope had no choice but to continue following the priestess. She lost track of how long they walked and how many steps they took.

Eventually, they came to a large, cavernous room with nothing but a large, silver bowl sitting on a pedestal in the centre.

The priestess tugged Calliope forward.

In the bowl, dark water appeared to be reflecting the night sky. Calliope didn't understand.

Even with the strange ceiling, the sun was shining brightly above them.

It must be magic. Whatever magic it was, it was far beyond her knowledge, but she could not deny that it was indeed the night sky reflected in that bowl, the bright Star of Oliantra gleaming in the centre.

The priestess let go of Calliope's arm.

The absence of warmth and pressure left Calliope feeling cold and hollow.

"Tell me, princess," the priestess said. "What is it that you wish to know? Which path do you wish to have laid before you?"

The question sounded so deceptively simple.

What do you wish to know?

Which path?

It should have been an easy question to answer, but as recently as the night before, Calliope had not even known that she would take the path that would lead her here. And yet, here she was, following the longstanding bridal traditions of Ailiar.

Then follow the tradition, she told herself.

That made sense. She was here to follow in the footsteps of the brides before her—she should ask the same questions they had. By entering into this union with Prince Di'Ath, would she be on a rewarding path? Would she be happy? Would they find love?

And, because she was the next in line for the Ailian throne – would this union benefit her people?

It should be that simple, and yet something nagged in the back of her mind, whispering that she was missing something, and that there were other questions she should be asking.

She shoved that nagging voice deep down, determined to smother it.

"I am to be married," Calliope said. "As soon as I come into my Affinity. My future husband arrived last week. So far, he has proven himself to be charming and warm, and I wish to know if this is the true him. I wish to know if our marriage will be a happy one or if this is a façade for the sake of our countries."

The priestess nodded as if she understood exactly what Calliope was thinking. She reached into a pouch that hung from the belt at her waist and revealed a handful of fine black powder. Like that on her face, the powder shimmered in the light.

The priestess closed her eyes, whispered a prayer over the powder, and tossed it into the water.

The water began to swirl. The stars depicted shifted and moved.

The priestess looked over the edge of the bowl.

Calliope could not make heads or tails out of it.

The priestess' smile faltered; her brow furrowed.

"What is it?" Calliope asked. "What do you see?"

Swallowing hard, as if she had taken a bite of food far too large, the priestess took a step away from the scrying bowl.

"You should leave, your Highness."

"What did you see?" Calliope asked again.

"Your Highness, I–"

"I am not leaving until you tell me what Oliantra revealed to you!"

The priestess offered her a smile so sad that it broke Calliope's heart.

"The dragon-prince of Zadanai will never be your husband," she said in almost a whisper. "His heart belongs to another."

Calliope stared.

"He loves someone else?" she asked.

The priestess looked pained. "Both the prince and the crown will belong to someone else. You will have neither."

Calliope could not stop staring.

It was not difficult to accept that Di'Ath's heart could belong to another. Neither of them had been given a choice in their marriage. It was possible—expected, even—that he had been involved with someone back in his home country.

But for there to be such a definite note as *he will never be your husband*? And the crown...

"I do not understand," Calliope breathed. "The crown has been handed down from mother to daughter for centuries – for millennia. It must be passed to the first-born daughter, just as the Gods decreed."

Otherwise, Ailiar would fall to ruin. It would be cleaved in twain by fire and flood. Brother would turn against brother.

And that would be nothing compared to the anger of the Gods themselves.

"I am sorry, princess," the priestess said. "But the path was clear. And there were no forks."

No forks. No choices. No way but towards this... nothingness.

Calliope felt as though she were moving through oil as the priestess guided her out of the scrying room.

"So," Jaena asked. "How did it go? Will the two of you be eternally happy?"

No, Calliope thought. *The two of us will never be.*

But she couldn't bring herself to say those words. Instead, she forced a smile and nodded. "We shall be the happiest. And Ailiar will thrive for our love."

FIFTY-EIGHT

ANIAIJA

DEI'NACH

ANIAIJA HAD SPENT A decade sailing upon the Sea Between Seas, and yet she could still not decide whether the moniker of *The City of Dust* was simply an apt description of the deserted port-town of Dei'Nach or if it was a cruel, mocking title.

As she stood at the prow of the *Mercy*, watching the port draw nearer, Aniaija tried to make out what the strange, thin spikes that reached into the sky like skeletal hands were. They looked nightmarish, horrific, as if they had been pulled out of stories written to ensure that children listened to their elders and behaved.

Aniaija could imagine the spires as the gnarled twisted fingers of a hag or witch placing a curse on some unsuspecting soul. Followers of the Tide might not believe in the Ancient Ones of the Ailian faiths, but they did believe in witches and hags – beings who used herbs and spells to achieve their goals. If Aniaija feared anything in this life, she feared these creatures.

A shiver ran down her spine. She shuddered and shifted her weight from one foot to the other.

"I guess it's almost time to say goodbye," Maida said, suddenly appearing at Aniaija's elbow.

Aniaija jumped and cursed herself. How had a human been able to sneak up on her like that? If she wasn't careful, Dapsa would get the upper hand

and she would be out twenty gold crowns.

"Almost," Aniaija replied.

"I wish you could come with us," Maida said. "All of you."

Aniaija's knuckles turned white as she gripped the railing tight. The sentiment was meant to be a kind one, she was sure, but that didn't stop the sting the words left.

She wished that she could go with her too. Though she hadn't liked the information that Geomar had relayed, the reasons why Maida and Aros had been on their ship, she wished that she had the luxury to just disembark. Even in a town like Dei'Nach, the abandoned project of someone with far too much money and not enough sense to manage it.

"Where will you go now?" Maida asked.

Aniaija chewed her lip before answering.

"The Oasis," she said. "We will take what we plundered from the ship you were on back to our families and loved ones and wait out the winter in the Oasis. After that... who knows. I truly don't know how much longer we can survive sailing on the Between. I suppose if Ailiar is on the brink of another war, it won't really matter."

Maida reached for the pendant at her throat. Aniaija turned to watch as she rolled the flower between her fingers. The sun glinted off the red gem in the centre.

"I meant to say something earlier," Aniaija said. "But that is a beautiful necklace. What stone is that?"

Maida looked down at the pendant, turning it so it caught the sunlight even more.

"Thank you," she said. "It belonged to my mother. It is the only thing I have of hers. I don't know what stone it is, though. The blacksmith in my hometown thought it might have been garnet, except it's not soft enough."

Aniaija's brow furrowed.

It did bear a resemblance to garnet. It was a brilliant, blood red. But it looked unblemished, and if it had been a piece handed down from mother to daughter, there would be signs of wear.

Aniaija could see none.

"I don't really care what it is or isn't," Maida said. "It's a part of my mother, and that's all that matters to me."

Aniaija forced a smile.

"Maida!"

Aniaija and Maida both turned to see Aros waving.

"I'll talk to you soon," Maida promised. "Before I leave, I'll make sure I say goodbye."

She smiled at Aniaija and turned to walk over to Aros.

Aniaija watched her for a moment. Only when she turned back towards the port did Aniaija realise that the twisted spikes she had observed were broken and abandoned pieces of scaffolding, ravaged by time and the unforgiving desert it bordered.

FIFTY-NINE

MAIDA

DEI'NACH

As THE *MERCY* SAILED away from the dock of Dei'Nach, Maida was unable to shake the feeling that by stepping onto the dusty, desolate docks of this so-called 'city,' she had made an irreparable, irrevocable decision that was about to change the course of her life once again.

Trusting that Aros would not lead her astray, Maida turned to look over her shoulder to watch as the once proud flagship of the Royal Navy sailed back into the Between. Perhaps, when all of this was over, she would search for them again. She had nothing to return to now—not really. Silktide was gone. Luvrahn had burned in the same way. She could not imagine finding a new home in Colosia or trying to carve out a life for herself amongst humans. Once she and Aros had fulfilled their duty of informing the Ailian Queen of Kaidos' treachery, perhaps Maida could find it within herself to join the pirates of the Between.

Or, perhaps she could settle down in another elven village. She could set up shop as a tailor. Perhaps Aros would join her, and they could try and find happiness with each other despite the losses they had both experienced.

Hoping for some kind of future for herself was necessary, she realised as they stepped deeper into the dilapidated city. Sheets of fabric flapped and snapped in the wind, somehow—impossibly—louder than the sails of the *Mercy*. Maida flinched with each loud *crack*, reminded of the brutal power that Kaidos wielded.

She slid her hand into Aros'. His fingers curled around hers, and he gave her hand a reassuring squeeze.

"Once we are on the other side, it will be easier," he assured her.

Maida was not so sure that it would be. They had another month at least of travel. By the time they arrived at Balliach, winter would be nearing its end. If they were delayed any further in their travel, spring might even beat them to the capital.

What if they were too late? What if war broke out while they were still so desperately trying to make their way to the city?

What if war had already broken out, and they just did not know it yet?

Maida knew her mind was reeling. She needed to think of something else, otherwise she would be less than useless.

"Where is everyone?" Maida asked.

"No one lives in Dei'Nach," Aros said. "Not for close to a century, anyway. A count tried to build a city around the bloodstone mine, but the Queen had stopped all bloodstone mining and the count ended up in debt. There may be a few stragglers, but I doubt it."

"Is that why it was safe for the *Mercy* to make port here?" Maida asked.

Aros nodded.

"But if they could make port here to drop us off, why couldn't they stop here and have everyone disembark and start new lives? Why do they choose to remain stuck on the Between?" Maida asked.

"They are hunted," Aros said. "They would only be on the run. Their best bet would be to make port in the southern provinces, and hope that they could survive long enough to make it to Colosia. Otherwise, the Queen's army would track them down for the rest of their days. Civilians would likely turn them in, too. They've been framed for treason. Their life now is hard, but they have a better chance of survival than if they were to try and live here."

Maida chewed her lip. She supposed she understood.

She certainly wasn't sure which option she'd prefer.

"Maida?"

Maida was so certain that she had imagined the sound of her father's voice that she did not turn towards the sound. She rubbed her itchy eyes, cursing the gods for such a dusty place and silently declaring that she would choose the Between over this forgotten, half-built city.

"Maida!"

She turned this time. She barely had enough time to register that a grimy, dirt-covered figure was running towards them before Aros gripped Maida's arm with such force she felt the tender flesh immediately bruise beneath his grip. He pulled her behind him and readied himself to defend her against whoever—or whatever—might be approaching them.

"Keep your distance!" Aros warned, his hand hovering over the blade on his hip.

"I mean no harm," said the figure. "Please."

The desperation in his voice encouraged Maida to peek around Aros' muscled frame. She gripped onto his shirt for security as she leaned.

The man looked years older than when Maida had last seen him. His once proud shoulders were hunched, his face was drawn, and his eyes were sunken. Yet despite the layers of dirt, sweat and other unmentionable muck, the man before them was unquestionably, undeniably, none other than Cillian Tailor.

Maida's father.

"Papa!"

She was not sure if Aros tried to stop her from going to her father, though he would not have succeeded in the attempt. She ran, closing the short distance between them with a speed she did not know she possessed.

Before she knew it, Maida was a tangled heap on the dusty ground, sobbing in her father's arms. A heavy iron collar around Cillian's throat dug into her cheek, but she did not care.

Her father was here.

He was alive.

"I thought you were dead," Maida cried.

"I thought I would never see you again," Cillian replied. "Oh, my dearest darling girl. What are you doing here?"

"We are passing through," Aros said.

Cillian and Maida both turned their faces up at him. Cillian looked sceptical, as though he didn't trust Maida's travelling companion.

Maida supposed that she couldn't blame him. He hadn't spent months finding a new family within them.

"We are headed to Balliach," Aros continued.

Cillian's face fell. "No," he said. "No, you cannot go there, Maida. It is not safe, not for you."

Aros' eyes narrowed.

"Why would it not be safe for her?" he asked.

Maida pulled back to get a better look at Cillian. Tears—his or hers, she could not be certain—had left pale tracks down his cheeks. She wiped her own.

"It is not safe for any human in these lands," Cillian replied. "But to take her to Balliach would be to take her to her death."

Maida sniffled. She leaned forward to look more at the collar around his throat. She could not see where it locked, and it was bare of any design save for a black stone in the centre that seemed to devour light.

"But the letter—" Aros said.

Somewhere towards the city limits, a horn was blown.

The three snapped their heads towards the sound. Cillian's face visibly paled, and he gripped Maida by her shoulders.

"Listen to me," he said, voice threaded with urgency. "You must leave this place and get as far away from Ailiar as you can. You cannot step foot in Balliach, and you cannot go to the Queen."

"Papa, I do not understand," Maida said. "Please, tell me what is happening."

"I don't have time," Cillian replied. He looked over Maida's shoulder to Aros. "Your Queen would not want her to go to Balliach. Not now, no matter what that letter says."

"What letter?" Maida asked.

Aros' breath caught in his throat.

"Take her and run," Cillian ordered, ignoring the pleading questions of his daughter. "Run and keep her safe. You will understand come—"

The horn sounded again, closer this time.

"I must go," Cillian said. He pressed a hurried kiss to Maida's brow, leaving a dark smudge in his wake. "I am so thankful that I was able to see you one last time."

"Papa," Maida said.

She reached for him as Cillian stood, but her father ran back the way he had come before she could stop him. Aros took her hand to stop her from giving chase.

"Come," he said quietly. "We must get out of sight. Now."

Reluctantly, Maida followed, a fresh wave of tears flowing freely down her cheeks.

SIXTY

ANIAIJA

THE SEA BETWEEN SEAS

FOR THE FIRST TIME in a decade, Aniaija Bahra stood at the stern of the ship, watching the port they had just as it shrunk and was swallowed by the horizon.

She should be at the bow, helping the other Saldhraos to split the sand so they could sail smoothly through the dunes. Yet she could not shake the feeling that she had forgotten or missed something. She had felt this way before, when she had realised that her friend had gone missing, just before Aniaija had found her about to sacrifice a child in a horrific, misguided attempt to bring back her golem. It was a rock in her gut, twisting in the bile, warning her that she was about to play a part in the world being thrown into chaos and confusion.

Tobie wound in and out of her legs in a never-ending figure eight. The tip of her tail whacked Aniaija's shins with each pass. Aniaija couldn't recall what her legs looked like before they were perpetually covered in black and blue bruises. Even her tan colouring did nothing to hide the evidence of Tobie's affection.

But, she supposed, there were far worse things to endure than a couple of bruises.

Something is about to go very, very wrong, warned a sing-song voice in her head. *And you can do nothing to stop it.*

It had been so long since she had heard such a warning. The last time had been when they were leaving Balliach, when those cannons had destroyed the *Mercy,* and she had barely saved them all.

She rolled her shoulders back in the hopes that it would loosen some of the tension that had been building since Aros and Maida stepped off the *Mercy*.

Surely, her apprehension had nothing to do with them. Ailiar was far more tolerant of humans than the neighbouring Rupaburg, and although uncommon, unions between elves and humans were accepted. Surely, Maida and Aros were safe on their journey to meet with the vicious, bitch-queen.

She reached up and toyed with the tie of her shirt, twirling it around her finger.

Really, Aniaija should get back to work. Now that Aros and Maida were off the ship, there was no reason to hold a place for them in her mind. She had hundreds of other people that she needed to take care of. She had families she needed to reunite before the Between became too treacherous with sandwyrms to traverse.

But she simply could not pull herself away from staring at the sight of Dei'Nach fading in the distance.

Images of Maida's pendant flashed before her eyes.

Maida had said it was a garnet. But the blacksmith had been right; it wasn't soft enough. If she had been wearing it her whole life, there would have been signs of wear. Scratches, maybe a crack under the surface...

But there had been nothing.

Briefly, Aniaija had tried to reach out with her magic to try and confirm its makeup, but she had been met with nothing but hollowness. At the time, she had thought she was just out of practice or that her mind was playing tricks on her, reminding her of how it felt to come across the empty space left by a body in the sand when the Dead Crew went searching for them.

But now...

No.

It was just a pendant. Beautifully crafted, yes, but a simple pendant, nonetheless. A flower made of silver-toned metal with a gemstone centre—it could be nothing of true importance if it were hanging from a human throat.

An idea reared its head, and Aniaija dismissed it immediately.

"It's not like a human could ever get their hands on..."

Her voice trailed off. It was as though speaking the words had allowed her to piece together the answer she had been skirting around. With wide eyes, she pushed herself away from the railing, nearly tripping over Tobie in the process. Dimly, she was aware of the people she was sending to the floor as she roughly pushed past them, too focused on her singular pursuit to apologise to a single one.

She would worry about explanations and apologies later.

"Geomar!" Aniaija yelled as she ran to the helm.

The old captain leaned over the railing, his sun-beaten brow furrowed as he looked down at her.

"We have to turn around!" Aniaija called. "We have to go back!"

The crew close enough to hear her turned to face her, the ship shuddering as the magic helping it move through the sand faltered.

"What are you talking about?" Geomar asked.

"We have to go back! It's Maida! She's in danger, her pendant—"

But Aniaija was unable to finish sharing her revelation before the *Mercy* was struck from beneath by a force so powerful it may well have been dealt by the gods themselves. Screams rang in Aniaija's ears as the ship was launched into the air, and the crew were sent flying.

SIXTY-ONE

MAIDA
DEI'NACH

MAIDA FOLLOWED AROS UP the crumbling scaffolding to the roof of one of the many unfinished buildings. From their new vantage point, they could remain hidden whilst maintaining a clear, unobstructed view of what Maida could only imagine had been intended to be the town square.

What else could it be? All roads and pathways seemed to stem from the large, rock-paved space. She could imagine dozens upon dozens of people—elf, human or otherwise—milling about the area, going about their business. She could see stalls set up along the perimeter for market days, and children jumping out from around the alleyway corners to scare their friends.

Even now, with the prisoners being rounded up by their guardians, it didn't look dissimilar to the town squares Maida had seen in Silktide and Luvrahn. The only difference she could gather, ignoring the dilapidated state of the Dei'Nach itself, was the absence of a well in the centre.

In its stead stood a tall, black stone column with a horizontal bar lashed to it. Even from a distance, Maida could see the iron cuffs dangling from the bar.

Her throat dried as the realisation set in.

Instead of a well, fountain, or anything else that may be considered functional or decorative for the most frequented part of town, stood a whipping post.

It was at the whipping post that the newcomers stopped. At the head of the group stood a broad, white-haired elven male. His complexion was as deep and dark as Aros'. He wore furs over black garb and silver armour, and carried himself with the air of kings.

Maida could not shake the feeling that she had seen this man before. Perhaps it was the resemblance. Perhaps it was in a dream.

All she knew for certain was she wanted to run in the opposite direction.

Beside him was a woman. The same sense that she had seen this woman before took hold of Maida. The elven female's hair was as bright and red as Maida's own. It seemed to float around her small, pale head like the flame of a candle as it was moved.

Perhaps it was influenced by magic.

Maida still didn't understand how magic worked. Aros' explanation as they fled from Luvrahn had done nothing to better her understanding. All she knew was that it fell under the four elements, and that everyone had a different level of control.

So why couldn't someone make their hair so weightless it floated around their head? Would it require constant thought and attention, or would it be a single desire made manifest until one decided they no longer wanted to have their hair behave like a cloud?

Maida likely would have lost herself in thoughts surrounding the logistics of altering one's hair with magic, if a short, thin elf male had not broken away from the ranks of newcomers.

He stalked over to the prisoners as though they were prey. His every stride, movement, and shift of muscle betrayed the predator that he was.

Still, Maida would happily choose to go against *him* rather than the brute at the head of the pack.

The pale elf slowed his pace only when he reached the prisoners. He inspected them all, one by one, as he made his way down the line. About halfway, he stopped, tilted his head, and pointed.

The prisoners parted like curtains to reveal Cillian Tailor.

Maida held her breath. She shifted her weight. Rock scraped against rock beneath her boots.

The warm weight of Aros' hand came to rest on the small of her back as though reminding her to stay still.

As desperate as she was to save her father from whatever horrors were about to befall him, Maida had no intention of drawing attention to them. If she wanted the chance to free him later, she needed to be quiet now. She needed to let whatever was about to happen play out.

No matter how much it broke her heart.

Cillian lifted his chin and walked through the parted prisoners.

The pale elf took him by the collar and dragged him to the whipping post.

The elf secured Cillian by the cuffs with his face pressed against the stone column. The elf unclipped a whip from his belt and let it unravel. A cloud of dust rose as the leather hit the dry ground.

Maida reached beside her. She found Aros' knee and gripped it tightly.

The pale elf in the square below raised his whip and brought it down with a sickening *crack* over Cillian's back.

Instead of gasping, Maida dug her nails into Aros' knee.

"Who are these people?" she asked in a low whisper.

Clearly, they were not good people. They were more like the elves she had been taught to fear as a child than the kind, welcoming elves she had come to know. She supposed it was only a matter of time before she met such terrible, fearsome creatures.

She wondered, of all the elves in Ailiar, which were more common – the kind and helpful, or the fearsome and terrifying?

Crack.

Cillian's pained groans were carried up to Maida with dust on a gust of wind.

She shuddered. Her heart beat wildly.

The large, white-haired male spoke. Maida could not hear him, but she watched in horror as her father spat at his feet.

A collective gasp emanated from the prisoners, interrupted by a third, flesh-splitting crack of the whip.

"Aros?" Maida whispered desperately. "Aros, what does he want? What is he asking my father?"

Maida Tailor would never know if Aros had planned on answering her this time. The white-haired male spoke again. Cillian mustered an answer that seemed to please him, and he turned his back. Relief flooded Maida.

Beside her, she felt Aros tense.

Then, she heard it.

It was a sound that had been haunting her for months. She'd first heard it in her dreams after she had fled Silktide. Then, her nightmares had been brought to life as Luvrahn burned and this unnatural thundering *boom* had punctuated the screams of people dying.

The sound that had robbed her of her hearing for hours after Nanos exploded in front of her.

It took a moment before Maida registered what she had borne witness to.

It was as though her mind had acknowledged that the white-haired elf had turned back towards Cillian. It was as though she could agree that she'd seen the elf move his hands to his stomach as if he were gathering something. It was almost as if her brain refused to admit that she had watched the air ripple around those dark hands before the elf threw the magic at Cillian.

Perhaps the greatest betrayal her mind committed at that moment, was replaying the death of Nanos while Maida watched her father's body be torn apart by magic. It had been dark when Nanos had died right in front of her, but she could see it so clearly now it may as well have happened in broad daylight.

As she looked down at the square in horror, she didn't see the chunks of her father's remains, or the shards of the black whipping post. She saw Nanos' remains, and the glistening white teeth and bone that had embedded themselves in her flesh.

Despite the need to stay silent, despite the need to stay hidden, Maida screamed.

She lunged forward. What she could now, with her father nothing more than a bloody mess on the dirt-covered stone, she didn't know. But upon seeing such destructive power, her body had reacted so instinctively that she couldn't control it.

Aros' hand closed around Maida's tunic, and he roughly pulled her back down. She landed hard on the stone and dirt-covered roof of the half-finished dwelling. She did not have time to register how painful her landing had been as the white-haired elf threw another destructive blast of magic up at them.

It hurtled past, slamming into a spire behind her. Dust and debris rained down upon them, and another pained cry tumbled out of her lips.

She looked over her shoulder. What had been a tall, rust-coloured column reaching into the sky was now nothing more than a cloud of dust. Rubble was still falling from the force of impact, collecting in mounds across the roof's surface.

If that had hit me...

Maida didn't need to continue down that line of thought. She didn't need to imagine what would have happened to her if the magic had met its intended target. She had seen it with her own eyes twice now.

Because that man was undoubtedly the same one that had killed Nanos.

Maida's chest tightened. Her ribs seemed to press into her lungs, making it impossible to pull in enough air.

"We need to run," Aros hissed in her ear.

Did she answer? Did she even acknowledge that he had said anything at all?

Maida had no way of knowing if she did. She knew only that Aros gripped her arm and yanked her harshly to her feet. He kept a hand on her back to keep her doubled over, hidden as they rushed back towards the scaffolding.

Maida followed Aros blindly.

She barely registered the jolt in her leg as her ankle twisted beneath her as she ran. Her mind shut out the sound of magic destroying brick and clay behind them. It refused to allow her to think about each step she took as Aros led her down from the building.

She existed in a void until Aros stopped and pulled her to a violent stop beside him.

SIXTY-TWO

AROS

DEI'NACH

AROS TUGGED MAIDA BACKWARD, positioning himself in front of her. Perhaps it was nothing more than delaying the inevitable.

As powerful as he was and as high as he had climbed amongst the ranks of Ailiar's army and its Court, Aros C'Asad knew that he no match for his brother.

"Aros," said that horribly familiar voice. "I thought that might be you."

Aros felt Maida shift behind him. How foolish he was to think that she would listen to reason and keep herself out of sight. Perhaps it was his fault. Aros had failed to truly make her understand just how dangerous this male was. Seeing him kill was one thing. Seeing him slaughter hundreds on a battlefield with a wild, bloodthirsty grin on his face was another.

"It has been far too long, brother," Kaidos said.

"You and I will have to disagree on that one, Kaidos," Aros replied.

He kept his voice low and calm. He didn't want to give away that he knew they were well and truly fucked. He wanted Maida to at least die with hope in her heart that they were going to get out of this.

"You always were so broody," Kaidos said. "Just what are you hiding behind you, brother?"

"She is none of your concern," Aros growled. "And we are just passing through. Let us be, and you can tend to your business here.

517

"Oh," Kaidos pouted. "Come now. It's rude not to introduce your friends, Aros. Don't you remember what mother taught you?"

Aros pushed Maida further behind him as if he could shield her from Kaidos' sight. Maida gripped the back of his shirt. She was trembling.

"You know as well as I do that a move like that is pointless," Kaidos said.

The shift in his tone had Aros reaching for his magic. Maybe—just maybe—he could move quickly enough. He just needed time so that the air he tainted with his magic could poison Kaidos before his brother could obliterate them with his cannon-like power.

"Give me the round-ear," Kaidos ordered.

"No," Aros replied.

"Your love for the humans has always been your greatest weakness," Kaidos spat. "A stupid, Ailian sentiment. Have you forgotten your roots so completely, Aros?"

Aros shook his head.

He had not forgotten his roots at all. He remembered being sent to live as a ward of the Ailiar family when he was a child. When Rupaburg declared war on Ailiar, Aros had believed that he would either be killed or used as bargaining chip. Instead, Meitranis had defended him. She had said that Aros' blood ran as red as bloodstone itself. It had been on that day when Aros had first made a blood oath to Meitranis Ailiar.

And besides—Aros had no love for the humans.

He had love for *one* human.

"She must be something special if you are defending her so fiercely," said a raspy, smoke-tainted voice from behind them.

Aros spun. He pulled Maida around with him, this time pressing her against his chest.

He wondered if she could hear his heartbeat.

He wondered if she would mind if it were the last thing she ever heard.

Still, he bared his teeth at Leilara Roaen—the Igdhraos that had shadowed Kaidos since he had found her a century ago. Leilara looked remarkably like Maida, he realised. They both had flame-coloured hair and pale skin. They were both slim, though Leilara more closely resembled a burned match in her figure than Maida did.

Even now, with their lives hanging in the balance, Aros couldn't help but notice that the four of them looked like distorted reflections of one another.

"Let us pass," Aros demanded again.

"I don't think so," Kaidos said.

Kaidos tilted his head ever so slightly, then uttered one more word: "Leila-ra."

If nightmares had mouths, their smiles would not compare to the feral way the red-headed woman's mouth twisted. It was the kind of predatory smile that reminded Maida of the stories she had grown up with—the kind of smile one would see on a wolf before it opened its maw and devoured its prey.

This was the type of elf that Maida had likely grown up hearing about. This was the unearthly creature that would hunt you for sport, steal your name and make you dance until your feet wore down to stumps.

"Are you leaving so soon, C'Asad?" Leilara crooned. "I am insulted. It is rude to leave without giving us so much as an introduction to your dear friend here. I'd almost believe she did not recognise me if it wasn't for that glimmer in her eye."

Maida swallowed hard, and she pressed ever more against Aros' chest.

"It was you," Maida breathed. "You were in Silktide the day it burned."

Leilara dipped into a dramatic bow so low Aros wondered how she didn't topple over.

"I am honoured you remember me," Leilara said. "Too bad you will have no use for memories where you are headed."

The elven woman straightened. Aros cursed himself for missing the movement of her hands pressing palm against palm before slowly pulling apart to reveal the flaming ball of power growing between them.

Heat radiated from that ball of fire.

Aros leaned down and whispered in Maida's ear: "Run."

"What?" she asked.

"*Run,*" he repeated, then he pushed her away from him.

Maida stumbled a few steps before she regained her footing. She screamed as heat licked up the back of her heels. Aros swore and, with a sweeping arc of his hand, pushed the flame away with his magic.

Blessedly, Maida kept running. Aros followed close behind.

"To the mines!" he ordered.

Maida turned towards the gaping maw of the mine across from the town square. Aros used his magic to keep the path clear, creating gusts of wind strong enough to blast away any elf or human that dared to step in their path. When they got close enough to the mine, Aros gripped Maida's arm, took over, and pulled her in.

Light did not exist down in the mines. The sun abandoned them after the first few twists and turns, and the two were forced to rely on the few faint and scattered lanterns that remained. Still, Aros pulled Maida deeper. Darker, deeper. Aros would take her to the earth's core if need be.

"You can't hide from me, Aros C'asad," Kaidos called. His voice echoed off the tunnel walls.

By the gods, was he that close? Certainly not.

Still, their legs propelled them forward. Each step became more precarious until the ground simply disappeared beneath Aros' feet. Maida's scream bounced off the walls, echoing in a seemingly endless loop down into the chasm he had fallen into. At the last possible moment, he had let go of Maida's arm and shoved her backwards, keeping her away from the ledge.

By chance and chance alone, he had managed to catch himself before he hurtled to his death. With a grunt, Aros pulled himself back up. He had just managed to pull himself back up to his feet when Kaidos rounded the last bend.

"Oh, he'll be so happy to know I've finally rid him of you," Kaidos purred. He sounded like a predator that had finally cornered his prey after playing with it for too long.

"You don't have to do this," Aros said.

Even as his words left his mouth, Aros knew they were useless.

Kaidos had not chased them into the depths of the mines to simply let them go.

"Oh," Kaidos said. "But I do."

Kaidos cupped his hands before him, gathering his magic at his core. All the air in the tunnel seemed to rush toward Kaidos like a vacuum, ready and willing to be used as his destructive weapon.

Aros pulled Maida close, readying himself for the death blow he knew was coming.

He was surprised to see, then, that Kaidos faltered.

Aros looked down to see what had caught his murderous brother's attention. From the pendant at Maida's throat, a red light was steadily growing. At fist it appeared dim. Then, as if it were devouring all the darkness in the tunnel, the light exploded. The earth shook, bringing Aros to his knees. He felt shards of metal slice his cheeks as Maida's pendant burst apart.

Then, all Aros could hear were Maida's blood-curdling screams.

SIXTY-THREE

MAIDA

DEI'NACH

MAIDA WAS SCREAMING.

She could feel the way her throat was being shredded and torn from the inside out. She could feel the burning in her lungs when they had no more air to give and the jagged talons of said air as it continued to be ripped out anyway.

But she could not hear it.

She could not hear anything.

She could not see anything either. It was as though the world had slipped from her fingers, and she had been cast into a void of her own making.

All Maida Tailor knew was pain.

Sharp rock and angry stones tore into her soft flesh like rabid dogs as she writhed on the floor of the dark mine. Dimly, she was aware of cloth catching and tearing as her thrashing caused her clothes to rip until they were nothing more than rags hanging from her convulsing body. Remnants of the fine fibres of the cloth became trapped, ground into the earth, and cursed to be forever a part of these gods-forsaken mines.

With needle-like talons, ice raced through her veins.

It froze every drop of her blood, transforming it into razor-edged, crystalline forms that sliced her open from within as the jagged points pushed towards the surface—desperate to break free of the skin that bound it.

The pain was everything.

Maida lost track of all sense of time as her body betrayed her in every manner imaginable. She had never known pain like this. No one had ever known pain like this. How could they? How could anyone survive this utter destruction of their own body? Because surely, that was what was happening. There was no other explanation. Her body was destroying itself, like a star—like a sun imploding under the weight of its own hubris.

Was there no end to the torment? Was Maida cursed to spend the rest of eternity having her entire being ripped apart, down to her very soul?

Just as she was about to give in to the inevitability of such a fate, the pain slowly began to subside.

As the burning ice ebbed away from her body, Maida's hearing began to return.

At first, all she could hear was her heaving breaths, and the low, keening whine that accompanied each exhale. She sounded like a pathetic, beaten creature. Someone should put her out of her misery.

Though the worst of the pain had gone, Maida's body still ached. She felt as though she had been lifted into the sky by a great bird, only to be dropped as they reached the clouds. She felt as though she had been trampled by an entire herd of kapriae.

She prayed that someone would end her soon enough. Perhaps Kaidos was close. Perhaps he would hurl his magic at her and she would finally be at peace. She didn't care how bloody her death was. She just wanted it to be quick.

And she wanted it to come soon.

Maida also wanted that incessant *thumping* to stop. Had she not suffered enough? Why would someone be hammering away at rocks while she lay dying and begging the Ailian gods to please just let her die?

Perhaps the gods were toying with her, torturing her.

Why wouldn't they? Maida had thought she could find happiness amongst the elves. She, a lowborn human girl with poor social cues and no mother, thought that she could find a home amongst a vibrant community.

It made sense that the gods were playing with her before finally letting her die. Otherwise, how else would she be able to see Aros' face?

She had not been able to see anything as they ran through the twisting tunnels of the mine. Maida had been forced to resort to blind faith and trust in the man she who had saved her twice already. And yet now? Now she could see him as though the tunnels were filled with twilight rather than the deepest night.

His dark complexion made it difficult to make out many of the details she had grown to love over the last few months. But she could see the curve of his cheek, the slope of his nose, and the outline of his braids around his head.

The hammering continued. It sounded like a battering ram, slamming into a stone wall over and over and over again.

"Am I dying?" Maida rasped.

Her voice was absolutely destroyed. No amount of honey in her tea would speed along her recovery. Only time would be able to heal the damage done—and Maida had no way of knowing just how much time she had.

Perhaps she had no time at all.

It would explain why Aros was not answering her or why he was cupping her cheek so tenderly as he ran his thumb across it.

Maida wished that heavy *thud, thud, thud* would stop.

"We need to find a way out," Maida croaked.

Aros' eyes glistened in the dim light. Was he crying?

As Maida's sight continued to return to her and her own eyes adjusted themselves to the darkness, she could confirm that Aros had been crying. She could see the tracks of tears that had run down his face. She could see the remnants of the mask he must have tried so desperately to continue wearing so as to not scare her with the simple truth that he was terrified.

Maida lifted her hand and brushed away the tears with the tips of her fingers.

"No!" Kaidos yelled.

His voice was muffled as though he were trapped behind a thick door.

Maida turned toward him and frowned.

She watched as Kaidos summoned his magic, pulling it from his centre and hurling it towards a large, translucent red wall. It hit with nothing more than a loud *thud*. Inexplicable laughter bubbled to her lips as she realised that the sound she had been hearing was Kaidos trying to break through this odd stone that protected her and Aros.

Where had it come from?

Maida would have recalled if it were there before the blinding light had erupted and her mind had given way to the searing pain that had her begging for death. If it had been there before, it would not be separating them from Kaidos. There were no gaps between it and the walls of the tunnel. The strange red stone seemed to have grown from the dirt itself.

"This is impossible!" Kaidos roared.

He ceased attacking the wall. He huffed like a wild beast as he paced back and forth. She had seen him obliterate bodies with his magic, yet he was not making a single dent in this blood red stone.

Kaidos pointed a warning finger toward them.

"This is not over, Aros," Kaidos growled. "I don't know what you're pulling here, or what *she* is. But I will have your head."

With one final violent display of power that did nothing but create a cloud of dust on his side of the red wall, Kaidos yelled out in frustration before turning and stalking out of the mine.

Maida watched him go. She listened as his footsteps faded. It took longer than she would have expected to stop hearing him. Was it the echo of the mine's tunnels that made it seem like she was hearing more than she possibly could?

Once she could no longer hear Kaidos, however, Maida slumped against Aros. She reached up to reassure herself with the familiar weight of the flower pendant at her throat, only to find that it wasn't there.

"My necklace," she croaked, sitting up far too quickly. White hot pain shot up her spine and she let out a choked cry. "Where is my necklace?"

She turned to Aros with her hand pressed to her now bare throat.

He had never seen such an expression on Aros' face before. It was as though every last muscle had given up holding his features in place. His eyelids drooped and his lips were curved downward. He looked positively defeated.

"What is it?" Maida asked.

Her throat burned when she spoke, and she was not sure how long it would take for it to heal. She realised, not for the first time, that she would need to rely on Sign for a while. She still did not know exactly what had happened to her. If she were being honest with herself, she wasn't sure she wanted to know. She didn't want to risk reliving those eons-long moments where everything felt as though it were shattering and fusing back together.

Aros took her hand in his. She always felt so protected, so comforted when he held her. Even when she had been terrified of elves, there had been something about Aros C'Asad that Maida had found comfort in.

She cast her eyes down to where her hand sat in his. It was pale and covered in cuts, bruises and blood. Some cuts had stopped bleeding, but others still glistened with fresh blood.

I should not be able to see this, Maida thought. *It's too dark. I should not be able to see my fingers, much less the cuts.*

She was so preoccupied with what she should not see that she did not notice Aros lifting her hand towards her face. She did not realise what he was doing until the tips of her fingers met the cool flesh of her ear.

"What-" she tried to ask, but between the pain and the finger Aros put to her lips, she fell silent.

Aros guided her fingers upward.

Maida expected to feel the familiar curve of her ear. She expected to feel that rise, the gentle arc, and the fall back down to the lobe.

Instead, they trailed upwards and back until they came to rest at a delicate, definite point.

No, she thought.

Aros pulled back as Maida lurched forward. She raised both hands to her head, patting, touching, feeling those ears that she had felt so many times over the past twenty years of her life. Even though she could not see them without a mirror, Maida was certain there was no mistaking her own ears.

No, no, no.

There had to be some mistake. She must be unconscious, hallucinating, or dead. Perhaps by thrashing about on the ground, she had cut her ears so severely that pieces had come clean off.

But if that were the case, her ears would be wet and slick with blood. They would be uneven, and smaller than before.

Not larger.

Not longer.

Not arching back to a thin, delicate, *definite* point.

Maida gave Aros one last pleading look as if he had the power to stop whatever horrid curse had just been placed upon her.

But Aros cast down his eyes, confirming the truth that Maida did not want to accept—the explanation behind her improved sight and hearing.

She buried her face in her hands and sobbed, the broken sound ringing in her pointed, elven ears.

EPILOGUE

CALLIOPE

CALLIOPE AILIAR'S BACK ACHED.

She had lost track of time, lost all sense of how long she had been curled up on the floor of the Hall of Queens, tucked beneath the portrait of the Maiden as she bent over the book in her lap. Perhaps if the Hall of Queens was more frequently visited, she may have been able to use the comings and goings of others to mark the passage of time. Then again, the desire to be left alone had been the driving force behind lugging the heavy, dusty tomes here rather than setting herself up in the library. Here, not even the Bloodmaids would dare offer their company.

Here, she was alone.

Here, her only companions were the portraits of her ancestors.

Calliope groaned. She rolled her neck, wincing at the popping sound of stiff joints rejoicing at being able to move once again. Despite the books stacked in piles around her, the hours she had spent pouring over them and the throbbing headache building behind her eyes, she had gotten nowhere. Not a single tome so much as hinted at what could happen should the Maiden's bloodline not take the throne.

Nothing, save for three words repeated in each tome and every scroll: chaos and ruination.

It was hopeless. Calliope had leafed through hundreds of pages. She had worn through the topmost layers of skin on the pads of her fingertips, and she had nothing to show for it.

There were theories, of course. And each scholar and historian had their own. None seemed to match up with the other, and not a single word of them was a part of the official texts themselves. The theories were scrawled into the margins in varying degrees of neatness. The newer notes were darker and scribed in fresher ink. The older ones were faint and contained words spelt with letters that no longer existed.

But in the end, it didn't matter how old or new they were.

They were theories. Ideas. Hopes, perhaps. Nothing that Calliope could point an aching finger to and confidently claim *this! This is what is going to happen if I do not inherit the throne!*

Each reference to floodwaters and raging fires was nothing more than mere conjecture. Each claim that the realm would enter a war that would not end until every Ailian was dead could not be substantiated.

Chaos and ruination.

Calliope slammed the book on her lap closed in frustration. The force caused the tome to topple end over end and off her lap to violently kiss the stone floor below. The sound echoed throughout the Hall. Calliope's ears strained to listen, hoping to hear some answering sound on the other side of the doors. But there was not so much as the scuffle of shoes to suggest that the Bloodmaid stationed beyond the door was about to charge in, brandishing one of her iron weapons, ready to protect her charge.

She would even welcome an untimely interruption from Gregory. The silver-clad palace guard had interrupted Calliope's routines more times in the six months than she had ever recalled seeing him before. If he were to walk through one of those doors at either end of the Hall, Calliope would stand from where she sat and run to him. She would fling her arms around his neck and weep.

She would apologise for being cold and distant, and thank him for showing up just when she needed him to.

But not even Gregory interrupted her solitude.

Calliope leaned her head back against the cool stone wall with a dull *thud*. She squeezed her eyes shut as tightly as she could in a fruitless effort to stop the tears from falling in warm streams down her cheeks.

Yet another reminder of how little control she truly held over anything.

"*Calliope.*"

A frigid hand closed around Calliope's heart, sending ice through her veins.

Her eyes flew open, and her chest heaved with a sudden inability to take in enough air. Her muscles tensed as though preparing to run even as she flattened herself against the stone wall as much as she could.

The voice was at once familiar and foreign. She was certain that she had never heard it before, but somewhere deep down in the very marrow of her bones, Calliope knew that she recognised it. It was as though the memory of it had been passed down in the generations of her lineage just as the blood of the Maiden had been.

She tried to rack her brain to find any trace of memory that would give her some clue as to the identity of the voice.

"*Calliope,*" the voice called again.

Calliope scrambled to her feet. She swung her head from left to right, frantically searching the empty Hall for the source of the voice. She found nothing. She was as alone as she had been.

Had the voice been in her head? Had she been staring at pages too long? Was her mind playing cruel tricks on her?

"Hello?" she called back.

Her wavering voice bounced off the walls, echoing until it reached each end of the Hall in nothing more than a whisper. She stood still, heart pounding, waiting for a response.

None came.

Perhaps it had been in her head after all. Calliope did not know anything about the intricate inner workings of the mind, but she was not completely convinced that her own could create an experience so realistic that her body would respond so primally.

No.

She *had* heard a voice. She was sure of it.

Gathering her skirts in her fists, she called out again.

"Hello?"

"*Calliope.*"

The answering call was an airy, raspy voice. It reminded her of trees scratching walls in the wind, of storms gathering strength in the bay, whipping waves into a frenzy.

"Who are you?" Calliope demanded. "I am not interested in your games!"

Silence fell again. Calliope took a few steps forward. Through the soft soles of her silk slippers, she felt her feet leave stone and find thick, plush carpet.

Something moved out of the corner of her eye, and she spun on her heel towards it. Still, the Hall was empty. Still, she was alone.

"This isn't funny!" she said.

She caught sight of a dark shadow moving past her, and again she spun. She had moved too quickly, and she stumbled. Laughter filled the Hall.

"Show yourself!"

"*Come find me,*" the voice said. "*Come find the answers you seek.*"

"What answers?" Calliope asked.

Slowly, she began to move in circles. Her path widened with every revolution as she tried to pinpoint the origin of the voice.

"*The ones that are not in your books,*" the voice explained. "*But if you are not willing to learn the truth…*"

It was moving. The voice was moving, and it was moving away from her.

Calliope chased after it, running down the Hall. The portraits of her ancestors watched her, numb to her plight.

"Come back!" she pleaded. "Please! Show me the answers."

"*You're getting closer, your Highness,*" the voice crooned.

Calliope continued to chase the phantom voice, passing Ailian Queen after Ailian Queen.

"*Here,*" the voice said suddenly.

Calliope slid to a stop and looked up, panting, at the portrait of Queen Dierma. The Mad Queen seemed to stare into Calliope's very soul with those wide, frantic eyes. Calliope shook her head and took a step back.

"No," she breathed.

No, the voice could not have brought her here. The Mad Queen would not have the answers she was seeking. Perhaps Calliope had imagined the voice. Perhaps she was following in Dierma's footsteps and lost herself to madness. Without an heir and without a sister to take the throne in her stead, it would surely lead to what Calliope had been trying to avoid this whole time.

Chaos and ruination.

"*Push,*" the voice urged.

Calliope's brow furrowed.

"What?"

"*Push.*"

Push *what?*

The only thing in front of her was the wall and the portrait. She could see no button, no lever, no piece of furniture that she could topple. What was it that this voice wanted her to push?

After a moment of thought, she stepped forward again. Calliope held her hands up, palms towards the wall. She gasped as the cold of the stone seeped into her as she made contact with the space directly beneath Dierma's portrait.

She had read somewhere that those with an Affinity over earth could feel the energy of stone buzzing like a hive filled with bees. Calliope felt nothing. She shoved the fear that came with that nothingness deep down within herself.

She did not have the time to deal with that now.

"*Push!*" the voice bellowed.

Calliope took a deep breath and pressed her whole body against the wall. She heard the faint ripping of the delicate embroidery of her dress against the stone. She felt the tiny beads from her bodice fall onto her feet as the threads snapped against the jagged face.

For a moment, that was all that happened. She barked out a single, mirthless laugh at her own stupidity before the wall suddenly gave way beneath her weight.

Calliope stumbled back, nearly tripping on her skirts.

She watched in awe as brick by brick, the wall opened to reveal a gaping dark hole with no sign of Deirma's portrait to be found.

Dust swirled in its wake.

Covering her mouth did little to stop Calliope from inhaling a lungful of it. She coughed and sputtered, doubling over in an attempt to simply breathe again. By the time she was pulling more air into her lungs than dust, the plumes of it had cleared.

As she straightened, Calliope could see the top of a staircase that spiralled down into the dark depths below.

Calliope's feet felt like lead.

Something deep within her screamed to run in the other direction.

"*Come find your answers,*" the voice called to her from below. "*Come learn what the gods do not want you to know.*"

A RETURN TO COURT
A PLOT REVEALED
A CONTENDER FOR THE
THRONE

MAIDENS & MOURNERS

THREADS OF AITHAR BOOK 2

The story continues...

Pronunciation Guide

Adarna Ah-DAR-nuh

Ailiar Ah-LEE-ar

Aerdhraos AIR-dreese

Aoife EE-fuh

Aniaija ah-knee-EYE-ah

Aros AH-ross

Balliach BA-lee-ack

Biyar BUY-yah

Bryha BREE-ah

Calliope Cah-LIE-oh-pee

Cillian KILL-ee-an

Colosia Coh-low-see-ah

Dapsa DAP-suh

Dania dah-KNEE-ah

Dhuina DEW-nah

Dorsa Door-suh

Dei'Nach DIE-Nack

Deija DAY-zhuh

Di'Ath DEE-ah-th

Di'San DEE-sun

Di'Tyan DEE-tee-ahn

Di'Wen DEE-when

Do'Mheirah Dough-MEER-uh

-dhraos Dreese

Eila EYE-luh

Eiv Eve

Fisa FIGH-suh

Geomar GO-mar

Holsten HOL-sten

Igdhraos IG-dreese

Jaena JAY-nuh

Kaidos KAY-dos

Kapriae kap-REE-ay

Kei KAY

Keivan KAY-van

Leilara Lay-LAR-ruh

Luvrahn LOU-vra-ahn

Maida MAY-duh

Meitranis May-TRAH-ness

Nanos NAH-nos

Oliantra Oh-LEE-ahn-truh

Oprianos Op-REE-ah-noss

Palis PAL-lace

Rupaburg ROO-pah-berg

Rych Rich

Saldhraos SAL-dreese

Sancor san-CORE

Sordi saw-DEE

Sy'da SIGH-duh

Thalia Tah-LEE-ah

Vaya VAY-yah

Yu'San Yoo-Sahn

Visdhraos VIS-dreese

Watren WHAT-wren

Windra WIN-druh

Wylden WHILE-den

Zadanai Za-DAH-nigh

About the Author

Elle Brockett has been a lover of all things fantasy for as long as she can remember. She has been an avid consumer of books since before she could even read, begging her grandmother to read every edition of Anna Sewell's *Black Beauty* that they could get their hands on.

When she doesn't have her nose buried in a fantasy world, she can be found living out her medieval dreams weaving, sewing, or engaged in combat.

She resides in Sydney with her husband, daughter, and their two cats—Annie and Renie—and dreams of owning property large enough to own goats and alpacas.

ACKNOWLEDGEMENTS

There are many people that deserve to be thanked and acknowledged for the creation of this book.

Naturally, my husband comes first. Tristan has been so much more than just a massive support for me. It is because of him that we figured out that it will take two weeks to cross the Sea Between Seas via ship, how long it'll take to get from Silktide to Luvrahn on foot (both for an experienced hunter like Aros and for a girl who doesn't even own the right pair of shoes, like Maida), and the type of armour and weaponry that the different factions of the world would wear and wield. You were always there when I came to a roadblock in the plot, every time something didn't make sense and when my knowledge of the medieval world failed me. I love you, and still can't believe that I met my soulmate all the way back in Kindergarten.

A massive thank-you to my best friend, Sirius, who will most likely be receiving a special Sirius-Edition of this book with all the unsavoury bits redacted so they can pretend that nothing bad ever happens to the characters that they fell in love with. They created the first-ever pieces of art for my characters, and they will never know how many times I cried looking over them. They are also the mastermind behind the map of Ailiar and the surrounding countries. It has always been my dream to publish an epic fantasy novel that includes a map, and thanks to Sirius, my first ever book has one! You bring my ideas to life, and I am so utterly grateful for your love and support in both my life and my creative endeavours.

To my Uncle Dan, who has taught me the importance of continuing to forge your own path, despite what others may say. I hope that when I say that I see parts of you reflected in the mirror, you take it for the compliment that it is. Remember – bears aren't always grumpy. They are seen as representations of strength, courage, protection and wisdom. I am so honoured to have you in my life, and hope for many more years of discussing Warhammer and battle goats.

Thanks also to my father-in-law, Phil, who pointed out that I had written "piles of ass" in my proof copy instead of "piles of ash". Without you, this book could be headed to a much different demographic. Who would have thought that the little girl with the Scooby-Doo schoolbag would have stuck around so long and written something like this?

To my grandparents, who always fostered creativity and supported my love of books. Who saw the boundlessness of my imagination and allowed it to grow. To my mother, who went with me to my first book convention where I realised that I could actually succeed in doing this.

To L.J. and Mila, who put up with my radio silence for sometimes days at a time when I got stuck in my own world.

To Sally, who popped up again at the most unexpected time but who has become someone I reach out to daily whether it's for my book or for other, general-life-stuff. I promised you I wouldn't forget you when this book makes me famous – I just didn't realise that you would be responsible for the first hundred pre-orders.

For all those in my BETA reading team, who put up with my ramblings and let me talk things through. I am so glad that you enjoyed learning about the etymology of the language within The Threads of Ailiar as it was created.

To Pete and Adrian, who essentially paid for me to write the first 30,000 words of this book while I was working in their café. I still dream about those ham and cheese toasties, and I have never had a soy caramel latte that compared.

To my editors, Kirsty Inic, who's advertising of her editing services at BookFair Australia 2022 was the catalyst for me to pick up this story again, and C.H. Folan, who's knack for bringing forgotten characters to the light is an inspiration every day.

Additionally, I would like to thank Aaron and Simone of Medieval Fight Club for their friendship and support.

And finally, to the authors that I have met along my journey, and who continue to inspire me every waking moment of every day: Kirsty Inic, Liv Evans, C.H. Folan, Emmie Hamilton, Mazrine L. Amaris, Megan Gilbert, Chloe Hodge, Emma Lombard, Tanya Nellestien, J.P. McDonald, Ross Kingston, Madeline Burget, C.S. Cooper, Athena Bliss and Selina Fenech. I highly recommend all the works of all these authors listed, and know that I would never be here without their influence and inspiration.